Praise for *New York Times* bestselling author Lori Foster

"Best friends find hunky men and everlasting love in Foster's latest charmer.... Her no-fail formula is sure to please her fans."
—*Publishers Weekly* on *Don't Tempt Me*

"Foster brings her signature blend of heat and sweet to her addictive third Ultimate martial arts contemporary."
—*Publishers Weekly* on *Tough Love* (starred review)

"Emotionally spellbinding and wicked hot."
—*New York Times* bestselling author
Lora Leigh on *No Limits*

"Storytelling at its best! Lori Foster should be on everyone's auto-buy list."
—#1 *New York Times* bestselling author
Sherrilyn Kenyon on *No Limits*

"Foster's writing satisfies all appetites with plenty of searing sexual tension and page-turning action in this steamy, edgy, and surprisingly tender novel."
—*Publishers Weekly* on *Getting Rowdy*

"Foster hits every note (or power chord) of the true alpha male hero."
—*Publishers Weekly* on *Bare It All*

"A sexy, believable roller coaster of action and romance."
—*Kirkus Reviews* on *Run the Risk*

"Steamy, edgy, and taut."
—*Library Journal* on *When You Dare*

LORI FOSTER

UNDER PRESSURE

HQN™

HQN™

ISBN-13: 978-0-373-78993-1

Under Pressure

Copyright © 2017 by Lori Foster

The publisher acknowledges the copyright holder of the additional work as follows:

Built for Love
Copyright © 2016 by Lori Foster

Recycling programs for this product may not exist in your area.

This edition published by arrangement with Harlequin Books S.A.

For questions and comments about the quality of this book, please contact us at CustomerService@Harlequin.com.

® and TM are trademarks of Harlequin Enterprises Limited or its corporate affiliates. Trademarks indicated with ® are registered in the United States Patent and Trademark Office, the Canadian Intellectual Property Office and in other countries.

www.HQNBooks.com

Printed in U.S.A.

CONTENTS

Dear Reader,

I'm so excited to introduce Body Armor, my new series, featuring some heroes who might seem familiar, plus a cast of all-new characters I hope you'll love as much as I do.

Those of you who read *Fighting Dirty*, the last book in my Ultimate series, will remember Leese Phelps, the MMA contender who'd decided to apply the skills he'd honed in the MMA ring to a brand-new job as a bodyguard. In *Under Pressure*, Leese has become a key security agent at the Body Armor agency—but he's about to take on his toughest assignment yet when he's hired to protect Catalina Nicholson. Because the more time he spends unraveling Cat's dangerous secrets, the more attracted he finds himself. Now he's not sure what's in more imminent danger—Cat's life or his own heart...

I hope you enjoy Leese and Cat's romance, plus the bonus novella "Built for Love"—about another tough, honorable hero and the woman who holds her own with him—at the end of the book. And of course, you're always welcome to reach out to me. I'm active on most social media forums including Facebook, Twitter, Pinterest and Goodreads, and my email address is listed on my website at www.lorifoster.com.

Happy reading!

Lori Foster

UNDER PRESSURE

CHAPTER ONE

LEESE PHELPS STOOD in the cold early evening air, his breath frosting in front of him. Lights at the nearby bus station blinked in an annoying mismatched pattern. A cascade of foil Valentine's Day hearts hung loose, almost touching the ground. Not exactly romantic, but then, he wasn't in a romantic mood.

Behind him, completely hidden in the shadows, his friend Justice complained, "My balls are freezing."

Still watching the surrounding area, Leese said, "You should try wearing underwear."

"The ladies would complain. They like me commando."

Leese started to smile, until a shadow shifted from the right side of an alley that bisected the station from a cheap hotel. He said, "Shh."

"This is it?" Justice whispered. "You see her?"

"Quiet." Leese pressed farther back into the darkness, his gaze alert, his senses zinging.

A woman, small in stature, emerged dragging an enormous suitcase with a broken wheel. As it tried to pull her sideways, she relentlessly forced it through slush and blackened snow. Her narrowed gaze scanned the area with nervous awareness.

Leese didn't move, but still her attention shot back

in his direction. She stared, watchful and wary, until he stepped out.

Trying not to look threatening, Leese propped a shoulder on the brick facade of the vacated building. He glanced at her, then away, as if dismissing her.

She continued to stare.

Now what to do?

"What's happening?" Justice whispered.

"Nothing. Be quiet."

The girl wore jeans with snow boots, a puffy coat that covered her to her knees and a black stocking cap pulled down to her eyebrows. Straight brown hair stuck out from the bottom.

When she finally looked away, it was to drop the suitcase and whip around, facing the way she'd come.

Two men stepped out, followed by a third.

The third smiled at her. "Going somewhere, Cat? Without saying goodbye?"

Suspicions confirmed, Leese watched Catalina Nicholson take a defiant stance. That didn't surprise him. As soon as he'd been given this assignment, he'd learned what he could of her.

She came from a wealthy family of lawyers and CEOs, people with far-reaching political and business connections. They were the movers and shakers of the world, influencing other powerful people effortlessly.

But Catalina had bucked convention by becoming an elementary school art teacher, something her family hadn't liked. She clearly enjoyed her luxuries, but wanted to earn them herself. Some inheritances helped to pave the way on that, but from all reports, she'd proven herself to be headstrong and independent. Small in size but not in attitude.

Here, in the slums of Danbrook, Ohio, she was far away from her usual routine of dealing with middle-class families and their grade-school children.

"That's right, Wayne," she said, her voice strong. "I'm leaving."

"I don't think so," the man called Wayne said, and his two cronies moved to surround her. "Not just yet. Not until you pay up on all those promises you made."

Strangely enough, Catalina looked back at Leese again, her expression a touch desperate.

Even from a distance, he felt her silent request for help.

"Stay put unless you see that I need you," Leese told Justice. He was pretty sure he could handle things without drawing his gun, but there was always a chance he'd cause a ruckus and then, to protect her, they'd need to make a run for it. "Be ready with the car."

Justice grumbled, "I miss all the fun."

His boots crunching in the frozen snow, Leese headed toward her in a casual stride.

Relief took the starch out of her shoulders. If he could defuse things without violence, that'd be for the best. Right now, the bus station was all but empty. But if a brawl broke out, for sure it'd draw attention from somewhere.

As he approached, the men all went still, watchful, before deciding he didn't matter.

Idiots.

Leese stepped up in front of her, blocking the pushiest guy, forcing him back a step.

"Hey!"

"Excuse me." Insinuating himself between her and the big goon, Leese insulated her from trouble, then turned to face her. Catalina was probably a foot shorter than him, and even in the thick coat she seemed slim all over. She tipped back her head and stared up at him with big blue eyes that were both wary and defiant.

By silent agreement, she trusted him, when that was the very last thing she should have done. No wonder he'd been sent to her.

Leese hefted her bag, which weighed a ton, and maintaining the casual vibe said, "This way," indicating where he'd been standing watch.

Without bothering to look at the other men, she drew a careful breath, braced herself and nodded in agreement.

Insane. The woman had no self-protection mechanism. She didn't know him from Adam, but was willing to blindly saunter off with him.

When he'd been assigned this case, not once had he expected it to be this easy. On the contrary. Everything he'd been told had led him to believe it would be a total pain in the ass to keep her safe.

She took two steps.

The closest goon said, "This is bullshit."

Pausing, Leese huffed out a breath. "Let it go."

"The hell I will."

Hearing the elevated voice, he turned just in time to dodge a thick fist. Still holding her bag, Leese landed a knee to the man's midsection, then flattened him with an elbow to the chin.

The guy's eyes rolled back and he collapsed like a rag doll, one leg bent awkwardly beneath him, his jaw slack.

Eyeing the remaining two, Leese popped his neck and waited. "Anyone else?"

Being wiser than they looked, they declined further violence.

As the downed man came around with a groan, Leese backed up with Catalina. "Get your friend out of the slush, before hypothermia sets in." It was so bitter cold, it wouldn't take long for the elements to affect a body, especially when drenched in wet snow.

While Wayne remained hostile, the other man rushed forward to help his friend back to his feet. Tottering, he made his way to a curb where he slumped, still unsteady.

There were no more smiles when Wayne said, "She owes me."

"How much?" Paying off the guy would be easier than debating it on such a bitter night, and more expedient than refusing them with his fists.

Wayne's eyes narrowed. "Not money."

"Ah, well, I can't even up with you, then. Guess you're out of luck."

Jaw grinding, Wayne glared at him. "I gave her a place to stay. I fed her. Bought her those boots and coat—"

"And you figured on getting paid how?"

Throughout it all, Catalina stayed behind him.

Wayne growled, "She knows what I expected."

Leaning around, tone apologetic, Catalina whispered, "Yeah, about that… I never planned to sleep with you, Wayne. I'm sorry. I promise I will repay you, I just can't right now. But I do have your address, so—"

"Fuck you," Wayne snarled.

Growing impatient, Leese said, "Apparently that's not happening." He set down the suitcase and pushed aside his open coat, showing the Glock in a belt holster at his side.

The men stared uneasily. Catalina sucked in a startled breath.

Ignoring those reactions, Leese looked at her boots, then lifted the collar of the coat, examining it. While they were decent protection against the elements, they weren't high-end items. Probably bought at a discount department store.

Definitely not worth Catalina prostituting herself.

He withdrew his wallet and pulled out a few hundreds. "This will have to suffice." He folded the money, walked up to Wayne and held it out.

After a ripe hesitation, Wayne took the cash.

With a dose of menace, Leese warned, "Don't come after her again."

Wayne nodded, said something low to the uninjured man and the three of them retreated behind the tall buildings.

Leese felt Catalina retreating as well.

Out of patience and feeling stern, he faced her. "Don't run."

Eyes huge, her face pale except for the pink of her cold nose, she swallowed hard. "You were sent to bring me home, weren't you?"

Body Armor, the agency where he worked, had sent him…but his job was to keep her safe, period. "You don't have to be afraid."

With a shake of her head, she stepped back.

Leese saw it in her eyes; she would run. "Don't."

She whirled to flee and plowed headlong into Justice. The impact was solid enough that she bounced back, her feet slid out from under her on the icy surface and she landed flat in the frozen snow. Given the way she wheezed, she'd knocked the wind out of herself.

She didn't sink in the snow as the other guy had. Nope. She might as well have hit solid ground. At least he didn't have to worry about *her* getting hypothermia.

Leese knelt beside her. "Shh." He cupped the back of her head. "Hold still." To Justice, he said, "You were supposed to wait at the car."

"I saw it was clear and wanted to hurry you along."

Justice was still learning patience. He was here today with Leese to get a handle on the job. So far, he failed with flying colors. "Carry her bag to the car. We'll be right there. And, Justice, stay sharp, *and stay with the car.*"

On his way past, Justice told her, "Sorry about that, honey. Didn't mean to startle you." He carried the bag as if it weighed nothing, but then, Justice was a six-foot-five former heavyweight MMA fighter made of solid muscle.

Drawing her into a sitting position and raising her arms over her head, Leese said, "Take it easy. You're all right."

She sucked in a strained breath, coughed and wheezed again.

"Running into Justice is like hitting the side of a mountain. Did you hurt anything?"

She got her breath back with a vengeance. "Who *are* you people?"

Her hat had come loose and silky brown hair tangled around her face. With very cold hands, Leese brushed it back. Gloves would have been nice.

But gloves skewed his accuracy whenever he needed to draw his weapon.

He never discounted that possibility, so no gloves.

"I'm a bodyguard with the Body Armor agency. I was hired to keep you safe."

"Oh God." Elbows on her knees, she dropped her head forward and rocked in agitation.

Sitting in the cold was not his idea of fun. "You're okay?" Instinct had him rubbing her back. She didn't seem to mind.

"Yes." She lifted her head and pinned him with her gaze. "You don't look like any bodyguard I've ever seen."

"Seen a few, have you?"

"Too many. They're pretty obvious, but not you. You don't fit the mold at all." She studied his face. "How did you find me?"

Leese was unaware of any mold, but he also knew Body Armor was vastly different from most other agencies. "I was told you were in this general area. It's a small town. Newcomers draw attention."

"I was two towns over the last time *bodyguards* found me."

So others had been sent to protect her, but she'd deliberately lost them, then tried hiding again? Leese wasn't sure what was going on, but he had an objective, and he'd see it through. "I showed your photo around and tracked you here."

Her eyes narrowed. "Since when do bodyguards track people?"

Since clients paid a small fortune to make it happen. Balanced on the balls of his feet, Leese let his wrists rest over his knees. "I learned a lot of neat tricks," he told her.

"Like?"

So she wanted to have this whole conversation while exposed to the elements? Appeared so. "Like how to locate people." He stood and pulled her to her feet.

She strained away. "What are you doing?"

Her unmistakable panic helped him to rein in his impatience. "Your seat is probably damp by now. The back of your coat too. You need to get somewhere warm and dry."

"Where?"

"Let's go to the car and we'll talk about it."

She balked. "So you're taking me home?"

That sounded like an accusation. Leese tried to ignore the cold. "Is that where you want to go?"

Her brows lifted. "Not really, no."

"Okay then, want to clue me in?" *His* balls were starting to freeze.

Puzzled, she narrowed her eyes on him. "You weren't told to take me anywhere?"

"I've only spoken to my boss, and she said to keep you safe, period." Why did he feel like he might be missing the big picture here? "That's the beginning, middle and end."

Incredulous, she asked, "For how long?"

He shrugged. "My understanding is that it's pretty open-ended at this point." Given her reactions so far, he could see why those who cared about her assumed she'd need protection.

But to be sure, at the first opportunity he'd give Sahara a call and have her fess up all the facts. Sahara Silver, the new owner of Body Armor, did like to do things her own way—and it was never conventional.

Catalina kept her gaze locked with his while working out something in her mind, and suddenly she stiffened. "Oh my God."

"Problem?"

Her hair whipped around as she searched the area again.

Who was she looking for? "Catalina—"

On a heartfelt groan of despair, she gripped the front of his coat. "You've probably led him to me."

Leese didn't know who she meant, but he saw honest fear in her expression. "Let's get out of the area, somewhere safe." He noticed that she limped a little as he led her quickly to where Justice waited with the car. "We'll talk more once I know you're secure."

Justice sat behind the wheel of the black Lexus SUV, the engine running, so the car would be warm.

Catalina balked again at the sight of him, then squared her shoulders and hastened her pace.

"You don't have to worry about Justice." Leese reached the SUV ahead of her and opened the back passenger door. "Colorful as he might be."

She said, "He's fine."

Right. Height and a brick build were enough to make Justice intimidating, but he also had black-as-sin eyes, a dark Mohawk and a goatee badly in need of a trim. His earliest fighting days had left him with a crooked nose from too many breaks and a right ear thickened from too many hits.

Overall, despite his massive size and capability, Justice was easygoing and considerate—especially to pretty girls.

"Let's lose the wet coat, okay? You'll be more comfortable."

She bit her lip, then quickly stripped her coat off. Leese took it from her as she climbed in.

She was so skittish that he didn't trust her to stay put and he definitely didn't want her trying to hop out of a moving car. Still holding the door open, he said, "Scoot."

"What?" Catalina pushed back her hair and blinked at him in question.

Rather than explain again, Leese took the expedient measure of getting in next to her, forcing her to make room for him. He watched her rump as she quickly crawled across the seat, moving as far from him as she could get.

As he draped the coat over her lap, he told Justice, "Go," and to Catalina, said, "Buckle up."

"Where to?" Justice asked.

"Head for the highway." Because she hadn't done it yet, Leese reached around Catalina and buckled her seat belt, then tucked the coat around her again. "We'll go south."

She pressed back in her seat. "Where's my suitcase?"

"In back," Justice told her, taking several peeks at her in the rearview mirror.

She confirmed that by twisting around to look in the cargo area. When she saw the battered suitcase, she dropped back into her seat and closed her eyes. "Thank you."

"Welcome." Then to Leese, he asked, "We expecting more trouble?"

"I don't know yet."

"Yes," Catalina said. "Expect it, because it's definitely coming."

Leese shared a look with Justice, but both chose to

stay silent. As they drove out of the small town, the streetlights faded away and only the headlights of the SUV and the few other cars on the road lit the area.

After about twenty minutes, Catalina slumped in her seat and yawned. "I don't suppose you have anything to eat?"

The guys shared another look.

Justice said, "Sorry, no. I take it you're hungry?"

"Mmm. I haven't eaten since lunch yesterday."

If true, that sucked, but Leese shook his head at Justice. "Don't stop yet."

"If I can't eat," Catalina said, "then do you mind if I nap? I've been even longer without sleep and now that I'm warm, I'm having a pretty hard time keeping my eyes open."

Every minute with her got more confusing. "Why haven't you slept?"

"I was planning my escape from Wayne's little cult. He considers himself this benevolent guide, but he's actually just creepy. I had to sneak out a window. Should have known he'd find out."

Tension knotted the muscles of Leese's neck. "You were in a cult?"

"Well, not an official cult or anything. Those are off in the woods or something, right? But Wayne has this weird setup where he takes in people in need."

"You?" he asked with clear disbelief, because her family connections alone would forever keep her out of the category of "in need."

She rolled one shoulder. "I had to lay low for a bit." Rather than expound on that, she went back to explaining the setup. "So Wayne has these two big Victorians and a bunch of people stay there on a temporary basis.

Homeless guys, alcoholics, a few addicts. Mostly men, but there was this older prostitute too. She helped me get away because, according to her, she didn't like the competition of having another female around. Guess she had a thing for Wayne. He's the only one who paid much attention to me."

"He bought you clothes?"

"The coat and boots, yeah. See, we all had to take turns keeping up the property. Clearing the front walk and driveway and stuff like that. I was the youngest and healthiest one there, so I volunteered to help the others. Only I didn't have the proper shoes and my coat was cloth and often got damp, so Wayne took it upon himself to replace them." She worried her fingers over the zipper of her coat. "He took a lot for granted, trying to give me gifts and getting enraged when I refused them. I'm not sure what he expected…well, I assume he eventually expected sex. I mean, that's obvious, right?"

Leese resisted the urge to look her over. "Probably a safe bet."

"But why he'd expect me to be into it…I couldn't figure that out. I never flirted, never led him on, not until I decided I couldn't stay there anymore. Then I acted interested only so I could put him off until after dinner."

"That's when you left?"

"Out a window, yeah. See, tonight he was planning for me to join him in his room for a late dinner instead of in the dining hall with everyone else. So I figured I had to go." She wrinkled her nose, which wasn't quite so pink anymore. "I was mean, telling him how I was looking forward to it and that I'd see him at seven. I told him I wanted to primp and make myself pretty for him."

She was already pretty, but as far as he could tell, she hadn't primped in a while.

"He liked that idea, so he wasn't hovering around me so much. It gave me an opportunity to sneak away. I dodged around for a while, figuring that was safer than making a beeline for the bus station, since Wayne would go there first to look for me, right?" Without waiting for Leese to reply, she continued, "But I guess he hadn't given up because he was watching the station all the same, knowing I'd show up there sooner or later."

Was the bus her only option? Her family was old money. Leese doubted any of them had ever stepped foot on a bus, much less made it their preferred mode of transportation.

That made about as much sense as her rooming in a shelter with a letch supervising.

"On principle alone, I'd have left the coat and boots, but when he gave them to me, he also swiped my old stuff. I didn't have anything else and I didn't want to freeze, so…" She slumped farther in the seat. "It was a gift, after all. And turns out, they are pretty warm."

Leese rubbed his jaw. When the headlights behind them drove closer, he looked over the seat to check it out. The car cut away and went down a side street to the right.

Gone, and yet his instincts sharpened with the probable threat. "Turn left here," he told Justice. If the other car had been following, hoping to circle ahead of them, he'd have to disappoint them.

The road was short and led back into a business district. New lights appeared behind them. There shouldn't be anything alarming in that, and yet, warning bells went off in his head.

Checking a map on his phone, he said, "Go through this parking lot, then left again. About five miles down you'll find an on-ramp for 75 north. We'll try that for a bit."

Catalina chewed her bottom lip, her arms folded around her.

She looked exhausted, apparently with good reason. He needed to make up his mind about what to do with her now, but there were too many unanswered questions.

Questions that would have to be answered later.

Hoping she'd have a suggestion, he asked, "Where would you like to go?"

Thinking about it, she inhaled and said, "If you want to find another bus station—"

"Not an option." Leese reached over, took her chin, and turned her face toward him. "Like it or not, I was hired to keep you safe. I can't do that if I can't see you."

"You also can't keep me safe indefinitely."

She sounded so sure about that. Did she really believe someone planned to do her harm? All he'd been told was that her father wanted her protected while she was out of reach, but he didn't know anything about a specific threat to her.

Was there a chance Mr. Nicholson had hired a bodyguard because his daughter was confused, maybe a little irrational…even delusional? She wouldn't be the first person to imagine a bizarre conspiracy theory.

As if she'd read his thoughts, she smiled sadly. "Bus station, after all?"

"No." Until he knew what was going on, he planned to keep her very close. "Do some weaving until you hit the highway," he told Justice, "then find us a place to stay for the night."

"Swanky or low-key?"

Leese thought about it, then asked her, "Preference?"

Her gaze traveled over his face, his shoulders, down his body. "Most would assume you'd go low-key, thinking that's what I'd want. But if we can afford swankier...?"

"We can." He had an alternate credit card to use, without any ties to the agency, just in case Catalina wasn't imagining anything. "It'll just take a little longer to reach."

Justice said, "We going to make her wait to get room service?"

Again, Leese deferred to her.

"I'd kill for a burger," Catalina said. "Loaded. With fries. And a malt." She made a sound of pleasure. "Man, that sounds good."

"I just fell in love," Justice said.

Ignoring Justice, Leese said, "A burger is doable, but we'll pick it up and take it to the hotel to eat. Okay?"

"You two might be my new favorite people." She curled into the corner, snuggling for a comfortable position. "At least for a little while." After a yawn, she said, "Wake me when we're there."

Leese watched her fall asleep.

A whole lot of things weren't adding up. For one, despite all the research he'd done on her, Catalina wasn't quite what he'd expected.

The situation, too, was off. He'd planned to keep her safe, but now he had to wonder: from what?

"She's out?" Justice asked with disbelief.

A soft snore was his answer.

Leese smiled, until she shifted, turning toward him and stretching out on the seat, her head on his thigh.

"Shh," she muttered. "So tired."

In the rearview mirror, Leese saw Justice's wide eyes. Hell, his own were probably bugging. What woman escaped danger, met strangers, mistrusted them, then decided to doze?

It wasn't normal. The idea of her being irrational seemed more plausible by the moment.

Justice turned the radio on low, and as she'd ordered, they both stayed quiet. But Leese stewed, at first in discomfort.

Where the hell was he supposed to put his hands?

Then he decided to hell with it and rested one forearm across her body. She shifted and his hand ended up on her hip.

Worked for him, and she didn't complain, so he just went with it.

The discomfort turned internal. Confused on all counts, he wanted to call Sahara and insist on some additional details, but not while Catalina might hear. He'd have to wait for the right moment and some privacy.

Using his left hand, he double-checked their route. With that done, he read a few private emails, did a little more research on the woman dozing against him and basically bided his time.

When it occurred to him that he was lightly stroking Catalina's hip without even thinking about it, he ceased...until she grew restless. Then he gave in to the urge again.

They drove for forty-five minutes before Leese decided they were close enough to the hotel to pull into a drive-through burger joint. In all that time, Catalina had slept soundly but now, as the car slowed, she stretched awake.

Feeling the lithe movement of her trim little body against him, Leese gave her a few pats. "Time to wake up."

"Mmm." Sluggish, she turned to her back, her knees bent against the door, and stared up at him, taking a moment to orient herself. Blinking in surprise, she asked, "How long was I out?"

Shadows kept her expression hidden, but he felt her intensity. "Less than an hour." His forearm was now across her stomach, meaning he practically embraced her. "Ready to order some food?"

Cautiously, she sat up and looked around, then turned to stare at him. "No trouble?"

"No." Did she think she'd have slept through it?

"Sorry I passed out."

"Not a problem." Odd as hell, but it had maybe made things easier, giving him time to sort through the altered situation.

She leaned closer to him to peer over the front seat and out the windshield. Several cars were ahead of them, and the line moved slowly. "Could we walk in? I need to use the restroom."

"We'll be at the hotel in just a few minutes."

Blue eyes stared into his. "I need to go now."

Leese wasn't sure how he knew—she didn't blink, didn't lose eye contact—but he had no doubt at all that she planned to run the second she got out of his sight. "All right. I'll wait by the door and Justice can wait right outside."

She scowled.

He grinned.

Giving up, she sighed. "I don't even know your name."

"Leese Phelps. The big guy up front—"

"You're *both* big." She peered toward Justice. "But yeah, you're gargantuan. Justice, right?"

"Yes, ma'am."

A dimple appeared in her cheek. "I like your style, Justice." Sitting back again, she turned to Leese. "Credentials?"

A little late, but at least she finally wanted to see them. Leese removed his folded leather holder and flipped it open to show his ID.

She studied it longer than necessary, looking from the photo to him to the photo again. "Okay, so you're really a bodyguard."

"You had doubts?"

"Sure."

By the second she became more of an enigma. "And still you went to sleep?"

"I was seriously depleted and needed the rest. Besides, what was I supposed to do? Try to fight my way free?"

Justice snorted.

"Exactly." As they pulled up in the line to buy food, her stomach rumbled. "Besides, even if I was a hulk like you two, I'm beat and I'm hungry. Fighting about the inevitable didn't seem worth it."

"Inevitable?" Leese asked.

"You were taking me, regardless of what I had to say about it. Right?"

What did she think? That he was holding her hostage? He was about to explain when it became their turn at the order window. Justice took and shared her food preferences, then ordered for himself and Leese too. Once they had two big bags of food, they drove away again.

Catalina sniffed the air. "Wow, that smells good."

"We're a block away from the hotel. Before we get there, you should understand something."

She awkwardly pulled on her coat, working around the fastened seat belt, bumping Leese a few times. "What's that?"

"I'm not holding you against your will."

One of her brows lifted.

"I'm here to keep you safe."

"So you've said. But if I chose to leave?"

He gave her the truth. "I'd follow."

CHAPTER TWO

"I HAVE HER HAT."

"What the fuck am I supposed to do with a hat? I need her, Tesh, not her wardrobe."

Refusing to be riled, Tesh fingered the hat, then stuffed it back into his pocket. "I meant it as a confirmation for you that I have her in my sights. She left the hat behind at the bus station after some idiots tried to accost her. The bodyguard stepped in."

"So he found her."

Making a sound of affirmation, Tesh said, "And I followed him." He could have found her on his own. Contrary to what little Cat Nicholson thought, she wasn't all that clever. But she'd have recognized him right off and booked again.

Having a different face, a less menacing face, track her down worked to his advantage. "I've been following her since, not too close because I don't want to spook her."

"Fine, what's the plan?"

"I'll grab her in the morning." Despite the wishes of anyone else, he didn't want her killed. Not his sweet, wild kitten. Given half a chance, he'd tuck her away and keep her safe.

All his, and his alone.

It'd be worth giving up everything. *She* was worth

it, and when he finished taming her, she'd be not only agreeable, but grateful.

"Keep me posted."

Tesh nodded. "Will do." He disconnected the call, and thought about how to proceed. He had his orders. And he had his preferences. If things went right, he could have it all.

CATALINA WASN'T SURE what to think. Leese Phelps, her new "bodyguard," looked sincere enough. But she knew how it worked.

For much of her life, and especially the last few months before she'd been forced to run six weeks ago, too many things had been done "for her own good." These days, she had a hard time knowing who to trust, but it was rarely those people claiming to have her best interests at heart.

Leese, with the gorgeous blue eyes and tall, solid physique, looked the part of a hero. But looks could be deceiving. He also said the right things, painting himself as a good guy. But good, too, could be subjective.

He'd made mincemeat of Wayne's bullyboy, taking him out in such an effortless way. Then with a look alone, he intimidated Wayne.

He had a gun and he spoke to his massive chauffeur friend as if the guy wasn't an enormous pile of muscle and badass 'tude.

She sighed. What to do?

Gaze teasing, Leese lifted one bag of food as enticement. "Why don't you come up to the room and at least eat before making any decisions? I have a feeling we need to talk out a few things."

The wind had played havoc with his dark hair, and

this late in the day he had sexy beard shadow scruff highlighting his lean jaw, making his incendiary eyes look even more compelling.

How unfair. Her eyes were a wishy-washy blah blue.

Not his. Nope, his eyes were the kind that made a woman's stomach tumble.

And though the food smelled good, it had nothing on Leese, who smelled incredibly delicious. The nap she'd taken, using his hard thigh as a pillow, was the best rest she'd had in a good long while.

How did that make any sense?

She had no idea how much, if any, she should trust him. But she'd slept peacefully.

"I guess if you wanted to murder me or some other heinous thing, you wouldn't have to take me to a nice hotel to do it."

"You see," he said, dark, level brows coming together. "It's thoughts like that we need to talk about."

"Then again," she continued, feeling constrained as they drove into a dark, concrete parking garage, "you could be luring me into a trap." Fear put a stranglehold on her throat. What if he only wanted her to come along peacefully because that'd make it easier on him? Then he'd hand her over without a single qualm.

Then what would she do?

"No trap," Leese said gently, and amazingly it helped to still the escalating alarm.

"No one else is waiting inside? Because it'd be beyond diabolical to lure me with food when I'm already so hungry, just to sabotage me and—"

One finger pressed to her mouth, silencing her. "I'm not sure who you think wants to sabotage you, but I promise, Justice and I won't let that happen."

Oh wow. He said that so convincingly while touching her mouth, and even through her fear, it affected her, making her toes curl in her boots. Believing him, even though that was an insane thing to do, she gave a small nod. "Okay."

"Good girl." His hand cupped the side of her face. "Now take a few breaths and try to relax."

She nodded, even as her thoughts scrambled.

Justice parked, then walked around and opened her door for her.

Hoping to hide her continued worry, she teased, "Such a gentleman."

Justice tugged at an ear. "Haven't been accused of that too many times."

When she stepped out, she felt downright puny next to him. It wasn't just his height, but also the breadth of his chest and shoulders. Boulder shoulders. Even through his leather jacket, she could see the unyielding strength in his body.

For whatever reason, even though she felt safe with Leese, Justice made her more at ease.

Could be the lack of attraction.

She saw Leese as walking, talking sex appeal.

Justice was like a big teddy bear…if teddy bears ate steel for breakfast.

A second later, his expression alert, Leese was at her side as he waited for Justice to open the back of the SUV. He had a leaner, more honed physique that was no less powerful.

Leese, clearly in charge, nearly vibrated with edgy awareness. Justice seemed to be along for the ride.

They made interesting cohorts, like mismatched bookends that would nonetheless get the job done. And if she wasn't so worried, she wouldn't mind her role as the only book.

"How's your ankle?"

She stared at him blankly. "My ankle?"

"You were limping earlier."

"Oh." She looked down at her feet, unaware of any problem. "Guess it's okay." She wiggled her toes. "Must have been a temporary thing."

"Good. Any discomfort, just let me know."

They each retrieved moderately sized overnight bags, and Justice lifted out her big suitcase.

"The wheel broke," she explained.

"Not a problem." Justice held it as easily as he would have a pillow.

That bugged her. She'd had a devil of a time hauling that awkward heap through the snow, sludge and ice in the alleys. If these two were going to corral her, they could have done so as soon as she'd left the shelter. Maybe then her back and shoulders wouldn't be so tired.

"He's a regular beast, isn't he?" she whispered to Leese.

Smiling, Leese shrugged, still looking around the area. "He's strong."

"Used to be a fighter," Justice said, proving he'd heard her whisper. "Same as Leese. We gave it up to be bodyguards, and gotta say, it's a lot less work."

Fascinated, Cat looked between them as they headed into the foyer of the hotel. "Fighters? Like boxing? Or do you mean street brawlers?"

"Professional MMA," Justice explained. "Mixed martial arts."

She knew little about it, but it probably meant they were well trained. "Why'd you give it up?"

Cutting off Justice's answer, Leese said, "This place isn't top-notch, maybe not what you're used to, but it's one of the better hotels in this area."

A change of subject? And what did he know about her preferences? She scowled at him. "It's better than the shelter, I'm sure."

"Book us two rooms," he told Justice, handing him a card. "If they have a suite, that'd be great. If not, a single and a double will do. Make sure they're near each other."

"Right." Leaving the luggage with Leese, Justice walked away toward the front desk.

"You can grab a seat while we wait." Leese indicated the cushy sofa behind her.

Luckily the lobby was nearly empty this time of night. Other than a couple headed toward the lounge, Cat saw only hotel employees. Big windows and glass doors at the entrance showed another light snow starting, each flake glistening as it danced beneath the lights. A boutique, decorated with hearts and flowers for Valentine's Day, as well as several restaurants lined the street across from them.

As she sat, Cat thought about the arrangements. Since she'd have a room to herself, she could sneak away if she wanted. But would that be wise? She was out of money, and if she hit the ATM that'd probably leave a trail. Then again, seeing Justice use the credit card at the front desk, she knew it'd be pretty easy to find her, just by tracking Leese and Justice, which had no doubt been the plan.

She'd thought staying with Wayne would completely throw off the bloodhounds. It was so far from her ordinary, everyday life that she hadn't imagined anyone would ever look for her there.

Then Wayne had to go and get grabby and ruin those plans. Not that she could have hidden indefinitely anyway. Sooner or later she had to work out a life for herself, a way to live safe and free.

Maybe it was time to confront things.

Could she?

For tonight, she'd try not to dwell on it. Showering in peace, sleeping without worry would be so nice.

And Leese did have that food…

It had been a while since she'd really enjoyed eating. With cockroaches running rampant, strangers staring and Wayne always on the make, mealtime at the shelter had been done in uncomfortable haste.

In contrast, a loaded burger seemed like a real luxury.

In the morning she could figure out an escape…perhaps over breakfast.

While she sat there thinking things through, Leese stood in front of her, hands in his pockets, his gaze brooding as he alternately studied the windows and door, and watched her.

When her gaze met his, he smiled. "Before you work out anything too elaborate, you should know that one room is for Justice, and the other is for us."

Her heart jumped. "Us?"

He caught her arm and pulled her back to her feet. "I can't protect you if I'm not with you. And I have a feeling you need more protection than I ever could have guessed."

His feelings were spot-on.

Justice rejoined them, handing out room keycards. "Got you the suite and I have a room across the hall."

So the big guy had understood the setup all along?

With a hand to the small of her back, Leese urged her to the elevator.

A bellhop took them to a private floor accessible only with a keycard. Nice. That gave her a little more added security.

On the ride up to the twenty-sixth floor, Cat tried to use the silence to plan, but she was far too aware of Leese standing closely at her back.

He intended to room with her.

She glanced at Justice standing at her side, and the big ape grinned at her as if he knew her thoughts. Scowling, she stared straight instead at the numbers as they changed for each floor.

Repugnant as it seemed, she should definitely go; Leese had said she could if she wanted. Maybe it was time to test that theory.

After they departed the elevator, the bellhop started to step off with them. Leese slipped him a bill and thanked him with an obvious dismissal.

He unlocked the suite door himself, then held it open for her.

Nervousness kept her glued to the spot. They were in such a private location, with only a few other doors around. She felt isolated, alone…but then she'd felt that way for a while now.

"I changed my mind," she blurted.

Silence ticked by until, tipping his head, Leese asked, "About?"

His calm only amplified her nervousness.

"This." She gestured at the room. At him. "I don't want to stay here."

Pausing at his own door, Justice waited.

"Okay." Hands on his hips, Leese held her gaze. "Where did you want to go?"

"Er…nowhere with you. I'm going to just…leave."

Dark brows touching, Leese considered her, making her squirm. He let the door shut. "All right."

Justice groaned with loud drama.

"Wherever you go," Leese told her, "I *will* closely follow. But it's up to you."

Damn it. Him being so agreeable left her only more perplexed. And truthfully, she didn't want to go anywhere. The nap had recharged her, but only a little. Problems pummeled her tired brain. And the thought of a shower was so enticing… "Can I take the food with me?"

A half smile curled his mouth. "Sure."

The easy agreement left her deflated, stealing the last of her resistance. "Fine. I'll stay."

Justice let out a long, relieved breath.

"But I'm not keen on sharing a room with you." *Liar.* She hated the thought of being alone. She protested on principle—because she liked the idea of being alone with him far too much. And why not? Could he be more striking with his beautiful eyes, calm, controlled nature and that ripped bod?

Her biggest dilemma was that he looked at her as a problem to solve, and she looked at him like any red-blooded woman would look at a sexy hunk of man.

She felt sparks, blast him, and he stayed cool and distant.

"If that's your only concern, I can stay out here."

Cat gaped at him. "Here, the…hall?"

"Yes."

Why wouldn't he just room with Justice? "I could take the single and you guys could—"

"Wherever you are," he repeated in a deep, serious tone, "that's where I'll be. Either in the room with you, or just outside the door."

Justice said, "Give in, honey. Leese takes this shit far too seriously, I swear. He'll stand out here like a guard dog all night, and then I'll feel guilty and want to spell him, and neither of us will get any sleep."

"I'll sleep just fine," she told him, though that was probably a lie too. Knowing the two of them stood vigil would keep her from resting.

"I meant Leese and me," the hulk grouched.

"Justice," Leese warned. "It's her decision. Don't pressure her."

Yeah, God forbid she be pressured. Such a laugh. She'd had more pressure lately than any woman should have to bear.

Justice plopped down her suitcase and took two big steps to swipe up the bag of food. "Fine." Rummaging inside, he said, "I'm at least going to eat while she decides." He withdrew two burgers.

Justice made her feel mean, and that, too, was unusual. "Open the damn door," she demanded.

Without questioning her, Leese did just that, holding it wide for her.

Justice, not taking any chances on her changing her mind, dug out his fries and malt too. "Glad that's settled." He balanced everything in the crook of one arm and deftly used his keycard. "Keep me updated," he said before going inside and letting the door close behind him.

Leese stood there waiting for her, patience personified.

After a deep breath, she lifted her chin and strode past him.

The suite was lovely, divided into a small kitchenette, a sitting area with two couches arranged perpendicular to one another, a large television, a desk, a round table with four chairs and a small half bath. One of the couches looked to be a narrow rollaway bed. Through open glass double doors she saw a separate bedroom with a full bathroom, including a wide tub and granite shower.

One bedroom. One shower.

Great.

Leese paid no mind as he got everything into the room. He put the bags of food on the table, then carried her suitcase to the bedroom and set it at the end of the bed for her.

Cat watched as he took his own bag to the end of one couch.

A promising sign. Sort of.

"What's it to be first?" He removed his coat and hung it neatly in the closet. "Food or talk?"

With his coat gone and his hands again on his hips, she couldn't help focusing on that menacing gun. Had he shot anyone?

Ever?

Recently?

In her experience, most bodyguards were older, thicker. Less appealing. Given her family's affluence, she'd grown up with them hanging around, always watching her like a prized possession.

She'd tried so hard to leave that life behind, but sadly, she'd taken just a little too long to make it happen.

"Catalina?"

Talking meant explaining, and she needed more time for that. Like…maybe a couple of days. "Food, definitely." Then if she had to make a run for it, at least she'd have a modicum of energy.

Stripping off her coat, she tossed it toward the suitcase. Given the amount of walking she'd done, the boots were starting to pinch her feet. Hopping on first one foot and then the other, she removed them, letting them drop to the floor by the side of the bed. Enjoying the freedom, she wiggled her toes inside her socks. That felt good enough that she also peeled off the thick sweatshirt, leaving her in jeans, socks and a long-sleeved T-shirt.

She pushed back her hair, freed the band from her wrist and secured a ponytail.

More comfortable, she headed to the table and chairs, unaware of Leese staring until she glanced up to ask if he was ready to eat too.

That hot gaze of his had been all over her body, but immediately jumped to her face. "Let me." He got close to pull out her chair, bringing with him that irresistible scent of fresh outdoors mixed with man.

She inhaled deeply.

In her old world, men were often well mannered and polite. They were also manipulative and mercenary, focused on a pampered social status that blinded them to the ugliness of reality.

The old world felt a million miles away, and nothing about Leese felt pampered. "Thank you."

He set out the food, napkins, even opened her straw and stuck it in her malt. "Help yourself," he said. "I'll be right back."

When he walked away, Cat turned to watch. He prowled around the suite studying the locks on the windows and closing the drapes, even in the bedroom.

Then he left.

As the door closed behind her, she froze.

An insidious sensation—fear, worry—crawled into her soul. They were such familiar emotions, usually with her every second.

But not since meeting Leese. Not like this.

The suite that only seconds before felt warm and comfortable now felt isolated.

The door opened again and he strode in, going still when he saw her face. "Hey. What's wrong?"

Her lungs filled with air, a refreshing breath of reassurance. *He hadn't left her at all.* Refusing to be pitied, she choked out, "Nothing."

His expression shifted from sharp awareness to soft understanding. "We'll need to work on that habit you have of lying." In only a few long, casual strides he stood beside her. Looking into her eyes, he asked, "Want to try again?"

Not really. She cleared her throat. "Where did you go?"

"Just checking on things."

"Like?"

"Staircase, other rooms, windows."

Oh. He'd once again been assuring her safety? Astounding. Her muscles further relaxed. Acting as if the panic hadn't happened, she gestured to the table. "Are you going to eat now?"

"Yeah." He took his seat, still attuned to her yet not intimidating her with his stare. He hesitated only a heartbeat, then said, "I'm not budging, Cat, okay?"

That was the first time he'd called her that. "You know my nickname?"

"I know a lot about you."

Wow, such a cryptic answer. She wasn't sure she wanted to ask, especially since he couldn't possibly know the most important things.

"I also heard Wayne call you that."

Oh yeah. He didn't miss much. "So, what's the plan?"

"Keep you safe." He took a big bite of a chicken wrap that looked to have tomato and lettuce on it, but nothing else. He followed that up with a drink of tea before adding, "Whatever it takes."

A not-so-simple answer to a very complicated question. He so easily shook her, mostly because he said things with such conviction she couldn't help but believe him.

And believing anyone right now was just plain foolish.

She picked up a fry. "Okay, that's long-term. But for tonight?"

"Once you're ready for bed, Justice can sit here while I go to his room to shower." He took another bite. "Then we'll get some sleep."

In bed. Or rather, one bed, one couch. She made a noncommittal sound and slurped down half her malt to try to cool a sudden rise in her temperature.

Amused, Leese asked, "What did you think would happen?"

"No idea, really. I've had supposed bodyguards after me for a while now, but none of them were like you."

She ate a few more bites, thinking, wondering how far she could push him. "You'll sleep here, right? I mean... on the couch?"

"Yeah." He finished off his food. "What kinds of bodyguards have you known?"

How to put it so that she wouldn't give away too much? If he was as up-front as he seemed and really didn't understand the ramifications and complications of the situation, she didn't want to clue him in tonight. He could react badly.

He could decide she wasn't worth the trouble.

Or that she *was* worth the payoff.

Just to see what he'd do, she settled on a tiny truth, saying, "Mostly the kind who worked for someone else."

He paused, then slowly sat forward to rest a forearm on the table. After studying her expression, he shrugged. "You already know someone else hired me. Otherwise I'd know nothing about you. But I think what you're saying is that these other bodyguards had ulterior motives...beyond your safety?"

In a nutshell. "Let's just say safety is subjective."

"Let's don't." Startling her, he put one big hand on her wrist. His palm was hot, his fingers rough, and the touch made her pulse gallop. "You're either safe from harm, *all* harm, or you're not. I intend to keep you safe from harm."

Cat swallowed to regain her voice. *Get a grip*, she told herself. He's only touching your wrist in *sympathy*, for crying out loud.

Because you're being so damned pathetic. And cowardly.

And because, as he said, someone paid him to look out for you.

"Yeah," she rasped. "That's how I figured it too."

His thumb brushed over her skin, then he patted her—like a dog, blast him—and retreated. "I was hired to keep you safe and that's what I plan to do. So rest easy on that, okay?"

No, she wouldn't rest easy. How could she now that she'd realized she was as sex starved as she was wary?

Not a comfortable combo.

Unaware of her inner turmoil, he continued, "It'd be easier to do that, however, if I knew who or what I was fighting."

No, it wouldn't. She figured she had a much better chance as long as he thought things were simple, instead of so very, very complicated.

But when she looked at him, he was so sincere, so *involved*, she almost caved. It'd help if he was an ogre. Or at least plain. But she didn't have that kind of luck. "It is so unfair."

"What?" he asked, as he stole one of her fries and bit into it. An expression crossed his face, as if he really enjoyed it too.

She watched his jaw move as he chewed, and even that was sexy. "That you should look so good."

He swallowed and slowly, cautiously, turned his head to face her.

Caught in his beautiful gaze, Cat sighed. "You really do. You realize that, right? And here I am, smart enough to know not to trust you no matter what pretty words you say or how sinfully sexy you are. I've had to deal with so much lately, but you're here now, looking like you look, and I don't mean just a handsome face or buff build. No, you have to be patient and nice and all alpha-in-control too, which is pretty damned appealing." She shook her head. "It's unfair. That's all I'm saying."

He didn't reach for any more fries. "That was saying an awful lot, actually."

She flapped a hand. "You don't need to worry about it. I mean, it's obvious you're not feeling the same." She knew it for a fact because he'd looked at her fries with more covetous greed than he'd looked at her. "Just sucks that I have so much on my mind and you keep trying to nudge in there—"

He choked a little.

"—but I'll block *that* from my thoughts somehow."

"That?"

"The attraction." Pushing back her chair, glad that she'd left him speechless, Cat stood and gathered up her empty containers. "Want the rest of the fries?"

"No, I'm good."

Sooo good. She swallowed her automatic sigh. Starting right now, she'd stop spouting nonsense. She probably needed a good night's sleep, then she'd be more mentally functional. "Are you on a diet or something?"

Narrowing his eyes at her, he sat back in his seat. It was a good pose for him, showcasing those flat abs and lean waist while at the same time his chest and shoulders strained the fine fabric of his button-down.

"Cat?"

When her gaze lifted to his, he shook his head, either in frustration or denial, she wasn't sure which. "What?"

"No diet," he said. "It's called healthy eating because I'm not into poisoning my body."

"Yeah, it shows." She didn't see any body fat on him at all. Was this a lifestyle preference leftover from being a fighter? She'd love to hear more about that. Later. If she stuck around. "Personally, I love junk food. If I ever start putting on weight, I'm in trouble."

"Fast metabolism," he said. "But you can eat right and still enjoy your food."

"Do they have fries in your food world?"

A grin twitched over his mouth. "Not much, no."

"Then I'll keep living in mine."

He stood too, and relieved her of the garbage. "I'll set it out."

Cat stared up at him. She barely reached his shoulder but instead of feeling insubstantial next to him, she felt oddly protected.

That had something to do with Leese's overall attitude.

His shirt, the sleeves now rolled to his elbows, fit his broad chest and hard shoulders as if tailored specifically for him. He wore nice jeans and boots, and he looked like a million bucks in a relaxed package.

Until now, she hadn't realized just how sexy "relaxed" could be.

"Did you want to shower?"

Her eyes flared.

Smiling, he chastised softly, "Alone."

Ignoring the tinge of disappointment she felt, she turned to escape. "Yeah."

Leese caught her shoulder. "Cat?"

Nope, she definitely would not face him. "Hmm?"

"If you're going to call someone, anyone, it'd be better if I knew so I could prepare for it."

"Can't," she said. "No phone."

"You don't have a cell?"

Well, heck, why had she just admitted that to him? He kept her rattled without trying.

She'd lost the use of the phone more than a week ago. At first she'd been too worried about someone using her personal cell phone to track her down. Some people had incredible reach and according to the movies, cell phones were a no-no when you were on the run. "I got a prepaid," she explained. "But it's done and I haven't had access to money to—"

"I could take care of it for you."

Pride made her rigid. "You already bought me food. And you're paying for this room."

"It'll all go on an expense account. Don't worry about it."

Oh God, that was even worse because she already knew who'd be covering those expenses—and that meant more control over her.

"We'll talk about it later." Again, Leese's thumb caressed her, this time on her shoulder. "For now, do you need anything?"

Sex, apparently. But that wasn't happening. "No." Somehow, some way, she'd figure out how to reimburse him herself. She wasn't without means, just temporarily unable to access them.

"Then for tonight, how about you put away your worries and just relax? In the morning after you're better rested we'll talk—about everything—and get it all sorted out."

A reprieve. Not a bad idea, considering she was dead on her feet. Now that she'd eaten, sleep beckoned, but first, a much-needed shower. "Sounds like a plan."

"I'll be here when you're done. Then I'll get Justice to come over while I shower."

"I won't be long." As soon as he released her, she practically ran to the bedroom, closed the glass doors and ducked out of view. Wow, the man packed a sultry punch, and he hadn't even been trying. What if he decided he wanted to seduce her? How easy would that be?

She knew she was already halfway there.

Gathering up what she needed, determined to stop thinking about him, she headed to the bathroom. But one thought led to another and as she stepped beneath the water, she thought of Leese doing the same.

No, no, no…shoot. Maybe she'd have to keep her own shower cold. If nothing else, it'd wake her up enough to prioritize.

And lusting after a near stranger was nowhere near the top of the list.

ON THE COUCH, arms stacked behind his head, Leese listened to the quiet.

Or more appropriately, to Cat tossing and turning.

He could picture her right now, how she'd look, that particular curious scowl she wore as if she couldn't decide whether to be pissed, scared, defiant…or turned on.

What a provoking case she'd already turned into, in more ways than one.

Cat might not realize it, but on many levels she appealed to him. Pretty, hell yes. Nice figure, definitely. But it was more her courage, her defiance and spirit that drew him.

Not that he could be drawn. Not during a case.

It didn't help that she made her own interest so apparent.

The shower had slightly revived him, helping to cool his lustful thoughts while also making him think about everything he didn't yet know. She had to have a valid reason for leaving everything familiar, avoiding her family and dodging their efforts to help. And then there was the fact that he was hired to protect her.

From what?

Her fear was real but elusive, there one moment, buried beneath pride the next, sometimes taking center stage and sometimes losing priority as other needs— like a nap and food—took precedence.

Tomorrow, as soon as they left the hotel, he'd take the opportunity to question her on the drive. She'd no longer be exhausted, no longer half-starved…

The amount of food she'd eaten still made him grin. The girl knew how to put it away. Her lack of reserve on that front had also been appealing. She showed no artifice, not about her hunger—or her sexual interest.

Nothing about her demeanor resonated with the idea of a rich pampered girl. She had daring, and she had guts.

When the bedroom door opened, every thought fractured beneath the weight of hot awareness. Saying nothing, he waited.

If she tried to sneak out, then what? He'd have to find a way to wake Justice and—

"Leese?" she whispered.

Her voice, rough and low, stroked over him. He watched the shadow of her slim form move closer. "Something wrong, Cat?"

Losing the hesitant edge, she said, "Sort of," and… sat beside him on the rollaway bed.

Yeah, not comfortable. For one, she was a near stranger, but more than that, she'd already proven herself to be very unpredictable.

With his arms behind his head, he felt…vulnerable.

So he quickly adjusted, coming up to a forearm and half turning toward her. "What is it?"

A slow, audible breath preceded the touch of her hand on his shoulder. "I should be sleeping."

Definitely. They both should. Had they been awake for the same reason? "But?"

"I can't quiet my thoughts."

Maybe they'd have their talk sooner rather than later. He started to sit up, but she said, "Wait."

For two seconds Leese considered things, then relented, resting back to his arm again.

"This is awkward," she said. "Bear with me while I sort it out, okay?"

Her nearness no longer worried him, at least not as any sort of threat from a stranger.

No, it had morphed into physical awareness real quick. "Sort out what?"

The silence grew strained, but she didn't move away. Leese shifted. "Cat?"

"Could I talk to you without you making assumptions?"

Since he'd already made a dozen or more, probably not. "I'll do my best."

"I don't know what it is about you, but it's making me nuts. You're like this assault on my system."

That didn't sound good. "An assault?" With every fiber of his being, he was attuned to her cool fingers lightly touching his now-fevered skin.

Rushing her words together, she stretched out next to him. "Could I sleep with you? *Sleep*, I mean? That nap with you today was the best rest I've had in a very long time but I'm still so tired. I just want to sleep, but I don't dare." She squeezed him, her small body pressed to his, her face against his throat. Her warm breath teased his skin with her agonized explanation. "I know I shouldn't trust you, but I keep wanting to anyway."

Leese tried to relax. "You can trust me."

As if he hadn't said that, she continued, "It's nuts to stay with you, I know that. You're so far out of your realm it only puts you at risk. I don't want that on my conscience, so I tried to convince myself to run—"

"Don't run." Cautiously, he put his arms around her. *Out of his realm?* She didn't have much faith in him.

"Every time I tried to make plans I ended up thinking instead about you being right here. So close and so... Jesus, I hate to say it, but you feel *safe*." She tipped her face up to his. "I need you to be safe."

"I am," he assured her, tucking her closer, folding his arms protectively around her. He gave her a gentle squeeze.

She snuggled in. "I need to make some big decisions, but tonight it just feels too difficult. I think if I slept well, that'd help."

"Sleep always helps." And now, with her body so soft and lax against his, he didn't want to let her go. Stretching out one long arm he rearranged his blanket to cover her too. "Let your thoughts rest, Cat, and tomorrow we'll work it out."

She gave a soft laugh. "Sure. Teamwork, right?"

Clearly she didn't believe him. "We can talk tonight if you'd rather."

"No." Shaking her head, she squeezed him again. "I still haven't decided how much to tell you—or how much you might already know."

He didn't know jack shit, and it frustrated him a lot. "Tomorrow, then."

She tipped up her face. In the darkness, she studied him. "You don't mind?"

Every nerve ending in his body sizzled, but… "No." She smelled sweet and felt soft, and if he let himself, he'd be hard in a heartbeat. But he'd once risked a woman through poor judgment.

He'd never make that mistake again.

"Where is your gun?" she asked.

Where she wouldn't get to it. "Don't worry about it," he said, then promised, "I won't accidentally shoot you."

"I figured." Sighing long and loud, she got comfortable again. "I didn't want to bump into it."

"You won't." He didn't mean to, but he kissed the top of her head. "Now sleep. We both need it."

She said nothing else, and within five minutes her breaths had turned slow, deep and even. Apparently her mind had finally quieted.

Unfortunately, his did just the opposite and he ended up spending most of the night thinking very inappropriate, erotic, explicit things that had no place between a bodyguard and the woman he was assigned to protect.

CHAPTER THREE

JUSTICE'S LIGHT TAP on the door stirred Catalina awake by slow degrees. She nestled closer and went still again. A second later she yawned and turned away from Leese. Her eyes opened, blinked heavily up at the ceiling, then closed again.

As she stretched, Leese dodged an elbow. "Easy now."

Jerking her head around, she stared at him.

He watched the awareness creep into her slumberous eyes and suddenly she bolted upright. The blankets fell away and he saw her body in the dim room. Nice.

"It's Justice," he said. "Time for us to rise and shine."

After turning to stare blankly toward the door, she gave her attention back to him and her eyes further widened at his naked chest.

Heat crept up her cheeks.

Smiling, Leese reached past her to the end table for his phone. He sent Justice a text: Five minutes—with coffee?

He got back an affirmative. Sure thing.

"Coffee in five," he told Cat.

She swallowed loudly, and blurted, "I don't remember anything!"

A grin fought to take over. She looked a little wild at the moment, and sweeter because of it. Catalina Nicholson, he surmised, was used to being in charge. Instead, with him, she'd let down her guard.

At least a little.

"Nothing to remember." Did she think he'd taken advantage of her through the night—and that she'd slept through it? "We both got the rest we needed, that's all."

"But usually I'm a light sleeper. I've had to be."

That bothered him.

"I remember you telling me to sleep, and then…nothing."

He pushed halfway up to his elbows. "You were exhausted."

"And you're a stranger." Using both hands she pushed back her hair and continued looking at his body. "I'm losing it."

Though he hadn't realized it last night, she'd come to bed in cotton sleep shorts and a T-shirt. The important parts were covered, but a lot of skin showed: her arms, her thighs… Seeing her now, Leese was grateful he hadn't had that image to add to his torment through the night.

The cool morning air had stiffened her nipples, now pressing against the stretchy material of the shirt. Small breasts, but that only added to the delicate look of her.

A deception, because he had a feeling that once you got beyond the physical, Catalina Nicholson was made of pure steel.

Catching the direction of his gaze, she folded her arms around herself. "These are the only pajamas I have."

"Yeah?"

With irony, she said, "I had to pack light when I left."

Mostly, he assumed, because she'd left under troubled circumstances.

The reality of that niggled at his brain, but with her currently in such a pretty pose—her wild hair, her eyes puffy and expression slumberous, the flush on her skin—he had a hard time concentrating on reality. When she'd come to him in the hush of quiet and the dark of the night, he'd focused mostly on her uncertainty.

Now, not so much, and morning wood became a very real possibility.

Testing his resolve, Leese tucked one side of her silky hair behind her ear. "Justice won't be long. Did you want to freshen up before he gets here?"

She turned her cheek into his palm. "Yes."

That single word, breathed so softly, sounded like agreement—or permission.

His jaw tightened and his body heated. "I'm not a saint, Cat."

She opened her eyes wide. "What does that mean?"

Stern, he held her gaze. "It means you're unwisely tempting me. We haven't even gotten to a measure of honesty yet, but you're giving off a pretty strong vibe."

Her eyes flared more. "A 'let's have sex' vibe?" Her mouth twitched. "Is that what you mean?"

Teasing? The woman had no idea of how she affected him. Deciding to clue her in, Leese caught her upper arms and swiftly turned her to her back. Looming over her, he gazed at her mouth. "Yeah." He badly wanted to taste her. "That's exactly what I mean."

"You do tempt me," she whispered, her smile in place. "I didn't realize it was mutual though."

"Now you do." And maybe she'd be more circumspect.

"Because I'm convenient?" she asked. "Or some-what—" her expression pinched "—desperate?"

The uncertainty twisted his guts. He glanced at her mouth. "Because you're hot."

Her teeth bit into her bottom lip. "You really think so?"

Intuitively knowing she needed to hear it, he shared his thoughts. It wasn't in the best interest of his sanity, but he liked seeing her blush.

He especially liked the way she looked at him.

"You, lady, are sexiness in a very small, sweet package."

"Usually I'm told I'm too thin."

Leese slowly shook his head. "You have the right look and the right attitude to push all my buttons."

Gifting him with that cocky smile he admired, she opened her hands on his chest. "Mmm. I think I like that."

"What?"

"Pushing your buttons." Her fingers trailed up to his shoulders, then around his neck.

Leese started to lean down when Justice knocked again.

Cat froze, then panicked. "Oh my God. That's Justice, right? I forgot all about him!" She pushed against Leese, trying to slide free.

He wanted to groan.

In truth, he should thank Justice for keeping him from doing anything insane. "Shh. Take it easy." He rolled to the side of her and watched her shoot off the bed, then make a mad dash around to the bedroom.

Her ass looked really nice as she did so.

After scrubbing both hands over his face, Leese

forced himself from the bed and went to the door. He peeked out first.

Justice stood there holding a tray with coffee and a basket of Danish pastries. Time to get the day started.

Past time to work through the puzzle of the current case: Catalina Nicholson.

CAT COULDN'T LOOK at him. She felt ridiculous.

And pretty wonderful.

She wanted him. And that worried her.

Moving on would be for the best. But where? And how?

And damn it, she didn't want to go. She wanted to snuggle up with him again. She wanted the unaccountable peace of mind he afforded her. *Why* he afforded it, she had no idea.

This morning, crowds filled the lobby and she realized what she hadn't last night: she looked terrible. In the nice hotel, most were dressed in expensive coats and leather boots, their hair salon-styled, their manners impeccable.

Standing to her right, Justice again hauled her big, broken suitcase and that made them stand out like a sore thumb. Not because of the guys, but because of her.

At her other side, Leese took her arm, drawing more than a few probing stares. "Ready?"

Did he touch her so she wouldn't feel so out of place? Probably. She wouldn't put much past him.

Or maybe the crowds made him as nervous as they made her. She could practically feel people watching, but with menace, disdain for her downtrodden appearance or curiosity given her man-candy bookends?

Maybe he thought she'd run if he didn't hold on to her.

Or maybe he felt the same remainder of simmering intimacy that kept her too warm. She'd slept with him—and loved it.

"Cat?"

She realized both Leese and Justice watched her. With a subdued nod, she allowed them to lead her outside.

Crisp, cold air filled the parking garage, undisturbed by the morning sunshine. She'd left her hair down to help keep her ears warm, and dressed in a bulky sweater over a long-sleeved T-shirt, jeans, thick socks and the trusted boots.

Still she shivered.

Of course Leese noticed. "Start the car," he told Justice. "I'll put the luggage away."

"You riding in back again?"

Leese gave her a long, level look. "Yeah."

Shoving her hands in the pockets of her coat and ducking her face, Cat said, "You don't have to babysit me. I'm not going anywhere." Probably.

"We have to talk, remember?" He brought up her chin. "That'll be easier to do if I'm sitting with you."

Insane that his fingers were warm despite the cold. "Suit yourself."

"I think I will."

The nice Lexus SUV hummed to life and a second later the rear door opened, apparently from a button Justice had pushed. Leese opened a back door for her, waited until she'd gotten in, then went back to lift in the luggage.

Stewing, Cat wondered what to tell him, how much she should trust him, until she heard approaching footsteps. Even before she looked, she knew. Her heart went into her throat. "Oh no," she whispered.

"Hello, Cat."

Smothered in the grip of dread, she looked up and into the face of Tesh Coleman. Of course he had two muscle men in tow.

The urge to run spiked her pulse just as Leese closed the back hatch and then her door. He stood there, blocking her view, his body between her and the three men.

She looked at the opposite door, gauging her chances of getting out as the automatic locks on the door clicked into place. Justice, one brawny arm along the back of the seat, stared out the side window at the men. "Don't be hasty," he told her.

Oh God, was he in on it? Was Leese?

Before that fear could fully take hold, Leese said, "That's close enough."

Given the quiet in the garage, Cat could hear every word. Hastily, she moved left and right, trying to find an angle so she could also see what was happening.

"Friends of yours?" Justice asked.

She punched him in the arm and snapped, "No."

"Then don't distract Leese."

Her heart maintained a wild drumbeat. "I have to *see*."

He hesitated, then moved his arm, making it easier for her to lean forward and look out the passenger window.

Tesh's black eyes immediately locked on to her and he slowly smiled. The fact that he looked so pleased to see her only amplified her terror, making it impossible to swallow, almost impossible to breathe.

He was as big as Justice, dark, menacing.

Dangerous.

"I have to go," she whispered.

As if her life didn't hang in the balance, Justice said, "Nope."

She had to try. "Leese said I didn't have to stay—"

"Yeah, well, for the moment, staying put is the way to go."

The awful silence outside the car left her shaking. The men stared at each other, Leese relaxed, waiting, Tesh and his two cronies quietly appraising.

Finally Tesh pulled off a stocking cap and ran a hand over his clean-shaven head. Almost with apology, he said, "I need the girl."

"No."

"I work for her father." Slowly, making sure Leese knew he didn't go for a gun, Tesh opened his coat and withdrew credentials.

Leese didn't bother looking. "Doesn't matter who you work for. You're not touching her."

Cat's spine turned into a noodle. *Doesn't matter.* Leese wouldn't hand her over?

Tesh scrutinized him, then gave it another shot. "Look, I understand your position. I really do. The thing is, her father hired me and I need to—"

"You're wasting my time."

Scowling now, an ugly, fearsome sight, Tesh took a step closer. He spoke low in an obnoxious man-to-man way. "There's no need for violence. I'm only going to take her back to her father, where she belongs."

"Actually," Leese said, his arms loose, his posture absurdly relaxed, "you're not taking her anywhere."

Nostrils flaring, Tesh jerked out a cell phone. "You can call Mr. Nicholson."

"Why would I bother? I don't work for him."

"The hell you don't! Who do you think hired your agency?"

Leese shrugged. "I wasn't told. My job is to keep her safe and that's what I'll do."

"From her *father*? Get real, man." And then, more gently, Tesh promised, "You don't want to do this."

Cat covered her mouth. She couldn't let Leese get hurt. She had to—

Justice nudged her. "You're being a silly girl. Stop it."

She was about to blast him when Tesh threw a sucker punch, making her jump with a startled screech.

Leese ducked, Tesh's fist hit the car and then somehow—it was all a fast blur—Tesh was on the ground with Leese standing over him.

There wasn't enough oxygen in the car to feed her starved lungs. Hands and nose pressed to the glass, Cat watched as Leese decided Tesh was done, then put his full focus on the other two men, beckoning them forward.

They didn't take the bait, choosing to wait for instructions from Tesh.

Leese showed his annoyance. "You walk away or not. Doesn't much matter to me. Either way, you're not touching her."

Appearing surprised, still flat on his back, Tesh touched his nose and stared at the blood on his fingers. Smirking, he sat up and dug a handkerchief from his pocket.

Who carried a hankie anymore? Tesh wasn't that old, maybe early fifties. And the man was definitely in his prime. If he wasn't so corrupt, she might have even called him handsome.

But her perception of his looks had been skewed for

a very long time, starting with the first time he'd looked her over in such an inappropriate way, and reinforced when he began referring to her as Kitten instead of Cat. She saw him only as an imposing terror—a very real menace…to her and to others.

With his gaze cutting her way, Tesh told Leese, "This isn't your fight."

"I have a job to do."

That regained his attention. "That's all she is to you? A job?"

Leese chose not to answer, which even Cat thought was sort of an indictment of his determination. He offered silent confirmation that her relationship with him, or lack thereof, didn't factor in. Either way, he'd protect her.

He'd said so, and for the first time in so very, very long, she felt a hint of promise, as if she could finally believe in someone. Tears stung her eyes and burned her throat, making Justice grouse.

"Don't get all mushy."

"No." She shook her head as the tears leaked out. "I won't."

He sighed. "When Leese is ready to get in, be sure you scooch over real quick and make room for him, okay? I don't want to waste any time peeling out of here."

Nodding, she wiped a wrist across each cheek and kept watch. "Should you help him?"

"Do what? He has it in hand." Justice patted her shoulder, and with the size of his hands it felt more like an assault. "Besides, if I so much as stick my big toe outta this car, he'd annihilate me." Bragging, Justice

added, "I'm supposed to be your protection in case anything happens to him."

Dear God. Her heart crawled right back into her
throat with choking uneasiness. "If you think that's
possible—"

"I don't."

Finally Tesh came to his feet. He meticulously folded
the hankie and tucked it away, and with every heartbeat
Cat expected him or one of his bullies to pull a deadly
weapon. She knew Tesh carried not only a gun but various devices all meant to bring about compliance.

In some ways, she feared him the most.

In other ways, she knew he was a mere tool, bought
and paid for.

"You're fast," Tesh said, his tone amused. "Trained?"

With no inflection at all, Leese said, "Yes."

Tesh smoothed the hat back over his head. "And
you're good?"

"I get by."

Eyes narrowing, Tesh said, "Now I know, and you
can believe I won't forget." A chilling smile slid across
his face. "Next time I'll be better prepared."

A promise, a threat.

Cat pressed a fist to her chest to contain her aching
heart. Tesh would come after her again, but he would no
longer physically engage. Instead he'd trap them, plan a
sneak attack, maybe even shoot Leese from a distance.
He wanted to take her back to her father, but to do that,
he'd have to eliminate Leese first.

How could she be responsible for that?

The gravity of the danger didn't seem to bother Leese.
He stood there, so casual he might have been bored,

until Tesh and the others retreated around the corner of the parking lot.

The second Leese opened the door, Cat made room for him. On her knees, she scampered over, then faced him and reached for his arm. She had to explain, had to make him understand. "Leese…"

"Buckle up." To Justice, he said, "Drive."

"My thought exactly." Already backing out of the parking space, Justice left the lot with enough speed to make her grab the seat for balance.

Cold from the inside out, she stared at Leese.

For the most part, he ignored her as he surveyed the area, his gaze sharp, his jaw locked.

As soon as he pulled onto the road, Justice asked, "Where to?"

"Right there." Leese pointed at the shopping center entrance almost directly across from the hotel. "Pull in to the side lot, but circle around to face the road. If I can see which car is theirs, that'd be helpful."

"Leese…" she said again, desperation clawing through her. She needed him to know what he was getting into. Yes, having help, any type of backup, would be amazing. But it would also put him in the crosshairs of so much danger.

Acknowledging her only with a hand on her thigh, he gave Justice instructions. "Go through there. Stay back though. You can use that truck to help conceal us. Yeah, right here. Good. Keep it in gear, your foot on the brake."

"I'm ready," Justice said, sounding anxious for a chase.

Her heart thumped painfully. She tried to make her voice strong, but it emerged a thin whisper. "You have to let me go."

Ignoring that, Leese gently pushed her back in her seat. "Sit back. I need you to put on your seat belt." He did that for her while also watching the road and occasionally checking their surroundings. "There." He leaned forward. "That's them." As if committing them to memory, he recited the plates out loud.

Justice used his phone to zoom in for a picture. "Got it." One hand on the wheel, he thumbed through some screens and texted the photo to Leese. "Do we follow?"

"No. Opposite direction. Go out the back of the lot."

She needed a way to dissuade him. Cat racked her brain, but nothing felt adequate to convey the level of trouble she would bring on him. "Leese, you have to listen to me."

He patted her. "Try not to worry."

Okay, that stole some of the numb fear and instead turned it into annoyance. "This is a mistake."

Turning a corner, Justice said to Leese, "Maybe she wants to nap again."

Of all the idiot… "No, I *don't*."

"Okay, okay," Justice soothed. "Don't get riled."

Eyes narrowing, Cat thought about telling him off. But truthfully, she didn't want to distract either of them, so she compressed her lips and stayed silent.

They drove down a few side streets, then left the commercial area for a residential neighborhood before finding another main road.

Leese kept vigil out the rear window for what felt like forever before he marginally relaxed. "We need to switch cars."

"You think they'll follow?" Justice asked.

"They obviously already did, that's how they knew we were at the hotel." Leese removed his cell from a clip on his belt. "They were waiting for us, so they might've tagged this car too. Who knows?"

Worse and worse, Cat thought. "Tagged, as in…"

"Put something on it to make it easier to track us," Justice explained. Then to Leese, he asked, "You really think so? That's a lot of expense and trouble, right?"

"I'm not sure cost is factoring in." Leese's gaze skipped to Cat. "But we can get filled in more on that in a minute."

Cat could do no more than stare in wonder. "You know they'll keep coming after me."

He thumbed in a speed dial number, then put the phone to his ear. "That's the one thing I do know."

"You also know my stepfather hired you."

"Stepfather? No, that's news to me." He lifted a finger when she started to speak again, then said into the phone, "I need to see Sahara. Yeah, today." He glanced at a thick watch on his wrist. "Two hours, give or take. Tell her I'm bringing a guest. Yeah."

Several times Justice sent her looks of sympathy in the rearview mirror.

Because of this Sahara person? Who was she and what did it mean to visit her?

While Leese finished his call, she curled into the seat, her arms around herself as a pervasive cold stiffened her bones and made her stomach cramp.

"Sounds good, we'll be there." Leese disconnected the call. "Head to Cincinnati. We'll switch up there."

"Switch up cars?" Justice asked.

"Yeah."

Clearly impressed by that, Justice clarified, "I'm sticking with you?"

"For now."

That obviously pleased him. "Got it."

"Turn up the heat a little too, will you? Cat's chilled."

A near-hysterical laugh bubbled up. Chilled? She was far, far beyond chilled.

If Tesh had his way, she could end up... *No.* She wouldn't think about that yet. She had to believe she still had a chance.

Worried, scared and, yes, still annoyed, she looked at Leese. "You led them to me."

"Seems so." Leese stripped off his coat and tucked it around her. "But now I'm going to ensure they don't get you." He lifted her chin. "You need to believe that."

Oh, how she wanted to, but drumming up enthusiasm for the possibility wasn't easy.

Leese stared into her eyes, brushed his thumb over her cheek, then shocked her silly by leaning down and putting his mouth to hers.

A rush of scalding heat chased off every shiver.

From the front seat, Justice let out a long, low whistle.

As he often did, Leese ignored his friend and current cobodyguard. Ending the kiss, he took in Cat's expression and smiled. "Better."

"Better?" she squeaked.

"You look a little less fatalistic." His gaze moved over her face, her lips, her throat, before returning to her eyes. "While I have your attention, how about you explain what's going on?"

Not like she had much choice now. Had he only kissed her to shock her out of her fear?

Apparently so, damn him. And it had worked—a little. But she couldn't explain anything while looking at him; he affected her too much.

Slumping into the seat, her cheek resting against the

cool glass of the window as she gazed out at the street, she lifted one shoulder and hit him with the truth. "I'm sorry, Leese, but you're a dupe."

HAVING ALREADY SURMISED THAT, Leese didn't overly react. He needed answers, and staying calm was always the easiest way to get them. "I figured as much. But how about you explain the details?"

"Webb Nicholson—"

"Your dad."

"My *stepfather*," she corrected sharply. "I was five when he married my mom."

Interesting reaction. "Go on."

She hesitated, emotionally withdrawing. "I don't know."

"Cat," he said gently. "You know plenty."

In quick protest, she said, "Honestly, I don't. I mean, I have my suspicions."

"Fine. Let's start with those."

She shook her head. "I also have my doubts."

"About me?"

She slanted a suspicious look his way. "Anyone can be bought."

Not true, but convincing her of it wouldn't be easy. "You still think I'm working against you?"

"I think it's very easy for someone to confuse what is right and what is wrong, depending on what they've heard, who they heard it from, what they're getting paid and who's paying them. Few things are ever black-and-white."

"Okay, let's start with that. I haven't heard jack shit. Your father contacted our agency and apparently said he wanted you protected. The agency assigned me. Period. The initial specifics I got from the owner and operator of the agency are that you come from wealth and you're out on your own. That concerned your father."

She snorted, then repeated stubbornly, "Stepfather."

"Stepfather," he conceded. "Through some research, I learned more about you. Recent stuff only, like your current job, hobbies, friends…that sort of thing." Clearly he hadn't dug that deep or he'd have known Webb Nicholson wasn't her biological father. But given it wasn't widely shared knowledge, he would have guessed they were close, that she considered Webb her father and he thought of her as a daughter.

"How would you know my friends?"

"Social media is always a start." And since he hadn't learned anything all that useful, he saw no reason to go into the specifics of how he'd been drawn to her even then. Her Facebook page had been left blank for more than a month, but prior to that, the things she'd shared and the comments she'd made were all humorous, optimistic, or inspiring. Nothing too deep or personal. Catalina Nicholson was not a woman who shared her life online.

She'd posted a few photos, mostly of artwork done by her students, or projects she'd organized for her community. Pics of her with friends, not family, and most of those settings were afternoon lunches with her girlfriends, movies, or casual dinners.

Not a single nightclub photo to be seen.

No dates with guys.

"So you completely snooped into my life?"

"As much as I could given the skills I have." When she looked disgruntled, he decided it was a good time to move on. "No one mentioned any specific threats to me. My assignment was just to ensure your safety. Not to take you to anyone."

"That's why you didn't hand me over to Tesh?"

Ah, so she definitely knew the creep from the parking lot. Interesting. "I'm not handing you over to anyone. That's not my job. If you want to go with someone, I'll follow. If you don't want to go—"

"I definitely didn't!"

"—then I won't let it happen."

They stared at each other until Cat again turned away. Unfortunately, dismissing him wasn't a luxury she currently had.

"I never met your stepfather. I only know he paid enough that I could stick by your side for more than a month." Leese watched her profile and saw her brows pinch together in obvious confusion. "What?"

Cat chewed over her thoughts before asking, "He paid up front?"

"Yes." Leese didn't know if it had occurred to her yet, but given she appeared to distrust the man, maybe he'd been buying his own alibi. Who could accuse him of wrongdoing when he was the very person who'd paid to ensure her safety?

Then again, Tesh—he needed to learn more about that man—had flat-out said he would take her to her father, and she hadn't appeared to disbelieve that part.

Which maybe meant he and Justice would have been removed as witnesses.

"He's used you to find me."

Certainly seemed that way to Leese, but that only opened up more questions. Wondering how much she'd understand, and what she would share, Leese said, "Why not just hire a private investigator to do that? Why hire a bodyguard?"

She turned her head and dissected him with a long look. "The thing is, I've gotten good at figuring out who is who. I recognize his men real fast."

"And you dodge them?"

Instead of answering, she said, "But you? You looked different to me. I didn't think you were one of them."

"I'm not." Unable to help himself, he asked, "Different how? Not threatening?"

Her mouth curled. "Oh, you look threatening all right." She sighed. "Just not toward me. Somehow I figured you were there to help, like… I don't know. A Good Samaritan or something."

Was he really so obvious? "Got all that in a glance when we first met, huh?"

She paid no attention to his humor. "People discount their instincts all the time. But not me. When my senses scream run, I run."

"Into people," Justice said.

"You snuck up on me!"

Justice grinned. "Honey, I'm nearly six and a half feet tall. I don't sneak up on anyone."

Peeved, she scrunched her brows. "Okay, so maybe I was distracted."

"With fear," Leese said gently. "Of me." But first she'd trusted him, so he'd hold on to that.

Now that the heat of the car had warmed her, she gave him back his coat, opened her own and pulled off her gloves. "You seemed one way, but then another when I realized you were working for Webb."

Despite all they needed to discuss, her understated curves and delicate bone structure drew his gaze. He'd always enjoyed shapelier women, but somehow, with Catalina, he couldn't imagine anything more perfect than her petite little body. Whatever she lacked in size she made up for with backbone—and wasn't that just about as sexy as it could get? Leese pulled together his fractured patience. "I already explained—"

"Yeah, yeah. No one hired you directly." She tucked back her fawn-colored hair and gave him the full force of those expressive blue eyes, currently filled with worry. "But don't you see? Until you came along, I knew who to avoid. I knew what they looked like, how they acted." She gave him a frown of pity. "Now I'm not the only one in trouble."

"What exactly do you think Mr. Nicholson plans to do?"

On a dramatic groan, she dropped back against the seat and closed her eyes. "I don't even know for sure if he's the one after me."

Okay then, he'd work with that. "So who else would you suspect?" In every problem like this, the victims always had an idea about who was after them.

Cat shook her head.

"You think it is him?" he guessed.

"I think it *could* be." She covered her face with her hands, but immediately lowered them. "And I *know* he can be dangerous."

It was like pulling hen's teeth, slow and impossible. Holding on to his temper with an effort, Leese said, "Dangerous how? What would he do that's so bad?"

"To me?" She rubbed her temple. "It's possible I'll just go under lock and key. But you?" Her attention flickered over him, then she looked away. "I'm sorry."

Leese sat back. She actually thought her father would

kill him? "If all that's true, why haven't you gone to the police?"

For far too long she held silent, staring out the window, her shoulders angled away from him. Plotting? Thinking?

Deciding whether or not to trust him?

Wasn't easy, but Leese waited.

Finally she answered with a question of her own. "Did any of that research you did on me include the basics on my family?"

Quite a bit, actually. "You have two brothers."

"Yes. The younger is a half brother."

Leese nodded his acceptance of that. "Your older brother is a CEO, the younger is still in school. Your mother passed away four years ago."

"Before my younger brother had even graduated high school," she whispered.

Feeling her pain, Leese covered her hand with his own. "Your father—*stepfather*—" he corrected himself before she could, "hasn't remarried or even really dated."

She snorted. "True, but not because he's lovesick over losing her."

"Maybe not." Leese wasn't sure what motivated the man, only that he was, indeed, motivated. "He's been a jet-setter for a while, but it seems he's thrown himself into pulling political strings, backing powerful men who, thanks to his wealth, eventually get elected and then return a lot of favors." He released her hand. That spontaneous kiss was inappropriate enough; he had to remember that she was a client and he had no business getting personally involved.

Wide-eyed, she blinked at him. "Wow. You say what much of the media won't. But it's true."

"Which part?"

She flagged a hand. "All of it, but I was talking about my stepfather. He wields a lot of power. Too much power. Sometimes it seems…he's untouchable."

"So what has your wealthy, powerful, untouchable stepfather done that has you running scared?"

Evasive, she picked at a frayed spot on the knee of her jeans. "My brothers, both of them, are good men."

"I didn't see anything in my research to tell me otherwise."

"Bowen will be an amazing doctor one day. He's always at the top of his class, and he's…well, he's brilliant. In so many ways."

"And your older brother?" Her full-blood sibling.

She smiled. "Holt loves the business. Webb has completely accepted him as his son and someday he'll inherit everything. Every time I see him, he has a new project that in some way benefits the community, the troops or the poor. He's pretty awesome too."

One thing stuck in Leese's mind. "You didn't like the family business?" From what Leese knew, her father had grown a highly successful empire supplying enhancements to new tech gadgets. Smartphone covers, special screens, camera lenses—he offered something for everyone, and had distribution throughout the country, as well as in select markets around the world.

"No." She wrinkled her nose. "I don't fit the mold. Honestly, though she faked it well, my mom didn't either. She could attend the fancy parties and appear to enjoy them. The transition was almost seamless for her. But when we were alone, she was herself. Really warm and funny, sometimes too strict and overprotective." She fell silent, then whispered, "Webb was different when she was here. I think she was a good influence on him."

"She passed away from cancer?"

"Yes. A terrible disease. Holt does a lot of fund-raising for cancer research. I think it's why Bowen went into medicine."

"Do you look like your mother?"

She flashed him a smile. "Everyone says I do. She was really petite too. Same color hair and eyes. I always thought my mom was really beautiful, and I know I'm not, so I'm complimented when people tell me that."

Justice, who'd been so quiet Leese almost forgot he would be listening, said, "Oh, I dunno. You're awful cute. I imagine if you dolled up, you could turn some heads."

She laughed. "Thank you, but I don't have many opportunities to 'doll up' anymore, thank goodness. That's one of the things I disliked most about wealth. Everyone expected me to look perfect all the time. And I'm just not the type who can pull that off."

Leese thought she looked pretty damned perfect, even in her tattered jeans, with her hair tangled and windblown and not a speck of makeup on her face. Her mouth, especially, drew his attention. She had full lips and when he'd kissed her—

"Teaching art to kids means wearing lots of smocks, not gowns. Usually the smock ends up being pretty colorful though—paint, clay, marker. I'm far better suited to a grade-school art room than an influential committee."

All in all, Leese thought that sounded pretty nice.

Justice asked, "You like kids, huh?"

"Very much. My students are terrific, even the more

troublesome kids. They're all creative in their own unique ways."

Leese let her and Justice talk about children and art, knowing it was a distraction for her. She didn't yet want to tell him about her stepfather, but time would soon run out.

When the two of them wound down and Justice ran out of teasing compliments, Leese said, "You can have a short reprieve, but when we get to the agency, you're going to need to decide."

A whole lot of wariness flooded back into her expression. "Decide what?"

"If you're going to make my job easier by coming clean, or if you're going to leave me muddling about in the dark, which could also be riskier for both of us."

She released a tense breath. "Maybe a better decision would be to leave so you guys aren't at risk."

Leese caught her chin, a surefire method to gain and hold her attention. "That's one choice you don't have. Whether you like it or not, you've got my protection."

Justice added, "If you're thinking of dodging him, think again. He's pretty good at surveillance."

Cat scowled at them both. "I think I'll take a nap, after all." She bunched up her coat and shoved it against the door like a pillow. "Wake me when we're there."

So she wouldn't rest against him this time? Too bad. But he wouldn't waste the quiet time. He had a whole lot more research to do, and this time his focus would be on her stepfather and his friends.

With or without her help, he'd get things figured out. Hopefully in enough time to keep her out of trouble.

CHAPTER FOUR

SHE SLEPT THE entire hour and a half it took to reach their destination. It was a testament to her level of exhaustion, and how much she intrinsically trusted him and Justice. There was very real danger, Leese didn't doubt that. Especially after meeting Tesh, who he discovered was actually Tesh Coleman, a fifty-two-year-old professional thug for the elite.

Justice glanced back at her. Her entire body was lax, her expression peaceful. Leese had had to move to the front seat to keep from touching her. Repeatedly.

"You're smitten," Justice accused. "And you told me that shit was a no-no."

"Concerned, not smitten. I'm wondering how long she's gone without a good rest to keep passing out like that."

"Maybe she's just a sound sleeper. This one lady I knew could sleep through an earthquake after a good boning. Totally knocked her out."

Leese grinned. "Maybe you bored her to sleep."

He only half listened to Justice's denials as they neared Body Armor's swanky main offices. He'd been with the bodyguard agency for a year now, and so far, it was unlike anything he'd imagined.

For one thing, he liked it a hell of a lot more than he'd expected to.

Playing protector suited him on a basic level. There'd been a time in his life when he'd been more of a jerk than he liked to admit. Much as he detested the truth, he believed in being honest with himself so he accepted that much of his attitude had stemmed from insecurity. As a mediocre MMA fighter, he'd had just enough skill to be cocky and obnoxious.

He wasn't insecure anymore.

And these days, with plenty of practice, his skill level was lethal.

After a lapse in his judgment had almost gotten a girl killed, his entire outlook on life had changed. The eye-opening close call had turned him around.

He planned to spend the rest of his life helping others, and if he got paid well in the bargain he'd count it a double win.

"She passed out whimpering my name."

Drawn back to the here and now, Leese said, "Probably begging you to quit and leave her alone."

With a smug smile, Justice said, "She still comes around for the occasional booty call."

"Maybe she has insomnia? She needs you to put her to sleep again."

Justice laughed. "Admit it, I'm a stud and you're jealous."

When Cat made a small sound, Leese again glanced into the backseat. She hadn't moved.

"Gotta say," Justice told him. "So far it's been interesting. But don't you miss MMA?"

Leese figured Justice asked because he was already missing it. "I still train," Leese told him. "I just don't compete, which is no big loss because we both know we weren't championship material." They were good.

A hell of a lot better than any street brawler. But champion? Only a select few could claim that title.

He'd come to grips with that, but maybe Justice hadn't yet. After all, it had taken Justice nearly a year longer than Leese to admit it. Leese had a feeling that once Justice got acclimated, he'd like the bodyguard business a lot more than he now realized.

"I guess." Justice tugged at his earring. "I'm actually better at shooting bullets than I ever was at takedowns."

"You'll try it as a bodyguard, and if you don't like it, don't stay." But Leese would bet he'd stay.

"You'd told me there weren't any hot babes to protect, but the little lady snoring in the backseat is pretty sweet on the eyes."

Very sweet. "She's an exception to the rule. It's mostly businessmen and high-profile local politicians." So far Leese's most exciting assignments had included coordinating protection for a touring musician, a movie production on location and a foreign dignitary. "In fact, the specifics of this case are an exception. Most of the time your job will be to check out safe routes for travel, research the backgrounds of people your client will interact with and search rooms where they'll be staying to ensure they're safe. Mundane stuff like that."

"You lucked out with this one, then."

"Maybe." He knew his boss, in her efforts to really promote the agency, reserved certain jobs for certain people. She was good at matchups, so Leese didn't question her.

Now she'd matched him up with Catalina Nicholson and while he felt like thanking her, because no way did he want anyone else in charge of her safety, he also needed to know what the hell Sahara Silver had gotten him into.

This was only Justice's second ride-along, sort of a training session, and so far, he was too impulsive in Leese's opinion. But he'd catch on soon enough.

"You think Sahara will keep us paired up?"

"We're not partners, Justice. I'm training you, same as I got trained."

"That's why you got to hit the bozos and I didn't?"

Leese resisted the urge to roll his eyes. "Usually there's no hitting involved, so don't get ahead of yourself." To further explain, he said, "For this case, I'm more like a close protection officer. Sometimes, depending on the job and the risk to the client, we might have a close protection group, but until meeting Catalina, no one thought that was necessary." Groups were generally used when a politician or ambassador suspected an assassination attempt, meaning different levels of surveillance would be needed.

But for one petite schoolteacher?

"With that one," Justice said, nodding toward the backseat where Cat slept, "I'm thinking a battalion might get a workout trying to keep up with her."

Leese was beginning to think the same.

"Know what, Leese?"

"What?"

"I'd consider it more fun if I got to do some hitting too."

With a lazy stretch and a purring groan, Cat came awake and sluggishly sat up. She rubbed her eyes while saying, "Then you're in for a good time, stud, because if you stick with me, I predict there'll be a lot of hitting in your future."

"Stud?" Leese asked, already guessing she'd been awake for a while.

"That's what he called himself, right?"

Justice grimaced. "You were playing possum?"

"More like caught between sleep and being awake. You're funny, Justice, in an overblown, overconfident, somewhat misogynistic way."

Leese elbowed him. "She's saying you don't have a healthy respect for women."

"Not true!" Justice lifted his nose. "I love the ladies."

Huffing a laugh, Cat turned to Leese. "And you're quick with the comebacks. You two should take your act on the road."

"Got our hands full keeping you safe, apparently." Her eyes still looked slumberous, but little by little, the wariness crept back in. "We'll be pulling into Body Armor in about five minutes."

"That's the name of the agency?"

"Yeah. Under new management."

"Oh?"

"Sahara Silver." Smiling, he spoke the truth. "And she's going to love you."

"Why?"

"Because she's always looking for ways to make the agency's rep sexier. And you definitely fit the bill."

SAHARA SILVER STEPPED into the polished foyer of the agency she'd recently inherited. How she loved this place, the high-end decor, the modern lines...and the testosterone in the air.

She breathed deeply, then shivered.

Perfect, just perfect.

As several people looked up, she smiled. She'd been

at the helm for a year now and still earned that curious, uncertain reaction. Her brother, God bless him, had been more sedate and far more serious. A wonderful businessman and an even better brother. She missed Scott every minute of every day, but being here, in the midst of all he'd built, she felt closer to him.

With her high heels clicking, she strode through, nodding to one and all on her way to the private elevator that'd take her to her office on one of the uppermost floors.

Anita, her lobby receptionist, rushed to meet her. "Ms. Silver, Mr. Phelps and Mr. Wallington went up about five minutes ago. They had a guest with them."

Excitement rushed into her bloodstream. "That's fine, Anita. Thank you." Leese Phelps, always early, always ready. He was her favorite find for the agency. An MMA fighter turned bodyguard with an ability so incredible, he would rarely ever need to use a weapon beyond his fists.

Leese had also brought Justice Wallington into the fold. Such a colorful character. Where Leese added suave, quiet power to the agency, Justice brought cocky, irreverent outrageousness.

Justice was still being fine-tuned, but she had no doubt he'd be an amazing addition to the new, more modern segment of the business. She'd be launching him out on his own very soon.

After greeting Troy, the armed guard who stood watch over the private elevator, Sahara waved off the attendant and stepped inside to ride up to her office. She could only hope that the surprise guest would be yet another fighter for her to hone into an asset.

When she'd inherited the agency from Scott, it was

like a lifeline, a way to remain attached to him even after he'd gone. Sixteen years older than her, Scott had practically raised her when their absentee parents chose to travel the world rather than be saddled with a "surprise" daughter. So many times Scott had brought her along to the office, let her observe and learn as she sat in on meetings both in preparation of assignments and in reporting outcomes.

Even then, when she was a fidgety preteen know-it-all, he'd encouraged her to voice her ideas and she always did. She was never short on opinions.

It wasn't until she'd turned nineteen that she'd told him, in front of all the bodyguards during a big meeting, that he needed employees with more sex appeal.

Her brother had choked on his drink, and the men—all of them middle-aged and less than impressive—had tried to melt her with heated glares.

Too fast for her to further explain, Scott had ushered her from the room and, she assumed, spent the next hour smoothing ruffled feathers.

Bodyguards, in her opinion, should not have feathers. They should be made of steel, and they should appeal to the masses.

Regardless of the less than promising reaction from the staff at the time, she hadn't been deterred. She'd thought about it more and more, a way to separate Body Armor from other agencies. Sex was in, the sexier the better.

Why couldn't her agents be top of the class in both skill and persona? Why couldn't they seduce with amazing talent and capability, as well as smoldering good looks?

The rich and elite, she knew, would pay a fortune

for appearances mixed with talent. Under her guidance, Body Armor would offer it all.

She kept the other employees and offered them at a reduced rate. They stayed busy, the revenue continued to pour in and already Leese Phelps was in high demand. Soon, with any luck, she'd find a few more new hires and round out the employee cache with something for everyone.

Thinking ahead, always, she strode toward her personal receptionist, Enoch, who jumped to his feet to present her with her day's agenda.

"Guests inside, Sahara. Leese and Justice, and they brought with them a young lady—"

She drew up short. "Not another fighter?"

He smiled. "Sorry, no. Or at least I assume she's not." He leaned in closer. "She's rather small."

Enoch knew her well enough to understand she preferred first names whenever possible, and because they got along so well, he was often very familiar. On any given day, Enoch was her right hand, her calendar and her friend. "Now I'm doubly curious."

"Would you like to go over your schedule first, or after you meet with them?"

"I have time?"

"At least an hour."

"Wonderful. Let's do the schedule after." Sahara smiled at him. "Could you bring us coffee and whatever... and see that I'm not disturbed while they're here?"

"I'll make a fresh pot." Off he went, always so quick at his tasks.

She did love Enoch's efficiency and understanding of her needs. If only she could find a man who—no.

The last thing she needed was a man in her life.

No time, not for that sort of nonsense, and not while shifting the agency into the powerhouse she wanted it to be.

Pasting on a smile, she opened the door and surged into her office. Leese stood looking out a window, hands in his back pockets. Justice took up most of the space on a small settee, his bulky arms stretched out along the back.

And in the chair facing her desk...

Sahara hurried in. "Hello." She circled the chair to face the woman, then stepped back in surprise. "You're Catalina Nicholson."

"Yes." With far too much caution, Catalina asked, "And you are?"

"Sahara Silver. I own the agency." Brows up, she turned to Leese. "You brought her here...why?"

Folding his arms over his broad chest, Leese turned his compelling stare on Catalina. "I'm hoping she'll tell us." He watched her a moment, then said softly, "Cat? What's it to be?"

Put on the spot, the girl glared back at Leese, then seemed to deflate. Her gaze shifted to Sahara, and damned if Sahara didn't feel a thrill go up her spine. She just knew this was going to be something unexpected and stupendous.

Anxious to hear it, she said, "Go on."

After a few more seconds of hesitation, Catalina asked, "Have you heard of Désir Island?"

Judging by Sahara's startled reaction, Cat assumed she had indeed heard of the island and was aware of its awful reputation.

The beautiful brunette inhaled deeply, then rushed

around to get comfortable in her chair. Forearms on her massive desk, expression rapt, she leaned forward. Both Leese and Justice were lost and, in truth, Cat was glad they didn't know about the island.

Enthralled, titillated without having yet heard the details, Sahara urged, "Go on."

Before Cat could, a man stepped in with a tray of coffee, fresh fruit, pastries and muffins.

Sahara didn't miss a beat. "Excellent. I definitely need more caffeine. Pour us each a cup, will you, Enoch?"

"My pleasure." Cups and saucers rattled as the assistant filled each cup. "Cream and sugar?"

"We can doctor them ourselves, but thank you." Sahara reached for a gooey pastry. "Fresh from the bakery?"

"Of course."

"You're the perfect man, Enoch. Thank you."

Smiling, Enoch departed and Sahara told Cat, "Please, help yourself."

She hesitated, but what the heck. If everyone else could be blasé, she'd give it a try too. "All right, thank you." After swallowing one big bite of a blueberry muffin, she asked, "You're aware of what happens on the island?"

"Yes, of course. Decadence. Perversion." Sahara waved a pastry. "Anything and everything sexual that money can buy."

Leese came around closer to Cat, which she appreciated, and propped a hip on the desk. After a sip of coffee, he asked, "Where is this place?"

"It's near the Virgin Islands. Uninhabited until twenty

or so years ago. Since then it's been built up and used for..." Cat swallowed, unable to say it.

Sahara didn't have the same problem. "It's a privately owned playground for the global ultrarich. Anything goes if you have enough money or influence, preferably both. Many politicians love it for the secrecy. It provides every luxury you can imagine with a small, posh hotel, a helipad for invited guests only and plenty of space for orgies."

"Orgies?" Leese asked, one brow climbing high.

Sahara nodded around another bite. "Lots of nasty business going on there. Like I said, anything can be bought if you offer the right price, whether it's legal or not, whether all participants are willing or not."

Now both of Leese's brows snapped down. "You're talking rape?"

"Sadly, yes. There've been accusations, some of them truly gruesome, but none have been proven because witnesses have a way of changing their tune, probably after being bought off, or they disappear, likely—"

"Murdered." The second the word left her mouth, Cat's stomach jolted. *Oh God, she'd said it aloud.* She fought off the panic, knowing she'd just crossed a line; she'd admitted the awful truth, *trusted* these people when for so long she'd been afraid to trust anyone, even her family.

But what choice did she have? She couldn't continue living her life on the run, and she didn't want to end up on that island, a victim herself. Sooner or later she had to share it all. For whatever innate reasons existed, she trusted Leese. Really trusted him.

By association, she trusted his closest colleagues. She couldn't believe he would bring her here, ask her to explain everything to Sahara and Justice, if he didn't know it would be safe.

On top of that, she was in a secure building, shielded from threats. Justice had already gotten past her guard and, as the owner of the elite bodyguard agency, Sahara seemed to have a measure of her own power.

When would another, better opportunity present itself?

Now that the truth was out there, it brought about a heavy silence. Disbelief? Uncertainty?

Accusation?

Without knowing what they all might think, Cat sipped her coffee and waited in an agony of suspense.

"Jesus," Justice rumbled, sitting forward now too. He snagged up a cup, black, and swilled back half of it.

Leese shifted uneasily. "And Webb?"

"I don't know!" Emotions propelled her from her seat. She set the cup aside with more noise than necessary and strode to the window, needing to see the view to breathe, to feel less trapped in the awful circumstances.

The vantage point of the office offered a view of the Ohio River, disturbed only by a few slow-moving barges. Ice and snow lined the shore and a sluggish sun struggled to shine through dark, rolling clouds.

The day looked as miserable as she felt.

Despite the bitter cold of the morning, cars filled the bridges and people went about their business. None of them had a clue what fate could dole out.

That was nice. She didn't want others to have to be as hyper-aware of threats as she'd recently become.

When she sighed, her warm breath frosted the window.

Knowing she'd stalled too long, Cat whispered, "My stepfather…he knows about it. He might only be involved in covering it up." *Or he could be guilty of the violent acts.* She shook her head. "I don't know."

Leese's hands settled on her shoulders and he drew her back against his chest, his chin atop her head. He said nothing, just held her, surrounding her in his size and scent and power.

In the reflection of the window, Cat saw Sahara look to Justice for an explanation, and she saw Justice shrug in a "haven't got a clue" sort of way.

So Leese didn't embrace every client? This was an aberration for him? Nice to know. But it was still confusing—to her, and obviously to his boss and his colleague.

Clearly, no one understood it, least of all her, but Leese made her feel as if all the bad things in the world couldn't touch her, not when he was close, and that robbed her of the debilitating panic.

She took one deep breath, then another. "A woman was killed."

"Who?" Sahara asked sharply.

There'd be no backing out now. Still, she couldn't tell them everything. She didn't dare.

The less they knew, the safer they'd be. She'd have to start juggling and, blast it all, she wasn't that coordinated.

"I only know her name." Cat pressed closer to Leese, stealing some of his strength. "And her age."

Leese waited.

Grateful for his patience, she sorted her thoughts. Though she'd already decided these people wouldn't hurt her, she needed further verification before she said anything more. "I can trust everyone here not to repeat what I'm going to tell you, right? If the wrong people find out—"

"You can trust us," Sahara assured her.

"Besides," Leese said, giving her shoulders a gentle squeeze, "I'm not going to let anyone hurt you, remember?"

He didn't seem to mind that others were watching, and Cat wasn't sure what to make of that.

Flustered, she stated, "It can't leave this room."

"Then it won't," Sahara promised.

Accepting that, Cat drew a breath and whispered, "Georgia Bell. She was only eighteen."

Justice cursed softly. "So young."

Wretched grief welled up. Every time Cat thought about it, about a young girl scared and alone and desperate, it broke her heart all over again. That poor, poor girl. How badly had she suffered?

And if the ones responsible found her, would Cat suffer the same fate?

Leese interrupted that thought by rubbing her shoulders. "Do you know how and why she was killed?"

The memory made Cat shiver. "From what I overheard, Georgia was hired to waitress at a private party on the island. Because she was offered so much money, she agreed—but only to waitressing. She didn't understand that the offer came with certain expectations regardless of how she'd feel about it."

"Like?" Leese asked.

This was the tricky part, where she had to dance around the truth without revealing too much. "One of my stepfather's more influential friends—" a name they'd all recognize, if she shared that much "—wanted her for…more. She agreed, to an extent."

As Cat spoke, the words came faster, more strained, matching the frantic beat of her heart.

"But I guess he took it too far because at one point Georgia wanted to leave."

"You're sure?" Justice asked. He scratched his left ear, thinking aloud. "If she said yes to something—"

Cat almost lost it. She jerked around to face Justice, wanting, needing a little violence. If he'd been closer, she might have slugged him.

As it was, Leese held her back when she started to lunge forward.

Fine. She still had her voice, and by God, no one would rob her of that. "She agreed to sex with *one* man. She said *no* to others joining them, and she obviously said no to being a sideshow. And no, as far as I'm concerned, *always means no.*"

Eyebrows shooting up, Justice said, "I agree one hundred percent, honey, so spew the venom elsewhere. Rapists are at the top of my list of scum of the earth, right up there with child abusers. I was just going for clarification. How do you know what happened? Were you there?"

"Oh God, no." She shook her head hard. If she had her way, that damned island would be blown to pieces. "I know Georgia refused, because that's what they said." The turbulent mix of anger and panic descended on her again. "They joked, laughing over how she wanted to leave but saying it was already too late for that and they couldn't let her, so they…they *killed* her." She squeezed her eyes shut, horrified anew at the blasé discussion of cold-blooded murder.

They'd talked about ending an eighteen-year-old girl with the same lack of empathy they'd have given to an annoying fly.

"Shh." Leese turned her into his embrace and his big hands moved up and down her back. "Take it easy."

Until he soothed her, she hadn't realized how badly she trembled.

No one spoke and by the second she felt more like a wimp. She knew Sahara watched them with wide-eyed incredulity, and that Justice was confused by his friend's familiarity. By letting Leese comfort her, she was putting his job at risk. He couldn't get in trouble over her.

Somehow she had to get it together.

But it was a struggle. Georgia Bell had been gone for months now, but for Cat, the horror was fresh, as if it had happened just yesterday. The cut felt raw and still far too painful.

A steadying breath helped a little. Trying to compose herself, she levered away from Leese's comfort. If this was her time of confession, she needed to get through it.

Leese kept his hands on her upper arms and dipped down a bit to look her in the eye. "How do you know all this?"

In the quietest of whispers, she confessed, "I overheard it all."

Leese's hands tightened. "And the killers know it?"

"I'm afraid so."

"See," Justice said, his hands out, "this is what I was trying to get to, the deets on how you know what you know." He grumbled low to himself, "Accusin' me of supporting abuse. That's bullshit."

He looked a little wrecked that she'd ever misunderstood, so Cat gave him an apologetic nod. "They were all in Webb's boathouse, only I didn't expect to find anyone there."

Leese barely breathed. "Webb too?"

She nodded. "It was too late in the season to take out the boat and it's not like Webb or his buddies like to fish. But we'd gotten that early freeze and I wanted to capture everything in photos to paint it later, maybe even to use as a project for the class, to show them how the ice sparkled and…" Dumb. So very, very dumb. None of that mattered now. "Anyway, when I got close I heard people talking. That didn't make any sense to me because no one used the boathouse in the winter. At first I listened, trying to figure out who was there. I was going to report them." To Webb, who she'd figured would run them off. *She'd been such a fool.*

"That's what most people would do," Leese assured her.

"If only it had been vandals, or someone just trespassing. But it wasn't. By the time I understood what they were talking about, it was too late." Over and over they'd said her name, Georgia Bell, a young lady who'd been used, and then murdered.

As if she was no one important, as if her death didn't matter.

To them, she'd been an expendable girl, easily discarded.

"I was standing there, I guess almost in shock, when they stepped out and…saw me."

Leese tightened his jaw.

"There was no place to hide. I was in my black coat, jeans and boots, standing in the white snow. It's not like they could have missed me. I tried to bluff, like I hadn't caught anything important. I tried to act surprised to see them, but welcoming." As usual, because she knew them all, had met them many times. Closing her eyes, she said, "But I guess they could still tell. They looked at each other as if coming to some silent agreement."

Hand to her throat, Sahara asked, "An agreement for what?"

"To get rid of me too. To remove the possibility of me telling anyone what I'd heard."

Gently, Leese said, "You can't know that for sure."

But she did. "Webb looked…" Devastated. Destroyed. But still resigned. "I could tell he wouldn't defend me. Or maybe it's that he couldn't. I'm not sure."

"Because you don't know for sure if he's involved," Justice said.

"I would never have believed it if I hadn't heard them all talking. They admitted having Georgia killed, her throat cut—" *What level of horror had that young girl faced?* "—her body disposed of on the island. When asked, Webb agreed to help provide alibis for them. The plan was that he'd claim they'd been with him, at his home, the weekend Georgia went to the island." *Believable, since the men had been to his home before.* "I'd say that makes him pretty damned guilty."

Leese nodded. "Agreed."

"But how would that cover all their tracks?" Justice asked. "They had to get to the island somehow, right? There must be records…"

Sahara answered. "For enough money, the helicopter pilots would keep silent, bury the paperwork—and do whatever was asked. The super wealthy always have those who will cover for them."

Cat drew a shuddering breath. "The way those men all looked at me…" She couldn't forget how Tesh had slowly smiled, his visible anticipation for what he probably saw as an opportunity.

For too many years that lech had wanted her and he'd seen this, her giant faux pas, as his best bet to get his hands on her.

"Cat?"

She met Leese's gaze.

"You keep saying 'them.' Who are we talking about?"

If she told the truth, would they even believe her? Cat had her doubts, so she hedged. "It was Webb and another man meeting, plus two personal guards."

"So four men, total?" Sahara asked.

"Yes. Tesh was one of them."

"He's associated with your stepfather?" Sahara clarified.

"Yes."

Leese glanced back at Sahara. "You knew he was her stepfather, not her dad?"

"Yes, but to me he seemed as concerned and genuine as any father could be. He said Cat was out on her own, and he wanted her protected because she'd lived such a pampered life. He was afraid her naïveté would get her into trouble." She frowned. "I hate that I was apparently duped."

Leese came back around to Cat. "Tesh works for Webb?"

"For the other man, actually. But Webb has known him for a long time. Since I was…" That invisible fist closed on her throat again. "Eighteen."

Because he didn't miss much, Leese muttered, "The same age as Georgia."

She nodded. "Webb considered him trustworthy, so there were times he 'borrowed' him for special tasks.

More than once Tesh was assigned to watch over me." During those times, he'd refer to her as Kitten even though he knew it annoyed her. As she'd matured she grew to understand that Tesh didn't consider her a person so much as his own personal pet.

"I met the man." With visible irritation, Leese said, "That's like hiring the fox to watch the henhouse."

Cat agreed. "I hated it. The way Tesh looks at me, it's always given me the creeps."

"Saw it," Justice said. "Dude wants you bad."

"More than that," Leese said. "He feels some ownership."

"No." Cat pushed out of his arms and backed away from him. "He has no reason to—" She squeaked when Leese pulled her right back in.

"I said he feels it, not that he has a right to it."

She blinked fast, startled by how quickly he'd moved, and pretty darned pleased to be close to him again. "Oh."

Keeping her *right there*, Leese turned them both to face Sahara. She looked fascinated. And once again titillated.

"We ran into Tesh on the way here."

"Do tell."

While Leese related the story to Sahara, Cat eased away from him and returned to her coffee. The caffeine kick could only help, so she took a big drink. When she caught Justice watching her, she frowned.

He nodded back. "You have guts."

How in the world could he think that? She'd been an awful coward. Rather than see justice for poor Georgia, she'd run away. She'd valued her own life more. She'd—

"Give me the names of the other men."

Uh-oh. Here's where it got bad. Refusing to cower, Cat faced Leese without blinking, and lied. "I don't know their names."

He gave her a brief but intense scrutiny. "Yes, you do."

"Sorry, I don't."

He crossed his arms.

Why was that so damned intimidating? "Please understand, Leese." Her palms started to sweat, especially with Sahara and Justice now scowling at her. "The entire reason I'm in danger is because—"

"The other man is a public figure," Leese guessed. "Recognizable name with a lot to lose if you share what you know."

Tread carefully, she warned herself. As if she didn't know more, Cat said, "He was with my stepfather, he'd been to the island, so yes, I assume he has amazing contacts everywhere, including with the police."

"Local police?" Sahara asked.

If only it was that simple. "I know Webb has influence with the highest levels of law enforcement." *Like... all the way to the US attorney general.*

With one finger under her chin, Leese brought her gaze back to his. "You can't keep it secret forever."

That had initially been her plan, to prove she wouldn't squeal until everyone calmed down. At first, it was the only thing she could think of, a blind panic sort of decision.

But it haunted her, what happened to that poor girl and how cavalier the men had been about robbing her of life. Staying silent wasn't the answer because the coward's way never worked.

If only she'd realized that sooner.

"We need the names of everyone in the boathouse that day," Sahara insisted.

"I know." She really did. "The other guard was familiar. I might be able to remember his name. I just need some time to think."

Not at all fooled, Leese said, "And your stepfather's associate?"

The public loved him, saw him as kind and caring. How could she trust they'd believe her, and even if they did, then what? "I've probably seen him before, but I don't remember." *Please let them believe me.* "I'll try to work it out." For too long, survival was all she'd had. Now, thanks to Leese, she could sit down and really decide what to do, and when to do it.

Just giving them names wasn't the answer; that'd only put them all at risk.

There was more Leese needed to know so he'd truly understand. Hopefully, in telling him some truths, she could keep him from breaking down her lies. "I ran that day, the same day I overheard them talking. Literally, I mean. I turned and ran as fast as I could. Webb called my name but I didn't acknowledge him. I kept waiting for a bullet to hit me in the back."

Leese went more rigid.

"But it didn't. They didn't even chase me that hard. I got to my car and then I wasn't sure what to do except drive. I was barely on the road when my cell started ringing."

"Your stepfather?"

She nodded. "He told me to come back, that he could explain. He promised we'd work it out. When I refused, he warned me that no one would believe me, that it'd be really stupid for me to start spreading tales about things

I knew nothing about." Tension crept into her neck and shoulders, making her temples throb. "It was so stupid of me, but I told him what I'd heard, that I knew he'd planned to cover up a murder."

No one said a word.

"He laughed at me. Actually *laughed*." It had been a sick, almost hysterical sound that escalated Cat's fear. "He said I misunderstood, that's all."

"Is that possible?" Justice asked.

God, how she wished. "No." Best to get it told quickly and have it out of the way. "I said I was going to the police. He stopped laughing real fast and instead told me the police were owned and I'd end up the victim if I ever again said anything that stupid. That's when I realized Tesh was behind me. When I told Webb that, he literally begged me to pull over, to let Tesh bring me home." *Home.* Once, long ago, that's what it had been to her. Even after she'd moved out, she'd still considered it home.

Never again.

"He said if I went to the police, he couldn't help me. That it'd be out of his hands. But with Tesh so close behind me, I couldn't think of another option to get away. Then I ran through a red light and Tesh tried to follow."

"Tried?" Leese asked.

"He got T-boned by a van." She met his gaze. "I slowed down long enough to see the driver of the van get out, then I took off again. Until I saw Tesh this morning, I didn't know if he'd survived that day or not. So many men had followed me, but none of them were Tesh."

"Maybe because he was the most recognizable," Leese said.

"Probably."

Sahara crossed her legs, her fingernails tapping on the desktop. "I take it you didn't go to the police after all?"

"I was closer to my house so I went there first."

"Cat," Leese chastised.

And yes, she felt like a fool. "It was stupid, I know. But I couldn't think straight. I wanted to get inside and lock my doors and maybe call someone."

"But?"

"Men were already there, peeking in the windows and trying the door, so I didn't stop. I called my brother, Holt, but another man answered and before I'd even spoken, he told me I needed to return to Webb. It was like a nightmare."

"No one got to you?" Leese asked.

She shook her head. "I didn't give anyone a chance. I realized then that if I went anywhere obvious—"

"Like the police station?" Justice asked.

"—more men would be waiting for me. I called Webb back and said I wouldn't talk. I hoped it would buy me some time, but he said there wasn't anything to talk about. Either I came home, or I was on my own."

Those words had felt so final, and so fatal.

"I told him I'd been on my own for a while. He really did sound apologetic when he reminded me that everyone knew how I'd separated from the family. Past actions, he claimed, had already discredited me, and if I forced his hand, he'd let the whole world know how... unstable I am."

"What did he mean?" Sahara asked. "Was there a big blowup when you moved out?"

"No, nothing like that. I just moved out, as many

young people do." That no one had protested, or seemed to care, still hurt her. "I continued to visit with my family, but I didn't do any more of the parties, the fundraisers, the galas. It was never my thing anyway. I'm more comfortable at a McDonald's talking to the other people in line or instructing my class of nine-year-olds on a project than I ever was at a big fancy party."

Sahara said, "I've always loved dressing up."

"Sure, me too. That part was great. But I'd mess up every time."

"How?" Leese asked, and he looked irate about it.

She rolled one shoulder. "I could never get the hang of the right attire. I'd have a knee-length dress when others wore long, or I'd wear bright colors when others wore pastels. I'd laugh at the wrong things. Or I'd laugh too loud. We'd start dancing and not until it was too late would I realize I was the only one really cutting loose."

Justice grinned. "Like to dance, do you?"

"Yes. But my idea of dancing and their idea were two very different things." Might as well admit all her flaws and get it out of the way. "I have no sense of direction either. I'd head for the powder room and end up in the kitchen. If I drank even a little bit, I'd get tipsy, which only amplified all the things I did wrong. Worst of all, the small talk never felt small to me. I was always worried about slipping up and saying something inappropriate." As in dumb. Or embarrassing. She gestured at Leese. "Ask him. He'll tell you that I speak without thinking."

Leese, brows still pinched, said nothing at all.

Justice grinned.

Feeling she had to defend herself, she said, "I moved out without fanfare and went about my life. Not mad, just…apart. Only there was gossip. Rich or poor, affluent or mundane, there's *always* gossip. Folks said I disappeared because I had a nervous breakdown, or that I was run off because I'm an embarrassment. One old…" She quickly censored herself. "…*busybody* even claimed I had a medical affliction of the mental sort, only she didn't put it that nicely. There was speculation on whether or not I was a drug addict, which would explain my weirdness, or if I'd gotten pregnant by a convict…all sorts of idiotic things. My brothers ignored it. Mother was furious so Webb tried to correct it. I honestly didn't care. In fact, at the time, I thought it was almost funny. Now, though…"

"It's a basis," Leese said. "A way for your stepfather to embellish what was already started. He can go back and rewrite history any way he wants."

"Yup. I'm afraid so." She looked only at Leese, not anyone else. "I know I'm odd." She shook her head, stopping his objection. "I still haven't learned the knack of thinking before speaking, or the right things to wear. With my students, it doesn't matter. I wear smocks and we laugh and we have a good time."

"You should always be comfortable," Sahara said, and with a shrug she added, "Create your own fashion and to hell with others."

If only it was that easy. "My mother always said I was too honest. Webb said I was immature. It's the truth, after moving out, I did what I wanted, when I wanted, without considering ramifications."

"Like running?" Justice asked.

"It wasn't the easiest choice. Nothing about it has been easy. But Webb and his cronies are powerful men with so much reach, I wasn't sure who to trust." And she needed to stop making excuses. Sitting a little straighter, she admitted, "I decided it'd just be best to take off for a while. So I did."

"An understandable reaction." Justice patted her shoulder with his massive paw. "No one blames you."

She wasn't sure about that. Leese watched her, but he didn't say anything. She should have been stronger, tried harder. *I should have found a way.*

"We're going to work this out," Sahara said, all but rubbing her hands together. "We won't let Georgia's death be swept away."

Cat feared it already had been. "What can you do?"

"What *can't* I do?" she replied. "But first things first. We need to keep you safe."

"I'll see to it." Leese again stood next to her.

So maybe he didn't blame her, after all. Didn't matter, since she blamed herself. But she'd hate to lose him as an ally.

"Yes," Sahara purred. "I can see that you will. Perhaps you'll also encourage her to remember that other name?"

"I'll do my best."

Cat gulped. His best was probably pretty damned awesome.

"What can I do?" Justice asked.

"Nothing," Sahara told him. "I have a different job coming up for you. You may as well stick with me the rest of the month. I'd like to assess you."

He shifted uneasily. "Assess me?"

"She does it with all the new hires," Leese assured him.

"This is my only chance," Sahara said, "since soon you'll accompany the client nonstop."

"I will?"

"Yes, you see, a certain actor—very hush-hush—who'll be playing a part in an upcoming MMA movie wants someone who knows the ropes to be his bodyguard. I sold you as the real deal who could not only advise him and teach him the lingo, the rules and routines, but also be his protection at the same time."

Justice blinked at her. "I... Wow." Then with accusation, he barked at Leese, "This job is *nothing* like you claimed it'd be."

"Complaints?" Leese asked.

"No." Somewhat dazed, Justice said, "Hell man, I'm lovin' it."

Sahara regained their attention. "I have an excellent PI who I'll have look into Georgia's death."

Sharp fear coursed through Cat. "Oh, but—"

"A girl can't just go missing without someone noticing, right?"

"PI?" Leese asked her, a note of mistrust in his tone. "Who?"

Sahara squeezed his arm. "The same one investigating my brother's death."

All news to Catalina, but Leese seemed to understand, so she figured she'd ask him later. If Leese trusted the man, she would too.

Except for one problem. "If you start digging, you'll lead them straight back to me. I'm sure they already have computer people watching for me to pop up anywhere. I haven't dared send an email or touch my Facebook. When I withdrew what cash I could from my accounts, I immediately took off. I was afraid the withdrawal could somehow lead them to me. I haven't used my name anywhere, or any of my credit cards. I've tried really, really hard to leave no tracks at all."

Unconcerned with her panic, Sahara said, "I promise we can be completely discreet. And until we uncover something, you can stay here, perfectly protected."

"Here?" Still shaken by the idea of anyone poking around—and possibly leaving her exposed—Cat again took in the posh office. Dark wood, plush furniture, massive television screen and full connecting bath; it had all the amenities except a kitchen. Still, she couldn't see staying in an office.

Not for any length of time.

"Here," Sahara explained, "in the building. Scott kept a suite but I haven't used it because…" She tapered off, then whispered, "He was my brother."

Catalina faltered. For only a flash she saw the same grief she felt mirrored in Sahara's eyes. She remembered Leese telling her that the agency was under new management—and then she understood. "I'm so sorry."

"Me too." Sahara let out a breath, then launched back into business. "There are women's clothes, makeup, lotions… I don't know. Many things. They belonged to one of Scott's girlfriends, who also supposedly died. The last girl was as slim as you, but somewhat taller—who isn't, right? Feel free to use whatever you can."

Harking back to the "supposedly died," Cat wondered what exactly had happened to Sahara's brother.

Shaking off the melancholy, Sahara said, "You'll find the suite quite comfortable and I promise you, the security here is top-notch. You don't need to worry."

She'd worry if she wanted to, and apparently she did because dread churned in her stomach. The questions were piling up, but she'd save them for Leese, after they were alone.

A tap sounded on her door and Enoch stuck his head in. "I apologize for interrupting, but you might want to take this call."

Unhappy with the intrusion, Sahara asked, "Who is it?"

"Webb Nicholson, and he says it's urgent."

CHAPTER FIVE

NEVER MIND THAT it was inappropriate behavior for a bodyguard—especially with his boss watching—but Leese needed to comfort Catalina, to reassure her. Later, he'd explain to Sahara. One way or another he'd make his boss understand—and if she didn't, well, then he'd find another job.

But regardless, he'd see to Catalina's safety.

Aware of her unease, Leese stood close behind her, silently reminding her that she wasn't alone. Like a deer caught in the crosshairs of a hunter's rifle, she'd gone deathly still the moment Enoch had announced the call. He could almost feel her gearing up to bolt, so he put his hands on her shoulders, and under his palms her muscles eased.

Amazing that he could have that much influence on her feelings. He didn't question it; she said she had good instincts and apparently she was right, because no way in hell would he let anyone hurt her. That, he told himself, was his own code of ethics, a protective nature toward women—now more finely honed given how he'd once inadvertently played a role in putting a woman at risk.

Never again.

With the phone on speaker so they could all hear, Sahara said smoothly, "Mr. Nicholson, how are you?"

"I understand you found my daughter."

"Me? No." She twittered a laugh. "I run the company, that's true. But I'm not in the field, so—"

Growling, Nicholson said, "Your man found her."

"Really?" Pausing for emphasis, she asked, "How do you know?"

A beat of silence passed. "You know damn good and well that he—"

"Don't raise your voice to me." The words hit like a whip, not loud, but sharp enough to draw blood.

Stunned silence proved that Nicholson felt the burn.

Clearly appalled at the way Sahara had just spoken to her stepfather, Cat tipped her head back to look at Leese in query.

He smiled and used his thumbs to further loosen her taut shoulders. She'd get used to Sahara, eventually.

"Now," Sahara said, "if there's anything else you'd like to say to me, I suggest you *calmly* say it."

"Your services are no longer needed."

"Odd." Sahara tapped one manicured fingertip to her bottom lip. "You already paid so substantially. I do believe it'll cover things for quite some time. Maybe even for a month or two."

"Keep the money, I don't care about that."

"Don't be silly." She gave another of her phony, teasing laughs. "We owe you the work. What type of businesswoman would I be if I didn't fulfill my obligations? And as I recall, you said it was of utmost urgency that we—"

"I'm firing you," Webb growled. "Your part is done."

Again Cat stiffened. Leese just waited.

"My *part*? Well, I'm so sorry you feel that way, Webb." Sahara softened her tone until it almost sounded pitying. The use of Nicholson's first name was a clear warning. "But understand, you merely paid. Catalina is our client. The transaction has been made, and we are on the job. At this point, only your daughter can fire us."

He sucked in an angry breath, but wary of her earlier warning, he didn't raise his voice. "Now you listen to me."

"Believe me, I'm all ears."

"Catalina isn't thinking clearly. I'm concerned. We're all concerned. She should be home with her family during this difficult time in her life. We *want* her home. Once she's here, she'll be fine."

"I have no doubt whatsoever. After all, family should always support each other in times of need. I promise, if my agent checks in, I'll ask him about it and then he can speak with Catalina. Not that I expect to hear from him anytime soon."

"What do you mean?"

"Well, I assume, being as good as he is and given your initial concerns and financial investment, he'll go to ground to ensure her safety."

"What are you talking about? He's not there with you?"

"Why ever would he be in the offices? I assure you, he's far from a desk jockey." Sahara propped her shapely ass on the edge of the desk and crossed her long legs, letting one high heel dangle off the tips of her toes.

How she walked in those things, especially in the winter weather, Leese had no idea.

"But...I thought..."

"Mr. Nicholson, you sound alarmed. If there are new concerns I need to know about, please let me know and I promise to share them with my guy as soon as he checks in."

Muffled whispering came through the line, then Nicholson asked, "When do you expect him?"

"I assume when he feels it's safe. No idea when that might be."

Impatience crept back into his tone. "There's no damn way you don't have contact with your men!"

The smile faded off Sahara's mouth. Her foot stopped swinging. Slowly, she slid off the desk to stand looking down at the phone. "Body Armor is by far the best agency you will find in the States, possibly in the world."

"I never said—"

Lacerating him with contempt, she cut him off. "I don't *babysit* my men because they don't need it, and further, if they did, you wouldn't have come to me."

After a gruff, "Harrumph," Nicholson said, "I apologize for losing my—"

"I understand. You're rightfully overwrought given your concerns for Catalina. Let me assure you, no one wishing her harm will get anywhere near her. Absolutely *no one*. You have my word. Now I must go. Have a good evening, Mr. Nicholson." And with that, she hit a button and ended the call.

Impressed, Justice applauded.

"This is awful," Cat whispered.

Wearing an evil smile, Sahara paced the room. "You should know, Catalina. I am a mean, mercenary bitch."

Intrigued by that, Justice leaned forward. "Really?"

"No, she's not," Leese stated. "Sahara, take a breath."

"Mean," Sahara insisted, still moving angrily around the room. "Mercenary. Bitch." She strode over to stand facing Cat. "And you need to understand that I will use this to my advantage."

Again, Cat glanced at Leese. When he shrugged, she turned back to Sahara. "How?"

"I'll ensure that you're protected," she promised. "And I'll do everything I can to see that Georgia Bell gets justice." On those insane heels, she crouched down beside Cat. "But that also means exposing every bastard involved, including, if necessary, your stepfather. The entire world will know what happened, the men—their livelihoods, their businesses—will likely be destroyed in the process. And this agency will take full credit for bringing them down. I will scrape up every bit of promotion I can to further our reputation as the best."

The overwhelming possibilities left Cat wide-eyed and shaken, but she didn't falter. She accepted that Georgia deserved retribution.

But Cat didn't yet realize that she did too.

"Anyone and everyone involved in hurting that girl needs to pay the consequences," Cat whispered. "Whatever they are."

"Excellent! Then we're in agreement." Rising gracefully again, Sahara smiled. "Now share the other names."

Pale, Cat shook her head. "I...I don't remember."

Sahara gave it quick thought, then shrugged. "Fine. I can start with your father."

"Stepfather." Appearing both fearful and guilty, Cat nodded. "And...okay."

Sahara turned her flinty blue eyes on Leese, taking note of the way he continued to hold Cat's shoulders. "Is there anything you'd like to tell me?"

He shrugged. "You're astute, Sahara. Do I really need to spell it out?"

She sighed. "And if I had a problem with this—"

"Then I'd understand and move on." But he wouldn't abandon Catalina.

"Don't be so dramatic. I have big plans for you." With a look of acceptance, she warned, "I'll want a full report. Soon."

To keep the peace, Leese nodded. But before he verbally made promises, he'd see what Catalina had to share. She knew the other men, he was sure of it. Would she trust him enough to tell him everything? And once she did, what then?

No idea. He knew what Sahara wanted, but he'd do whatever was best for Cat.

"They know you're here. Both of you. That much was clear." Sahara paced away, a vibrating bundle of energy. "Even though it's secure, we'll want to throw them off to give you a little breathing room. So I have an idea."

Very unsure of any plan she might contrive, Leese said, "Care to share with the class?"

"We're going to get each female employee to hide behind a scarf and glasses, then scatter in different directions—" she fluttered her fingers "—to all corners of the city and beyond. How fun will that be?"

"Fun?" Cat twisted her hands together. "Not fun at all. More than anything it sounds dangerous. I don't want to risk anyone else."

"We'll take care. Don't worry. And unless they have a lot of people out there watching us, they won't be able to follow everyone."

Cat asked, "How many female employees do you have here?"

"Counting me?" Sahara grinned. "Ten. But currently in the building? Only seven. It'll have to do, even though they're not all bodyguards. For a case like this, we need everyone on deck." Before anyone could question her participation, she went to the door and summoned Enoch. "Could I beg an enormous favor from you?"

Already to his feet, Enoch said, "Of course. What is it?"

"I need you to round up all the ladies, and then you'll need to run across the street to that decadent little boutique and do some fast shopping."

Two HOURS LATER, Enoch escorted them to the penthouse apartment. Leese wasn't sure what to expect, but he could tell that Cat was at the end of her rope. She needed some downtime, so the accommodations no longer mattered.

Trembling from head to toe, Cat entered the private elevator. "You're sure she'll be okay?"

Enoch looked as worried as Cat, so Leese reassured them both. "She has Justice with her."

Using an exclusive keycard, Enoch pressed the button to access the penthouse. "You said he's new."

Enoch stood a foot shorter than Leese, and probably didn't weigh a whole lot more than Catalina. But he had a keen intelligence, an aptitude for fast learning, was loyal to the core and often seemed to know what needed to be done long before being told. Leese liked him, and better than that, he trusted him.

"Justice is new to being a bodyguard, but he's a veteran at kicking ass. He can handle things, believe me." Justice might not have been refined enough to win a title belt, but few could ever reach that elite status. Match him up to any four or five street fighters, and he'd annihilate them.

"They're in your car." Cat stood in the corner, her gaze on the elevator numbers, her face set. "They're going to be the obvious ones to follow. Tesh and his crew will—"

"Scatter to cover their bases in case we're pulling a fast one, just as Sahara said. They won't take chances. But Sahara took the car on purpose," he reminded them, "because Justice can damn well handle himself. Now stop fretting, both of you."

At the uppermost floor, the elevator stopped and the doors opened directly into a secure vestibule with yet another locked door. On one of the walls, a sconce lit the area. On the other wall, a heavy door opened to private stairs.

Seeing the direction of his gaze, Enoch said, "The stairs are necessary in case of a fire."

Leese valued the multiple barriers.

Enoch removed an actual key and opened two different locks, one in the doorknob, the other a dead bolt. "I have duplicate keys for you," he said to Leese while avoiding Cat's gaze. "And you should know there are around-the-clock guards at the elevator and stairs on the lobby level. They protect Sahara from anyone reaching her office on the floor below."

He'd already been aware of that, but appreciated the reminder for Cat's benefit.

Opening the door, Enoch added, "I've been in charge of the upkeep here. No one has been here unescorted, not even the monthly cleaning crew. I'm always here if anyone needs to get in the suite, and I can promise you it's safe." He stepped back and allowed Cat and Leese to enter.

Wow. Cat, who was used to such decadence, only said, "This is very nice."

Leese didn't know what the hell to think. Towering ceilings with massive hanging lights, floor-to-ceiling windows with an astounding view, open spaces, a central fireplace... He looked around, taking it in.

"The kitchen has everything you need, pots and pans, dishes, canned goods...everything except for perishables. If you'd like to make up a grocery list, I can take care of that for you." He strode to an elaborate bar. "The liquor is stocked, so please help yourself."

Cat dropped her purse and coat on a massive contemporary couch overloaded with pillows, then wandered to the expanse of windows to look out at the city. "I bet this is stunning at night."

"It is," Enoch confirmed. "Would you like to see the bedrooms?"

Multiple rooms? Leese immediately wondered if Cat would prefer to sleep with him again.

Insane as he knew it to be, he hoped so.

Following behind the two of them, he lost track of the penthouse layout because his attention zeroed in on Cat's small but perfect ass. As they stepped into one room, he managed to concentrate.

"This is the master suite."

The enormous room boasted more floor-to-ceiling windows, a sitting area, a flat screen TV and an oversize bed with decadent bedding. Leese barely resisted the urge to whistle.

"There's a bathroom through that door." Enoch opened another door to show off a walk-in closet big enough to be a room of its own. "Clothes are still in the closet, including some things for a female. As Sahara said, help yourself, although there are more things in the guest bedroom."

"If this was her brother's room," Cat whispered, "maybe we shouldn't use it."

"Sahara isn't shy. If that had been her preference, she'd have said so." Enoch lifted a remote from the nightstand and closed the drapes, then opened them again. "Mr. Silver worked hard at making this space exactly as he liked it. It has all the bells and whistles you could imagine. I think in some ways, Sahara enjoys the idea of it being used again. She just can't bear to be the one doing so." He turned and headed out, so Cat and Leese followed.

"This room is a library-slash-television-slash-gaming room. The Wi-Fi is secure, so feel free. Every television in every room is connected to the satellite for the building, so you'll have plenty of choices on what to watch. This television, of course, is set up for theater-style viewing. And if you open the cabinet under the TV in here, you'll find some gaming systems and the most popular games." Again walking, he led them to another room. "This is the guest suite."

Leese peeked inside. This bedroom had more padded furniture instead of the heavy wood. No seating area, but a cushioned window seat.

Enoch smiled gently at Cat. "There's another connecting bathroom, and inside you'll find makeup, nail polish…a plethora of toiletries preferred by ladies. Again, please help yourself."

"I couldn't," Catalina said. "If they belonged to her brother's girlfriend—"

"No one special," Enoch assured her. "Mr. Silver had many girlfriends, and he was far from ready to settle down. Sahara would have thrown everything away, except she seldom comes in here because of the memories."

Ill at ease, Cat nodded. "Thank you." She sat on the edge of the full-size bed, stroking one hand over the plush comforter. "It's very nice."

So she'd be choosing the guest room? Looked like. Leese didn't like it, but he wouldn't protest. More than anything, he wanted her to be comfortable. She'd earned herself a break from worry.

"Please," Enoch said, "use whatever you like. Sahara will like it if you do."

Catalina bit her lip, then reluctantly agreed. "All right then. I'd actually love to."

"Wonderful." Enoch looked genuinely pleased. "Any questions, don't hesitate to let me know."

"I have a few." Leese glanced at Cat. "Why don't you get settled while Enoch and I talk? I'll be back in a minute."

"You're leaving?"

The pitch of her voice gave her away—and broke his heart. To reassure her, he stared into her eyes. "Just going into the other room with Enoch."

"Oh." She let out a nervous breath and nodded. "Okay."

"Cat? I won't make any plans without telling you. If I do have to step out, it won't be for long, and you'll know beforehand."

"Sounds good." Trying to appear unconcerned, she smiled. "Thanks."

Giving up, Leese stepped out and closed the door. Sooner or later she'd stop doubting him.

"Something private?" Enoch asked.

"A favor, really. Can you find out for me the nearest place to get a couple of burner phones?"

Enoch lifted his brows. "Your company phone isn't working?"

"It is, but I'd like some prepaids," Leese explained. "Disposable phones."

With no further questions, Enoch explained, "Actually a phone store right across the street offers them. Would you like me to run the errand for you?"

He shook his head. Leese preferred to do some things himself. "I'll take care of it, but could you come back in about an hour? Maybe keep Cat company while I'm gone?"

He flashed a grin. "You mean you want me to ensure she doesn't budge?"

"That too." If need be, Enoch could reinforce Cat's cooperation by alerting the guards. Or calling Sahara.

Leese wanted to trust Cat, but she'd already made so many references to booking it, to thinking her best option was to run, that he—

Peering around the hall, Cat said, "I wouldn't sneak off."

After a roll of his eyes, Leese turned to fully face her. "Eavesdropping?"

"Yes." She came out the rest of the way. "And good thing. Enoch doesn't need more duties piled on him. Seems to me he already has a full plate."

Protesting that, Enoch said, "Believe me, Sahara makes it more than worth my while."

"I hope so. The scope of your job seems to cover… everything. I don't want to add to it."

"Sahara is the very best boss I've ever had. Always polite and caring. She gives me requests, but if I said no, she'd be okay with it. She wouldn't fire me. So far, though, I've never even considered saying no to her. I love this job too much."

With fresh curiosity, Leese asked, "Was her brother the same?" Of course he'd known about Scott Silver. The man wasn't a secret. But Sahara had never really discussed him much.

"Scott was very similar. They were close and shared a lot of personality traits. Smart, motivated, considerate… Sahara, though, is far more driven, personally and in business. Around her, there's never a dull moment." He opened the main door, but hesitated. "She normally doesn't talk about him at all. She keeps everything inside—she's super private that way. If you don't mind, it'd be better if you don't ask her anything about him."

Since Leese was the same, he understood. "Sure."

"Thanks." He stepped out. "I'll be back in one hour."

Soon as he left, Leese turned to Cat. She'd removed her sweater and now wore only jeans, socks and a pullover long-sleeved T-shirt that hugged her modest curves. Somehow, on her, at this particular moment, it looked like the sexiest outfit ever.

"You doing okay?"

She nodded, but it was a lie. He saw it on her face, in the darkness of her eyes and the pallor of her skin.

Taking both her hands in his, he pulled her closer. "Fibber."

"I'm here," she countered. "Safe. I'd call that okay."

"You're chilled." Her fingers felt like ice. "Want me to adjust the temp?"

"Did you see that thermostat? It'd take a mathematical genius to figure it out." She tipped her head back to look up at him. "Besides, my hands and feet are always cold this time of year."

Damn, but it was tempting to kiss her, especially since she looked to be waiting on it. Instead he took a step back. "Since we're going to be playing house, why don't we go through the kitchen and see what groceries we'll need? I'll pick them up while I'm out getting us phones."

In silent agreement, she headed that way. "Why do you need the phones? You don't trust the landlines here?"

"They're secure. Sahara would have seen to that." But trust that no one in the building would listen in? There were a lot of people in an agency this size—too many to vet them all, too many that he didn't know well. "But I'd still rather you not make any calls. If there's anyone you want to talk to, let me know."

As she stepped into the kitchen she trailed her fingers over the polished granite bar. "You called them burners."

"Usually burners mean a phone you use once and toss. I won't do that, but I will use different phones in different locations so I can mix it up, and once one runs out of minutes, I'll be done with it. It's just a way to up our chances of dodging them. That's all."

"I'm glad you're more serious about this than Sahara." She knelt to look in a cabinet, found big bowls and stood again. "I can use one of the phones?"

"Yes." He watched her go on tiptoe to open another

cabinet. Her body was slim but supple, looking leaner as she stretched.

This cabinet held staples like salt, flour, sugar and spices. None of that interested her though.

Curious, Leese folded his arms and asked, "Who do you want to call?"

She rolled one shoulder. "My brothers first. I don't know if they're worried or not, but just in case..." She opened a drawer and found a pen and paper. Drawing them out, she asked, "Can you cook?"

"Sure. You?"

"Pretty much." She wrote on the paper, then went back to checking cabinets.

Leese stepped closer to read: *cereal, milk, cookies, cola...* He shook his head. "You're going to kill yourself eating that—"

"Shush it." After glancing in the freezer, she said, "Put ice cream on there too, will you? And maybe chocolate sauce. Or ooh, whipped cream."

No, he wouldn't. "Why don't you let me take over meals?"

With an exaggerated shudder, she said, "Because you'll have me eating tofu or something nauseating like that."

"I promise that's not true."

She closed the freezer and opened the fridge. "I need my junk food in times of stress, and Leese?" Glancing over her shoulder, she emphasized, "This is definitely a time of stress."

Gently, he wrestled the refrigerator door from her and closed it, then with his hands on her shoulders, he turned her to face him. "Who else will you want to call?"

On a groan, she said, "So many people."

"Let's hear it."

"People at the school. The boy who usually shovels my walk and driveway. I have a neighbor who probably wonders what happened to me. At least he'll be able to tell me if my house is okay."

Every possessive instinct came to attention. Leese tried to ignore the unruly urges, even as he repeated, "He?"

"Mike. He's like… I don't know. Eighty-five or so. Scrawny little guy but real protective. Sometimes he'd walk over in the morning with coffee. See, he belongs to this coffee club and sometimes he likes to share."

And she was kind enough to make time for her elderly neighbor. Nice. Hell, everything about her was nice.

Leese knew he wasn't only attracted to her physically. So far, he actually liked everything about her.

He considered her a job. His responsibility. In some ways, he already considered her…his.

Dumb. Dangerous. But looking down at her, needing to protect her, wanting her, he couldn't deny the truth of his feelings.

"If you call your neighbor, it's going to lead to a lot of questions about where you've been. It could even put him in danger. So how about I go by your house instead? I can check it over, make sure—"

"What?" Eyes flaring, she insisted, *"No.* Absolutely not. Don't even think about going to my house."

Mystified by her reaction, Leese asked, "Why not?"

Her hands fisted in his shirt. "Promise me right now that you won't." When he didn't answer fast enough, she tried to shake him.

Silly.

He untangled her fingers from his clothes. "Settle down, Cat."

That earned him a punch in the ribs. Not that she had enough strength to hurt him, especially without room to really draw back.

Going on tiptoe, she said straight into his face, "They know what you look like, damn it! By now they probably know who you are. You can't go poking your nose around places where they might be."

Leese wasn't sure if he wanted to kiss her or set her straight. He decided to go with setting her straight first. "I'm not worried about them."

Her eyes widened even more. "Oh my God, you *were* going to poke around, weren't you?" In a huff, she started to turn away.

He caught her, then trapped her smacking hands behind her. Irked that she thought so little of him, Leese growled, "Let's be clear on something here."

Uncaring that he'd hampered her with his size and strength, she snapped, "I won't be a part of your suicide."

That was one insult too many. Leaning down, Leese said an inch from her face, "Just because I'm holing up here with you—to keep *you* safe—don't expect me to run from them. Because, Catalina, I can promise you that's not going to happen."

Temper sent her voice higher. "You won't have to run if you don't get within shooting distance!"

Irritation deepened his voice. "How damned incompetent do you think I am?"

"I didn't say you're incompetent!"

Only slightly mollified, he asked, "Then how do you figure I'd get myself shot?"

She tightened her mouth. "You're too naive to realize how bad they are."

Oh hell no. In a deadly whisper, he repeated, "Naive?"

"Yes!" She struggled against him, but finally stopped to glare. "Man-to-man, sure, you can beat up any one of them. But you won't get that chance because they don't play fair. You're not familiar with guys of their caliber."

"Why don't you enlighten me?"

As if challenged, she snapped, "Fine." Nose up, brows down, she said, "I've been around them much of my life. They're well-dressed, well-paid, articulate thugs hired by the elite to solve problems in any way necessary. Not a one of them has a conscience, they're completely ruthless and, as I've recently learned, they're capable of anything, including cold-blooded murder."

"You think I didn't already know that?"

"I…" Doubt darkened her eyes. "I don't know."

"No, you don't. You definitely don't know me well enough to presume I'm that dumb or helpless." Leese arched her a little closer. "I do know my job, damn it."

"Your job includes taking insane chances?"

"My job is taking care of you."

They stared at each other, him frowning, her doubtful, when sudden awareness arced between them. Leese felt her soft breasts pressed to his midsection, her slender thighs aligned with his. Her eyes were big and bright, her lips soft, parted.

With a catch of her breath, Cat's attention dipped to his mouth. Watching her anger melt away all but singed him.

By small degrees she rested against him, her breath warm on his throat, her body easing into his. Leese didn't move, didn't even breathe...until she touched her lips to his, barely there, ultrasweet.

Every emotion—anger, annoyance and that powerful protectiveness—merged into consuming need. He forgot about what was smart or professional.

On a groan, he released her hands to gather her as close as he could get her, taking her mouth in a devouring, out-of-control kiss. Her arms immediately came up around his neck in full participation. She welcomed his tongue, stroked back with her own, every bit as frenzied.

Without really thinking about it, Leese clasped her waist and hoisted her up to sit on the counter, then pressed her slim legs apart to step between them. She didn't break the kiss, but she did lock her ankles behind him.

On autopilot, blind with lust, he anchored one hand to her ass and rocked her against his straining erection. With the other hand he found her left breast. Small, firm but soft...*perfect*.

Freeing her mouth, she moaned and dropped her head back, her eyes closed, her lips now swollen.

He liked that reaction a lot, especially since it mirrored his own. Using his thumb, he strummed the tight nipple pressing through her bra and shirt.

Her fingers clenched on his shoulders and she drew a ragged breath. So sensitive. So hot.

Letting the anticipation build, Leese kissed his way along her jaw and down her throat, nudged aside the neckline of her shirt to kiss her collarbone, then dipped down and lightly bit her nipple through the material of her shirt.

"Leese," she whispered, sounding a little desperate.

He wanted her out of the shirt, right now, so he could get to her bare skin. He slipped both hands under the hem, and his cell phone rang.

They both froze.

Damn. He had a near-lethal boner, but he could guess who was calling.

As much to himself as her, he said, "I'm sorry."

She swallowed audibly…and her legs fell away, freeing him.

Leese stepped back, then made the mistake of looking at her. Jesus, she looked beautiful when turned on— blue eyes dark, skin flushed and hair mussed.

Breathing too heavily, Leese cupped her cheek, brushed his thumb over her heated skin, then, with extreme regret, he turned away to answer the call.

CHAPTER SIX

CAT COULD BARELY think beyond the disappointment and, yup, embarrassment. Good grief, she'd all but molested Leese. The ringing of his phone had brought her crashing back to reality and she'd realized she had him locked to her with her legs around his waist.

Not that he'd been complaining.

She touched her lips while staring at his broad back, seeing it expand with his every heavy breath. God, the feel of him—those delicious, defined muscles in his shoulders and biceps, the way his thighs flexed as he moved against her, the strength in his abs... She closed her eyes and remembered how hard he was all over, how he'd tasted, how good he smelled...

"Sahara, hi. Everything okay?"

Sahara? Cat opened her eyes again, and found Leese watching her with piercing intensity. He had his cell to his ear, but his scrutiny flustered her all over again.

Hopping off the counter, then quickly steadying her rubbery legs, she asked, "Everything okay?"

He nodded. "Sahara, Cat's concerned. I'm going to put you on speaker."

After pressing the screen, he set his phone on the bar and went back to watching her.

"All went well," Sahara said, her voice chipper. "We did have a tail, but lost him."

"She drives like a demon," Justice said in the background.

That got Leese's attention back on the phone. "I thought you were driving."

"She made me pull over!"

Sahara laughed. "He's a cautious driver and that's not what was needed."

"By cautious, she means I didn't scream through red lights, drive against traffic or take turns so sharp the SUV nearly rolled."

"Calm down, Justice. You survived."

"Barely," he groused.

Starting to grin, Leese looked at Cat again.

She couldn't blunt her own smile, but it faded as she asked, "Was it Tesh following you?"

"It's possible," Sahara started to say.

But Justice interrupted. "I didn't see any damn tail! I swear, I think she made it up just so she could play speed racer."

Leese laughed outright.

"The important thing," Sahara insisted, "is that we're both fine. I also heard from everyone else and it appears we all escaped unscathed. So, Catalina, rest easy."

That news buoyed her. Maybe she could blame stress as the reason she'd accosted Leese? Never before had she been sexually aggressive. But one minute she'd wanted to clout him, and in the next she'd badly wanted to crawl all over his very fine body.

"Catalina?"

She cleared her throat. "I'm here, Sahara. Thank you. I'm relieved that everyone is okay."

Leese asked his boss, "Are you returning to the offices?"

"Maybe later," she said. "Since I'm already out and about and I have a hunky escort—"

"Me?" Justice asked.

"Of course, you. I figured I'd do some shopping—" Justice groaned.

"—*and* I can use that time to see how aware you are of your surroundings, plus we'll have a chance to talk about your upcoming client."

His groaning stopped. "The movie star?"

"Yes."

Justice quickly agreed and they said their farewells.

As silence fell, Cat couldn't quite meet Leese's gaze. "You weren't worried about her using your cell?"

He shook his head. "Not just yet. The phone is supplied by the company, not registered to me. Her phone is secure, so we're good."

She didn't entirely understand that, but only nodded. Now that they were post-make out session, she felt pretty awkward. "Justice is a funny guy."

"He has his moments." As Leese slid the phone back into his pocket, his concerned gaze held hers. "Listen, Cat…"

"I'm glad Sahara won't be alone," she said quickly, hoping to divert the conversation.

Leese ignored her efforts. "I should apologize."

"You already did." And she didn't want to talk about it. "No worries." Trying for a strategic retreat, she turned to leave the kitchen, but Leese stopped her by catching her hand.

"I'm sorry," he stressed, "that we got interrupted."

She turned fast to face him. "Oh." Did that mean he intended to pick up where they'd left off? That'd work for her.

Already the burn ignited deep inside her.

"Damn, honey, don't look at me like that." Stepping back, he ran a hand over his neck. "We both know it shouldn't have happened."

"Speak for yourself." She and her body both thought a whole lot more should have happened. In fact, she was hoping it still might. "I enjoyed it, *you*…the diversion." Hoping he'd understand, she admitted, "You make me feel things."

He popped his neck. "Yeah, I know what you felt."

The way he said it, she understood just what he meant. "Gratitude?" she choked, because damn him, she did feel gratitude. But so much more.

"Yes. And you shouldn't confuse that with anything else, okay?"

Simmering anger crawled into her bloodstream. "You had your tongue in my mouth."

"Cat…"

"And your hands on my butt." She thrust her chest forward, adding, "And a boob. I'm not at all confused about that."

His gaze skipped over her body, but shot back to her face and resolutely stayed there. "I got carried away."

Thumb to her sternum, she said, "And I liked it."

A tortured expression crossed his features. "It shouldn't happen again."

She snapped back, "I'm hoping it does."

"Because you're—"

"What? *Confused?*" She almost dared him to say it again. "You can't imagine, can't know, what it's like to be only around strangers for so long, feeling only worry, or sometimes fear. Six weeks has seemed more like six months. Sometimes like six years. So many times

I wondered how others live with it, the uncertainty of not knowing what will happen the next day, maybe even the next hour, if I'd have any money or any food."

His shoulders tightened. "You shouldn't have gone through that."

"People do, all the time. They don't have a safety net, they're alone without family or friends to turn to. I met some of those people in a shelter. I liked them, but I couldn't stay long because I knew, eventually, someone would look for me there."

Leese said nothing, but listened as if he truly wanted to learn more about her. Normally that would have been her cue to shut down. She didn't—*couldn't*—trust anyone who was too interested in her situation. Until now.

"Before all this happened, I'd never experienced that. Even as weird as I am—"

"You're not weird. Not at all."

"Compared to my family I am. I stick out like a sore thumb, and I'm okay with that. It's one reason why no one in my family protested too much when I quit hanging around for their social functions and instead did only the occasional private visit. They were as tired of the awkwardness as I was. But even then, being aware of how they felt, I knew I had them, that they were there." Her heart seemed to skip a beat, and she whispered, "Right up until they weren't."

Right up until it was all snatched away.

She didn't want to think about that now. When she did, it brought her down and, currently, life was hard enough without dwelling on yet more things she couldn't control.

"You're not weird," Leese reiterated one more time, as if it mattered to him what she thought of herself.

"I am." She'd long ago accepted it. "But you know what? You should give me some credit, because I've learned a lot about myself, some of it good."

"More than some."

The compliment was nice, even though it changed nothing. "I've always been a woman of means. I had resources others never had. I grew up secure, without a worry, filled with the confidence that a pampered life had given me. If I didn't have something, it was because I didn't want it or I'd chosen to give it up, not because it was out of my reach."

Hands in his pockets, Leese rested a shoulder against the wall. "Car? Education?"

"Everything like that. Nice clothes. Every new tech gadget. Spending money. But more important, I had family. I had backup." She went quiet, then laughed with irony. "I *thought* I had backup. Turns out I was wrong."

Sympathy brought him nearer. "Okay, so Webb isn't who you thought he was. But what about your brothers?"

"I don't know yet. I hope they believe in me, I hope they'll know the truth when they hear it, but they're close to Webb. Far closer than I ever was. They trust him, share with him." It was so dumb, but seemed to represent so much. "They still love the parties."

"I'm not a party person either."

Cat drew a breath, appreciating his support. "The thing is, Leese, despite how awful this has been, I'm proud of myself for finding my survival instinct and being able to make it entirely on my own, from scratch, without any of the things I'd always taken for granted." She put a fist to her heart. "I didn't have anything, not even my name, but I've made it this far. With money and power used against me, with trained men hunting for me, I've dodged them for six weeks. That's something of a miracle, don't you think? And I did that."

"You're smart," Leese said, "and you're resilient. No one can deny that."

Damn it, plenty of people denied it. If Webb had his way, they'd all think her insane. For that reason, Leese's faith in her tightened her throat.

"I'm smart enough, and resilient enough, to know what I want." She stared at him to ensure he didn't misunderstand, and then as a parting shot, she added, "Next time, without an interruption."

He stayed silent as she walked away, down the hall and into the guest bedroom. She hesitated, but when he didn't follow she closed the door and collapsed facedown on the bed.

How was it her life just kept getting more and more complicated? Having a wealthy, entitled, corrupt lunatic or two after her was bad enough. Living on the street, surviving with nothing? Plenty difficult.

But now she had an ultrahunk in her life who, damn it, didn't want what she'd repeatedly offered.

How often did men turn down willing women? In her world, apparently too often.

It seemed like she rested there forever, her thoughts churning as she tried to decide what to do next. Not that she had a lot of options. She wasn't sleepy. Wasn't yet hungry. Leese was too big for her to coerce, and apparently kissing her and groping her hadn't sufficiently seduced him.

Maybe she should crash in front of the TV.

Or...she rolled to her side and stared toward the

walk-in closet. She could take inventory on the clothes. See if anything would fit. If anything appealed to her.

It'd be nice to wear something other than the same pair of jeans for a change. Maybe she'd find something pretty, even sexy. What difference did it make if no one would see her? No one except Leese, and he'd just sworn off touching her, so he didn't count.

When the tap sounded on the closed bedroom door, she almost hit the ceiling. Going to her back, heart pumping hard, she asked, "What?"

He peeked in, saw her there on the bed, balanced on her elbows, and his gaze heated. "You okay?"

No doubt she'd be better if he joined her. "*Okay* is a subjective term. All in all, for what my life has turned into, yeah, sure, I'm peachy."

He stepped farther inside but stayed near the door, the chicken. Maybe she tempted him. That'd be a nice thought.

"Putting aside everything before this morning," he said, "still fine?"

"Sure." Pride had her sitting up and shrugging as if she hadn't a care. "You're not the first rejection I've gotten, so don't sweat it."

Almost against his will, he looked her over. "You're not stupid, Cat, so don't pretend to be."

No, she wasn't, but she asked anyway. "What's that supposed to mean?"

His attention drifted back to her face. "You know I want you."

Even while irked, hearing that sent a shiver down her back. *Guess my radar isn't as wonky as I thought.* But whether he wanted her or not, he'd still rejected her, and she was still stung by that. "So you backing off is... what?" With a sneer, she asked, "Nobility?"

Her deliberate laugh intensified the heat in his gaze. "I've known you less than a day."

"Ah, so it's scruples?" She tsked and asked with an overdone dose of sympathy, "You've never had a one-night stand, huh?"

"I never said that."

No, he hadn't, which only confirmed that it was something about her that had him refusing.

"Not that it would apply anyway," he added. "We'll be together for more than one night, maybe even weeks."

Weeks? Good grief. Could a woman die of unrequited lust? "So it's that you need me to wine and dine you first? I can give it a try. That is, if you'll add wine to that grocery list. No, wait. I bet there's some here in the penthouse somewhere." She looked over his very fine body and murmured, "I'll see if I can find it."

The provocative words brought him closer. "You keep pushing and pushing." He stood right next to her feet, which hung over the side of the bed. "I'm taking off now. Enoch is here. To give you privacy, he said he'll stay in the office on the computer. I guess he can loop in to his own files from any location. He'll work—here, with you—until I return."

No, and no again. "I don't need a babysitter." What she needed was some private time to reflect, to mope, to do whatever the hell she wanted to do—without an audience.

Leese crossed his arms. "I'm not so sure about that. Half the time I think you're plotting to run off. The rest of the time I figure you're plotting something worse."

Cat tried to stare him down, but blast him, he was right. Out of necessity, she did do a lot of plotting.

Hoping to placate him, she said, "What if I promise I won't leave?"

"How do I know your word's good?"

Slowly, she scooted to sit on the edge of the bed very close to him. "Okay, I'm not going to take offense at that. Like you said, we haven't known each other that long. But you could look at it this way—where would I go? Tesh is out there, keeping watch. Others might be too. I know it. I *feel* it. Obviously I don't have a death wish or I wouldn't have worked so hard to stay safe, right? Sahara made me a terrific offer. I want to move forward with my life, not always be on the run. Believe me, it gets old quick."

He considered that. "So right now, staying put is your best option?"

Her only option, but not a heinous one. "That's how I see it." She glanced back at the closet. "I was going to play a little. Shower with the good stuff, do my hair." She pulled forward a hank of dull, dry hair. A deep conditioner would really come in handy. "Like you said, we might be here a week or so."

"More than a week."

No, she wouldn't even consider that. "Since this will be my current residence, I want to explore the place." She deliberately pouted at him. "I'm not comfortable doing any of that with Enoch hanging around."

After studying her, Leese must have decided she told the truth, because he patted her knee and stepped away. "I'll be gone a couple of hours, tops. The elevator and the stairs will be watched. If you do try to sneak off, someone from here will follow you until I can catch up."

"I'll be here," she promised him. Then, since she'd gotten her way, she teased, "Waiting for you."

Given how he inhaled, it was a direct hit. He waffled a second more, then blew out a resigned breath. "Be good, okay?"

"I'm always good," she countered as he went back through the door and closed it. Deflated, she whispered, "Just not good enough."

NEEDING SOME RELEASE, even in the way of violence, Leese half hoped someone would approach him. If he couldn't screw away his tension, maybe he could demolish it.

Unfortunately, he got through the phone store without a single incident. When he stepped out again, the area remained clear of any threats.

Enoch had given him the keys to another car at the Body Armor agency, this one a nondescript sedan. To keep anyone from tinkering with it, he'd avoided the parking garage and instead pulled up at an empty spot near the curb right out in front of the store. As soon as he got seated inside, he locked up and pulled away. Still vigilant, he used one of the new low-tech flip phones to make a call.

Miles Dartman, a fighter and a friend, answered on the third ring.

Since Miles wouldn't know the number, he said, "It's Leese. I'm using a different phone."

"Hey, Leese, what's up?"

"Not a lot." He still talked to the guys often enough that a call from him wasn't surprising. "Work." *A woman.* "Saw you won your last fight. Congrats on that."

"By decision." His disgruntlement was loud and clear. "I needed a knockout."

Didn't they all? It was never ideal to leave the decision in the hands of the judges. "You creamed him."

"But couldn't finish him." After a bitter huff, Miles said, "You didn't call to hear me bitch. Hell, *I* don't want to hear me bitch. How about a change of topic?"

"Sure." Leese turned the corner, heading for the grocery. "I was wondering if you'd have time to do me a favor."

"Probably," Miles said. "I won't fight again for a while and I have a few minor injuries to nurse. What and when?"

As briefly as possible, Leese gave the bare-bones update about Catalina as a client. "I don't want to go into detail—just know that I need someone I trust to stick with her for a few hours while I take care of something." Cat was the type of woman who, if cooped up too long, would get stir-crazy. Hopefully, if he got her a few of her own things, she'd settle into the situation without as much conflict.

And maybe she'd be less inclined to seduce him too.

He was as far from a saint as a man could get, but he didn't want to take advantage of her.

So regardless of what she said, Leese planned to go by her house and get some of her belongings for her. If Cat was right, he just might be able to kill two birds with one stone.

"I'm not saying no, but isn't Justice there with you?"

"He was. Now he's otherwise occupied, and I trust you more than him anyway."

"Trust me to keep her safe, or to keep my hands to myself?"

Locking his back teeth, Leese admitted, "Both."

When he finished laughing, Miles said, "You're a couple of hours from me. When do you need me there?"

"Day after tomorrow would be good. Think you can swing that?"

"Shouldn't be a problem. Let me get the address from you."

Once Leese finished giving him directions, he added, "One more thing. I don't want you to tell her why you're there."

"Because…?"

She'll know what I'm doing, and she thinks I'm such a terrible bodyguard that I'll get murdered. No, he wouldn't admit that to Miles. "Like most women, she's a worrier."

"Uh-huh. And hot?"

He pulled into the lot for the gigantic grocery-slash-department store. "Yeah, she is. She's also been through hell and I don't want to contribute to her anxiety."

"So I'll be keeping watch over a hot, tortured worrier, but she can't know why I'm there, and I can't come on to her."

"That's about it." Used to being heckled by his friends, Leese didn't take offense. "Think you can be here by noon?"

"Sure. Should I plan on spending the whole day, a few hours, or what?"

"Whole day. She'll enjoy the company." Maybe. "I'll treat you to dinner."

"Sounds good. See you then."

After he disconnected, Leese looked around, but from what he could tell, no one had followed him. Had

Sahara's ploy really worked? Possibly, but he wouldn't buy it just yet.

If he got back to the Body Armor agency without incident, then maybe, just maybe, he'd start to believe.

For now he only wanted to concentrate on feeding Catalina a good, *healthy* meal that she'd enjoy. And if he could resist her, that'd be terrific too.

WHILE SOAKING IN an enormous tub filled with scented bath bubbles, her hair covered with a deep conditioner, her face caked with a mud mask, Cat sipped the best bourbon she'd ever tasted.

Gawd, it felt good to pamper herself again.

Until now she hadn't realized how much she missed primping. And alcohol. Yup, she missed that too. Not that she was a lush. Far from it. What she'd told Leese and Sahara was true—it didn't take much to give her a buzz. But it felt so good to be comfortable enough, secure enough, to imbibe and not worry about putting herself at risk.

For too long she'd had to be sharp, on guard, always watching for an attack.

Sighing in pleasure, she examined her fingers and toes and decided a mani and pedi were also in order.

When the water started to cool she drained the tub and turned on the shower to rinse her hair and face. She felt soft all over—and liked it.

Using a round brush, she blow-dried her hair into loose waves. Scott's girlfriend had loved her beauty products, and Cat found an array of makeup to choose from. She wrinkled her nose at most of it, but did play up her eyes with shadow, coal liner and two layers of mascara, then slicked pink gloss over her lips. She knew from experience the gloss wouldn't last; she almost always licked it off without thinking. But she liked the way the makeup enhanced her eyes.

Wrapped in a towel, she finally examined the closet and found so many beautiful clothes that she felt guilty for her excitement. After all, Sahara's brother and his girlfriend had both died.

Cat bit her lip, then gave in and went through the clothes, finding a few pairs of skinny designer jeans that fit once she rolled up the hem. She tried on sweaters, blouses, shirts, sweatshirts—enough to last her for a good long while. The yoga capri pants, in multiple colors and patterns, worked perfectly. She even found socks, two nightgowns, a robe and slippers.

Then she withdrew a slinky black dress made of stretchy material meant to hug the body and show off curves. Ohhhh, nice.

Never mind that she lacked the usual curves necessary to really make the dress work. It was snug enough to ensure a decent fit.

Skipping panties and knowing she *couldn't* wear a bra, not with the cut of the dress, Cat pulled it on over her head, then tugged and adjusted until her breasts were cupped by just enough material to emphasize her meager cleavage. The hem dragged the floor like a train, but a side slit cut up along her leg nearly to her hip, leaving her almost indecently exposed.

Now that she had the dress on, she didn't want to take it off. Not yet.

What would Leese think? She grabbed up her drink to sip again, then poured another before deciding she'd leave the dress on. Just as she appreciated the pampering, she also liked the male attention. It had been even longer since she'd had that—at least from a good man.

In her old life, she'd never have worn anything this daring, but she'd owned similar quality gowns. Even being apart from her family, she'd celebrated special occasions with them. The last time had been her oldest brother's birthday at a swanky restaurant. Each of her brothers had brought a date, but she'd gone alone.

That night, two different men had approached her, but she'd ignored them both. They were smooth, polished and made assumptions as only the entitled could. She'd wanted less of that world, not more.

Leese wasn't like that. Sure, the man had confidence in spades. But it was different. She had a feeling he'd earned everything he'd ever gotten.

The way he'd looked around when they entered the penthouse told her he hadn't often seen that type of luxury, but he didn't let it intimidate him.

In fact, she couldn't imagine anything or anyone intimidating Leese.

Remembering how easily he'd leveled Tesh left her breathless in awe. Thinking of the muscled strength on every inch of his body, the heated way he looked at her and the hungry way he'd kissed her left her breathless in an entirely different way.

There'd been nothing refined in his touch or attitude— and something very basic inside her thrilled at that fact. She'd bet her own safety that Leese had never taken a shortcut through the hardships. No, he'd probably just worked his way past them.

Twisting, Cat looked at the rear view in the mirror. The straps were cut in a way to leave her back almost entirely bare. Inspired, she darted back to a dressing table and pinned up her hair in a casual twist that left a few long tendrils free.

For once, she actually felt sexy.

The shoes were all a size too big for her, so she ignored them and went for the jewelry, settling on long chandelier earrings in sparkling silver.

Getting dolled up made her want to dance, so she headed to the living room and a state-of-the-art sound system. As she left the carpet and her feet touched the smooth tile floor, she realized it was heated.

Heaven.

After wiggling her toes, she examined the stereo. Much of the available music didn't interest her; she'd never had mellow tastes in that regard. Another way she was weird. Her family liked classic music…and she rocked to heavy metal.

She scrolled through every option until she found some hard rock. Immediately her heart picked up the beat and, feeling free, she stood to dance. Sure enough, the bourbon gave her a nice buzz to go with the music that now played throughout the penthouse. Carefree for the first time in ages, Cat let herself go—and forgot about everything else.

APPARENTLY THE PENTHOUSE was well insulated, because Leese had no forewarning until, arms filled with grocery bags, he shouldered open the door and got hit with the loud screeching of a metal band.

Even more surprising was Cat, looking like sex personified in a slinky black dress that left tantalizing swaths of her body exposed as she danced, arms up and eyes closed, in the middle of the floor with abandon.

Ridiculously captivated, Leese closed and relocked the door, then just stood there and took it in.

She'd dolled herself up with makeup and she'd done something sexy and loose with her hair. He also noted the half-empty tumbler on the table.

So dressed up, dancing and drinking?

Not wanting to startle her, he quietly set the grocery bags on a foyer table, then went to the stereo and turned down the music.

Slowing her dance, Cat opened her eyes and focused on him. "Leese." With a silly smile and a limp wrist, she brushed back a wayward curl. "You're back."

"Yeah." And now he wanted her more than ever. All the lecturing he'd given himself was shot to hell the second he'd seen her. "What are you wearing?"

Smiling, she struck a seductive pose then twirled, sending the material to fan out around her legs. "Do you like it?"

The way the dress parted, she had to be naked underneath. For damn sure she wasn't wearing a bra. "Yeah," he growled, looking at her small bare feet. "I like it."

"I'd hoped you would."

Why the hell did she purr like that? "I thought your feet and hands stayed cold in the winter."

"I decided to dress for dinner, except the shoes were all too big. Luckily, the floors are heated." Dropping her voice, she whispered, "I feel a little pagan, all dressed up but barefoot."

More like undressed, but whatever. "It's sexy." She was sexy—and he was definitely in trouble.

Wearing a sultry, seductive expression, she started toward him. He almost backed up, but then decided to stand his ground instead. "What are you doing?"

When she stood right in front of him, she smiled and reached around him to turn up the music again. "Dance with me."

"I don't dance."

"Now's a good time to start." She curled both small hands around one of his and said again, "Dance with me."

Desperation unfurled inside him. There was no way he could get close to her in that getup and still deny himself. "I thought you wanted me to cook dinner?"

"We haven't even had lunch yet."

And she'd been drinking on an empty stomach. "Sorry about that. I know you have to be hungry."

"I'd rather dance." She began swaying her hips.

"I got the phones. You said there were calls you wanted to make."

"Later." Back-stepping, she brought him toward the open floor.

"I need to put the groceries away."

Her gaze darted to the door where he'd left several bags. Pouting, she said, "You have more excuses than I have lies."

Jumping on that, Leese said, "What lies?"

Her smile slipped, then she frowned. "You don't want to have sex, you don't want to dance. You're such a party pooper."

Knowing he absolutely couldn't talk about sex, especially with her in that dress, Leese cupped her face instead and concentrated on what she'd said. "What lies, Cat?"

"Forget it." She shrugged free of his hands. "You're the king of denial. Fine. Let's go with that. But I'm dancing."

She turned her back and sashayed out to the middle of the floor. Knowing he couldn't stand there watching, Leese said, "I'll get some food together."

"Don't be too long." Hiking up the skirt, pretending he didn't exist, she moved to the music.

Leese had to admit, the woman had rhythm.

CHAPTER SEVEN

TRYING NOT TO watch her, Leese carried the groceries to the kitchen and did a quick reorganization that made more sense than the present setup. He liked everything orderly, but this time the skill came with an effort.

Repeatedly his attention got drawn back to Catalina.

Was it his imagination, or were her gyrations more deliberately sensual now?

The sway of her slim hips, the ecstatic look on her face… Jesus, he almost felt like a voyeur, especially when he imagined her naked.

Would she look that hot during sex?

Would her face have that same expression of abandon if he pinned her to the wall and—

He didn't need to visualize that.

He needed to concentrate on setting up the kitchen. Not an easy order when with every fiber of his being he knew Cat was *right there* moving in a way designed to make him insane.

With the groceries put away, he went about making a pitcher of fresh unsweetened tea. Next he sliced up the strawberries he'd bought and put them in a covered container. One way or another, he'd get Cat to eat a little healthier. And thinking of that, now would be a good time to let the chicken marinate—

"What are we eating?"

He turned fast and found her standing far too close. All her dancing had intensified her scent, that of sweet lotion and her sweeter skin. His nostrils flared on a deep breath as he filled his head with her.

"Leese?" Teasing, she swirled her drink and took another sip. "Everything okay?"

"Yeah." He would stop letting her work him, starting right now. Covering her hand on the glass with his own, he tipped it forward and sniffed. "Bourbon?"

"It was that or gin, whiskey or beer." With a wrinkle of her nose, she said, "No wine."

"Really?" Gently, he took the tumbler from her and set it on the counter. "Judging by your glassy eyes, I'd say you've probably had enough."

"Why are you forever trying to curb my appetites?" She stepped against him, all warm, fragrant woman on the make.

God help him. "Cat—"

"First you rule out junk food, then sex, then dancing. And now—"

For the sake of his own sanity, Leese smooshed a finger to her lips. "Stop baiting me."

She lightly bit him, then sucked his finger into her mouth. With a soft sound of pleasure, she twirled her tongue around him.

Instant boner.

Watching her only made it worse, seeing the way her heavy lashes lowered to hide her eyes, how her lips closed around him.

With both hands holding his wrist, she kept him right there, making him think of blow jobs and release.

By force of will, he got himself together. "Enough, Cat. This isn't going to happen."

She bit him lightly, the released him. "You're so mean."

"And you're drunk."

"Just tipsy."

Holding her by the elbows, he kept her an arm's length away. "This situation hasn't gotten better. If anything, now that you're *tipsy*, you're more off-limits than ever."

For the longest time she looked at him, judging his sincerity, probably considering ways she might get around his decision, and finally accepted that she couldn't.

"I looked around the penthouse," she told him. "Checked out all the rooms, what's stored where and all the windows and doors and...everything."

Familiarizing herself with her new surroundings, just in case. Smart. He planned to do the same before bed. But he didn't want her worrying, and beyond that, he wanted her to trust that he'd protect her. It was his job, so she could relax now. "You're safe here."

"I know. I believe it." She stepped away from him and pulled out a bar stool. It took her a second to maneuver with the dress, but she got that stellar little ass onto the stool and propped her elbows on the bar. Not looking at him, she said, "Sometimes knowing and believing something isn't enough to shake the fear."

What would be enough? No, better not to ask her that. He already had an idea of what she'd say, and he didn't need to be further provoked.

The dress fell to the side, showing her trim calf, smooth thigh...all the way up to her hip.

His abs tightened.

"What does that mean, exactly?"

"It means this place seems secure enough, but old habits die hard. I've gotten used to barely sleeping, listening for trouble, being ready to run in an instant if need be." She tipped her head to see him. Her hair was now more down than up, as if she'd just been laid. "Sleeping with you was the best rest I've had in weeks."

Ah, hell. That hit him on two levels; it made him want to strip her naked, and it made him want to hold her protectively close.

He wanted to hear her scream with a climax, and he wanted to feel her resting easy against him.

"I'll back off," she promised, her gaze locked on his. "If you let me sleep with you again."

Leese barely suppressed the groan. It was what he'd wanted; hell, keeping her that close would make it a whole lot easier for him to sleep too. He'd be able to rest secure in the knowledge that she couldn't sneak off.

But now, after seeing her like this, after she'd been teasing him?

Sleep probably wasn't on the agenda, no matter what.

Still holding his gaze, Cat whispered, "I'm sorry. I can see by your expression that you're not much interested in that either. And if I wasn't so weird, if I was more like my family, I'd back off. But I can't, because I don't want to sleep alone. Not when you're here."

Him, specifically, or would she have felt the same about any other dude?

As if she'd read his mind, she said, "I trust you. At least a little."

"Enough to sleep?"

"Yes."

He hoped that was true. Nutting up, he nodded and said, "You're not weird, so stop saying that. Especially

since I was hoping you'd want to sleep—*sleep*, Cat—
with me again. We both need to catch some shut-eye."

A slow smile added to her appeal. "You really are
a good guy."

Leese braced himself, but after she slid off the stool,
she only hugged him—a platonic, friendly, grateful hug.

"Thank you." Stepping back, she dusted her hands
together and said, "So what are we eating? I'm starved."

THEY HAD QUICK, crunchy tuna wraps that were surprisingly good, especially since it was real food, fresh and
she didn't have to help make it. Even though she could
taste some baby spinach in there, it didn't detract from
her enjoyment. They were delicious, and would tide her
over for a few hours.

She popped the last bite in her mouth, and after she'd
swallowed, she asked, "What are you doing for dinner?"

"So you agree that I'm the chef?"

"Sure. Unlike you, I don't like to deny people."

He pretended to take that on the chin, then laughed.
"If I'm cooking, you have to eat it."

"Deal." She could make the basics, but she didn't
have a lot of interest in it. Usually she was drawn to
her sketchbook and food was forgotten.

She did help with the dishes, then took the time to
show him everything she'd discovered. The balcony was
her favorite. It overlooked…everything, with heated
handrails to keep the ice and snow away, and a cozy
electric fire pit that gave the ambience of a real fire with
the ease of flipping a switch.

"Why," Leese asked, "would anyone heat an out-
door area?"

"To enjoy it in the winter, of course. Maybe we can eat a meal out here."

Leese tested the air, even opened his coat, then shook his head in wonder. "Sure, maybe," he promised her. "Not today though."

"Why?"

"I want to do some more surveillance first."

Ah. If they were sitting outside, in the open, they could be targets. Cat nudged him with her shoulder. "I like the way you think. Come on, I'll show you the rest."

He was as curious about the setup of the penthouse as she'd been, all the egresses, the nooks and crannies, closets, an attic, the security system... Leese also thought of things she hadn't, like where to hide weapons.

"I'll be with you," he told her. "And when I'm not, I promise you'll be protected. But to be even safer—"

"When won't you be with me?" She felt like a nag asking. Even though he was her bodyguard—*for the time being*—no one was responsible for another person 24/7.

"I had to go out today for food, right? Assuming we'll be here awhile, stuff like that is bound to come up again."

It was more than that. She sensed it. Would he turn her over to someone else? A different bodyguard from the agency? Maybe Justice?

Justice was nice enough, but he wasn't Leese.

"Pay attention, Cat. When I'm not here, I want to know that you have every advantage."

Then you should always be here. But she didn't interrupt again to say it—his instruction fascinated her too much. He covered every eventuality. Any room she went into would give her both a place to hide and a means of defending herself with a weapon already stashed there.

Cat thought he might have been so meticulous about the details for her benefit, but then again, Leese was a detail-oriented neat freak, so it could just be part of his personality.

By the time he finished, she knew where to find a hidden cell phone to call for help, how to block the doors to any room to make them more impenetrable, where to find hidden butcher knives and a few other sharp objects, and how to use hair spray, an ink pen or even an electrical cord to defend herself.

"We'll work on all that," he told her, his gaze skimming her thigh bared by the slit in the dress. "Tomorrow."

"Can't wait." It'd be fun to learn some moves, more so with Leese as a hands-on teacher.

He popped his neck. "We'll run some drills too. What to do, how to do it and how fast to do it in case of an emergency."

"If you want, but I'm not sure I'd remember." When she got scared, she went deaf and blind with panic.

"That's why we do drills. Do something often enough, and it becomes automatic." Quickly he grabbed for her.

Ducking, her face turned away, she jumped back, realized what she'd done and glared at him.

Leese smiled.

Suspicious, and more than a little flustered, Cat demanded, "What are you doing?"

"Proving a point. If I'd reached for you like this..." He gently closed his hands over her shoulders and pulled her closer, soothing her temper in the bargain. "No problem, right? But anyone lunging at you causes a programmed response. You protect your face and move away. That's muscle memory."

"That was fear!"

He smoothed back her hair. "It's smart to be afraid when someone acts out of character—like me grabbing at you. In doing drills, you'll get conditioned to do certain things the most efficient way, and you'll learn how to counter attacks, which the attacker won't expect. It'll give you an edge."

"Wow." Now that he'd drawn her near, she took advantage and nestled closer. "You're a fount of information. This is going to be fun."

He laughed, and released her before she could get too cozy.

To keep him there with her, she said, "Explain this 'muscle memory' stuff to me."

Shrugging one big, hard shoulder, he complied. "It's how fighters learn. For every punch, there's a counterpunch or a way to block it. If you have to stop and think, you're already hit. So it has to become second nature. Often it's not enough to duck, as you did. You not only need to avoid getting hurt, you have to be able to disable your attacker so you can advance, or in your case, escape."

Cat lifted her chin. "Maybe I'd want to advance too."

He clutched his chest theatrically. "Now you're just trying to give me a heart attack." Going serious, he said, "You will run and, when necessary, you will hide. That's the plan, okay?"

Seeing the intensity in his gaze, Cat gave him the reply he wanted. "Okay." *For now.* And in the meantime, once Leese started instructing her, she'd learn as much as she could.

By the time they were sitting down to dinner, Leese had learned how everything in the penthouse worked, especially the security system. He discovered that all the drapes, not just those in the bedroom, were on a remote and out of an excess of caution he closed them, denying her the view. Then for more than two hours, he researched the surrounding businesses. If he could see the building from the penthouse, he wanted to know all he could about it: who ran it, who was employed there, how long they'd been in operation and the hours they were open. When she asked him about it, he said if he could see them, they could see him, and he didn't like leaving things to chance.

Would Webb hire people to spy on her in the penthouse? The thought gave her the creeps, and she decided the view wasn't that interesting, after all.

Anyone who could "see" her could also put her in the sights of a high-powered rifle. How easy would it be to shoot her through the window, then disappear without a trace?

She'd seen it in movies plenty of times, but she had no idea if that related to real life or not.

After Leese finished his surveillance, he finally unpacked in the master bedroom. He didn't have much more with him than she had—a few changes of clothes, a shaving kit, more cell phones than she had imagined, keys to several cars and a laptop.

While he did his thing, she trailed behind him, bored but not in the mood to be alone. He didn't seem to mind.

For the most part he didn't appear to notice her presence.

As he finished up dinner prep, she sat in the kitchen and watched. He looked so good there at the stove, his shirtsleeves rolled up, his hands deft at everything from chopping onions to tearing lettuce, that she knew she had to draw him.

Rummaging around in the drawers, she found the small pad of paper and a pen.

Good enough.

Leese glanced at her as she sat again, got comfortable and began to sketch.

"Making another list?" he asked with near dread.

"Nope."

"So what are you doing?"

"Math."

He laughed and, with his hands held out, wet from the salad prep, he looked over her shoulder. "Not math." He studied the vague outline. "What is that?"

"Go cook, and I'll show you again when it starts to take form."

Skeptical, he shook his head and retreated. "Dinner will be done and on the table in five, so don't get too involved."

When it came to her fascination with him, she was already so involved she almost didn't recognize herself. It always helped her to draw. Even doodles. This time, though, she composed a picture of Leese from the back, standing at the counter, preparing dinner.

Ink wasn't an ideal medium for this because she couldn't really shade. With pencils or chalk, she'd have emphasized all those gorgeous muscles and innate strength. But she made do, using small lines and squiggles to add texture, leaving some spots lighter, layering others for depth, and by the time Leese turned to her, arms folded over his chest, plates on the table filled with fragrant chicken, broccoli and rice, she'd all but finished.

Her imagination had delivered what sight couldn't.

"Let's see it."

She wasn't a shy or modest person, but what Leese thought mattered. And shoot, she'd only been quickly sketching, not doing a portrait or anything. Would he understand? Was he a natural-born critic?

For all she knew, he might be offended by the way she'd drawn him. He could—

"You're blushing."

Yup, she was. She could feel the heat in her cheeks. Scooting off the stool and keeping the picture turned toward her, she said, "It's nothing. Just a doodle. If you want, I'll actually draw you something. Later. After I've gotten some supplies, maybe."

His eyes narrowed the tiniest bit and a small smile curled his mouth. "No way. You've made me curious." He strode to her.

"Leese—" She waffled between wanting to run or maybe just scrunching up the paper. Both reactions felt infantile, so instead she stood there, flushed, as he took the sheet from her and studied it.

"You drew me naked."

Cat cleared her throat. "Yeah, I know, see—"

Caught between humor and disbelief, he said, "You drew my ass."

Leaning around to see the paper, Cat inhaled. "Yup." And a very sexy ass it was, as taut and sculpted as the rest of him—at least in her head.

He glanced at her. "Who the hell cooks naked?"

Another deep throat clearing, and she said, "I didn't start out with the idea of losing your clothes."

He lifted one brow.

"It's just…you were moving around and stuff, and I could see your muscles flexing through your clothes, and I sort of… I went with it. My imagination, I mean." Feeling defensive, she tried to reclaim the picture but he held it out of reach. "It's not like your clothes hide a lot."

That made him laugh. "My clothes hide a hell of a lot more than that dress you're wearing."

"I'll change after dinner." She went on tiptoe to get the paper, but he just lifted it higher. "Give that back to me."

"No." He smiled down at her. "Sign it, and give it to me."

The request completely took her by surprise. "Seriously?"

"Yeah, why not?" He looked at the pic again, then grinned. "You made me look really good."

What a way to pique her curiosity. Sticking close to him as he headed for the table, she asked, "It's not accurate?"

"I'm not telling. You're too curious as it is." He laid it on the table and handed her the pen. "Sign it, then let's eat before everything gets cold."

As the evening faded away, Cat had to admit in some ways it had been fun. What a concept, her having fun while people who wanted her dead searched for her.

She didn't delude herself; the threat remained. But for once, while being insulated from harm, she could block it from her mind and think about other things.

Like Leese.

Was there anything he couldn't do? On top of being a stellar fighter and meticulous protector, he was a patient teacher, an understanding listener, a gorgeous man, honorable role model and a damn fine cook.

She'd all but inhaled her food, even the broccoli, which had been cooked just right and seasoned in a way that made it delicious.

Or maybe it was sharing the meal with Leese that made everything taste better.

His dinner conversation stayed light, steering clear of anything that might have ruined her appetite. He'd talked about his fight training, being very humble while answering her many questions. He'd told her about his family, how he'd grown up poor, always dressed in hand-me-downs. And he asked her questions, about her goals in life, her classrooms of kids, her favorite art projects.

More than once she'd caught him eyeing her meager cleavage.

Despite her lack of assets, he wasn't immune to her, but he was pretty darned honorable. Much as she might tease him, she understood his reservations and respected him for them.

Didn't make it any easier to accept.

And no way would she *stop* teasing him. Not yet anyway.

After dinner, she insisted on helping with the dishes, which didn't take long, then they settled on the couch to watch a movie. It was getting late, but she was far too restless to sleep.

As Leese used the remote to thumb through the movie menu, he said, "You sure you're not tired?"

She yawned and said, "Not yet."

He glanced at her, tucked back a loose hank of hair and smiled. "Your eyes look so different."

"It's the makeup." She battered her lashes at him, then thought to ask, "Do you think it's gruesome of me to wear a dead woman's dress and makeup?"

For the longest time he continued to study her eyes, then finally seemed to snap out of it. "I think it's nice that the stuff is being put to use."

A very no-nonsense answer. Cat smoothed her hand over the material of the dress. "It's actually comfortable. Almost like a nightgown. Well, except that I'm showing too much leg."

Leese said nothing.

The "too much leg" was wasted on him.

They agreed on a comedy. The movie started, but neither of them looked at the large-screen TV.

Stretching out, Cat propped her bare feet on the coffee table, letting the dress fall away to expose both her legs.

True, she was on the slight side, and she didn't have a lot of curves up top, but she'd always liked her legs. They were long enough, shapely enough, that she didn't mind showing them off. She flexed her toes—and again caught Leese watching.

Playing it cool, she asked, "Do you know what happened with Sahara's brother and his girlfriend?"

"Only the very basics."

"Will you tell me?"

He hesitated, then sat forward and, making her heart beat hard and fast, lifted the material of the dress and tucked it around her legs. "I can't concentrate with you in this."

"What if I take it off?"

"Cat." He chastised her with a frown. "You promised."

Laughing, she scooted into his side for a hug, and to her pleasure, Leese used one arm to return it.

Rather than push her luck, she leaned away, grinning, and said, "All right." She left the couch with a yawn and stretch. "I'll go find some pajamas, and then we can watch the movie."

"Something really ugly would help," he called after her. "And make sure it covers you from head to toe."

In the guest bedroom, Cat realized she was still smiling as she pulled the remaining pins from her hair. If she'd met Leese under different circumstances, she felt positive she would have gone after him. Everything about him appealed to her, including his wit.

But if the circumstances were different, would he have given her a second look? That was anyone's guess, and she didn't like speculating on what-ifs, so instead, she concentrated on the here and now.

Locating pajamas wasn't easy; apparently Scott's girlfriend like sexy lingerie only. She settled on women's gray yoga pants and a man's black T-shirt, the front imprinted with the vintage KISS tongue logo.

She liked Scott's style.

While she was at it, Cat went ahead and removed the heavy makeup and even brushed her teeth. After another lusty yawn, she returned to Leese and found him sleeping, his head resting back, his wide chest moving with deep, slow breaths.

Guilt held her in the doorway; desire kept her watching him.

She knew he hadn't slept much the night before and yet she'd insisted on a movie. Thoughtless. Going forward, she'd try not to do things like that. After weeks of concentrating only on herself and what she needed to survive, it would actually be nice to consider someone else for a change.

His disheveled, dark hair looked a little more mussed, as if he'd run a hand through it. With his inky lashes resting on high cheekbones, she couldn't see the intensity of his light blue eyes, but she'd never forget them. Loosely, his hands rested over his firm abdomen, legs stretched out, his knees relaxed.

Deep inside her, a hot yearning unfurled and spread into every corner of her awareness. Breathing faster, she inched toward him...

Lazily, his voice deep, he said, "You're not drawing me again, are you?"

Cat jumped. *How had he known she was there?* Hand to her heart, she accused, "Playing possum?"

He turned his head to see her, looked her over, then met her gaze.

"Better?" she asked.

After his own inspiring stretch, he sat forward. "At this point, nothing is going to be perfect. But yeah, at least you're better covered."

With her heart beating a little too fast, she stayed near the door. "Describe perfect?"

"Drab enough that I can keep my thoughts off inappropriate things."

Happiness mixed with desire in a potent combination. "Thank you for admitting that you're interested too."

His level gaze never left hers. "I don't recall ever denying it."

No, he hadn't. He'd just denied her. "I'm ready to keep my promises if you're ready to go to bed."

"I thought you wanted to watch a movie."

She wanted him, but she'd take what she could get. "I'm sleepier than I realized." *And so was he.* Holding out a hand, she said, "Come on. We're both tuckered out."

After the slightest of hesitations, Leese stood and took her hand, walking silently with her to the bedroom. Once inside, he released her and said, "I need ten minutes. Go ahead and get settled in. And, Cat?"

"Yes?"

"Don't even think about trying to sneak off."

Ha! All she could think about was cuddling up to Leese in that big comfy bed.

Deliberately, she patted back a yawn. "No worries. I'm too exhausted for shenanigans."

He touched her cheek. "Good." After running two fingers along a lock of her hair, he turned away and went into the connecting bathroom.

Cat released the breath she'd held. Heaven help her, behaving would be tough, especially when he was so gentle and attentive.

The shower came on, but she knew Leese wouldn't linger. Leaving on only one small light, she turned back the covers on the bed, plumped the pillows, then crawled in.

Damn it, she felt like a virgin all over again and sex wasn't even on the agenda.

But truth be told, the idea of sleeping up close and personal with Leese was more exciting than sex had been with other men. She thought about that kiss he'd given her earlier, and her toes curled.

She was a mass of taut nerves and anticipation when Leese stepped out of the bathroom wearing only his boxers.

Why hadn't she left on more lights?

He set his neatly folded clothes on a chair. Put a gun and a few other things she didn't recognize on the nightstand and, after turning off the bedside lamp, he got into bed.

The mattress dipped, making her body turn toward his, but she didn't get a chance to take advantage of that because Leese's arm came around her, drawing her against him.

"Is this how you sleep?" he asked. "On your back, the blankets in a death grip?"

Sounding strangled—*with lust*—she said, "No."

"So what do you prefer?"

Being under you. Or over you. She scolded herself for making things worse. *Get a grip, Catalina.*

"Usually on my side." And she still sounded strangled.

"Left or right?"

How could he be so damn friendly about everything? "Right."

"Okay, so how's this?" He settled on his back, then with one muscled arm behind her head, tucked her in close so that her head rested on his shoulder, her arm draped over his lower chest and her feet brushed his hairy calves.

Cat barely bit back the moan of excitement. "Perfect," she croaked. *For torture.*

After a perfunctory kiss on her forehead, he let out a deep breath. "Great. Let's get some sleep."

Oh sure. That'd be easy. *Not.* Heat radiated off him, intoxicating her with his unique scent. It took all her willpower not to brush her nose against him, to resist taking a small bite of his sleek skin and to still her twitchy fingers from exploring his body.

To distract her hormones, she said, "You were going to tell me what happened to Scott and his girlfriend."

"It's a long story."

"I need something, damn it!" Feeling more than a little irascible, she said, "Think of it as a bedtime story." The words no sooner left her mouth than she gasped at her own insensitivity. "I didn't mean that the way it sounded," she promised. "I just thought talking a little would help to redirect my thoughts." From sex. From Leese. Feeling like an ass, she sighed. "Okay?"

Leese gave her another one-arm hug and agreed.

Hopefully he needed the distraction too, because she wasn't into suffering alone.

"Like I said, I don't know all the details. But my understanding is that they were out on Scott's yacht. Something happened—no one is sure what—but they found the yacht floating at sea, blood everywhere, but no bodies."

Okay, so definitely not a bedtime story. With her heart breaking for Sahara, Cat closed her eyes. "Scott's blood?"

"Both of theirs. It's believed they were attacked and their bodies thrown overboard. Sahara did an extensive search, but was never able to find anything. She hasn't given up though. She's kept a PI on retainer ever since then."

"How awful for her."

"Yeah. Not knowing for sure what happened makes the loss even harder to take. When her brother went missing, she stepped in to run things. After he was declared dead, she inherited the business. She loves it, but she'd hand it back over in a heartbeat if Scott re-appeared."

Wondering if there was any hope of that, Cat asked, "You think he might?"

"No."

So tragic. She understood well the awfulness of not knowing. "Thank you for telling me."

"No problem."

In her own case, if she knew she'd be on the run for a year, or even five years, she could deal with it better than wondering when, *if*, it'd ever end. With no light at the end of the tunnel, she couldn't plan, couldn't organize.

Couldn't reclaim her life.

Would her job still be there if she was able to return? Weeks ago, she'd used a pay phone to call the school and take a leave of absence, but that would only last so long before they'd find a permanent replacement. And what about her house? She couldn't pay any bills, couldn't maintain the property, couldn't collect the mail from her mailbox… Would the city declare it abandoned?

When she heard Leese's breathing even into the deep rhythm of sleep, she forgot about her problems and peeked up at him.

Only a soft blue light shone from the alarm clock radio, putting his features in deep shadow. Lethargy pulled at her, and after daring one soft kiss to his ribs, she closed her eyes…and quickly faded.

CHAPTER EIGHT

A LOUD SCREECHING shot Leese out of a sound sleep. He was on his knees, gun in hand, in an instant. Searching out the threat, he flashed his gaze over every dim corner of the immense room, but found nothing.

Beside him, Cat stirred. "Leese?"

He glanced at her.

Meekly, she pointed to the alarm clock radio. "Don't shoot it, okay?"

Ah, hell. He inhaled a deep, calming breath, turned and slapped the stupid alarm to silence it. Who the hell woke to that every day?

His heart beat in the slow, hard way it did when he faced an opponent and he took a second to get a grip. Dim morning light barely penetrated the thick curtains. He carefully set the gun back on the nightstand, turned the automatic alarm off so he wouldn't have a repeat heart attack tomorrow morning, then finally allowed himself to look at Cat.

Fuck, she looked irresistible.

Messy tumbled brown hair, sleep-puffy blue eyes, flushed cheeks and a totally lax body. Still drowsy, she stared back at him. Not kissing her was one of the hardest things he'd ever done.

"Sorry about that." How long had it been since he'd slept that soundly? Dangerous. He couldn't afford to lose himself that way. He'd put the blame square on Catalina. Her small, warm body had fit so perfectly to his, had felt so right, that he'd relaxed in unfamiliar ways—even while sporting a boner.

"You're fast," she whispered. "I barely heard that alarm, and you were ready to shoot it."

She'd probably tease him forever—no, not forever because he wouldn't know her that long. "I was out," he admitted. "Dead to the world."

"Me too."

"Usually I'm a light sleeper."

Her gaze lowered to look at his body. "I used to always sleep hard, but it's been different since all this started." She pushed back her hair, then scooted up to sit against the headboard. "You know how usually if you hear something in the night, you assume it's the house settling, or the wind outside, or…whatever?"

"Sure."

Pulling the covers up to her lap, she bit her lip, then gazed toward the curtained window. "These days," she softly confessed, "when I hear something, the first thing I do is panic. I assume I've been found and I go into that fight-or-flight mode, with flight being my preference."

Leese moved to sit next to her, their shoulders touching. "That's understandable given your current circumstances."

"Maybe. But with you, I sleep like I used to. That is, once I fell asleep." Smiling, she nudged him and said, "Took me a little while last night. With you right there, looking like you look, feeling like you feel—"

"You felt me?" He tried to pretend affront, but mostly he tried to hedge off another erection.

"You're hard and hot, and man, Leese, you smell good."

"And you're small and soft and smell good too. But if we're going to continue sleeping together—" *Weirdest conversation he'd ever had with a woman, period.* "—then we need to make an agreement."

"I think we need to make coffee."

He stilled her when she tried to leave the bed. "I'll make the coffee in a minute."

Groaning, she flopped down flat on the mattress again. "Okay, but hurry before I expire."

This was the tricky part. How to explain without hurting her feelings, or worse, encouraging her. He'd strained his control as far as he could; she needed to work with him.

"Let's put the seduction on the back burner, at least for a week." When she started to protest, he cut her off. "One week, Cat. You can rein it in that long, and if after a week—" which was about as far as he could push himself "—we're still holed up together, and you're still sure of what you want, well then—"

She bolted up to face him. "You mean it?"

Damn, when was the last time anyone wanted him that much? And how could he resist it? Sure, he'd always accepted that too much familiarity was a major no-no in the biz. Made sense.

Until he met Catalina.

Now that he did know her, the rules didn't seem to matter. Sahara already knew the score; the woman was neither blind nor obtuse. She might've kicked up a fuss about it, and if she had, he would've resigned without hesitation. It was her business and she had to run it the way she figured was best.

What he couldn't do was resist Catalina forever. He understood his own limitations. When he'd lectured Justice on the rules, never, not once, had he ever figured on meeting a woman like Cat. If he only had to fight himself, then maybe he'd be successful. But knowing she wanted him too, that she had from the start, well hell…he was only a man.

With his proposed time frame, she looked like a kid being promised a pony on her birthday. He took in her expectant expression and laughed, not at her enthusiasm, but in pure pleasure because of it.

It felt damn nice to be wanted so much.

She mistook his humor, though, and slugged him in the midsection. Hugging her tight, Leese pinned down her arms. "So it's your violence and your lust we need to restrain?"

"You're laughing at me."

"No, I'm just flattered, that's all." He loosened his hold enough to give her a brief, firm kiss. "And if I can manage one week, surely you can too, right?"

"Okay, fine." She pushed against his chest, putting some space between them and giving him a good look at her frown. "But I want it on record that I'm agreeing under duress and if those bastards get me and I end up dying without knowing what it'd be like to sleep with you, I'll—"

She squeaked when Leese took her to her back on the mattress. Looming over her, he said, "Nothing is going to happen to you, because I won't let it."

"—come back and haunt you," she finished.

She was the most infuriating, and the most amusing, woman he'd ever met. Here he was, tense over the mention of her being hurt, and she didn't even notice. That helped him to clear his head.

He meant what he said. She'd be safe, because he'd damn well keep her that way.

To lighten his own mood, he teased her. "Haunt me, huh? Now I'm scared."

She sighed, very put-upon. "No you're not, but that's the best threat I could think of, since being dead would make it pretty hard to exact any other revenge."

Having her under him felt even better, and just as natural, as cuddling her close through the night. "You need to have a little faith."

"All right." She lifted her chin. "But you better plan on paying up at the end of the week."

Smiling, he promised, "Count on it." In a week, Leese reasoned, she might be feeling secure enough that he no longer looked like her White Knight. Maybe she'd remain grateful for his help, but without the sexual component.

Or, he accepted, she could want him even more.

He wasn't entirely sure which he'd prefer. Getting sexually involved with a client would bring its own complications.

But not having her…he didn't want to think about that yet, even though he knew it'd be best.

"Okay then." She shoved at his chest until he let her up, then she rolled from the bed, a warm, sleep-rumpled, sexy temptation. "I'll use the guest room bath and you can have this one." With a scowl, she warned, "I expect coffee when I emerge."

Feeling ridiculously content for a man who'd slept chastely with a smoking hot woman, Leese murmured, "Yes, ma'am." Catalina Nicholson affected him in too many ways. He wanted her. She made him laugh. She wrenched his heart. And he was determined to keep her safe.

Leese left the bed, popped his neck and pondered the coming week. Hopefully it would go by fast…otherwise he'd never make it.

WEBB DISMISSED THE housekeeper and carried his coffee out to the sunroom at the back of the house. All around him, the pristine white landscape glittered under a full sun, unmarred by even the footprints of animals. From here he couldn't see the lake.

But the image glared at him all the same, pounding in his brain like a repeat, flashing photograph. Catalina, standing there in the snow, dressed in black that showed stark against the frozen white ground. No one could miss her, and one look at her face confirmed she'd heard enough. Maybe even everything.

Why the hell had she ventured to the boathouse?

His temples throbbed and he set aside the coffee with a clatter. A different man would punch the wall in frustration, but not him. He was fucking refined.

Jesus.

Catalina's unaccountable behavior had caused problems before, but nothing like this.

Nothing life-and-death.

Stomach churning, Webb paced the room. He didn't know what to do. Ms. Silver—Sahara—claimed she hadn't heard from her man. Probably a lie. Definitely no one else believed it, even if Webb did.

So where was she? Holed up somewhere safe? Still on the streets? Exposed?

"Mr. Coleman is here to see you, sir."

Fuck, *fuck*. He was in no mood to talk to anyone, definitely not a shady "bodyguard"—a man Webb knew as competent, but who also walked a very fine line. It was the other side of that line that concerned Webb currently.

Taking a breath, he turned to face Tesh. "I wasn't expecting you."

"I know." Tesh came in with his own cup of coffee. Because he'd occasionally worked for Webb, the staff knew him well, always greeting him with respect and consideration.

Pulling out a chair, Tesh asked, "Any news yet?"

"No." Many times in the past, Tesh had been assigned to keep an eye on Catalina. He was a tough son of a bitch, capable of tackling any problem, deadly when necessary. "I'm worried."

"She's your daughter," Tesh said, discounting the lack of blood relation. He sipped his coffee, gazed out the window at nothing in particular. "I'm going to find her," he said low. "You can rest easy on that."

Webb believed him. But would Tesh find her in time? And if he did, what would he do with her…to her? His muscles tensed anew. He had money, he had power. But right now, he felt far too vulnerable.

"Senator Platt wants a meeting." Tesh stood and pushed in his chair. "Today, noon." Already on his way out, he said, "Don't be late."

It didn't matter that Tesh had worked for Webb in the past. Right now he was working for the senator, and they both knew that gave him clout.

Webb ended up punching the wall, after all. It hurt like hell and did nothing to alleviate the problem.

Catalina.
Where the hell are you?

BODY ARMOR HAD a workout room in the basement that the agents could use to stay in shape. It also had an indoor shooting range. Getting hold of a gun to use for practice might be useful, but she'd tackle that another day.

For now, just getting Leese to the gym had taken an effort.

He'd have preferred to keep her locked up in the penthouse, curtains drawn. But already she felt claustrophobic. She needed to do something, and watching TV wouldn't cut it.

So she'd convinced Leese to get in a little exercise. She had no idea what she was doing, the machines all looked intimidating, but hey, she could do some jumping jacks or something.

"Where do you want to start?" Leese asked.

"Umm…" She looked around. "Where do you usually start?"

He crossed his arms and gave her a knowing look. "You're not exactly a gym rat, are you?"

Judging her? For some reason, she didn't want to be found lacking. "I'm not a fighter like you, but I get by." She'd occasionally taken lengthy walks.

On sunny days.

With designated trails.

Without hills.

"I'm ready." Out of necessity, she wore only socks. She'd found workout clothes—yoga pants and a stretchy sports bra—but again, the shoes were too big and she wasn't about to put boots on with athletic pants.

When two other men entered the room, Leese stared at them until they turned around and left again.

She almost choked on her amusement. Warning off other guys? Nice. Or maybe it was that he didn't trust them. That gave her pause. "We're safe in here, right?"

"Wouldn't have you here if we weren't."

Wow, touchy much? She crossed her arms and jutted out a hip. "Okay then, what was with the mean mugging? You scared off those poor guys."

His gaze went to her exposed midriff, then away.

"What?" she asked. "Am I showing too much skin?"

He stepped into her space. "Did you want to exercise or not?"

"Fine," she said with a lot of attitude. Tweaking Leese was currently one of her favorite pastimes, maybe because she didn't have much else to do. "I'll start on that." She pointed at a machine that looked easy enough to figure out where her feet and hands went.

"The elliptical, huh?" He eyed the machine, then her. "If you're not used to it, set it on low resistance. You don't want to overdo it."

Just being in a gym was overdoing it, since she'd never ventured into one before. But she wasn't about to tell him that. "Don't worry about me. Go do your own thing."

"I'll use the heavy bag. Let me know when you need to switch up."

Switch up? It'd be a wonder if she lasted on one machine for half an hour, much less take on something else.

Luckily the heavy bag was right across from her, so she could easily keep an eye on Leese. With no idea how to change the resistance to low or otherwise, she used

the current setting, found it tedious but not too difficult and was more interested in what Leese would do.

First he took off his shoes, then stripped off his shirt.

She almost fell off the machine.

Mouth going dry, she concentrated on pedaling in an
even cadence and watched Leese hit the bag.

Not with his hands, but with his feet.

He did a lot of various kicks, impressing her with
each one. Every fluid strike sent a loud *crack* to echo
around the enclosed room. The bag swung, Leese
turned and kicked from a different angle.

Fascinating.

An hour later, just as Cat was about to cry uncle,
Sahara breezed in. She wore impossibly high-heeled
booties, a knee-length skirt and a cashmere sweater.
To Cat, she looked like a fashion model.

Hair damp, his muscles all pumped, his body glistening, Leese paused in his workout. He didn't sound
at all winded when he said, "Something up, Sahara?"

"Not at all." As if she saw gorgeous, ripped, mostly
naked men every day, Sahara didn't even blink.

"Did you hear from your PI?"

Cat's heartbeat tripped. Had they discovered her secrets?

"He's on it now," Sahara said. "We need to give him
some time, but I'm sure he'll have information for us
soon."

And when he did? Cat thought. When he found out
who was with Webb at the boathouse, then what?

Then, she assumed, it would all end—for her.

"I'm here," Sahara said, beaming at them, "because
I wanted to talk to you both about a wonderful idea I
had."

Intrigued, Cat stepped off the elliptical and stumbled on rubbery legs. Good grief. Maybe if she hadn't been so involved ogling Leese, she'd have realized her legs were shot.

She limped forward. "An idea?"

Wary, Leese held silent.

"Valentine's Day will be here before we know it," Sahara said.

Cat's stomach sank. So much time had passed in a blur. She'd missed the festive holidays with family, but she hadn't exactly been checking days off a calendar.

What would she do if Leese had a sweetheart he wanted to visit over the romantic holiday? She didn't think he was involved; he struck her as being too honorable to kiss her if he had anyone important in his life.

"Around here," Sahara said, "public relations are key and I use every opportunity available to throw a party."

A party? Cat almost groaned. Would Leese be expected to attend?

Yes, of course he would be. And that left her…where? Alone?

Just thinking about it made her feel exposed, vulnerable—

"Yeah?" Leese said to Sahara. "So?"

"You both need to attend the company party."

Wait—what? Cat did a double take. "You want *me* there?"

"No," Leese said. "It's too dangerous."

"We're having it here," Sahara told him, all smug and satisfied, "So she won't even need to step outside. We'll decorate the third floor."

"With what?" he asked. "Paper hearts?"

Clearly Sahara didn't appreciate his sarcasm. "It'll be sophisticated and perfect."

"Wait a minute…" Cat said, mentally trying to catch up.

"I don't know," Leese told her. "Something could go wrong."

"Oh, please." Sahara flapped a dismissive hand. "What could possibly be safer than a party filled with bodyguards, in a completely secure building?"

Still dubious, Leese said, "Plan to work everyone during the party, huh? You don't think anyone will object?"

"When I'm handing out generous bonuses for their participation? Of course not."

Leese glanced at Cat, then rubbed the back of his neck. "I don't know."

"She can be by your side all night," Sahara assured him. "Surely you trust yourself to see to her safety?"

Reluctantly, Leese agreed. "I suppose it wouldn't hurt."

Cat looked at each of them, and couldn't hide her uncertainty. "A party?"

"I'll take care of everything you need. Just get your dress and shoe size to Enoch, and of course let me know your favorite color." Now that she'd gotten her way, Sahara turned to leave. "It's going to be very productive. You'll see."

And with that, she left as suddenly as she'd arrived.

"Wow," Cat said, "that woman is a whirlwind."

"Agreed."

Hating the idea of mingling with crowds, she glanced at Leese. Did he anticipate the party? Probably. She tried a smile. "You didn't sound too keen on her plans."

He watched her, his expression enigmatic. "You're

already antsy. Before long, you'll be climbing the walls. A party will help break up the monotony."

The monotony of hiding from murderers. "Okay." If he wanted to go, she'd go, and she'd even pretend to like it. Leese would keep her safe, she believed that.

With that settled, she moved on to the next worry. "Do you have anyone special hoping to see you for—"

"I don't," he replied even before she'd finished asking, and now he looked insulted.

Cat sighed. "But…" He seemed dead serious, so she let it go and moved on to another concern. "I've been thinking only about me, about what I needed, but now it occurs to me that you have a life too. You have family, friends and—"

"Yeah, I do. Not that it matters. Until you're in the clear, you're stuck with me." He eyed her up and down, probably noting her somewhat bowed posture, then shook his head. "You overdid it, didn't you?"

In a big way. "Maybe a little." She needed time to think about things. She didn't want Leese forced into isolation because of her. But she also didn't want to be left alone, a sitting duck.

"Come on. It's time to get you back upstairs. You can rest up while I shower and take care of a few things."

Cat didn't know what those few things might be and she didn't ask; all her concentration was on trying to walk without groaning.

Once they returned to the penthouse, she decided to soak in the whirlpool. Not only would it feel good, but it'd give her a chance to sort through some things.

Villains, a party…and Leese all warm and pumped up from exertion, wearing only shorts and a lot of machismo.

THE NEXT MORNING after breakfast, Leese noted the stiff way Cat walked and had to hide his grin. "Feel like working out again?" he asked.

She groaned, swallowed and said with convincing enthusiasm, "Sure."

He snorted. "Get real. You can barely walk."

"I'm walking."

"No, you're shuffling." She'd spent the rest of the day yesterday drawing, watching TV… and resting her over-worked legs. From experience, he knew today she'd be even more tender, and tomorrow would be the worst.

From what he could tell, her leg muscles were now so tight, she could barely get her feet off the floor. He urged her to the sofa. "I should have realized and better monitored you." But he'd been too busy trying to work off sexual tension. Out of necessity, that required blocking Cat from his mind. He hadn't looked at her, and he'd done his best not to listen to her heavy breathing.

She dropped down, groaned and went flat to her back.

Understanding, Leese lifted her legs up so she fully reclined. "Want to try the whirlpool again?"

"No, I'm good." She closed her eyes. "Right here."

He let the smile go. "I'll get you some aspirin."

After she'd taken that, he kissed her forehead, covered her with a soft knit throw, turned the television down low and literally watched her doze off.

Twice last night he'd awakened when she shifted around, trying to get comfortable. He should have realized why she was restless. Instead he'd tortured himself by spooning her, feeling her plump behind pressed to his groin, draping one arm over her waist. Her soft hair had teased his nose, and the rest of her teased him everywhere else. It had taken a little while, but eventually he'd faded back to sleep.

Had she?

Without the alarm jarring him awake, he'd slept till his usual 5:00 a.m. When he awoke, Cat was already alert, facing him, her nose in his chest hair.

He'd had a hand on her ass.

Every hour with her made a week of celibacy seem more impossible.

While she napped, he dug into some computer work, confident in the security of the Body Armor servers. Sahara's PI would be doing similar research on Webb Nicholson, but that didn't assuage his own need to dig around. He needed to know all of Webb's closest associates, and whether or not the man had ever been to Désir Island.

He started a list, breaking down names by business, politics and family. He'd cross-check those against known visitors to the island. Although, the more he learned about Désir, the more he realized that most visits were kept top secret.

After finding more names, he added a column for actors to the list of associates.

Webb Nicholson got around. Leese found plenty of information about Webb getting cozy with people who'd been to the island, but nothing specific about Webb himself going there.

Pushing back from the laptop, Leese lifted the paper and slouched in his chair to study it. None of the names jumped out at him as being obviously corrupt enough to murder. One actor had been busted for cheating on his wife, another for posting an explicit sex video. A businessman had been arrested for embezzling. One politician was under indictment for attempting to steer a federal grant. Another for accepting bribes and kickbacks. Yet another for sexual harassment.

Only a few on the list were squeaky-clean…and those men actually drew Leese's attention more than the obviously shady ones.

He picked up a highlighter and went over their names. When he leaned back to the laptop, Cat groaned, drawing his gaze.

"You okay?"

She went still, then drowsily sat up on the couch. Seeing him at the bar with his laptop, she asked, "What are you doing?"

"Research." He waited a beat, curious as to how she'd react, then said, "On your stepfather."

She didn't make a sound, but her face went pale.

Rather than push her, he waited, giving her time to get her thoughts in order. He knew there was so much she still hadn't told him.

Soon she'd have no choice.

"You…you probably should leave that up to the PI."

"Why?"

"It could be dangerous?"

"Is that a question, Cat?"

Irritation finally set in. "No, it's a fact. I told you he's dangerous. You know what he did—"

"No. I know what you heard, that's all. Until you tell me the names of the other men there that day, we can't know what role Nicholson played in it."

She tossed aside the throw, swung her legs over the side of the couch and went still with another deep groan. "God Almighty," she complained, "you killed my legs."

"That was all you, honey." He put aside the paper

and joined her, gently rubbing a thigh. "The aspirin didn't help?"

"I guess a little." She stared toward the area where he'd been working. "Leese…"

Bringing her face around, he asked, "What are you afraid I'll find?"

"I don't know." She looked away from his gaze. "If you research Webb, you're bound to find an article or two about me."

"I saw them." And he'd ignored most of it.

"What if you see something that convinces you I'm nuts?"

"Won't happen. You're more grounded in reality than anyone else I know. In fact, I'd say you're unique." He brushed his thumb over her cheek. "A very nice unique."

CAT SIGHED. IN a different world, maybe in a romantic movie, this touching moment would mean a kiss, possibly more. But she couldn't count on that, not from Leese.

And even if he was inclined to a little hanky-panky before the agreed-upon week had passed, she had other things to worry about.

He'd been poking around on the internet.

"You realize any searches can be traced back to you, right?"

His shoulder lifted in a don't-worry-about-it shrug. "Body Armor has the best firewall available."

Would it be good enough?

"Still…" What else could she say? *You're going to alert them, they'll assume I'm talking and none of us will survive.* It wouldn't matter. He was determined to unravel the threat.

"Why don't you let the PI do his thing?" she asked.

"He is. I'm just doing my thing too. You need to trust me."

She couldn't hold back her frown. "Webb said that very thing to me."

Leese sat back, his eyes narrowing. "Don't do that, Cat. Don't compare me to him."

"I'm not. I mean, I was, but not the way you mean."

"You want to explain that?"

How? Leese was nothing like Webb, but the point now was to dissuade him from digging in. "For a right-brained dreamer, living in a family full of left-brained workaholics felt a lot like 'nuts,' and not the nice kind. Before my mother passed away, she was a buffer, making the differences easier to take. But now that she's gone…"

Gone forever.

Heartache left her quiet. In so many ways, she still missed her mom. Every day. Sometimes every minute.

"Now?" Leese prompted.

It shouldn't still affect her, any of it, but it did. "Webb always thought I was immature. He'd often said I needed a better dose of the real world."

Leese snorted. "I'd say you've swallowed a pretty big dose lately."

"Maybe." She certainly felt like she'd dealt with her fair share. "But the thing is, Webb told me that I was going down the wrong path, throwing away my opportunities by not taking advantage of family connections. He told me to trust him, to try things his way—"

"His way is not my way."

"And I'm not into blind faith."

They stared at each other, the tension growing, until a sudden buzzing split the quiet.

Startled, Cat jerked back, ready to run, to hide.

"Easy," Leese said. "It's just the intercom." He walked to the door and pushed a button on the wall. "What is it?"

"Sorry to disturb you, Mr. Phelps," said an eerie, disconnected voice. "You have a visitor. A Mr. Miles Dartman."

Horror washed over Cat. What visitor? An imposter? Someone trying to find a way in, a way to reach her?

She meant to make the denial loud and clear, but her "No" sounded only as a breathless whisper.

Watching her, Leese said into the speaker, "Allow him up." As he stepped away from the door, his gaze never wavered. "I'm going out for a few hours. Miles is going to stay with you."

CHAPTER NINE

ALREADY SHAKING HER HEAD, Cat said again, louder this time, "No."

It hurt Leese to see her like this, so afraid, expecting the worst. From the moment he'd met her, she'd seemed genuine to him. His instincts had told him to believe in her, in the threats she detailed.

Seeing her now, the unmistakable fear she couldn't hide, he knew he'd been right. "It's okay. I won't be long."

"You can't leave."

Needing to reassure her, Leese strode closer. "I'm only running a few necessary errands. Miles is a friend. He's here to keep you company."

"You're supposed to stay with me."

He could see the panic, and it gnawed on him. "I trust Miles. He's a good friend, a good man, and he's skilled."

Looking smaller, hurt, she whispered, "I don't want you to go."

Leese considered how to handle her very real panic, what to do to snap her out of it. Most of the time Cat was strong, independent, determined. She'd barely awakened, and then he'd thrown her for a loop. He regretted not telling her sooner.

If she hadn't napped, or if he hadn't gotten so involved researching her father... But that didn't matter now. She wouldn't like showing so much blatant fear, not to him, definitely not to Miles.

He settled on a method, and said with feigned indifference, "I'm going all the same. Just do me a favor and don't give Miles a hard time."

The callous comment rid her of the vulnerability real fast. Jaw tight, eyes glittering, she slowly stood to face him. "Afraid I'll pick on him? If I can, then how badass can he be?"

"Very badass." A knock sounded at the door. "Now behave."

He heard her indignant gasp as he turned his back and went to answer. He checked the peep hole first, saw Miles looking around in awe and opened the locks.

"Hell of a setup you have here," Miles said as he stepped in.

"Yeah, it is." They exchanged a quick, gruff bro hug. "Thanks for coming."

"No problem. You've got me curious."

"Curious," Cat asked, "about what?"

Miles looked toward her, then lifted a brow. "Hi."

Guessing there would be fireworks, Leese beckoned her forward. "Catalina, come meet Miles."

Unfortunately, an unholy light had entered Cat's eyes.

She sized up Miles, head to toe, sent a provoking look at Leese and purred, "My, my, my. So you're my new protector?"

Immediately charmed, Miles smiled at her. "Seems so." He, too, looked at Leese.

"No," Leese said to him, answering a question he hadn't asked, then to Cat, he repeated, "No," to curb any ideas she might have.

She asked, "You're still leaving?"

"Yes." He didn't want to wait any longer before going by her house. If anyone had rifled through it, he'd know.

"Do what you must." Her chin lifted and she strolled closer. "Tell me, Miles, do you have the same scruples as Leese?"

"Scruples?" Miles asked, his amusement growing.

"Cat," Leese warned. He was relieved to again see her stiff pride, but she didn't have to push it so far. "This won't change anything."

"Go on," she said, shooing him away. "I'm sure Miles and I will be fine. Isn't that right, Miles?"

For a split second, Leese wasn't sure. Would she really throw herself at Miles as payback because he insisted on going, or was it an idle threat, a show meant to annoy him?

He trusted Miles. Hell, he trusted Cat—even when she was in a vindictive mood.

But just to be sure, he went to her, tipped up her chin and said again, "Behave." Before she could reply he took her mouth, doing his best to singe her—and ensuring Miles understood the lay of the land.

ON THE LONG drive to her house, Leese thought a dozen times about what she and Miles might be doing. He'd warned Miles that they were both to stay put. No phone calls. No visitors. No surfing the web.

Cat had replied that she'd find plenty for them to do, but Miles had only laughed.

Right before he'd walked out, she'd asked how long he'd be.

When he'd admitted he wouldn't be back until the

evening, he'd seen another flash of fear in her vivid blue eyes, but she'd quickly hidden it beneath attitude.

She had bravado in spades.

She was also the most vulnerable woman he'd ever known.

Leese parked two blocks from her address then walked the rest of the way, constantly keeping watch. He saw kids playing, dogs barking, but no one suspicious.

To alter his usual current appearance, he'd dressed down in sloppy jogging pants, a hooded sweatshirt, high-top sneakers and a ball cap, with sports sunglasses to hide his eyes. The different look, reminiscent of his fighting days when he'd jogged for hours, should keep him from being easily recognized.

The neighborhood surprised him, being one of those communities where the houses sat close together with postage stamp-sized yards filled with enormous trees. Nothing about it said privilege or wealth.

Her house, a small brick ranch, looked quiet, but the walk had been shoveled, and someone had tromped across the yard—kids, the one who'd done the shoveling, or her father's cronies?

Acting as if he belonged, hoping none of her neighbors would notice him, Leese went up the walk with a whistle, quickly picked the lock on the front door, then went inside and listened.

Nothing.

It took him a mere minute to go through the house— three bedrooms, one bath, an eat-in kitchen and a small living room. He was truly alone. After that quick survey, he ensured both doors and all windows were locked. He didn't want to risk anyone busting in on him without notice.

With all that done, he looked around with a critical eye.

Oddly, only a small amount of mail littered the floor from the mail chute. He checked the postmarks and saw they were all from the past week.

Had her stepfather been by to get the mail? Perhaps he'd even spoken with the neighbors so they didn't get too nosy? That'd make sense. He could have also asked them to let him know if she showed up.

She'd had a few plants, now dead. So someone had shoveled the walk, collected the mail, but hadn't bothered watering the plants?

Good thing she didn't own a cat.

At every window the drapes were drawn.

Still in protective mode, he used a special device to sweep for electronic bugs and mini cams. He found only one tiny audio mic, no video, tucked inside a lampshade.

Furious that anyone had tried to spy on her, Leese crushed it under his heel, then put the demolished pieces in his pocket to dispose of in a Dumpster on the drive back.

Finally taking a relaxed breath, he felt free to notice more about the house—the plump sofa and chair, the paintings on the walls, the books on her bookshelf.

Everything was colorful, bright, coordinated. Organized, but not overly so. She'd arranged the furniture for function, filling up the limited space of the living room.

Going through each room, he took note of her decorating tastes, saw artwork he knew to be her own, some from other painters. Her bedroom was tidy, but with an unmade bed. Had she left in a hurry her last morning here?

The guest bedroom had a futon, a rocking chair, a bookcase and small TV. She'd turned the third bedroom into sort of an office. Standing racks held art supplies. School papers and stacked folders nearly buried a desk painted bright red.

In the kitchen, on the front of the refrigerator, she'd secured several childish drawings, no doubt from her students.

It was easy to see how much they liked her.

Not wanting to push his luck, he decided against lingering any longer. With every minute he remained he ran the risk of a neighbor getting nosy.

Tucked inside a pantry, he found a large grocery tote and went back to the office. He couldn't take it all; he'd look far too obvious leaving her house and walking back to his car with an overflowing floral tote. Being selective, he chose a moderately sized sketch pad, a box of paints, brushes and pencils. Back in the living room he took several DVDs from her shelf, then also selected a few books and the iPod he saw on the end table.

Now for some clothes.

The closet was ajar, a nightstand drawer slightly open and the covers tossed to the foot of her bed.

First things first, he straightened the covers to provide a spot for sorting things. From her closet, he picked out warm clothes and stacked them on the bed. A sweatshirt, two sweaters, dress slacks. On the floor of the closet he found ankle boots, sneakers and snow boots.

Could he manage to take it all?

When he turned back to the bed, he again noticed

the nightstand drawer. He waffled for only a moment, then peeked in…and saw a gun.

Frowning, he opened the drawer wider and found a .38, a box of shells, cough drops and a small key.

The gun was loaded.

At least she had some protection. Smart for a woman living alone, especially for a woman with affluent relatives who could be hit for ransom.

Thinking the key must go to a lockbox for the gun, he looked around, didn't see it and bent to peer under the bed.

He found the security box along with a dark, mid-size suitcase. Perfect.

Setting them both on the bed, he loaded the moderate suitcase—which would look a whole lot less conspicuous than the flowery tote—then took the key from the nightstand and opened the box so he could store her gun.

Well, hell.

The box wasn't empty. Nope.

Catalina had a vibrator. And a pack of rubbers.

What type of woman left a loaded gun loose in a nightstand drawer, but locked up a vibrator and rubbers?

Catalina Nicholson, of course. He had to grin.

He was about to put the box back under the bed when he heard a noise, and knew his time was up.

Things were about to get real. Time to do some damage.

"So," Cat said, keeping a safe distance from Leese's buddy. "I take it you're a fighter too?"

As she walked to the other side of the bar, bright

green eyes tracked her movement. "What gave me away?"

The ripped body, the air of confidence. "All the boo-boos."

Grinning, he ran a hand through inky hair and laughed. "Yeah, that last fight was a bitch."

"You lost?"

"No, ma'am. But I didn't win as decisively as I would have liked."

Something about him helped her relax. Could be that crooked smile, or the obvious amusement he felt at her wariness. "Did Leese tell you why I was here?"

"Bare bones." Coming closer, he indicated a bar stool. "Mind if I sit?"

She minded that he was now much closer, but wouldn't tell him so. "Suit yourself."

"Thanks." He shrugged off a coat, hung it on the back of the bar chair, then sat and braced solid fore-arms on the bar. "I know Leese is a bodyguard, so it stands to reason you need protection. He said you had to lay low, as in invisible, until they got things unrav-eled. That's all I really know."

What a relief. "So." She hobbled over to the coffee-maker to prepare a fresh pot. "Tell me about the fight."

"I'll tell if you will."

She glanced back in question.

"You walk like someone who went five rounds with a Muay Thai kickboxer. I walked like that once, after I'd been slammed in the thigh about a dozen times. From my knee up I was black-and-blue for days."

Wow, such a graphic picture he'd painted. "I had a similar experience."

"Yeah?"

Nodding, she said, "I went sixty minutes with an elliptical machine."

He laughed, a rich, deep sound. "Pushed it a bit much, huh?"

"Probably fifty-nine minutes too much."

"Exercise virgin?"

"Afraid so." While the coffee perked, she studied his face. "Stitches?"

He touched the small patch under his right eye. "Caught an elbow and it swelled enough to split the skin. Seven stitches." Standing, he lifted the edge of his T-shirt to show off colorful ribs. "These are from a kick."

"Uh-huh." Cat stared at some impressive abs. The bruises were bad, but the abs were badass. "You fighter types sure are ripped."

"Not all of us." He sat again. "Some of it is selective gene pool. Some is hard work. But I know some guys who work at it just as hard as Leese and I do, and they still have soft middles. It's just not in their DNA. Doesn't make them lesser fighters."

"Probably makes them lesser studs though."

His lips curled into another crooked smile. "I'll take your word for that."

When the coffee finished, she asked, "You want a cup?"

"Sure. Black, please."

She poured both, then joined him closer to the bar. By the minute she felt more comfortable. "So why you?"

"Why me, what?" He sipped and said, "Mmm. Strong, the way I like it."

"Why did Leese ask you to babysit me?"

He looked her over, cocked a brow and said, "You'd have rather been alone?"

She'd have rather Leese didn't go, but clearly that hadn't been an option. "I guess not."

"So you needed company, not a babysitter."

Okay, she'd buy that. "But why you specifically?"

Miles scratched his chin. "I've known Leese for a while now, back to when he was still a shithead with a lousy attitude. We've gotten close, so he trusts me."

No way. She stood a little straighter, full of disbelief. "You mean Leese wasn't always perfect?"

"Perfect?" That cracked him up. Miles laughed, caught her frown and laughed some more.

"Why," Cat asked, "is that so funny?"

"Let's just say Leese stumbled into our group by default after using some pretty poor judgment. He corrected what he could, then he stayed and now he's one of us."

"Us?" she asked.

"Fight camp. It's where a bunch of us train at the same gym. We're as much like brothers as friends. Several of the guys married recently and the ladies are all tight too." He gave her a sideways glance. "For some reason they're extra close to Leese. Cannon and Armie don't mind much, but it makes Stack and Denver a little nuts. Stack's wife, especially, is cozy with him, like he's a confidant or something. She was pretty broke up when he left fighting to be a bodyguard. But he usually gets back to town every other week or so, and we all get together then."

Cat blinked at that outpouring of unique names and detailed information. She hadn't even needed to coerce him to spill his guts. She appreciated how easy he'd made it, but... Leese was friends with the ladies? *Close* friends? The thought of that made her neck hot.

To cover her reaction, she asked, "What about you? Not married?"

"No." Appalled, he leaned back in the seat as if distancing himself from the very idea. "Not interested, thank you very much."

Tone dry, she said, "I wasn't personally asking."

"Still, it's never good when hot ladies bring up marriage."

Oh, nice. "You think I'm hot?"

He gave her a mocking don't-be-coy glance. "Yeah, I do."

She damn near preened. "Thank you."

"You're welcome." He went back to drinking his coffee.

Deciding to go with her gut, Cat stopped worrying and instead came around to join him on the other bar stool. "Tell me more about Leese."

Eyes warming, he asked, "What do you want to know?"

THROUGH THE OFFICE WINDOW, Leese barely lifted a curtain and peered out. He could just see the driveway, the front yard and a part of the stoop where two men, gazes shifty, looked up and down the street, then went to work on the door.

Only two. Good.

They'd parked a noticeable black sedan at the curb. Idiots. The slick, polished car stood out against the minivans, hatchbacks and compact vehicles.

One man was dark, his hair cropped short. The other

had brown hair. Both wore suit pants and long black coats.

Way to announce yourselves, assholes.

Two he could handle—piece of cake. No need to sneak out the back, Leese decided. He wanted to know who they were and why they were here.

No sooner did he have that thought than he overheard the men muttering to each other.

"She's turning into a major pain in my ass."

"We'll have her soon."

"Won't be soon enough for me. I hope she's made to pay before she's taken out. Bitch deserves it."

A gruff laugh. "Yeah, this hasn't been the cakewalk I expected."

Fuckers. Every muscle in Leese's body tensed before he forced himself to relax again. Invested rage, he knew, wasn't a benefit. He needed a cool head. He needed to be detached.

Damn near impossible, but he'd manage.

Being less efficient than him, it took the goons a full minute longer to pick the lock, and by then Leese was in the living room, behind the door. More than ready.

They continued to rumble to each other, voices low and testy. Yes, it was bitter cold outside. Yes, the wind howled.

No reason to cry about it.

When the door quietly opened, Leese released a breath, and both men stepped inside. Being obtuse as well as assholes, they started to close the door before finally noticing him.

Surprise had them fumbling, and by then it was too late.

He didn't want to destroy Cat's house, so he didn't

play around. The closest guy got a kick in the temple that stiffened his entire body. Eyes rolling back unevenly, he collapsed into his darker, bulkier friend.

Before the muscle man could draw his gun, Leese lifted his own. "I'd really hate to cause a ruckus," he said. "In a neighborhood like this, the cops will come swarming in."

"That'd be a problem for you too," the man said, his gaze calculating, seeking an escape.

"Not so much." He was legit, so he'd deal with the cops just fine if it came to that. Using his foot, Leese nudged the door shut. *No reason to advertise this conflict to the neighbors.*

"Make this easy on yourself." Shifting in a way that his coat moved away from his hip and exposed a holster, the thug said, "Give up the girl and we can go our separate ways."

"Yeah? And what do you plan to do with her?"

"Not your concern."

Leese stared into his black eyes. "There's where you're wrong. She is very much my concern."

The man laughed. "Bullshit. She isn't involved with anyone. She hasn't even dated for a year. Cut your losses before it's too late."

Leese ignored most of that. "Are you the one who planted the bug?"

The near infinitesimal flaring of his eyes showed his surprise.

While he gauged the situation, Leese asked, "Who do you work for?"

"You're in over your head, man. Back off."

That brief conversation took only seconds, yet it felt

so momentous it should have been an hour-long interrogation.

"With two fingers," Leese instructed calmly, "take
out your gun and set it on the table. Do it slowly." When
he started to move, Leese added, "Understand, I won't
hesitate to end you."

One palm up in the universal sign of surrender, the
intruder carefully removed his weapon and gingerly
placed it on the table.

"Back up." Maintaining his aim, Leese waited for
him to move, then took the relinquished weapon, stuck
it in his own pocket and withdrew nylon cuffs. "Fasten
your friend's hands." The downed man wouldn't stay
out much longer. "Now."

Going to one knee, he did as told. "You are making
a big mistake."

"Not over his coat," Leese said with impatience. "His
bare wrists." Once they were nice and tight, Leese said,
"Good. Now lie on your stomach, hands locked behind
your neck." Without taking the gun off the intruders,
Leese flipped the lock on the door.

Thinking he was distracted, the darker man rolled
fast to his back and grabbed for his friend's gun.

He wasn't fast enough.

Leese kicked out, sending the gun to skitter across
the floor and probably breaking the man's hand in the
process. Dropping a knee to his chest, Leese used his
left hand to slug the man in the jaw twice. He wanted
to hit him more. He wanted to annihilate him.

But the asshole had already blacked out.

Damn. Hard to question unconscious men, but how
was he to know they both had glass jaws?

"Shit." Tucking his own gun away, Leese flipped

the man back to his stomach and bound his hands behind him, drawing the nylon cuffs tight enough to stifle circulation. For good measure, he went ahead and bound their feet as well, then searched them for any additional weapons.

In total they'd had three guns, a big blade and a Taser.

When Leese imagined men of their ilk ever getting within speaking distance of Catalina, icy rage slid through his veins. He took a few seconds to think about what to do, then made up his mind.

Minutes later, as both men came around, Leese lifted the razor-sharp blade and smiled in evil anticipation.

DRESSED IN COMFY flannel pants and a sweatshirt, seated on the sofa with a big bowl of popcorn and a Coke—something Leese would have frowned over, *if he'd been there*—Cat watched the screen. Every couple of seconds she had a question, and each time Miles patiently answered.

Who knew MMA was so exciting?

As one sweaty man twisted another man's arm to the breaking point in some complex, pretzel-like move, she lifted the bowl to hide her eyes. "What is he *doing*?"

"Kimura," Miles said. "It's a double joint armlock, used to get your opponent to tap."

"Oh my God, *so why doesn't he tap already*?" She was so tense, it felt like her own arm was being twisted in that unnatural way. *"Tap, tap, tap,"* she insisted.

Miles laughed. "Why would he tap when he can get out of it? Watch."

Reluctantly, she peeked over the bowl, and seconds

later, somehow, the positions were reversed. "That's absolutely amazing."

"For every move," Miles said, "there's a counter. It's just remembering it, being strong enough or agile enough to do it and doing it at the right time to make it work."

It all sounded very complicated. She tried to imagine Leese in that type of fight. Picturing him in the shorts was easy enough. Such a nice visual. But the rest... "Did Leese ever get in those awful positions?"

"Those and worse, sure. Happens to every fighter at one time or another."

Sympathy made her wince. "It looked really painful."

"Because it is. But pain is temporary. Losing is forever."

That was about the dumbest thing she'd ever heard. "Pain is pain."

"I guess. But there's pain that just hurts, and then there's pain that causes damage. Most fighters learn the difference. If something just hurts, you fight through it. If you know a bone is going to break, or you're going to tear cartilage, then you tap and plan to come back better prepared the next time."

Imagining the snap of a broken bone, she shuddered. "Why did Leese quit? Do you know?"

Rolling one shoulder, Miles said, "He's good, but he decided he'd never be a title contender. That's the main reason he switched up careers. Being second best doesn't suit everyone, and only a select few fighters can be the best. Leese still stays in shape—"

"Yup." He most definitely did.

"—but from what he's told me, he doesn't regret quitting the fight scene." He turned to face her. "Next time I see you, I'll show you some of Leese's fights if you want."

He figured on seeing her again? Cat wasn't sure how that would happen, since she didn't even know how long she'd have with Leese. Not that she'd go into all that with Miles. Sharing a portion of her secrets with Leese had been difficult enough. "You've recorded his fights?"

"Most fights are recorded. That way we can go over them again, see where we messed up, what we need to work on, stuff like that."

"I'd love to see them, thank you." They'd already gone through two whole competitions, but she could have watched for hours more. Unfortunately, when the next fight ended, so did the MMA. The sports channel moved on to football.

How much longer would Leese be? It was past dinnertime already, and she could really use another whirlpool.

Miles caught her rubbing a thigh and asked, "Still uncomfortable?"

Being truthful, she admitted, "Not as much. It's easing up." She no longer felt like Frankenstein when she walked.

"You should have taken an ice bath right afterward."

Appalled at the idea, she gasped. "Not happening, *ever.*"

A devilish light entered his green eyes. "So you're not only an exercise virgin, you're a wuss?"

"When it comes to ice?" She shuddered. "Absolutely. I don't do cold. I did lounge in a hot whirlpool though."

"Wrong. That should've been after the ice."

Pointing her Coke at him, Cat said, "I don't want to hear that word again."

He twisted toward her and gave her legs a quick survey. "Massage helps too. Want to stretch out?"

"Um…" Nervous tingles ran up her spine. "No?"

He took the drink and bowl from her hands and set them on the coffee table. "I'm not going to make a move, promise. But there's no reason for you to sit there and be uncomfortable when I can help."

"But…" He was Leese's friend, not hers, and while Leese might trust him, she didn't know him. Sure, he seemed okay, as harmless as Justice, but he was still a stranger and anything was possible. He could be working for Webb, he could—

Miles caught her ankles and, ignoring her yelp, pulled her flat on the couch. Before she could totally shift in the usual fight-or-flight mode, he flipped her over so that her face was in the sofa cushions.

"Now just relax. This'll ache a little at first, but it'll feel better quick."

Eyes wide, hands flattened at either side of her head and her body light-years away from relaxed, Cat prepared to launch away.

Then she felt his large hands begin kneading her calves.

Oh, *heaven.*

She drew a shaky breath, but couldn't think of anything to say.

"Okay?" Miles asked, still working on her muscles through the flannel pajama pants.

"Mmm," she replied, going all squishy inside. She'd had massages before, but none had ever felt this good.

With a grin in his voice, he murmured, "I have no idea why Leese didn't already do this."

She sighed. "He's resisting me."

"Yeah?" Miles's fingers went higher, to the backs of her thighs, but remained impersonal as he worked her muscles. "How come?"

She felt too lax to reply.

"Did you fall asleep, Catalina?"

"No." Another deep breath, and she managed to put some words together. "He doesn't want to take advantage of me."

"Ha!"

Well, that sounded rude. When she started to turn to him he stilled her by holding down her legs.

"Sorry. Didn't mean to laugh." He dug deeper into her muscles, making her groan. "You just don't strike me as the timid type who can't speak her mind."

"No," she murmured, "I'm not." She was just the type who got in over her head with ruthless murderers.

"Seems to me that if Leese is saying no, you haven't presented your case very well. I mean, it could be a firing offense for him, right? You'd need to make it worth his while."

A firing offense? She twisted to frown at him. "Why would he get fired if I was willing?"

"He's your bodyguard. Pretty sure sex with a client is a no-no."

Grumbling, she relaxed again. "Maybe bodyguards should worry more about pleasing the client instead of protocol."

She could hear the grin in Miles's voice when he said, "And maybe you need to spell it out."

She considered that. "I could promise to explain to his boss for him."

Miles outright laughed. "Probably not a good idea. Leese wouldn't like that. But you could explain that your interest isn't about you being grateful just because he's protecting you. I assume that's his biggest conflict, the reason he thinks he'd be taking advantage of you."

It wasn't easy to think while Miles turned her muscles to mush. "I suppose." Apparently Leese thought she was fragile and weak and didn't know her own mind.

Perhaps Miles was right. She needed to state her case a little differently.

When the tap sounded on the door, her heart shot into her throat.

A second later, a key sounded in the lock and the door swung open.

Leese stood there, his gaze locked on them both. Slowly he stepped in and set a large pizza box on the foyer table, then dragged in a suitcase, a few bags and...

Oh. Dear. God. He had her lockbox.

Miles stood from the couch. "Is that pizza I smell?"

Leese's gaze never left Cat. "I promised you dinner." He pushed the door closed and folded his arms. "So. What did I miss?"

CHAPTER TEN

IT WASN'T EASY to keep his attention off Catalina, especially when she looked miserable, guilty and mortified all at the same time.

From the second he'd stepped in, she'd been blushing.

Not because Miles had been rubbing her legs either. He swallowed back the growl that automatically came each time that particular image crawled back into his brain.

Miles's casual "muscle massage" explanation had covered the scenario. Neither of them had looked involved beyond that, so despite his surge of possessive jealousy, Leese let it go.

In fact, he acted like it hadn't bothered him at all.

He should win a freakin' Oscar.

"Did you fill up on popcorn?" Leese asked her, seeing her pick at the crust.

"No." She took a bite, her eyes wide and cautious and not meeting his.

Miles refused to note the tension and instead dug into his pizza. "Gotta tell you, Leese. I was expecting home-cooked. But this is good."

With his attention still on Cat's flushed cheeks, he shrugged. "I figured now that you're between fights, you could indulge a little."

"Yeah." Miles wolfed down a slice in two big bites. "What's the rest of that stuff?"

Cat choked.

Feeling unaccountably tender, Leese reached over and rubbed her back. "Chew your food."

She glared, went redder in the cheeks and looked away again.

It was sort of sweet that she was so embarrassed. He couldn't do a damn thing about it until after Miles left, which probably wouldn't happen for another hour or so.

He could have left the lockbox behind, but after finding people in her house, he decided it might save her embarrassment by bringing it along.

What if someone else, one of the damned thugs, had opened it?

"I went shopping," he said, to answer Miles's question. "I'll put it all away in a little bit."

"I'll do it," Cat offered, ready to leave her seat.

Leese stopped her. "I'd rather you didn't. Some guns are mixed in, a knife and a Taser."

Her wide eyes rounded even more.

"No kidding?" Miles looked toward the pile again. "Sounds like a story I want to hear."

Leese wasn't sure about revealing too much to Miles, so he censored the story a little. "I had to check on a house—"

"My house," Cat growled, her eyes narrowed. "And I thought we agreed you wouldn't."

Maybe, Leese thought, the new topic would help her to forget about her "toy."

"It's a good thing I did, because a few goons showed up."

Worry rivaled rage, and finally she demanded, "Who?"

Letting her know it wasn't Tesh or the buffoons who'd been with him, Leese said, "No one I recognized."

Some of the tension loosened from her shoulders. "What did you do?"

"I disarmed them." He glanced at Miles. "And since I didn't have time to stick around for an interrogation with the police, I bound their hands and feet, took their weapons, wallets and cell phones, cut their clothes off them and dumped them out the back door in the snow, in their boxers."

"Ha!" Dropping back in his seat, Miles cracked up. "Frostbite, dude. That's harsh."

Wearing his own grin, Leese explained, "They were flopping around like fish when I locked up and left. I figure they'll get loose before they freeze. Ought to be interesting to see how they get home though. I drove their car back to where I'd left mine a few blocks away, but they won't know where to find it, if it's even still there. I left it unlocked with the keys in it."

"Diabolical," Miles praised. "I can see why you prefer this shit to fighting. It sounds like it's a lot more fun."

Less amused, Cat quietly asked, "Now what?"

"I have their wallets, so I'll share the details with Sahara's PI." He thought about that, then said, "And I might do a little research too, see if I can make any connections."

As if expecting the worst, she slowly closed her eyes. "How was the house?"

He sent Miles a look, letting him know to play it easy. "The walk was shoveled."

Her eyes popped open. "Really?"

"Most of your mail was gone too. Only the past week's worth or so was on the floor. I brought it with me."

Puzzling over that, her gaze drifted away.

"Electric still on, water running. The curtains were all pulled."

She said nothing.

"Other than a few dead plants—" *and an audio bug in your lamp* "—everything seemed okay."

Her face fell. "My plants are dead?"

That's what bothered her most? He looked at Miles and saw his friend bite off a grin.

"I'll buy you new plants."

She let out a heavy breath. "No, it's okay."

He knew that, but did she? The fact that people had intruded into her home, not just the assholes from today, but whoever had been collecting her mail, would have to leave her feeling even more helpless.

On the drive home, he'd called Sahara and given her details from the drivers' licenses. They were likely fake, but who knew? He'd chase down every detail he could.

By morning, Sahara's people should have some news for him. Until then, there wasn't much either of them could do.

When Miles gave her shoulder a sympathetic squeeze, she smiled her gratitude at him.

He's a friend, Leese reminded himself. *You trust him.* But jealousy had a way of destroying logic.

"So," Leese said. "That was my day. Now let's hear

about yours." He tried a smile that felt just a little like a warning. "Other than massages, what'd you two do?"

Eyes back on her pizza, Cat said, "Watched fight videos and talked about you."

Shifting his gaze to Miles, Leese asked, "Is that right? What'd you tell her?"

"That you were a shithead when I first met you." He grinned. "But you're okay now."

Leese felt Cat watching him. "I can't really disagree, now can I?" He hated the truth, but he wouldn't run from it, and he wouldn't lie. Back then, he'd been a punk—a punk who almost got a very nice girl hurt. It still sickened him to remember it.

Going serious, Miles said, "It was short-lived, and hey, we've all been there a time or two."

"Not all."

"Okay, so Cannon is a saint. He's also out of the norm, so he doesn't count. The rest of us have had our moments."

"Cannon?" Cat asked. "He's one of the fighters, right?"

"Cannon Colter. His nickname is Saint," Miles explained, "and it suits him. He's a freaking paragon, and a hell of a great fighter."

"It is such a fascinating world," she said, and then to Leese, "But you're so good at everything, I can't imagine you not being perfect too."

He laughed.

Miles said, "Had the same reaction. You've got the poor girl completely deluded." He gave Leese a friendly shove. "You should probably keep it more real than that, let her know you're a flesh-and-blood male." He winked at Cat, then pushed back his chair and stood. "Time for me to go. I have a long drive home."

"Thanks for coming by," Leese told him. "Appreciate it."

"No problem." After pressing a kiss to Cat's cheek, he said to Leese, "Keep up the massage, it seemed to help."

Refusing to take the bait, Leese walked him to the door. Voice low, he said, "Watch your back when you leave. I don't think anyone's keeping track, but you can't be too careful."

"Yes, Mom."

"I'm serious."

Miles studied him, then nodded. "Okay, sure. I guess I can play the stealth game, same as you." He looked past Leese to where Cat had begun tidying the kitchen. "She's nice, Leese. Pretty hilarious too."

"Yeah."

"And like you said, damned sexy." He clapped him on the shoulder. "Don't underestimate her, okay?"

What the hell did that mean?

Whistling, Miles pressed the door button on the private elevator that would take him to the lobby, and the doors closed behind him, robbing Leese of the opportunity to come up with a reply.

Thoughts colliding, he stepped back into the penthouse and secured the door. For a moment, he watched Cat moving around. True, she seemed less stiff now, her gait a little more natural.

Massage, huh? Yeah, he could handle that—maybe.

He joined her and they worked in silence until everything was tidy again. Not wanting to wait any longer, Leese said, "Let's talk."

Her face immediately went hot, her expression guarded.

"Not…" Sighing, he took her hand and led her to the sofa. They could talk about the contents of the lockbox later. Right now he had something more important he wanted to cover. "I found a listening device—a bug—in your apartment, inside the lampshade in the living room."

The embarrassed color washed from her face, leaving her pale with shock, yet a second later angry heat flooded in again. "Those bastards were spying on me?"

"It's probably safe to assume they put it there after you busted them conspiring, not before. My guess is they assumed you'd eventually return there, and when you did they wanted to know."

Her jaw worked. "So if I had, they'd have *greeted* me?"

It turned his stomach to imagine her at their mercy. He kept the rage in check because Cat needed his calm control right now, not additional fuel for her fear. "That's the likeliest scenario. But they misjudged you, didn't they? At every turn, you've outsmarted them."

"I can't run forever. Eventually they're going to catch up to me."

"No." He held her face in his hands. "Eventually they'll trip up and be caught."

Sadness kept her smile dim. "Maybe. I hope so. But God, I want it over."

"I know. And I'll do everything in my power to make it happen." His thumbs brushed her cheeks. "Even if that means doing things you don't like."

Straightening with irritation, she poked his shoulder. "Like going to my house after we agreed you wouldn't?"

"I never agreed to that."

She grumbled, "Well, you should have." With new umbrage she muttered, "You could have been shot today."

"Not even close." When would she accept his skill level?

She touched his chest with her fingertips, then slowly opened her hand against him. Finally she lifted her gaze to his. "Do you think they're still in my yard?"

"I doubt it, but if they are, they're probably sharing body heat."

That nonsense answer, meant to defuse her worry, got her started snickering, and then she couldn't stop.

Hysterics? Leese wondered, even as he smiled with her.

"Picturing that," she said around her chuckles. "I hope parts of them freeze off." With new hilarity, she fell against him, her shoulders shaking with her robust laughter.

Leese put his arms around her.

Hysterics or not, this was nice, a hell of a lot nicer than her looking so lost.

He didn't mean to bring it up so abruptly, but as he stroked his fingers through her silky brown hair, it just came out. "Don't be embarrassed."

That ended her giggles real quick. Stiffening, she tried to shove back from him but he held on.

Trying to reassure her, he said gently, "Every woman I know has a—"

"Don't say it!"

The smile played with his mouth, but he kept it contained with an effort. "Okay," he soothed. "Just know that it's not a big deal."

She groaned, long and loud.

Leese squeezed her, and couldn't resist just a little teasing. "I am curious about one thing."

Another groan, this one more heartfelt.

"Why did you lock it up, but leave your gun out in the drawer?"

After a huff of breath, she mumbled something indecipherable against his sternum.

"What's that?" He tried to tip her back, but now she was the one holding tight. "I can't hear you."

Shoving back suddenly, she took him by surprise and surged to her feet. Her face looked scalded, making her accusing blue eyes brighter by comparison. "I don't want anyone knowing my private business, that's why it was locked up. And I kept the gun close so I could shoot anyone who snooped."

Fighting another grin, Leese cautiously stood in front of her. "So the gun was strictly to protect the locked up—"

"Ohhhh…" she growled, snapping away from him and stalking away. "Just be quiet!"

"I think you're adorable." Following on her heels, Leese caught her elbow, turned her and pinned her to the wall. When she turned her mulish gaze up to him, he fought the urge to kiss her attitude away. "I also got you some of your own clothes, shoes, books, art supplies—"

Her gaze shot to the door where he'd left the luggage. "That's what all that is?"

"And the weapons and lockbox, yeah."

She dropped her forehead to his sternum. "You know, just because you don't want to have sex, you didn't need to bring *that*."

"What?" he teased. He'd love to hear her say it.

She glanced up at him. "I can promise you, it's not a substitute."

Well, hell. Now he was envisioning all sorts of things. As briefly as he could manage, he kissed her. "There were men in your house, honey. Who knows if more will show up, and if they'll search the place looking for a clue about where you've gone." Another kiss, this one a little longer. "I didn't want anyone else knowing your personal business."

"You're right." She hugged her arms around him. "Thank you."

Heart and resistance melting, Leese said, "You're welcome."

"I'm very glad you weren't hurt."

"Not even a scratch," he assured her.

"Thank you too, for getting rid of the bug and the jerks."

Against her temple, he said, "That was my pleasure."

"Leese?"

He liked her agreeable like this, all soft and sweet, especially after the show of anger. "Hmm?"

Slipping her arms up and around his neck, she said, "We need to talk."

Not what he was expecting at this particular moment, but he'd take it. "About the other men who were with Webb?"

She screwed up her expression and sighed. "You have a one-track mind."

He felt her hands traveling down his back and said, "That's the pot calling the kettle black."

Lips quirking, she agreed. "True enough." She stepped him back and held out a hand, palm up.

Leese lifted a brow in query.

"The key."

Oh, right. He dug it out of his pocket and placed it in her palm. "About that talk…?"

"It'll wait." Her fist closed tight around the key. "I'd rather put away my things—and no, I do not need your help."

WEBB STOOD INSIDE the private horse stables of Senator Platt, his irritation growing by the second. What was he, a fucking lackey? How dare the senator order him here and then keep him waiting?

Tesh watched him, his thoughts cloaked, his mood as touchy as ever. There was a time that Webb considered him reliable, capable and even somewhat trustworthy. Less than two months ago, but it felt like decades.

The stable smelled of horse sweat, leather and hay. Tack hung on the walls, but no one else intruded. Likely the senator had told them all to stay away.

As one of the richest and most powerful men in politics, his orders were always followed to the letter.

Except that Catalina had dared to defy him.

Tesh glanced out a window, then murmured, "Here he comes now."

Thank God. Already Webb felt as if he might crawl out of his own skin. He liked to be the one in charge. He enjoyed mingling with the movers and shakers. Exchanging favors, no problem. Rubbing elbows with the rich and famous—it's what he did.

But this bullshit, jumping at someone's beck and call, damn it, he should have been above that.

Platt stepped in flanked by two bodyguards. The protective detail wore faces void of compassion, flesh-and-blood robots ready to do the senator's bidding, whatever it might be.

Murder, of course, was not off the table.

"Senator," Webb said, taking one hand from the pocket of his coat and extending it.

Platt smiled as he accepted the greeting.

He was in his late sixties, his frame tall and thin, his accent Southern, his smile warm. Such a ruse.

The senator was a perverted son of a bitch, but no one knew that. Or rather, anyone who had learned it was later found dead.

None of that boded well for Webb, since not only was he aware of the senator's proclivities, but his daughter knew what had happened on that cursed island.

"How are you, Webb?" As if a life wasn't held in the balance, he put his arm over Webb's shoulders and walked him a few steps away. "Tesh," he said in his soft Southern drawl, "join us."

Without a word, Tesh trailed them to the back of the stable. A horse shuffled, stomped the floor and whinnied. Another gave a soft nicker. The senator owned many horses.

He also owned many people. Webb didn't want to be one of them, but how to extricate himself and still live?

With a measure of privacy between them and the bodyguards who stood at the entrance of the stables, they stopped.

Smile fading, pale eyes narrowing, Platt said with soft menace, "Where is she?"

"I don't know."

"Hmm." He rubbed his mouth with a hand gnarled by arthritis. "You need to find out."

The pleasantly implied "or else" made his muscles flinch.

Webb tried not to shift uneasily; Platt fed off fear. It was there in his eyes, watching for a sign, hoping for it. "I've done what I know to do." *The rest is up to you, Catalina.* "You heard me on the phone with Body Armor. You were there, so you know I spoke to Sahara Silver herself. I insisted as much as I dared, but I don't think she knows any more than I do." *Such a lie.* "Even if she did, I can't force her to tell me."

"No," Platt said, his condescension gentle. "I suppose a man of your limited means can only do so much."

Limited means? Webb took the hit rather than attempt to refute it. Compared to Platt, he was a pauper.

"I have news," Tesh announced.

Webb froze, not breathing, not moving.

"Two men went to Catalina's house to check on things."

"They found her?" Platt asked, lighting up with pleasure.

Webb waited in agony.

"No, sir. Sorry. She wasn't there."

As carefully and quietly as he could, Webb let out a tense breath. *What men?* He had his own crew keeping up with his daughter's home, ensuring neighbors didn't get suspicious by keeping her yard maintained, her bills paid. To anyone who had asked, they'd offered up the excuse that Catalina was away for a family emergency.

If the current catastrophe didn't count, he didn't know what would.

But he hadn't sent anyone lately, and it was news to Platt, so who had sent them?

Tesh explained, saying, "I figured it wouldn't hurt to take a look around."

"We'd done that," Platt said.

"Yeah, but in case she'd returned or anything, I wanted to know."

"So you could bring her to me." Platt nodded. "Ah, good. Go on. I sense there's more."

"The same man who sucker punched me also leveled them." Tesh touched the bridge of his nose, maybe in remembered pain. "He punches like a fucking sledge-hammer, and he's fast."

"He killed them?"

"That's the really messed-up part. See, he stripped them down to their shorts, bound their hands and feet, and tossed them outside in the snow."

Good God. Webb waited to see what the senator would do.

Staring at Tesh, Platt made a strangled sound that might have been a chortle. It came again, blossoming more and more until he laughed out loud. "Genius," he crowed with pleasure. "Damn, I wish I could have seen the men. Did they die of exposure?"

Tesh shook his head. "Once they got loose, they jacked some old minivan. Had to drive home in their boxers. My understanding is that they have some frost-bite, their wrists are stripped raw from fighting out of the restraints, but they'll be okay."

Still chuckling, Platt said, "Get rid of them."

"Sir?"

"They're obviously useless, except for a laugh." He smiled. "I like this bodyguard you hired for your daughter, Webb. I really do. The man is inventive."

"Apparently." More so than Webb ever could have known.

Glancing at Tesh, Platt said, "Maybe it's time we visited Ms. Silver. What do you think?"

"Consider it done."

"Report back to me." He patted Webb on the shoulder. "And see that our friend gets home safely. It wouldn't do for anything to happen to him. He's the most direct solution to our problem."

The senator walked away, talking softly to the horses, pausing to stroke a few, before joining the armed detail and exiting the stable.

Webb's knees shook and he thought he might puke. "The men he told you to kill—"

"Would likely have hurt Catalina if they'd found her. You know as well as I do that she wouldn't have come along without a fuss."

True. Catalina had always been different. He'd never realized quite how much until recently.

"C'mon," Tesh said, leading the way out.

As he had for weeks now, Webb did as told. What choice did he have?

Once in the car, Tesh started the engine but didn't pull away. "I'm going to get Catalina."

Webb had no idea what to say to that.

"If you repeat this, I'll kill you."

Nodding seemed to be answer enough.

"After I get her," Tesh said, "she'll be mine. Do you understand?"

Not even a little.

"She won't be a problem to the senator or to you. She'll be *my* problem. I promise. So if you do learn anything, let me know. I'll take care of it, and you can finally get on with your life."

"All right," Webb agreed slowly, even while wondering: Would Tesh protect her, enslave her or would he cut her throat?

CHAPTER ELEVEN

LEESE RETURNED HER gun to her.

That simple act of faith still astounded her.

While she'd been putting away her clothes in the guest bedroom, he'd walked in and given it to her. It was hers, so that made sense. But by handing it over without a fuss, he showed that he trusted her. At least, that's how she chose to take it.

The only thing he'd said was, "You know how to shoot it?"

She'd replied, "I took a class, and then I spent a few weeks at the shooting range practicing. I wouldn't say I'm a great shot, but I know how to load it, shoot it and clean it."

"Good enough." He'd also given her the ammunition that went with it, then left her to decide where to keep the gun.

It went back in the nightstand drawer next to where she slept, which was beside him. Every night.

The lockbox was safely hidden where neither Leese nor anyone else would easily see it.

Every time she thought about it, it mortified her all over again. Like he'd said, she was hardly the only woman with a battery-operated-boyfriend, but that didn't make it any easier. Her romantic involvements had been few and far between, never serious, and she'd definitely never discussed anything so incredibly private with a man.

Not that Leese was anything like other men. Not in any way.

Everything about him was wonderful: his incredible good looks, his intelligence, his sense of humor and his patience. But it was his trust that she appreciated the most.

The thought of ever betraying that trust made her stomach churn with regret, but if she needed to run to protect him, at least now she'd be armed.

She'd also have some of her own clothes—another bonus.

Not that she anticipated taking off. So far, the setup worked perfectly for her. In fact, other than missing her job and knowing her life could end at any moment if she was found, she was happier than she'd ever been.

She felt a connection to Leese unlike anything she'd ever experienced. And that had led her to another decision.

It was a big "if," but *if* they found a way to resolve her problems, could she and Leese possibly have a real relationship? Once he no longer had to protect her, would he consider dating? Without the threats surrounding them, without her secrets as a wall, with no barriers at all between them.

She hoped so.

Multiple times she thought about asking him. But for some reason, she held back. He'd taken on enough responsibility without her possibly making it awkward. Out of necessity, they were insulated together in the penthouse, shielded from the outside world and the usual day-to-day interactions with work, family, friends. If she screwed up—and with her record, that wasn't exactly a long shot—their remaining time together could be miserable. She didn't want that.

So instead of speaking her mind, as was her norm, she reined in the emotions and just enjoyed the next three days. Since Leese didn't leave her, it was easy to do.

While counting down their time to the end of the weeklong agreement, Cat lived in a deceptive cocoon of happiness. Leese taught her some fight moves, making them more exciting by occasionally kissing her once he had her pinned down. She never knew which type of kiss to expect—a soft smooch, a quick peck, a teasing nuzzle or a full-blown eating kiss that left her wanting so much more.

Whenever he allowed her the upper hand, she kissed him and her choice *always* involved heat and tongues and lots of body contact.

As promised, he'd also run her through multiple drills, going over every possible scenario.

If intruders got into the building, what to do.

If anyone made his way into the suite, what to do.

If Leese got taken—a scenario she hated—what to do.

"I don't expect any of that to happen," he'd told her, "but on the off chance it does, I don't want to leave you unprepared." Then he'd taken her through the numerous drills again.

Whenever he worked out in the gym she joined him, but she went by a workout plan he'd drawn up for her. Already she felt a bit stronger, definitely faster, and there was something very satisfying, very calming about exercise. Funny she'd never realized that before.

At least twice a day, Leese cooked while she sat at the bar and talked with him about anything and everything. She ate each meal with appreciation, then helped with cleanup.

While he did research online or spoke privately with Sahara, she sketched.

And each night he held her close.

When it all ended, she'd miss that the most, the warmth and comfort of sleeping in his arms, knowing she was safe, feeling his heartbeat against her cheek.

Somehow she had to convince him that they could continue a relationship outside this tragic circumstance.

It was late afternoon when they returned from a workout, and Cat was thinking of how to broach the topic. It was never easy to think after an hour or more of seeing Leese in only shorts.

If he didn't give in to her soon, she was likely to go nuts.

"Leese…"

He paused on his way to the kitchen with their refillable water bottles. His gaze moved over her and he asked, "You okay? Muscles sore again?"

Ever since she'd overdone it, he checked on her often. She regretted that he felt the need. "No, I'm fine." She'd be better if he gave up abstinence, but still… "I was just thinking, maybe we could—"

The intercom buzzed, interrupting her.

"Hold that thought." With his T-shirt sticking to his back, the ends of his hair damp with sweat, Leese went to the door and pushed the button.

Sahara came through loud and clear, saying, "I'm heading up to see you in five minutes. I didn't want to take you by surprise."

"Anything wrong?" he immediately asked.

"Not at all. I have a few party dresses I want Cat to take a look at...and a few other things to discuss."

It was the last part that had Leese going into bodyguard mode. "Make it ten." He locked his gaze on Cat. "We just left the gym and we both need to shower."

"I'll see you in ten."

The second he disconnected, Cat squawked. "I can't be ready in ten minutes!" She forgot all about her proposed conversation, and so did Leese.

He strode past her. "I can. Go ahead and take whatever time you need. I'll let Sahara in."

Suspicious, Cat wondered if he'd done that on purpose, ensuring he'd have time to talk privately with Sahara. It appeared so. Well, she'd thwart that plan. Whatever news Sahara had, Cat deserved to hear it too.

She all but raced into the guest bedroom, grabbed clothes to wear and ran into the bathroom. Unfortunately, sweat left her hair lank so she had to wash it, and that took more precious minutes.

After wrapping a towel around her head, she dressed in jeans and a sweatshirt, pulled socks onto her feet and rushed back down the hall to the living room.

Sahara was already there, seated on the sofa with Leese in a chair pulled close across from her. Their knees almost touched.

Before they noticed her, Cat picked up on the conversation.

"My PI has men who've been watching her stepfather's house. Discreetly, of course. He's already had a few rendezvous with this Tesh Coleman character." Sahara gave a delicate shiver. "That one is like a badly drawn cartoon villain, he's so clichéd."

Cat agreed. There was something very wrong with Tesh and the way he'd always focused on her.

"However, as far as my man can tell, Webb Nicholson has never visited Désir Island. In fact, for the past two years, each of his trips is well documented, and he has a rigorous business and social schedule that occupies his time at home."

Leese braced his hands on his thighs. "Time that can be confirmed with alibis?"

"Many alibis," Sahara confirmed. "Her stepfather is a very busy man. Interestingly enough, he's also very generous."

"Generous how?"

"He supports several charities, and it doesn't appear that he's motivated simply by the tax write-offs. He gets personally involved."

"How?"

She shrugged. "Visiting a boys' home, purchasing and dropping off books to hospice patients, helping to build an on-site clinic at the local animal shelter."

So Webb had continued with her mother's work? Out of love, Cat wondered, or a sense of duty?

Or did he actually care as much about those in need as her mother always had?

Leese wasn't impressed. "So maybe we should saint him."

Laughing at the sarcasm, Sahara said, "Let's not go that far. After all, he is associated with Tesh Coleman. There's no denying that."

"I did some research on Coleman." Leese pitched his voice low. "His profile is genuine, but his reputation doesn't mesh with any real business. Word is, he's more of a cleanup man."

Cat barely stifled a gasp. *Leese had been poking into Tesh's history?* Dear God. She hadn't known that, and now that she did, icy apprehension rolled down her spine, making her tremble all over.

She had to trust that Leese knew how to cover his tracks, because if not, Tesh would be coming for her; she knew that deep down in her soul. And since Leese stood in his way...

No! She wouldn't let him be hurt because of her. If it came to that, somehow she'd figure out another way.

"A lot of powerful men have hired Tesh," Leese continued. "Some straight up, some more quietly. He's known as a problem-solver, the guy you bring onboard when you want to make something go away."

Sahara gave that some thought. "He must be successful, given the men who hire him. My PI said that he stays in high demand."

"Who is your PI?"

"A very trustworthy person. That's all you need to know." She followed that rebuke with an explanation. "I, too, need to keep some things private."

Leese gave her a long look, then let it go. "Some of what Coleman does is legit, probably as cover. If you do an aboveboard job here and there, it helps to hide the dirt, blood and bodies."

Knowing he was right, Cat wrapped her arms around herself. Tesh was the undertaker...and he'd always seemed obsessed with her.

Sahara patted Leese's tense forearm. "We're looking into it, I promise. Anyone Tesh might be associated with, who he's dedicated to, visited and who he occasionally works for. But given his discretion, that's going to take more time. Somehow it's all related."

Leese gave a grim nod. "Cat, Tesh, Webb...the truth."

"I sense Webb Nicholson is the weakest link, our best bet at finding answers. He's cagey when he leaves the house, having his driver do a lot of evasive moves so that he's difficult to follow without being obvious. But eventually we'll figure it out."

On the arm of the chair, Leese's hand curled into a fist. "He's cagey because he has something to hide."

"Possibly," Sahara agreed. "But many wealthy people are the same. Guarding their privacy is important to them, which is one reason Body Armor gets so much business. We, too, can be discreet." Turning smug, Sahara said, "Our loyalty is part of what will carry us through. The villains in this play have power, but so do I."

"Powerful clients?"

She smiled. "I've done high-profile work, and I've kept some jobs very quiet. People owe me favors, and when necessary, they'll gladly repay."

Somehow, Cat knew that while Sahara might have done some things very secretly, she'd never accepted a job to hurt others.

Without looking convinced, Leese said, "Keep me posted on whatever you find."

"There's one more thing."

Wondering if she could deal with more, Cat eased farther around the wall, ensuring she could see them both and that she wouldn't miss a single word.

"It's possible that the agency is being watched. Not visibly," Sahara explained, "but from the cover of other businesses."

"High windows," Leese confirmed.

"Yes. Tall, adjacent buildings make it pretty easy to spy."

Biting back the groan, Cat put a hand to her heart. So even here, in this sanctuary, she couldn't hide. She couldn't open the curtains, couldn't enjoy the balcony...

"I'd checked for that myself," Leese said, "but I couldn't find anything concrete. Not from here."

"You're where you're needed most," Sahara assured him.

"The suite is great and we both appreciate it, but it's not complete insulation. Unfortunately, nothing is. I need to know exactly what I'm dealing with."

Sahara sat a little straighter. "I can tell you which businesses have new hires with sketchy backgrounds, and which businesses might be susceptible to infiltration, but you are *not* to act on it, not alone and not without my approval." After that stern warning, she patted his arm. "I won't have one of my prized agents getting hurt."

Droll, Leese said, "Your lack of faith rivals Cat's." He covered her hand with his own. "Speaking of that, I hope you're taking extra precautions as well?"

"As a matter of fact, Justice is currently my very own private protection."

"Lord," Leese groaned.

"He's actually pretty good. I've been watching him, gauging his situational awareness. He sees everything, and he's very suspicious. Perfect qualities for a bodyguard."

"Suspicious, huh?"

Sahara smiled. "True, he stands out, especially in the company I often keep. And he's a bit too preoccupied with pretty ladies, but he's getting better. It doesn't help that the ladies look back, but at least the men seem wary of him. Of course, the way he watches them is different, far more menacing." She laughed at that. "He has a very effective death stare."

"He honed it in the cage, trying to use it to intimidate other fighters."

"I gather it didn't work on you?"

"Different weight class," Leese said. "But when he fought, yeah, sure, sometimes his size and attitude gave him an edge."

"What does Catalina think of him?"

"She seems to like him okay." Leese turned his head and looked right at her from where she peeked around the corner. "Isn't that right, Cat?"

Busted.

"You can quit eavesdropping now. We're done discussing business."

Feeling self-conscious with her towel-covered head and thrown-together outfit, Cat stepped out. "Sorry."

"No, you're not," Leese said.

She lifted her chin. "No, I'm not." She had a right to know…everything.

Even though she kept secrets? Cat winced, ignored her conscience and came closer.

"And yes, I like Justice. He's really sweet."

Leese rolled his eyes at her description.

Sahara stood with a dress bag. "I have three choices for you to try on. I know you told Enoch that you preferred jewel tones, so these should work. I love each of them, but if you'd like, we can let Leese help decide."

Umm… She looked at Leese, at those light blue eyes studying her so intently, and had to clear her throat. "I should have dried my hair if I was going to—"

"It's fine." Smile taunting, anticipatory, he said, "Go ahead, try them on."

In full support and approval, Sahara handed her the zippered garment bag. "Once you decide, we'll move on to shoes and jewelry. And I'd be happy to send my own stylist to take care of everything else. Manicure and pedicure, makeup and hair."

Did Sahara consider her incapable of the task? Cat forced a smile and said without commitment, "Thank you. We'll see." Escaping any rebuttals to that, she went down the hall with the dresses.

Rather than attempt this in her current state, she removed the towel and twisted her hair on top of her head, then secured it with a few pins. Not exactly elegant, but it was definitely better suited to the beautiful dresses.

After opening the bag and laying out the dresses, she groaned. Yes, they were jewel-toned. They were also far sexier than what she usually wore.

She thought of the long dress she'd borrowed from Scott's girlfriend, the dress she'd danced in—with Leese watching.

These dresses were less revealing, so she stopped waffling and chose first the red dress made of stretchy midweight lace, with a sweetheart neckline and a hem that hit just above her knee. The material hugged her body and, amazingly, it flattered her figure.

Sahara was pretty good at this dress-picking stuff.

With a bit more confidence, she went down the hall. Leese and Sahara, who'd been in conversation, went silent as they saw her.

Slowly Leese stood.

"Turn around," Sahara said. "Let him see the back." The back dipped low, meaning it'd be impossible to wear a bra, not that she'd need one with the structure of the dress. Inhaling, she turned, waited a few heartbeats, then turned again.

Leese's eyes were narrowed, but not with irritation. He said gruffly, "It's nice."

The small smile came without her permission. "On to dress number two," Cat sang. "Be right back."

Next she tried on the green one. Strapless, with a flirty skirt. Good thing they weren't actually going outside, or she'd freeze to death. Not that most ladies ever let a little discomfort get in the way of their fashion choices.

Anticipating Leese's reaction, she strode back to the living room.

His gaze devoured her.

Without being asked, Cat turned, twice, to show how the skirt drifted out around her.

"Lovely," Sahara announced. "Leese? What do you think?"

Attention on her exposed neck, upper chest and shoulders, he gave one sharp nod. "Pretty."

"Wonderful," Sahara said, and then to Cat, she added, "It's the blue dress I liked the most though. It's a softer color and matches your eyes. I'm glad you saved it for last."

She, too, had liked it the best. Hurrying back, Cat changed into the beautiful blue dress, then looked at herself in the mirror. The color of the dress did indeed complement her eyes, making them seem brighter. She smiled and, feeling giddy, went out to show Leese. This time she didn't rush. A strange shyness came over her, so she moved slowly, tried to remove the hopefulness from her expression and stepped out where he could see.

He'd been watching for her, and now, with her in sight, he moved closer.

"Oh my," Sahara breathed. "You look *beautiful*."

The A-line, one-shoulder dress with a fitted bodice and flirty tulle skirt made her feel like Cinderella. Little jewels decorated the top and glittered along the asymmetrical strap, a contrast to the soft material of the skirt.

His steps methodical, Leese walked around her until he once again stood in front of her.

Sahara said, "I had thought we'd need some alterations, but—"

"No need," Leese assured her in a soft growl. "It's perfect."

His tone was so intimate, Cat felt heat flushing her body. In contrast, she sounded forcibly jovial. "Guess we all agree, this is the one."

He ran his finger along the single strap and in the process grazed her skin. His gaze lifted to hers. "Definitely the one."

Was it her hyper imagination, or did he include her, not just the dress, in that equation? She wasn't sure, but oh how she'd enjoy being "the one" for him.

Either way, with Leese as an audience, she just might enjoy the occasional party.

"Well." As they continued to look at each other, Sahara said with dry humor, "Clearly there are repercussions I hadn't considered when hiring sexy bodyguards."

That snapped Cat out of her trance. "Just so you know, I'm the one insisting—"

Leese cut her off. "Was there anything else, Sahara?"

"Not unless you have some names to share with me."

He shook his head. "Not yet, no."

She sighed. "Then I suppose I should go so you can... work on it."

"I'm sorry," Cat said. "Give me one minute to get the other dresses ready for you."

Never mind Sahara's not-so-subtle prodding. After those long, maybe meaningful looks from Leese, Cat was more than anxious to get him alone. Changing took her only two minutes, then she returned with the dresses repackaged for Sahara. She dutifully answered questions about heel height and jewelry preferences, agreed to a mani and pedi, thanked Sahara profusely and then, finally, she and Leese were alone.

After securing the door, he turned to face her. "You're okay?"

"Yup."

The corner of his mouth lifted in a crooked smile. "Always so resilient."

Tipping her head, Cat wondered what he meant. "You thought trying on dresses would...what? Make me upset?"

Slowly, he shook his head. "You looked good enough to eat."

Oh wow. That sweet compliment seemed like the perfect opening, so she cleared her throat, ready to segue into seduction—

And Leese interrupted. "You don't ever have to apologize or explain to Sahara. I'm the one working for her, so let me handle it."

"I don't want to get you in trouble."

"You won't."

Meaning...what? That he wouldn't do anything to cross the line? He didn't give her long to ponder that awful possibility.

"Everything you overheard, about the PI and Tesh and Webb… I don't want you to worry."

She'd definitely heard a lot. Talking about it later would have better suited her, but if it had to be now, she'd get it out of the way. "I'm going to assume you didn't leave a trail when you poked around online, looking into Webb's or Tesh's business."

"Good assumption."

"And," she said, inching closer to him, "I figure as long as we keep the drapes drawn, no one can spy on us here. Sucks, but I'm still safer here than I've been in quite a while."

"Completely safe," he assured her, meeting her halfway. When they got within touching distance, he lifted her chin. "I'm on it, okay? And what I can't do, Sahara has others doing. No one is going to touch you."

"Well, that's the thing." Cat slipped a hand up to his chest. "I know we're a couple of days shy of the agreement. But I was sort of hoping for a few touches." She stepped against him. "From you."

Such a temptation.

Leese had to admit, kissing Catalina topped the list of the hottest things he'd ever experienced. The softness of her lips, her immediate response, the natural way she would press against him… Catalina Nicholson wore her heart on her sleeve.

She kept dark secrets, true, but not about how she felt.

It was an amazing combination—her physical honesty with her obvious mistrust—that made him more than a little nuts.

Lately, he'd given in to the urge to kiss her, taking

her mouth when he knew she wanted him to, which was pretty often.

She gave new meaning to practicing moves.

For so many reasons, *good reasons*, Leese had denied himself. But it seemed impossible to wrestle with her and not kiss her, so he'd quit fighting it.

"Leese," she groaned, going on tiptoe to better fit herself against him in that now-familiar way.

Encouraging her, he scooped one forearm beneath her bottom and lifted her up.

Before she could show her surprise, his mouth took hers. For only a moment, she stiffened…then sank against him with a soft, hungry sound of approval.

The problem, Leese knew, was that every kiss made him want her more. There were times at night, with her small body tucked close and her scent filling his head, that he couldn't remember why he waited.

To prove something to her—or to prove something to himself?

He'd figure that one out later, he decided. Now, after Sahara's visit, he sensed things were coming to a head. It wouldn't be much longer before the players made a move, and then he'd have them.

And Cat would be free.

Before that happened, he needed to cement his relationship with her. For him, that's what it was: an intimate relationship beyond the obligation of a bodyguard to a client.

How much more, he didn't yet know.

But he damn sure wanted an opportunity to find out.

Did she feel the same? Only one way to tell for sure.

Still holding her, he headed for the couch; if he made a beeline to the bedroom he'd lose his cool and rush things. After all their teasing, she deserved more than that.

To ensure she didn't disappear from his life, he needed to make an impression on her.

He needed *her*, period.

As he sat on the couch, he arranged Cat to straddle his lap. Her slim thighs opened around him, her knees aligned with his hips. "Touching," he said against her mouth, "sounds good to me."

Eyes heavy, lips damp, she whispered, "Really?"

"That," he promised her, "and more."

She inhaled deeply. "How much more?"

She might fight total honesty, but he could give it. "As much as you want."

"Perfect." Without hesitation, she tugged his T-shirt free from his jeans. "I want everything."

Leese surprised her by leaning forward far enough that he could strip off his shirt and toss it aside.

He'd definitely changed over the past couple of years but he'd never been modest.

She gave a throaty groan of approval and stroked those small curious hands down his chest, dragging her fingers through his dark chest hair, over his pecs, back up again to his shoulders and then his nape. Without a word she leaned into him and kissed his jaw, his neck, lightly bit his shoulder, opened her mouth on his upper chest.

"Hold up, honey." It was enough to have her sweet ass warmly snuggling his dick. Now, with her hot, damp mouth touching his skin, he was damn near a goner. Setting her back, he said, "You need to play catch-up."

"Okay." In quick agreement, she started to peel off her sweatshirt.

Leese again stopped her, this time with a short, tortured laugh. Pleased with her, he said, "Let me, okay?"

"Okay, sure." She held up her arms.

So damn ready.

During his adult life, he'd had easy conquests, but never had a woman wanted him as much as Catalina did.

Rather than do as she expected, he drew her in for a hungry, openmouthed, tongue-twining kiss, and while she melted against him, he slipped his hands under the sweatshirt.

Her warm, silky skin enticed him. More than anything, he wanted to strip her naked and kiss her all over.

And he would. Soon.

Until then, he traced her spine upward...

No bra strap.

Well, hell. Knowing she was bare beneath the sweatshirt stole a good chunk of his control.

Bringing both hands around to the front of her, he opened his palms over her breasts. So soft and warm. He rasped gently over her already tight nipples, taking her groan into his mouth.

When he caught her nipples in his fingers, gently rolling, her legs tensed and her hands on his shoulders clenched. As if she needed the added contact, she pressed more snugly against his cock, slowly rocking, setting him on fire.

Okay, so maybe he couldn't take things slow. Apparently neither of them wanted or needed that. "Arms up again, babe."

Without a single word of protest she sat back and did as he asked.

More clumsily than he would have liked, Leese

whisked the sweatshirt away, then had to pause and just…look at her.

God, she was beautiful.

Using only his fingertips, he traced over her shoulders, her collarbone, around the outside of her breasts, down to her small waist and then the flare of her hips. The low-fitting jeans left her belly exposed. Dipping one finger inside the waistband, he brushed back and forth over her satiny skin.

"You're such a tease," she complained, her breath strained. Tunneling her fingers into his hair, she leaned forward.

Knowing what she wanted, Leese licked around one taut nipple, stroked his tongue over it and, when she shuddered, he slowly drew her in, sucking softly.

She gave a husky, barely there whimper. "Oh God…"

Her ragged breathing, the flush of her skin and the stirring words she murmured, all pushed him.

Knowing his own limits, Leese turned her to her back on the couch and settled between her legs. Going back to her nipple, he nipped her carefully, caught her in his teeth and tugged, then moved to the other breast.

Head back, eyes closed, Cat breathed fast and deep while keeping up that tantalizing rhythm, grinding herself to him in growing need.

Lost to the pleasure, Leese kissed his way down her body, tasting her heated skin, licking, leaving behind the occasional love bite. He dipped his tongue into her navel, brushed his teeth over her hip bone and nibbled his way to the waistband of her jeans.

"These need to go," he muttered thickly, and opened the snap.

Cat said nothing, and with a quick glance he saw her

holding her bottom lip in her teeth, her eyes squeezed shut, her expression an agony of anticipation.

So fucking hot.

He wanted to hear her come, taste her on his tongue, feel her body twisting with pleasure.

Sliding both palms inside her jeans and panties, he cupped her plump bottom, caressed her and dragged down the material to midthigh.

Again, he soaked in the sight of her, those soft upper thighs and hips, sweetly curved belly and her now damp sex. His chest worked, trying to find enough oxygen.

He sat up long enough to push the denim lower, out of his way.

Coming back to her, he deliberately wedged her thighs wider, used his fingers to further part her and then, with just his fingertips, he touched her, playing over her slick flesh, spreading the moisture up and over her clitoris…

"Leese," she groaned, her hips shifting sharply, trying to follow the touch.

He gave in to the need and pressed his face to her, breathing deeply of her musk scent, stroking his tongue into her. He didn't think about seducing her, but instead, for the next few minutes, he just took what he needed.

It must have been enough, because as he drew in her clitoris, rasping with his tongue, sucking softly, she stiffened beneath him, tangled her fingers in his hair, and arched hard, crying out as she came.

CHAPTER TWELVE

WHEN LEESE LIFTED HER, Cat barely managed to put her arms around his neck. Every part of her felt liquid. And hot. And a deep throbbing remained in her blood, a pulse beat of incredible pleasure.

After a slow inhale, she murmured, "Where are you taking me?"

"The bedroom." His incendiary gaze bore into hers. "I need you naked."

"Yeah." She let out a shuddering breath. "I need that too."

His hard mouth tipped in a predatory smile.

"Um… I mean…" It was difficult to think around the residual pleasure. "I'd like us both to get naked."

"Works for me." He entered the master bedroom and lowered her to the bed.

Before she could think, he had her jeans tugged off completely, taking her panties at the same time and leaving her utterly bare. That might have been a little unsettling, except that he stepped back and, keeping his gaze on her body, unbuckled a thick black belt.

With her heart beating harder, she came up to her elbows to watch.

Reaching toward the small of his back with one hand, Leese caught a belt holster as he pulled the belt free.

He'd been packing? Good grief. She nodded at the

heavy Glock he set on the nightstand. "Do you carry that always?"

"Yes." After toeing off his shoes and kicking them aside, he lifted a foot to the bed, pulled up one pant leg and opened an ankle holster too.

Her eyes rounded. "Always?"

He stared at her breasts. "Always." The smaller revolver joined the Glock on the nightstand.

A hundred questions vied for priority. But Leese stepped back, eased down the zipper on his jeans and stripped them away.

Cat forgot how to breathe.

The fact that he tossed the pants aside rather than fold them, as was his norm, showed the level of his interest. Leese was a neat freak, but his jeans had just hit the wall and slid to a pile in the corner.

After scouring her hungry gaze over him top to toes, she slowed and looked again, this time taking it all in.

She started with his large feet, currently braced apart, then let her attention crawl up to his strong, hairy calves. Muscles roped the length of his thighs, tapering in to narrower hips, and an impressive erection. Her palms tingled with the need to touch.

"Catalina…"

"Shh." She took in those shredded abs, the firm pecs and wide shoulders. "You're incredible." She'd never before known a man built like him, much less had the opportunity to see such a man naked.

There was so much to appreciate that it took her a second to return to his jutting erection.

Everything on Leese was proportionate and hard, especially that part of him. Unlike a bulky bodybuilder, his muscles were flexible, made for power, not display.

But wow, what a nice picture he made.

There was no mistaking that he wanted her—probably not as much as she wanted him, but she didn't mind that.

She licked dry lips. "You're the most impressive man I've ever seen."

Smile strained, he touched her calf, drifted his fingers up to her knee and lightly pressed, urging her legs to part again. "I'm glad you think so, because I've been craving you since we met."

She'd never really been insecure, or a woman who needed compliments. But she heard herself ask, "Do I measure up?"

"You're hotter than even my imagination." His gaze met hers for one searing moment. "And I imagined you naked a lot."

When his fingers teased higher, she caught her breath. "I'm average."

"There's nothing average about you." He stroked over her. "You're small and soft and, God, Cat, I'm dying to get inside you."

Her toes curled. "Do you have protection?" She quickly added, "And I don't mean weapons."

"Yeah." Buck-ass and glorious, Leese walked to the closet.

She thought of the picture she'd drawn, and smiled. She'd gotten pretty darned close to the reality.

While she tried not to pant, he got out his overnight kit and removed two condoms.

More revived by the moment, Cat watched him return to her.

Out of necessity, the drapes were drawn as usual. But it was still early enough that plenty of light penetrated the room, showing the flex and shift of his body as he came back to her.

His attention burned over her like a tactile touch.

She opened her arms, expecting Leese to come over her.

Instead he settled beside her, his large hand opened over her breast, his mouth at her throat.

Oh, well yeah, that worked too.

Now on sensory overload, Cat felt the crisp hair on his calf covering one of her legs, the roughness of his fingertips playing over her sensitive nipple, his hot breath on her shoulder and the hotter touch of his erection against her hip.

The man was not idle. He stroked her gently, occasionally caressed roughly, somehow always knowing her preference. By the second her need escalated to a fever pitch.

He trailed small, damp kisses over her temple, opened his mouth over a special place on the side of her neck, took a gentle bite of her shoulder and made his way back to her nipples, using that hot tongue to turn her into a mass of quivering sensation.

"Let's see if you're ready."

"I am," she promised breathlessly.

But he only smiled against her breast, then pressed his broad hand between her thighs, his long fingers slipping over her, spreading her moisture. "Mmm," he murmured. "Maybe. But let me…" Slowly, he worked two fingers deep, then groaned. "Nice."

Cat arched up on a throaty cry of pleasure.

"Yeah," he growled low in approval. "You're wet and ready."

Because she was very close to losing it.

"Come for me again," he urged, and he brought his thumb up to her clit, idly stroking in a maddening way.

With the tension rapidly building, it would be so easy to give in. But she wanted to touch him too, she *needed* to touch him, had been thinking about it since meeting him, so she caught his wrist and held him still as she struggled against the tide of release.

"Catalina?" He kissed her ribs, though *kiss* didn't quite cover the bone-melting way he used his mouth. "What is it, baby? What's wrong?"

Speaking wasn't easy. Heck, breathing was a struggle. "Next time I come," she managed to whisper, "I want you in me."

With sultry satisfaction in his voice, he promised, "We'll get there."

"But before that—" she turned to face him, then very deliberately pressed him to his back "—I want to play a little too. After all, this was my idea."

His pale eyes smoldered. "I don't mind playing, but know that it was a *shared* idea all along." He eased her hair away from her face. "Before we went this far out of bounds, I wanted you to be sure."

"I've never been more sure of anything in my entire life."

Appearing pleased by that admission, he searched her face until his focus settled on her mouth. "Then have at it. I'm all yours."

Oh, if only that was true. If only she knew that when this dark fairy tale ended, Leese would still be with her...it'd make every day, every minute, so much easier.

But all she had was right here, right now, and she wanted to make the most of it.

She brushed her mouth over his. "Stay still," she whispered.

Now it was her turn to taste him all over. With her breasts pressed to his chest, she leaned over him and drew his earlobe between her teeth.

Leese put those beautiful arms of his around her, stroking her back, playing with her bottom, doing his own share of kissing her wherever he could reach.

He felt so good, his skin hot and sleek against her palms, muscles taut over large bones.

Crisp chest hair, just the right amount, added to his machismo. He shuddered when she lightly bit his pec muscle, then licked over one flat nipple.

He tangled a hand in her hair, and didn't object as she began kissing her way down his body, much as he'd done to her.

From his navel down, she teased her nose over the happy trail that bisected his body, then grew thicker around his testicles. With her so near, his erection flexed in spontaneous reaction. The heated scent of him filled her head and, losing herself to the moment, she wrapped her fingers snug around him.

"Damn," he muttered, his thighs tensing.

She brushed her cheek against him and whispered, "You smell so good, Leese." When he shifted restlessly, she stroked once, twice, then licked her tongue from the base of him up and over the head.

He breathed harder; his hand in her hair urged her closer. Knowing what he wanted, Cat put one soft kiss to the underside of him, then opened her mouth and drew him in, taking him as deep as she could.

"Catalina," he whispered, his whole body strung tight, his breathing labored.

Wow, he was in worse shape than her, and that was saying something given how badly she wanted him.

Thrilled, even more turned on by his response, she stroked him with her tongue, then slowly retreated before taking him again. Over and over, she worked him, sucking as she withdrew, licking with her tongue while she took as much of him into her mouth as she could. She tasted his salty pre-cum, heard the broken, almost pained sounds he made and felt the tautness of his big, hard body.

Only a few minutes in, his hands shifted to her cheeks and he held her face. "Enough," he growled. "You need to let up."

Rising to an elbow to see him, Cat took in his expression. She'd expected him to be concentrating, eyes closed, teeth locked.

His teeth were locked all right, but he stared at her, watching, his gaze incendiary.

Still holding him in her fist, she asked, "You don't like it?"

He groaned a laugh. "I like it too much."

Good. She wasn't exactly a pro at this sort of thing, so she'd been going mostly by instinct. Now, seeing how she'd affected him, she wouldn't mind starting all over again. "I can feel you throbbing." Lightly fondling him, she whispered, "I like doing this to you, Leese. A lot."

He didn't smile. "I need you now, Cat."

"I need you too." Wanting him to know, she said, "Understand, it's not just your smokin' body, and not just because you're a barrier between me and crazy killers."

"Cat," he admonished, because he'd already told her many times he wouldn't let her be harmed.

She moved her free hand over his abs, up his ribs to his chest. So warm, so strong. So perfect in every way.

Leese didn't know it yet—how could he? Until this moment, she hadn't even realized it. Finally getting this close to him, this intimate, she couldn't mistake her feelings.

She loved him.

Crazy, over the top love.

If it came down to it, she'd sacrifice herself before letting him be hurt in the line of fire. "It's everything about you." Her throat felt thick with sudden tears, but that wouldn't do, not at this precise moment, so she smiled. "You're the most amazing man I've ever known."

"Good," he said, the single word so gravelly, it was almost inaudible. "Now come here." He caught her under the arms and drew her up the length of his body, then in the same movement, turned her beneath him.

"Leese—"

He took her mouth in a hot, demanding, we're-done-talking kiss that made her forget everything except the desire. His hands were on her again, causing the most delicious friction, teasing in all the right places. For only a moment he moved away, no doubt to roll on the condom, then he settled over her again.

Unsmiling, he kneed her legs apart, held her gaze with his as he reached between their bodies, adjusting, then filled her with one deep thrust.

She was so wet, he entered her without resistance, but it had been a long time for her and she gasped at the unfamiliar sensation.

The *incredible* sensation.

"That…" She took two breaths and whispered shakily, "That almost did it for me right there."

Looking very tender, he pressed a sweet kiss to her parted lips. "Let me see if I can improve on it." Still watching her, he began a slow, deep rhythm, pressing deep, almost leaving her, then driving in again. With each heavy thrust, the pleasure ratcheted up.

Yup, even better.

Curling her legs around his waist, Cat held on, unable to do much more than welcome the expanding need. In this new position, each glide of his body both filled her and stroked her clitoris until, without warning, the waves of sensation spiraled through her.

She cried out, closed her eyes against the intensity and just held on to him. Seconds later he pressed his face to her neck and groaned out his own release, his body shuddering, heat pouring off him.

As the fog slowly receded, Leese went to move to her side.

Cat hugged him, wanting him to stay over her, unwilling to give up the connection. Her body still pulsed and throbbed and a very sweet ache remained in her heart.

God, she loved him so much. She'd been drawn to him the moment she met him and the emotion grew thicker every day until it almost consumed her. It didn't matter that she hadn't known him long, she knew everything important. From the start, even with questions unanswered, he'd protected her. He not only believed in her, he gave her blind faith, trusting that she told the truth without pushing her for more than she was willing to share.

She'd already spent more meaningful time with Leese than she would have with anyone else she'd been dating for a month.

With an obvious effort, Leese shifted, coming up on his forearms at either side of her face. He looked mellow, his dark hair over his brow, his face relaxed in a way she'd never seen before.

His gaze searched hers.

Lazily, he brushed his thumbs over her cheeks, then bent to sweetly kiss her. Against her lips, he whispered, "I'm glad I brought your lockbox."

Immediately, Cat turned her head away to protest.

But he didn't give her a chance. "I only have one more condom, and I can't see sending Enoch out for more."

"Absolutely not!"

"And since I'm not leaving you today, we're going to need your supply."

"Oh." So he wasn't talking about the vibrator, but about condoms. *How many times did he plan to have sex?* "Okay, then."

"Love it when you're agreeable." He kissed her neck, his tongue soft and hot against her pulse point. "What do you say we go get something to eat first?"

That worked for her. "Sure."

"Then we can shower together."

Better and better. She nodded agreement.

"Tomorrow," he promised, "I'll go out for more rubbers. A couple of boxes at least."

Her toes curled. "Sounds good."

"After all the teasing you've done, you and I are going to make up for lost time."

She smiled, but at the same time her heart broke a

little. Forget lost time, she needed to make memories for the future—just in case this special time with him was all she'd ever have.

"THE CURTAINS ARE never opened on the top floor."

Tesh paced as he talked on the phone. That probably meant Catalina was in there. His mind jumped ahead, formulating possible ways to get her out of the Body Armor offices. That place was like a fortress. Maybe he could call in a bomb threat, then everyone would have to evacuate. Once he had her out in the open...

Unfortunately, during a time of chaos like that, she'd likely be circled by every damn bodyguard in the building. *Fuck.*

The low-level lackey who he'd recruited spoke again, interrupting his internal rage. "The windows are always dark on the two floors below that too."

Running a hand over his head, Tesh tried to reason through possibilities. Maybe those floors were just empty. He'd need to get the blueprints of the building, see if those floors were set up as offices or storage space or...whatever.

Since her brother had passed away, Sahara Silver had taken over, restructuring everything. It was possible there'd been a loss in business. Maybe she'd had to cut back. If so, that could explain the empty floors.

But maybe his little Catalina was inside, held prisoner by her own fears, fears that he'd play on, use to his advantage, fears that he'd nourish to make her his in every way.

Fears, he knew, that were well warranted.

As usual, when he thought of Catalina, his heart beat

harder, slower. Soon he'd have her—and he wouldn't let anyone take her from him.

BECAUSE OF A steadily falling sleet, Sahara held Justice's arm—more like a tree trunk—on the slippery walk to the car. It was late, nearing 9:00 p.m., thanks to the lead she'd followed on the web. Sometimes tearing herself away from her work was harder than the work itself.

It was only knowing that Justice waited for her that convinced her to call it a night.

Her high heels were rarely a problem; she could run across snow-covered gravel in them without a single slip. But ice? It wouldn't matter if she wore athletic shoes, she would still welcome a supporting arm.

"You've kept a lot of late nights," Justice observed.

Which meant he, too, had suffered the same.

Over the past three days, she'd checked in with Leese on the progress each of them had made in their research. It wasn't easy to talk privately with him when he and Catalina shared such close quarters. Generally she'd wait until they were leaving the gym so she could catch him while Catalina showered.

At first she'd been mildly irked about the breach of professionalism. But alas, she was a romantic at heart. While neither of them had mentioned love to her, even a blind man could tell that their relationship was beyond casual.

Sahara was far from blind.

The way the two of them clicked was actually heart-warming to see, and though she might be a barracuda in the business world, she was still a woman, and she enjoyed witnessing true affection.

So it was taboo. So what?

She ran the business and she could break any rules she wanted. Since she didn't want to lose Leese as her number one agent, and since Catalina clearly wouldn't be issuing any complaints about the familiarity, what could it hurt?

Now if only Catalina would come clean on the rest of the details. But she remained too wary to openly trust.

So far, without Cat's knowledge, Sahara and Leese had narrowed down Webb Nicholson's most likely cohorts to three men, two of them in politics. Before either of them said anything to anyone else, they needed more facts. Any accusations that couldn't be proven would result in disastrous lawsuits that could cripple the company.

She couldn't risk that.

Her PI was one of only a handful of people she trusted. Leese and, amazingly, Justice, were two others.

"Have you minded being my bodyguard?" Sahara asked.

Because he'd been too quiet, his gaze going everywhere around the lot, her question took him by surprise. "Why would I mind?"

Casting a knowing look on him, Sahara smiled. "I've seriously cut into your free time."

He rolled a massive shoulder. "Not a big deal. I like this shit. It's interesting, I'm learning the ropes and you're easy to talk to."

"Thank you." She patted his arm. "You'll enjoy the next job more, I'm sure."

"I'm looking forward to it," he admitted, then tugged at his ear in what she'd learned to recognize was a nervous gesture.

Justice was an attractive man. Not GQ gorgeous like

Leese, but more rugged, earthy and real. He had that "from the streets" look, and all the authenticity of thickened ears and a few scars that proved him a *real* fighter.

"But...?" Sahara asked.

"Guess I'm kinda edgy about it too."

"You'll do a wonderful job. I have complete faith in you." She liked Justice and saw great potential in him. "Look at it this way. An actor would only hire you to get the authentic experiences, yes? So you can completely be yourself, but maybe with a little understanding that he is the client and he's paying. See what I mean?"

Without a lot of conviction, he said, "Sure."

Smiling, she hugged his arm. "Just be the big, bad-ass, cocky dude that you are, and I promise he'll appreciate it."

"I guess I can do that."

"So, Justice." She stepped around a patch of ice. "Do you have a regular girlfriend?"

He stalled, cleared his throat, frowned and then coughed. "Um, Ms. Silver..."

With the night so dark and the air so still, her laugh echoed everywhere. "I'm not hitting on you, Justice, I promise. Unlike our friend Leese, I never mix business with pleasure and besides, as much as I admire you, we're hardly suited."

Relieved, he flashed her a sinner's smile. "No, ma'am."

The awkward politeness from such a hulking, muscular guy tickled her. On Justice, even the Mohawk worked, adding to his unique persona. "I asked because this profession can be very demanding. There will be jobs that keep you away from home 24/7. It won't be easy to carry on a committed relationship."

"Works for me."

So he enjoyed the singles scene? Given his appeal, that didn't surprise her. "Well, if it ever does become an issue, I want you to know that you can come to me. I like to keep my agents happy. So if at some point you fall in love, talk to me and we'll see if we can adjust the jobs to accommodate romance." After all, she was being quite accommodating for Leese. She would do no less for Justice.

He skipped right past any possibility of romance and asked, "Does that mean you plan to keep me around?"

"Most definitely." It fed her business-savvy soul to have male employees who were not only large, capable and sexy, but also possessed a certain cocky savoir faire.

They'd just reached the big SUV Justice preferred to drive. Ice encrusted the windows and door handles on the passenger side, which faced the open end of the lot. "You should have let me get you at the door," he complained. "I could have had the ride heated up already."

"I'm not a flower," she promised. "I won't shrivel in the cold."

Suddenly, with no warning, Justice's head snapped up and he took one big step in front of her. Being so massive, he completely shielded her, backing her into the car at the side of the door.

"Get in," he told her, reaching back to hand her the keys.

That particular tone alarmed her as much as the possible threat. She took the keys, but given the ice, she didn't think she'd get the door open without circling to the driver's side—in the direction Justice stared. "I can't. It's frozen shut."

He muttered a low curse word, took her arm, and—

"Please, Ms. Silver, don't go running off."

Immediately Justice put her behind him again. She tried to peek around, but he didn't let her. With a hand on the gun in his holster, he ordered, "Get in on the driver's side."

The intruder said, "I'm here to talk to you, Ms. Silver."

Making a guess, she asked, "Is that you, Mr. Tesh?"

The heavy pause gave away his surprise at being so easily identified. "Just Tesh, and yes."

"Justice," she said with authority, "you will let me handle this."

Conflicted, he tugged at his ear again.

"Justice," she warned.

Reluctantly, he took one step to the side of her. He still protected her with his body, but he'd allowed her to see the men.

She knew right away which one was Tesh, though two others accompanied him but definitely not anyone powerful. Powerful people stayed hidden and sent others to do their dirty work, like cleanup.

"It's a dreadful night, and I'm sure none of us prefer to stay in the weather any longer than necessary. So tell me, Tesh, how can I help you?"

Her amiable tone confused him further. Apparently deciding Justice wasn't an issue, Tesh stepped forward. "You can stop fucking around."

"Language," Justice snarled.

Incredulous, Tesh barked a laugh.

Even Sahara was surprised by the defense. "It's fine," she told Justice, patting his tensed arm. But because she didn't like his humor at Justice's expense, she tacked on, "Some men have a very limited vocabulary and vulgarities are all they can manage. We certainly don't want to tax Mr. Tesh's abilities, now do we?"

Justice grinned. "Guess not, ma'am."

Taking the bait, Tesh narrowed his black eyes. "You're a mouthy bitch, aren't you?"

Sensing she'd hit a nerve, Sahara stilled Justice's automatic reaction. "There are security cameras everywhere," she said as much for the intruders as for Justice's benefit. "I don't want to have to defend a murder over something as childish as foul language and insults."

"If he doesn't censor his mouth, it's happening anyway."

Oh my. Justice truly was heroic. Best to move on quickly. "In answer to your question, yes, I can be quite 'mouthy,' if by that you mean I trump your insults with ease."

The men behind Tesh shifted impatiently. Tesh just pulled off a stocking cap, ran a hand over his shaved head, then, presumably with his rancor controlled, announced, "I want the girl."

"So many people do." Stepping farther away from the protective wall of flesh and bone Justice provided, Sahara tapped a gloved finger to her lips. Playing a dangerous guessing game, she said, "Webb Nicholson isn't the only man who'd like to recover Catalina, is he?"

"Others want her," Tesh said. "You already knew that. It's why you were hired."

Hardly the motivation, but she let it go. "Ah, yes, but I meant another good, well-meaning man. Someone who cares for her and only wants to protect her. Someone she's accused, but who surely is innocent." She held his gaze without blinking. "You work for that man as well, don't you?"

Going more lethal, Tesh asked, "Where did you hear that?"

"Oh, please." She laughed as if not afraid, as if she didn't have a clue why she and Justice had been stopped. "I'm good. Better than good. And I do my homework. So I assume this other man is involved?"

He tightened his mouth and stayed mum.

"Is Webb aware that you have divided loyalties?"

More silence, more dead staring.

That was admission enough for her. "If you can meet me halfway, Tesh, I'd like to set an appointment with him."

Justice tensed in disapproval, but she ignored him.

"I've spoken with Catalina several times now—"

"So you have her in your building?" Eyes hard with expectation, Tesh took an aggressive step forward. "You have her here?"

Justice snarled again, so Sahara put a hand on him, restraining him with just a touch.

"Now, Tesh." She gave him such a pitying look that he ground his teeth. "Did you really think it'd be that easy? Even a man of your meager accomplishments should know better than that."

Tendons strained in his neck and his temples pulsed. Through his teeth, he rasped, "You're pushing your luck, lady."

That proved too much for Justice. "She'll say whatever she wants to say, however she wishes to say it and you'll damn well shut up and listen."

Tesh's jaw flexed with more teeth-grinding until he finally appeared to get a handle on his unruly temper. "Why the hell can you curse, but I shouldn't?"

"I work for her." Justice shifted his massive shoulders. "And you don't."

Good Lord, Sahara thought. *It's like trying hold back an enraged bull.* Justice now chose to take everything as offensive. "Before we all freeze to death, I'd like to get to the point."

"Yeah," Tesh said. "Why don't you?"

"Catalina Nicholson has been under our protection. Given you butted heads with the agent assigned to her, I'm sure you're aware of that much."

Voice clipped, he said, "Yes."

Making her words as effective as possible, Sahara said, "Perhaps you're not aware of how delusional the poor thing is."

Tesh's brows went up in cautious surprise. "Delusional, you say?"

"Clearly. The convoluted stories she's told, the stretch of her imagination…they are not the ramblings of a girl based in reality."

Edgier than ever, Justice whispered, "Sahara—"

Hedging off his protest, she snapped, "Know your place, Justice." Turning her back to Tesh, she stared directly into Justice's eyes, doing her best to convey the need for trust. "You've interrupted quite enough."

After a moment, he grudgingly relented, so perhaps he did understand.

Facing Tesh with a bright smile, she said, "I don't know if anyone she's mentioned is associated with Webb Nicholson, but surely you do."

"I know everything there is to know about the Nicholson family."

Bragging? Excellent.

"Who has she mentioned?"

"She's yet to give me a specific name, but I do believe I can convince her. And once I do, it'd be wonderful if you could help to facilitate a meeting, sort of provide neutral ground so that Catalina doesn't panic too much." In a conspiratorial whisper, she confided, "She is entirely too dramatic and prone to great exaggeration."

Tesh looked like a dog salivating over a meaty bone. "Not usually. More often than not she's stubborn and determined to do things her own way."

Was Tesh insulted for Catalina? It did look that way. Odd. Just how attached was he to her?

Rather than try to convince him that Catalina had undergone a complete personality change, Sahara said, "Oh, believe me, she's still quite stubborn, and *very* determined to make us believe that otherwise-reputable men would do her harm." She flapped a hand for good measure. "It's beyond silly."

"I know who she's accusing."

"You do?" Heart tripping, Sahara asked with feigned disinterest, "Who?"

Tesh stared at her, his expression carefully blank while his eyes burned with rage. "It's better if I don't say. No reason to further the tales. Just get her to me."

"I see your point." Such a dangerous game to play, but Sahara had to believe it'd be helpful in the end. "I would suggest giving her to her father, but she's so terrified of him, she'd bolt the second she saw him."

"Yes," he agreed. "She would."

"These other men, though…perhaps we could meet someplace neutral? A park or—"

"I know just the place. Once I have everything arranged, I'll let you know."

"That would be grand." Sahara shifted her purse off her shoulder and brought it around in front of her.

Just as quickly, Tesh's men reached for their guns, halting only when he lifted a hand.

Good Lord. Did they think she'd go for a weapon? That she hoped to shoot it out with them? Murder Tesh outright with witnesses?

With Justice bristling beside her, Sahara cleared her throat. "I was going to give you my card."

"I have your contact info."

With her hand still half in her purse, she asked, "My private number? I'd like to give you that as well."

His eyes narrowed, but he nodded consent, watching her closely as she withdrew the card case and opened it to get a linen business card.

As if he wasn't a scumball cretin with questionable intentions, she approached him and handed it over, then covered his hand with her own before he could withdraw. "I can't tell you how much I appreciate this." She stared into his eyes too—and saw soulless evil. "Just let me know when you have something arranged and I guarantee, I'll get her to you."

He pulled away and stuck the card in his coat pocket. "What about the bull watching over her?"

"My agent?" A very real laugh slipped out. "Oh yes, of course he'll come along. She wouldn't go anywhere without him." And Leese would never let her out of his sight. "But he, too, understands that she needs help. I'm sure he'll thank you himself."

Tesh gestured to his cohorts and they began to back away. "I'll be in touch very soon."

"I look forward to hearing from you."

He paused once more. "You should know, Ms. Silver. If you're jacking me around, spinning a trap, you're going to regret it." His black gaze crawled down her body. "And you know what? I almost hope you are."

With that last implied threat, he turned and strode away.

Furious, Justice said, "What the hell—"

"Shush." After a telling glance, she squeezed Justice's hand. "Let's get out of the cold before we talk. Even my bones are starting to shiver." Of course, that could be pure reaction to Tesh. In every way, on every level, he repulsed her.

Catalina was smart to run from him. But she couldn't run forever.

Justice reached for the back passenger door, where she usually sat.

"I'll ride up front tonight."

He didn't question her on that. He got her door open with a little effort, thanks to the ice, then waited for her to get in before going around to the driver's side. Once he started the vehicle, he cranked up the thermostat and flipped the switch for the heated seats.

"I need to scrape the windows, but keep an eye out, okay?"

"Of course." Not that she could see much through the ice.

Justice worked with quick efficiency, clearing each window with a scraper while also continually checking the area. Normally the car would have been protected in the covered lot, but he'd parked close enough to the opening that the ice had blown in everywhere. As she'd said, it was a miserable night. Hopefully they wouldn't lose power.

Once back in the car, Justice put it in gear and pulled

away. As soon as they were on the main roads, he said, "Leese is going to be severely pissed."

"On the contrary, he will be thrilled, because now, Justice, we have a way to get to them."

The light of realization dawned in his eyes. "You aren't handing her over?"

"Of course not. I'll forgive you, just this once, for doubting me. Just don't let it happen again."

Justice slowly unleashed an enormous grin. "Yes, ma'am." He waited a moment more before laughing. "You're scary, you know that, right?"

Flattered, Sahara smiled at him. "Why thank you, Justice."

"Welcome." He shook his head. "Honestly, I don't know what you have planned, and neither did Tesh. That makes him even more dangerous."

"Yes, it does." And somehow they had to keep Catalina safe. She drew out her cell and dialed Leese.

After she explained, she found out that Justice was right, after all.

Leese was pissed.

She thought about reminding him, despite her very lenient attitude, that he worked for her. But in truth, she enjoyed the protective anger. It reminded her of her brother.

Scott, too, had often worried for her.

But he'd also taught her to be strong and smart and independent. Tomorrow she'd meet with Leese and they'd work out details.

"Until then," she told Leese, "you should worry about Catalina, and let me worry about me." She disconnected on his protest, smiled at Justice and asked, "How would you like to spend the night?"

CHAPTER THIRTEEN

LEESE'S MEETING WITH Sahara didn't happen.

Shortly after he'd gone to the store for more protection, the snowstorm worsened and they ended up with the second largest snowfall to ever hit Ohio. From Toledo to Portsmouth, record cold, snow and ice shut down cities. Road crews couldn't keep up and the mayor declared a snow emergency, recommending that everyone stay home for safety reasons.

Sahara got through to him twice, but the landline connection was iffy and speaking over the cell phone was too dangerous. Only a few people had made it into the agency, and Sahara wasn't one of them. Given how many wrecks were reported, Leese was glad she didn't try.

He figured Tesh and his cohorts were equally disabled by the weather, so it was probably a wash; he and Sahara couldn't make plans, and the people after Cat couldn't cause problems.

Through the next two days, the power went off, came on and went out again. There were plenty of candles in the penthouse, they had enough food and the propane fireplace in the center of the room radiated heat everywhere. The switch, of course, didn't work, but Leese was able to manually turn it on.

The building was still secure; even when the power

blipped, the auxiliary power, run by a generator, kept everything locked up right and tight.

It didn't make sense, even to him, but he didn't mind being snowed in with Cat. In fact, it felt like a forced respite, an ensured time period with her. He couldn't research, couldn't go out, and that meant no one else could either.

All he could do was enjoy her.

And he enjoyed her a lot. "You know, Cat, I could get used to this."

Glancing over her shoulder at him, she asked, "What? Posing?"

Leese smiled. He rested in bed, naked, his shoulders propped against the headboard, one corner of the sheet barely covering his lap.

Catalina, equally naked, stood in front of a make-shift easel sketching him. She'd pinned up her fawn-colored hair in a loose, tousled bun that threatened to drop free at any minute.

"Actually, I meant watching you work naked."

"It seemed fair," she said in a distracted way, leaning close to use the side of her baby finger to add smudges to the charcoal drawing. She blew softly on the paper, then leaned back to get a different perspective. "And I don't mind you looking." She flashed him a quick smile. "I'm not super modest or anything."

"No reason you should be." She had a cute, sexy little body, all soft curves and satiny skin. Her breasts were moderate, her waist tiny and that heart-shaped ass... He loved holding on to those firm cheeks while driving into her.

And if he didn't curb those thoughts, he'd get a boner and ruin the picture. "I wish I had your talent."

Absently, she asked, "Why's that?"

"I'd draw you too. Just as you are right now." *Her body bare, expression focused, looking like the perfect wet dream.* "With the candlelight on your skin and that particular concentrated expression on your face." He saw her smile and added, "You're beautiful, Cat."

She paused in her sketching. Bit her lip. Then turned to him. "You really think so?"

God. How could she not know? He took in the sight of her soft nipples, her smooth belly, the neat patch of downy pubic hair. "Yeah," he promised, his voice brusque. "I look at you and I want you."

"Even though we just had sex?"

"That was..." He glanced at the clock. "An hour and a half ago."

The smile played with her lips before she turned away again. "Thank you. I've never really minded how I look. I mean, for the most part, I don't think about it that much. I have what I have and there's no changing it. I know I'm short and far from stacked, but it's not like I can somehow make myself taller. I'm not an ogre, and I have my health, so..." Her shoulders lifted. "It's nice to hear that you're not disappointed."

"Far from disappointed." She finished up and, with coal-blackened fingers held out to her sides, stepped back from the sketch. "What do you think?"

Leese sat up to see the large drawing. Bemused, he draped his forearms over his knees and couldn't resist smiling. He felt a little self-conscious, a lot complimented and pretty damned turned on.

They were both naked, after all.

Cat had drawn him in the bed, a smirk on his face as he stared right at her. She'd caught the sexual interest in his gaze, the tolerant amusement on his mouth. It was a novel thing to be with a woman who saw him so much better than he saw himself. "I think you're too talented to just teach art."

Casual as you please, she strode to the dresser and picked up a damp cloth to clean her hands. "You're sweet, but I'm not good enough to make a living off my art, and I like eating too much to go the starving artist route. So I teach, and that's okay, because I love kids."

With her hands now free of charcoal, she returned to him. On hands and knees, she crawled over the bed and sat on his abs. "Drawing you seems like a good reason to keep you naked."

Laughing, Leese automatically put his hands on her thighs, coasted them up to her hips, then around to that lush bottom he appreciated so much. "Ever thought about having kids of your own?"

"Sure. Someday I'd love that." She continually touched him, occasionally pressed a kiss to his chest or throat. "I've just never met the right guy." Her gaze strayed away. "You?"

"Met the right guy? No." He jumped when she tweaked his chest hair. "Ouch, hey." Laughing, he caught her wrist and freed her fingers before she got him again. "Take it easy."

Eyes narrowed, she said, "I will—if you don't dodge my question."

She looked so serious, Leese knew she asked out of more than idle conversation. So did she care? He thought so. Cat didn't try to hide her feelings. But was the caring based on gratitude, lust…or more?

She scowled. "You're taking an awful long time to

think about it." In a huff, she tried to move off him. "Forget I asked."

"I thought I was in love once."

That stilled her. "Really?" Slowly she settled back onto him, that sweet ass snuggling his groin, her beautiful breasts right there for him to see. To touch.

Taste again…

As if to soothe, she stroked his shoulder. "It didn't work out?"

Leese had to laugh at himself. He'd gotten quickly mired in sexual need, and she wanted to chat about past relationships. "For good reason, it never really got started."

"She was a horrible person?"

There was no way to hold in his humor. Catalina's faith in him was both humbling and amusing. It forced him to own up to his own disreputable past. "Why do you assume it was an issue with her?"

Stretching out over him, Cat tucked her face under his chin and stated, "Because you're so perfect."

She'd said that too many times; he had to set her straight. "You're delusional, honey."

"I don't think so."

Damn, he hated making confessions, but Cat deserved to know. He couldn't let her go on thinking he was some damned paragon of virtue, when the reality was nowhere near that.

He folded his arms around her, breathed in the scent of her hair and admitted, "I used to be a real ass."

"I know Miles jokingly accused you, but—"

"It wasn't a joke. I was totally obnoxious."

Disbelieving, she said, "Yeah, right. When you were ten?"

Yes, he'd probably been a jerk back then too. "Not that long ago, really." One stroke of his fingers and the bun tumbled down. He adored her hair, the soft shade of brown, the silky feel.

Cat waited, so he started to talk, all of it shaming him. "You're partially right that I was a dick when I was a kid. My parents didn't have a lot of money, and I resented that."

"Why? What was it you missed?"

"I didn't miss anything."

She looked up at him. "Of course you did. If the budget was tight, there had to be things you wanted that you couldn't have."

Hell, he'd wanted everything—and gotten none of it. Talking about his childhood still made him uncomfortable, but maybe if he opened up more, she would too.

"Until I turned fifteen and got my own job, all I'd ever worn were hand-me-downs."

She stared at him a moment, then ducked her face and went back to hugging him. "Hand-me-downs from who?"

Fuck. Trying to sound as if it didn't matter, Leese said, "They were donated by the community."

"Were they at least nice?"

Not always. "I don't think it would've mattered." But he knew it did. Wearing clothes that didn't fit, with stains and tears, had made him stand out, and not in a good way. "I always wanted a dog." There were times he'd beg, and while his dad wasn't mean about it, the answer was always the same. "We couldn't afford one though."

"I always wanted a dog too! But when I lived in Webb's house, he wasn't keen about animal messes, as he put it. He'd tell me to get a horse, mostly because horses lived in stables."

Leese smiled. "Can't let a horse sleep at the foot of your bed."

"No." She tipped her head. "And that's what I wanted. You?"

"Yeah."

"Now," she said, "I don't know. I'm just not sure I'm home enough."

"Same here. And you know, after I got that job and started getting paid, I didn't want to spend it on a dog either. Not when there were other things I needed too."

"Like clothes?"

"That, and I started saving for a car." Memories made his chest tight. "I knew my folks were always broke, but it never occurred to me to see if they needed any financial help."

"They had jobs?" she asked, without censure.

"Yeah. Dad worked in a factory, Mom at a convenience store." He thought of the long hours they put in…without ever getting ahead. "They never seemed to want more and I couldn't understand that." Because he'd wanted everything. Possessions. A savings account.

Pride and respect.

"Hard jobs," she said.

"Definitely." His father now suffered joint problems from so many years on his feet. His mother looked a decade older than she was.

Now that he made good money, Leese tried to help them out when he could, but they usually refused his efforts. For them, having a roof over their heads and food on the table was more than enough. "Through the years, Dad got offered promotions. But it would have

meant a different sector of the factory, working with
new people, and he wasn't interested."

"He liked the familiar?"

"I guess." For Leese, poverty could never be familiar.
"He was happy with the little run-down house he rented,
but I wanted a house of our own. He and Mom shared
a rusted old sedan, and I wanted a decent running car
that didn't look like it belonged in the junkyard."

Cat came up to her elbows, her gaze soft and serious
and understanding. "You have a nice car now?"

"Yeah, and a house of my own." With her looking at
him, he traced her eyebrows, feathered a fingertip over
her thick lashes, then along the narrow bridge of her
nose. Finally he outlined the shape of her lips.

He loved each individual feature; together they made
the most gorgeous woman.

"You resented their attitudes."

"When I shouldn't have."

"Not true." She brushed her nose against his. "People
are individuals. They wanted one lifestyle, you wanted
another. There's nothing wrong with that."

"If you say so."

She lightly kissed him, her teeth nibbling, her tongue
teasing. When he started to deepen the kiss, she cupped
his face and smiled down at him. "If you don't mind
me saying so, I think it's unfair of parents to try to
force a lifestyle on kids, especially if they're uncomfortable with it."

Was she thinking of her own conflicts? She hadn't
fit in with the status of her family, but unlike him, she
hadn't resented anyone. She'd just gone out and forged
her own way.

Eventually Leese had done the same, but it had taken a close call to make him see things clearly.

Having Cat nose to nose with him, he couldn't avoid her gaze. There was no way to hide from his discomfort, so he gave in and admitted, "Making a good appearance matters to me."

One side of her mouth curled and she squirmed atop him. "You could just stay naked. I promise you, that would always be a good appearance."

From the moment he met her, Cat had lightened his mood and often made him smile. "You have sex on the brain, woman."

"How could I not when I have you under me?" After one sweet, very emotional kiss, she added, "How does all that relate to you and this woman you cared about?"

Yeah, he still had to go there, didn't he? With a disgusted sigh, Leese said, "College wasn't on the agenda, but I was athletic, so I started working out in a gym, training."

"As a fighter?"

"Yeah. And I thought I was good, until I got around guys with real talent. I had a shitty attitude about it all and I carried a massive chip on my shoulder."

"You're saying you weren't a nice guy?"

He'd been a real asshole, but no reason to spell it out that plainly. "I was always trying to prove something. To myself, but to others too. Then I met this girl…" She was everything Cat wasn't. Stacked, definitely. Bubbly, yes. A blonde bombshell and the life of the party, whereas Cat was petite, serious and preferred quiet time in front of a canvas.

The biggest difference, though, was how Cat affected him. He'd admitted defeat with the other girl, but for Cat he'd take on the world. From the get-go, she'd stirred an innate need to protect, shelter—and claim.

"How did you meet her?"

Never before had he known a woman who wanted to hear about past crushes. Cat didn't look offended or snarky, just curious. "I did the local circuit fighting, and she hung out with fighters. Since we were often at the same MMA events, I'd been hitting on her for a while. She was always nice, not really encouraging me, but not kicking me to the curb either. One night we were dancing at an after-party when I found out she was pretty hung up on someone else."

Cat winced. "You were filler?"

He idly stroked her satiny bottom, thought about it and shrugged. "The other guy was dragging his feet, so she needed a distraction."

"Ouch."

He smiled. Yeah, at the time it had stung. But now he realized it was mostly because he'd chosen to misunderstand. "She'd never led me on. We'd dance, talk, but nothing more, and honestly, she danced with a lot of guys. Everyone knew the score, except for me."

"So you never had sex with her?"

"No."

"Wow, poor girl doesn't know what she missed."

How could he remain maudlin with Cat smothering him in compliments? For far too long, he'd been disappointed in himself. His single goal had been to be a better person.

Cat made him feel like the best man around.

"Since she's very happily married now, I doubt she sees it that way."

"To the foot-dragger?"

"Yeah. He's a good guy. One hell of a fighter."

"Is he as good-looking as you?"

Grinning, Leese turned her under him and settled between her warm, slender thighs. After feathering kisses along her jaw, he said, "I'm not weighing in on another dude's looks."

She moved right past that to ask, "Are you still hung up on her?"

"Definitely not." And now Leese knew he'd never really been emotionally involved, because what he felt for Cat was far richer, stronger and more real than anything he'd felt with any other woman, period. Every past relationship paled in comparison. "It was physical attraction, that's all."

"So...you lusted after her?"

"Yeah." And Cat didn't look happy about it. "But I still acted like a dick when she turned me down." He rested on his forearms over her, enjoying the way her small breasts plumped against his chest. It'd be nice to wrap up this conversation so he could move on to more important matters—like planting himself firmly inside her, hearing her cry out, watching the beautiful way her face contorted as she climaxed.

He had to draw a deep breath to regain his control. Time to condense the story. "Like you, she had some people after her. I was feeling burned, and I didn't know they wanted to hurt her..." It still pissed him off to remember how stupid he'd been. "They claimed to be related to her, and when they chatted me up, wanting information on her, I stupidly shared."

Cat went still. "Did she get hurt?"

"Luckily, no. It didn't take me long to realize they

were bastards, so I went to the big guy she liked and told him everything."

"Wow." She wrapped her legs around him and locked her ankles at the small of his back. "That took guts."

"Honestly, I didn't know what else to do. There were three of them. They spiked my drink, then beat the shit out of me while asking me questions."

"Oh my God," she breathed.

Leese felt his ribs ache at the memory. "I tried not to tell them anything, but—"

She touched his mouth. "You were *drugged*."

"Yeah." But if he'd been smarter, he wouldn't have found himself in that situation. "I don't know what they gave me, but I couldn't fight back. It was like my legs wouldn't work. I woke up that next morning and realized how badly I'd fucked up. Going to her boyfriend was the only thing I could think of to do."

A sheen of tears softened her blue eyes. "You are the most remarkable man."

Taken aback, Leese said, "How the hell do you figure that?" Jesus, he'd given her no reason to cry. "I just told you—"

"That you owned up to things," she finished for him. "And you corrected what you could. Very few ever do that. But even though she'd rejected you, you faced her boyfriend, explained what had happened and tried to help her."

Maybe. But in his heart, Leese knew that didn't exonerate him.

Sniffling, smiling at him with admiration, Cat asked, "Did it all work out for her?"

Leese occupied himself by cupping her breasts; it

was easier than seeing her tears. "Yeah, it did." No thanks to him.

"And the guy she married? How did he take it, when you told him your role in things?"

That was the part that had always stunned him the most. "Instead of being pissed and stomping me—which he could have done—he thanked me, involved me, confided in me, and his friends, *her* friends, made me a part of that group." It had been a life-changing moment. "It felt good, being on the honorable side of things."

"You know what I think?"

Given her starry-eyed infatuation, he could guess.

"You were always honorable. It's just that sometimes we aren't tested, so how can we really know? Most of us go through our lives with mundane problems that are easily resolved if we don't dwell in melodrama. But some people face life-and-death situations, and they come away with proof of their convictions." She searched his face. "You, Leese Phelps, now have proof."

He'd never really thought of it that way. "Part of my learning curve involved admitting that fighting wasn't for me. I'm good, but I knew I'd never be the best, so what would be the point?"

"That's how I feel about art. I love it, and by teaching I can make a difference with it."

So damned wise.

Prodding him, she said, "Sort of like you becoming a bodyguard, right?"

Made sense. "I do like protecting people. A few times in my life I was lucky enough to be around when someone needed me. And damn, it always feels good to know I could help."

Pride gave her a small smile. "You're a natural-born hero."

"And you're an optimist, determined to paint me in the nicest way."

"Naked," she quipped while bobbing her eyebrows. "I still say that's the nicest way for you." Then, more seriously, she added, "I see you as you are, Leese. Very smart and caring, capable, and most definitely honorable and protective. So yes, you're a hero, and that's that."

Leese knew he'd happily spend the rest of his life doing what he could to live up to her expectations. But at the moment, the tightening of her nipples distracted him. And he could feel the damp heat of her open thighs. "Mostly," he whispered, "I'm a man who wants you."

Her gaze warmed and her breathing deepened. "Again?"

Always. "Yeah." Reaching between their bodies, he opened her, not so he could sink in, but so he could rock his cock against her, spreading her wetness, slowly stroking over her clit. "What do you think?"

Her nails bit into his shoulders. "I think we can talk more later." She kissed him, her mouth open, hot. Drugging.

Enjoying her escalating excitement, Leese kept the friction steady until she bowed under him.

He damn near came with her, but he held off, unwilling to take a chance without protection. This particular game was risky enough already.

When her harsh groans receded to soft moans, he moved away, grabbed the rubber and seconds later was ready.

"Over you go," he said, turning her to her stomach, drawing her up to her knees, then opening her legs. Palming her ass, he growled as he slowly pressed into her.

So fucking hot.

He loved seeing her body accept him, the delicate pink lips glistening with her release, snug around him, taking him deep.

She clutched at the sheets, her hands fisted; all along his cock he could feel her squeezing him, the little aftershocks of her pleasure.

Holding her hips, he began a strong, heavy pace that rocked the bed, each thrust and retreat pushing him closer to release. Cat kept her head down, her bottom raised in a carnal position so erotic, Leese knew he wouldn't last. When she cried out, the sleek muscles in her neck and shoulders strained.

He put a hand at the small of her back to keep her right where he wanted her. Awkwardly, she thrust back into him, taking what she needed to finish, and he liked that enough that he stopped trying to hold back and instead joined her.

Depleted, his body thrumming, Leese eased her flat and rested over her, his face beside hers. With his heart still thumping, catching his breath wasn't easy. Damn, she pleased him.

She sighed. "Leese?"

Satisfaction leveled him, so he only managed to say, "Hmm?"

There was a moment's hesitation, then she whispered, "Every time seems better."

He gave her a squeeze, and wondered what it would be like...for a lifetime.

THE NEXT MORNING the weather finally cleared enough that everything returned to normal.

Leese stood at the stove cooking breakfast and Cat sat at the counter sketching. She wore thick white socks, yoga pants and an oversize pink sweatshirt.

She was the sexiest, sweetest thing he'd ever seen.

Being with her like this, in a domestic routine, felt right.

As he removed eggs from the skillet, he asked, "What are you drawing this time?"

Before she could answer, the intercom buzzed.

More relaxed now, Cat merely glanced toward the door, then started to rise.

Leese stopped her. "I'll get it." She might be less wary, but he would continue to take every precaution. On his way past her, he saw that she'd drawn birds, a cluster of them on a broken fence with a small ramshackle shed to the side.

It should have been a depressed scene, but she made it pretty. The background faded, making the plump little birds the focus, and damn, it made him smile.

In his youth, maybe he should have noticed the birds more and he'd have been a happier kid.

Cat might deny it, but she was incredibly talented.

He hit the intercom button and said, "Hello?"

"I'm sorry to disturb you, Leese." Enoch sounded jovial. "Sahara is on her way in, but since I got here before her, she asked that I check on you both."

Leese unlocked the door and welcomed Enoch. "Thanks, we're fine. Come on in."

Nose and cheeks still red from the cold, Enoch strode in. "You had enough to eat? Stayed warm enough?"

"It was an adventure," Cat said from the kitchen. "I enjoyed it."

Enoch smiled toward her. "Good morning, Catalina."

"Good morning."

To Leese, he said, "I'm making a run for Sahara, so is there anything either of you need?"

"Making a run?" Cat asked.

"She wants to welcome everyone back to work with coffee and fresh pastries." He set aside a briefcase and chafed his hands together. "There's a little bakery right across the street. It won't take me long. But while I'm out…?"

"We're good." Leese led him toward the kitchen. "We were just about to eat. Want to join us?"

"Thanks, no. I'm short on time." He lifted his briefcase. "I haven't even been to my office yet. I came straight here to check on you, as Sahara requested."

"Then the least I can do is give you a cup of coffee before you go." Leese needed a chance to talk to Enoch alone. Stalling was his only option. "Cat insists on having it every morning."

"Oh, okay." Picking up on Leese's unasked request, Enoch nodded. "I think I have time for half a cup. Thank you."

Cat stared toward him. "You mentioned pastry?"

Leese handed a steaming mug to Enoch, then slid a plate of eggs in front of her, scrambled with a little cheese and ham, a small dish of mixed fruit beside that. "You have breakfast."

"And I'm sure it's delicious," she countered. Then with a begging expression, she added, "But fresh pastry? Like something with jelly or icing. Come on, Leese, you can't seriously expect me to skip that."

She looked so mulish, Leese bent and kissed her pinched mouth, leaving her pink-cheeked and blinking. "I don't expect you to skip anything." He asked Enoch, "Would you mind bringing us two?" If he missed his opportunity to talk to Enoch now, he'd catch him on his return.

Cat cleared her throat. "I only need one."

"I'll eat one with you."

She brightened up, making him laugh. To Enoch, he said, "She's easy to please."

Enoch wasn't listening. While he sipped the coffee, he studied the drawing on the counter in front of her. "This is incredible." He took in the pencil she held, the charcoal dust around the art mat under the drawing, and his eyes widened. "Did you do this? It appears you have, but still…"

Cat lifted her smudged fingers. "It's a charcoal pencil, a little messy but with a lot of versatility, and yes, it's mine. Do you like it?"

"It's amazing. The birds look so real." He leaned closer.

Cat warned, "Careful, or you'll get it on you." She tipped her head at him. "If you really like it, you can have it."

His eyes widened. "You're serious?"

"Sure. Being cooped up here, I've done a lot of drawings."

"May I see the others?"

She went pink again. "Um…"

Because many of the sketches were of him naked, Leese said, "She can pull them all together for you to see soon. Right now, I don't want the eggs to get cold."

"Yes, that would be wonderful. Just let me know

when you're ready." He stared reverently at the sketch. "You're sure you don't mind if I take this one?"

"It's not a problem at all. Let me spray it first so it won't smear." She left down the hall toward the bathroom.

Propping a hip on the counter, Leese said, "She's good, isn't she?"

"Very good." He sipped his coffee. "I had no idea."

"Took me by surprise too."

"I'll frame it and hang it in my den," Enoch told him. "I have a fondness for birds."

Leese was about to get to his more pertinent questions when Cat strode back in, shaking a hair spray can. "This will help it to set."

"Sign it first," Enoch said, and then with glee, he added, "I'll have an original."

She laughed, but scrawled her name on the bottom of the drawing, lightly sprayed it, blew on it gently and then put it between two other blank pages. "Here you go."

"Thank you so much." Enoch carefully slipped it into a pocket of his briefcase. "I don't know what to say."

"I'm flattered that you like it."

"I *love* it."

Appearing very pleased, Cat put away her supplies and went to the sink to wash her hands.

Knowing it might be his only opportunity, Leese led Enoch back to the front door. Hoping the running water would keep Cat from hearing, he said low, "Could you tell Sahara I need to talk to her right away?"

"No need. She had the same request for you," Enoch explained in a reciprocal tone. "She'll probably need another thirty minutes. Everyone is running behind."

"Understandable. I'm sure a lot of the side streets are still a mess." He'd peeked out the window earlier and saw snow piled everywhere. It'd probably be a few more days before they got it all cleared up.

"I know she wants to talk to everyone as a group, and then you privately." He glanced toward the kitchen. "I imagine I can entertain Catalina while you're with Sahara. It'll give me an opportunity to ask her more about her art."

"Sounds good." Leese opened the door. At the end of the vestibule, the private elevator doors stood open, and the adjacent door to the stairs remained secure. "Let me know when and I'll be there." After he closed and locked the door behind Enoch, Leese turned and saw Cat waiting for him to join her before eating. He needed to talk to Sahara, to tell her he wanted to end this, whatever it took.

He wanted Cat free.

And then they could decide about the future.

CHAPTER FOURTEEN

"Isn't that the little dude who works in the agency?"

Hands jammed deep in his pockets, his collar up and a scarf around his neck, Tesh gave up his perusal of the deadly icicles hanging from the gutters of the building where he planned to hole up. The owner, who worked for one of Platt's associates, was late and that pissed him off. It was too fucking cold to stand outside waiting.

But the building was a good choice. It gave him a clear view of the Body Armor agency. With the roads finally cleared, he and two of his men had arrived half an hour ago. Already it felt as if his nose might fall off, it was so cold. He'd been about to head back to his car to wait when Johnson pointed out the man leaving Body Armor.

Enoch Walker. "Well, I'll be damned." Most everyone who left or entered the building did so through the parking garage doors.

He recognized Enoch from a detailed report he'd gotten on all the employees, from Sahara Silver down to the cleaning crew. The security for the building was top-notch, but here was Sahara's right-hand man, waltzing out as if on a mission.

As he watched, Enoch tucked a briefcase under his arm and secured the buttons on his coat all the way to his throat, then turned up the collar.

"Get him," Tesh said, the anticipation already heating his blood. "*Discreetly*. Take him to our car. I want to see what's in the briefcase, if it gives us any clue about Catalina."

"Sure thing."

"I'll join you in a minute." As an afterthought, Tesh added, "Don't hurt him too much—until I'm there."

Wearing the slightest of smiles, Miller led the way, making a beeline across the cleared parts of the street. Johnson followed.

Both men liked to act, not wait. Giving them a focus was like throwing a meaty bone to a rabid dog.

Watching them work could be amusing, but right now, Tesh had his own need to work.

No longer cold, he watched as the little man was stopped. As alarm flared in Enoch's eyes, Tesh breathed deeper. He loved seeing that moment of recognition, that split second of time when people realized they were in real trouble.

Enoch looked ready to scream, then Miller leaned close, said something in his ear and the little man clammed up in terror.

No doubt Miller told him he had a gun to his ribs. Since he kept his hand in his coat pockets, no one would know until it was too late.

With terror making his gait awkward and his face pale, Enoch allowed himself to be led away. Miller carried his briefcase.

Perfect. Absolutely fucking perfect.

Tesh flexed his fingers and, after ensuring no one had noticed and he wouldn't be followed, he headed after them at a discreet distance.

He'd done many things in his life and had never

been caught. He sure as hell wouldn't blow it today... not when he was so close to having Cat.

They'd parked the SUV with darkened windows in a private lot less than a block away. Tesh followed the footsteps in the snow and, with every beat of his heart, the turbulence built in tandem with the excitement.

A very dangerous mix. A mix that inspired extreme violence from his soul.

When he got close, Johnson opened the door and stepped out. "He's in the back."

"Then that's where I'll be as well."

"I figured." He opened the door and waited for Tesh to slide in, then closed it and got back behind the wheel.

He now had Enoch trapped between himself and Miller.

Immediately, Miller held up a sketch. "This is signed by her."

Enoch's audible breathing filled the interior. From the top of his head to the bottom of his feet, the little man trembled.

"Ah." Tesh took the drawing. "Even without a signature, I'd have recognized my kitten's work." His gaze pierced Enoch. "So you have Catalina?"

It took two tries before Enoch squeaked, "No. That is, the agency is working for her but—"

With a single nod, he unleashed Miller, who viciously punched Enoch in the temple. The blow blindsided him, knocked his head to the side and sent him so close to oblivion, he almost slid off the seat to the floor.

Before welcoming blackness could close in, Miller hauled him back up.

"Now," Tesh said, enjoying the ultimate power of being in control. "You have her in the building?"

"Oh God," Enoch whimpered, his shoulders hunched and his eyes going red.

Miller let loose with a barrage of punishment that left Enoch gurgling with pain. Sections of his face turned purple, one eye swelled shut, blood seeped from a cut at the corner of his mouth and his nose looked decidedly bent.

Superficial wounds, but they had to hurt like hell.

Miller rubbed his bruised knuckles, but surprisingly, Enoch didn't confess Catalina's whereabouts. At the moment, Tesh wasn't sure he could. He looked dazed into a stupor.

Tiring of the game, Tesh took the briefcase and rifled through it. He found papers he didn't care about, files and an itinerary that didn't pertain to him but perhaps would be useful later. He folded them, put them in his pocket…and then he found a smaller pocket with keys and keycards.

"Ah. This is what we needed." The keycards would get him on the elevator, and the actual key would be used to—

"No," Enoch said, making a grab for it.

Miller hauled him back with a hand in his hair, then landed a harsh blow to his soft gut.

"So this is the one, eh? Good to know." Tesh thought of those darkened windows on the upper floors and guessed he'd find Cat there. Not that he'd risk going after her himself.

He wasn't stupid.

"I'll stay with our friend," he told Miller and Johnson. "I need you to take the guard at the elevator."

"Sure," Johnson said right away. "Piece of cake."

"He's armed," Enoch warned in a rush, the words

slurred by his swollen lips. "He'll shoot before he lets you overpower him."

"Maybe," Tesh mused. "But not if he thinks he has to save you. Perhaps a deadly car accident? With this ice, it's more than possible." The plan formed in his mind, entirely plausible. "Take the briefcase. Hold it so the guard can see it. Explain that there's been an accident and a man is hurt."

Enoch shook his head. More to convince himself than them, he said, "It won't work. He won't leave his post."

That he was so worried about it only reinforced for Tesh that he was on the right track. "Go quickly," he told his men. "Before anyone else shows up. Check the top two floors. And if you find Cat, bring her to me."

"What if we run into anyone else?"

Tesh smiled at Miller. "Kill them." Anyone who stood between him and his kitten definitely needed to go.

CAT INSISTED ON doing the dishes while Leese showered. It seemed fair since he'd cooked, but she had to leave everything *perfect*. If she left a single crumb behind, he'd find it. He wouldn't say anything, but he would definitely clean behind her.

She understood him better now and assumed his upbringing had helped to forge him into such a neat freak. He hadn't said it, but she got the impression his folks hadn't taken much pride in anything, not better employment, not better clothes for their son and likely not in their home either.

He'd been in her house, so he knew she didn't share his affinity for organization. Not that she was a slob;

she did like things neat and orderly. But Leese took it to a whole new level.

Not a terrible trait at all.

Besides, tidying the kitchen after their breakfast gave her some much-needed alone time, allowing her to drop the bubbly facade.

Loving Leese was bittersweet, both the easiest and the hardest thing she'd ever done.

It was past time she confessed everything. Continuing the lie was no longer an option now that she cared so much for him.

It felt like a massive betrayal.

Yet telling him the truth could put him at added risk.

Bracing her hands on the counter, Cat dropped her head forward and fought off the desolation.

There had to be a way to handle things on her own, but no matter how she considered all the angles, it remained impossible.

She pushed away from the sink and hugged her arms around her middle.

Leaving, walking away without a word, wouldn't guarantee Leese's safety—especially since she had the distinct feeling he'd come after her.

Staying would be worse, because once he knew, Leese would insist on confronting the trouble instead of running from it.

Unfortunately, it was a fight he couldn't win.

And she'd just brought herself full circle.

Honesty now was her only option. Maybe, though, she should try confessing to Sahara first. That indomitable woman might find an alternative that eluded Cat.

Knowing Enoch would be back any minute with the pastries, she decided to hurry Leese along. She wanted him to see the kitchen all spiffed up before she got it messy with crumbs.

She started down the hall and a noise at the door made her pause.

Not the intercom, and not a knock. Curious, she looked toward the door, listening.

The doorknob moved.

Instincts rioted but, undecided, she took one step toward the door. It was probably Enoch, probably fine.

She was still safe.

No.

No, she wouldn't take that chance. Not with Leese in the shower, naked, unprepared...

With fear steadily building, she back-stepped, one foot behind the other, until the door started to open. Alarm bells clanged in her brain and, breathless, she turned to run silently for the bedroom. Her sock-covered feet didn't make a sound, and she didn't call out.

Timing was everything, she knew that.

She needed a weapon, and she needed to alert Leese.

Slipping into the bedroom and slowly closing the door, trying to lock it without the ridiculously loud click, she secured them the best she could. Next she dived for the nightstand and her gun.

Thank God she kept it fully loaded.

In a few long strides, she opened the bathroom door, strode to the shower and turned off the water.

Leese took one look at her face, then at the gun she held, and without a sound he comprehended it all. Wasting no time, he stepped out of the shower. Bypassing the towel, he grabbed her arm and drew her back into the bedroom, pushing her down beside the bed to keep her concealed. As hushed whispers came down the hall, he snatched his own gun off the nightstand, but also his cell.

Sliding his thumb across the screen, he unlocked it, pressed a button and handed it to her. With a finger to his mouth, he warned her to silence.

Cat saw that the phone was dialing, but who? The building was all but empty. Even Enoch was off buying treats.

Crouched there on the floor, her heart in her throat, Cat set the phone aside and braced her gun over the bed.

She was as ready as she could be, but the dreaded moment—a moment she'd prepared for the best she could—rattled her even more than she'd ever expected.

When Leese shifted, her gaze went to him. Naked, water trickling down his powerful body, he seemed rock-steady, determined to defend her against unknown threats.

Dear God, have I waited too long to tell him everything?

Giving her a silent order, he pressed down on her head, wanting her to stay entirely hidden, then he moved around the bed and silently positioned himself behind the door. Unlike her, he held the gun only in his right hand, lowered to his side with the barrel aimed at the floor.

He didn't look at her again, but she couldn't pull her gaze from him.

Hurting in her heart, Cat prayed they'd make it through this.

Someone tried the doorknob, and when it didn't open, a laugh sounded.

"You can lock the door, girl, but we're coming in anyway."

Both she and Leese stayed silent, her shaking with fear, him loose and prepared as the door exploded, kicked open with a lot of force.

Cat got one look at a big man, grinning with sick delight as he stepped into the room…

Then with double the force, Leese kicked the door back into his face. Blood spurted from his crushed nose, and the man staggered until he hit the hallway wall hard and slumped to the floor.

Barking a foul curse, a second man lifted his gun. Leese caught his wrist quickly, and keeping the man's gun aimed at the ceiling, jerked him into the room and against the door to close it. The guy fired off several shots before Leese snapped his wrist and the gun fell.

The noise was deafening—gunshots, shouts of pain, the cracking of bone.

Leese didn't stop with mangling the man's arm. He punched him hard in the throat, kneed him in the groin, then kicked his knee. The man's leg buckled backward and he went down, his face blue, his eyes bulging, his body distorted.

No longer a threat.

The gruesome damage made Cat's stomach pitch. So much violence, happening so quickly and effortlessly on Leese's part. She couldn't think, could barely breathe past the noise and motion and the fear, so much thick, consuming fear.

Her heart punched frantically with the need to somehow help, but at the same time, she saw him handling things with frightening efficiency.

He'd completely disabled the first man without firing a single shot—but not in enough time to completely protect himself.

The man with the smashed nose dived back into the room, already firing his gun before he'd landed. The shot hit Leese in the side, knocking him back, and Cat watched in horror as blood splattered on the wall, bloomed from the wound and snaked down his side.

The cry of outrage strangled in her throat. She didn't recall standing, didn't realize that she'd taken aim until she fired.

Not once, not twice, but over and over. Driven by pure reaction, she squeezed the trigger until she ran out of bullets and heard only empty clicks.

"Cat, it's okay." Leese's hand, warm and firm, curled around her wrist. "He's done. Let up now."

She stared ahead, seeing the carnage, the motionless bodies of the men who'd attacked. So much blood, so many bullet holes…

"Baby, it's okay."

She sucked in air on a sob. "I killed him?"

"No. You shot him in the shoulder and then I took him out. The rest of the bullets hit the wall."

She took in the scene before her. Bullet holes, all over. Dear God, she was a lousy aim. "I could have hit you!"

"But you didn't. You helped me."

Terror receded enough for her to see Leese, really see him—standing tall, hurt but not hindered. With his gun hand, he pressed a T-shirt to his side. With the other he again pushed her to sit, then gently cupped her chin.

"I need you to stay down, babe. Don't move. I'll be right back."

What? "Wait!"

"Not now, Cat." With one hard look, he repeated, "Stay down." The order given, he retrieved something from the nightstand, then went back to the downed men. While constantly searching out the now-broken door, he disarmed them both, tossing multiple weapons onto the bed. He checked each for a pulse, bound their hands and feet together, then glanced back at her and reiterated, "Do. Not. Move."

Numb, Cat nodded.

He stepped over the men and disappeared into the hall.

Oh my God. Alert, terrified, she listened but couldn't hear a thing. Thirty seconds aged her like thirty years as she stared at that door, aware of the unmoving men, the smell of gunfire still in the air, the proof of her own incompetence before her.

She badly wanted to trail Leese, but she didn't want to get in his way. Staying silent, her fingers in a white-knuckled grip on the bedding, she waited in agony until he stepped back in.

The blood now darkened his hip and much of a thigh, making her throat close up in horror.

"I think it's clear. I relocked the front door. No one else is in the penthouse." He strode back to her and urged her toward the bathroom. "Stay there." He retrieved the phone. "Sahara?"

So that's who he'd called?

Her knees went weak and she sank to the floor.

Leese said, "Shit," only a second before she heard the new commotion.

Renewed fear didn't have a chance to take hold before she heard Sahara shout, "Leese? Answer me, damn you!"

Thank God. She put her head on her knees.

"We're okay," he called out. "Two men down. Check the building for any others."

Bleeding, but still issuing orders. God almighty, he was an impressive man.

Cat tried to fill her lungs and retched instead.

"Hey." Coming to his knees beside her, Leese stroked her head. "You did great, honey."

She gave a shaky, half-sick laugh.

Justice made it into the room first, Sahara behind him. Their gazes went everywhere, skimmed over the now stirring men, then zeroed in on Leese, naked and bleeding.

"Do I wanna know?" Justice asked.

Sahara just raised a brow.

Grabbing for a towel, Leese explained, "I was showering when they got in." He wrapped it around himself. "No time to get dressed."

With a confusing lack of alarm, Justice asked, "You got hit?"

"A flesh wound." Disgusted, Leese said, "I'll be fine, but I don't know about those two. Did you send men to search the rest of the agency? There could be others."

"She did." Justice nudged Sahara with an elbow, and almost knocked her off her heels. "I haven't seen her shook up before, but taking that call from you, she was squealing like a little girl ready to burst into tears and—"

"You're bleeding a lot," Sahara interrupted.

That snapped Cat out of her trauma. She looked at Leese's side, just above his hip bone, and saw the awful damage done to his flesh. The bullet appeared to have torn across him, leaving a three-inch-long furrow, blackened around the edges, constantly oozing blood. Already his skin started to bruise.

"Oh my God, Leese," she whispered. "You were *shot*."

"Grazed," Leese corrected. He looked at his side and said, "It's not deep."

Not deep? "Are you nuts?" Finally having a purpose, Cat grabbed more towels and a wet washcloth, then hurried back to him. Leese tried to take a towel from her, but she didn't let him. "I need to see—"

Justice stilled her hand. "Let me, okay?"

"Why you?" she snapped, on the ragged edge.

"Well, for starters, I'm not shaking. And I'm used to seeing blood since fighters get hurt all the time. Odds are I've had more experience than you."

Dubious, Cat asked, "With gunshot wounds?"

"Well, no…" Justice eased the cloth away from her and began cleaning the blood. "But I've seen broken bones, dislocated joints, head wounds that bled like a mother, split lips and brows, gouged eyes—"

Cat backed up. "Fine. You do it."

After flashing her a smile, he said to Leese, "Sit down, will you?"

"I don't want to ruin the bed."

Cat was about to scream when Sahara said, "The other men will report to me if they find anything. Sit, cooperate. Please."

Compromising, Leese propped a shoulder against the wall and, watching Justice work, asked Sahara, "How did they get in?"

To Cat's critical eye, Leese looked merely curious, not in a lot of pain. Then she saw him wince and tears rushed to her eyes.

He could have been killed—*and it would have been my fault*.

"Troy, the elevator guard on duty this morning, is missing." Sahara rubbed her forehead and stepped cautiously around the fallen men. "Given the mess here, I'm worried about him."

Cat put a hand to her heart. Two broken bodies on the floor, a guard missing, Leese shot. *What have I done?*

"You need stitches," Justice decided. "Not many, but enough to close it. Looks like the bullet sliced a chunk out of you. Not that deep, though I'm sure it burns like a son of a bitch."

Leese ignored him to ask, "How many men do you have with you?"

"Just two," Justice said, "but others on the way."

"You call the cops yet?"

Sahara leveled a meaningful look on the unconscious intruders. "I wanted to talk to you first, given we have many things we're currently keeping from the cops."

He nodded.

"When you call them," Justice said, "have 'em bring an ambulance for nature boy here." He thwacked Leese on the bare shoulder.

Leese shrugged him off. "Cops, yes, but no ambulance. I can drive myself."

Sahara's cell beeped, making Cat jerk. Only Leese seemed to notice as he watched her with concern.

Sahara answered with alacrity, turning her back to them to speak quietly. When her shoulders relaxed, something also loosened in Cat's chest.

"Troy is okay?" she asked hopefully. Cat didn't know him, but she couldn't bear the thought of anyone else being hurt because of her.

As Sahara ended the call, she turned with excitement. "They found him. Knocked in the head, shot in the shoulder and stuffed in a closet, but he's alive and it appears he'll recover." She pointed her phone at Leese. "The ambulance has already been called, so please don't be difficult. As Justice so rudely pointed out, it's been a trying morning for me."

Skipping past all that, Leese frowned. "So they attacked the guard to get on the elevator. That doesn't explain how they got into the penthouse. The door was locked, I know, because I saw to it myself after Enoch—"

Horror made Cat cry out. She covered her mouth, but only long enough for the pieces to come together. "They had keys. I heard them at the door and at first I thought it might be Enoch, but he always knocks and they didn't. They unlocked the door and they came right in. Enoch—"

"Enoch," Sahara repeated, back on her phone.

Everyone waited...while the phone rang and rang, without an answer.

TESH WATCHED THE commotion at the agency, and knew his men had fucked up. Worthless imbeciles. He hoped they were dead. That would be preferable to them being held, possibly being coerced to talk.

Not that it would do them any good.

When Enoch's phone rang, Tesh accepted that things had gone very wrong. No doubt it was Sahara or one of her underlings calling to check on Enoch. Any second now they'd begin a search, going to the bakery, looking on the street when they couldn't find Enoch inside.

Finally the ringing stopped. Enoch hadn't moved,

but his eyes, now bruised and bloodshot, badly swollen, stared at Tesh with crushing fear.

Such a nuisance.

"No witnesses," he muttered, grabbing Enoch by the throat, squeezing hard with both hands. Against the feeble struggles, Tesh watched him gag and gasp, until finally he went limp and his eyes rolled up…completely blank.

Leaving the huddled, lifeless lump splayed awkwardly in the backseat, Tesh stepped out of the car and started walking. Head down, hands in his pockets, he trudged on for a few blocks, then made his call.

He'd be picked up in ten minutes. The car and the body would be disposed of.

No one would ever peg this on him.

He'd remain free and next time he'd get Catalina for sure. When he did, he'd make her pay for putting him through so much trouble.

CHAPTER FIFTEEN

IT WAS THE screeching of a siren that roused Enoch. When he shifted, sharp pain stabbed into every inch of his body. His throat hurt so badly he couldn't swallow. The blackness called to him again, but around the edges of consuming agony, reality wormed in.

He got one eye open and through a blurry haze he saw...no one. Taking only shallow breaths, he listened, but all he could hear was the noise outside the car, not a peep within it.

He'd never been hurt before, and now he knew it was terrible. Throbbing torment pulled at him, making him want to pass out, but he pushed himself upward.

Sahara depended on him. Catalina was a target.

I have to move.

If he stayed in the car, people might die. *He* would die. He knew it.

Hell, he'd already thought himself a goner.

Were the others okay?

Pain, humiliation and regret turned his stomach, but he didn't dare vomit. He could only imagine the added discomfort that would bring.

He'd been incompetent, ineffectual. But he wasn't an agent, and he definitely wasn't a fighter. His value was in being the very best and most attentive assistant.

With extreme effort, he crawled off the floor and

onto the seat. When he tried to open the door, he realized he had a broken finger or two. Biting back the automatic groan, he struggled and finally the door opened, spilling him out.

The fall sharpened every ache, but he slowly breathed in the crisp, cold air and resisted the urge to call out.

Given the strain of his throat, he didn't think he could anyway.

He used the open door of the car to help him gain his feet.

Gingerly, trying not to disturb his oddly bent fingers, he withdrew his cell and fumbled until he could press in Sahara's number.

She answered immediately. "Enoch?" Voice shaky and anxious, sounding suspiciously like tears, she asked, "Where are you? Are you okay?"

No, definitely not okay. Swallowing hurt so bad. But he had to tell her. Ahead of him he could see a crowd forming, an ambulance, police.

But would he reach them?

At any second that awful man or one of his goons could return.

Enoch tried to speak, but nothing came out.

"Enoch! Please, *please* answer me."

Hearing the upset, knowing his brave, vibrant Sahara was near to losing it, he tried again, and finally, in the faintest, raspiest of whispers, he managed to say, "Outside."

"I'm on my way, Enoch!"

It seemed only seconds passed before Sahara and Justice burst through the entrance, their gazes wildly searching. When they spotted him, Justice rushed to him, Sahara doing her best to keep up in her heels in the snow.

If his mouth hadn't been so grotesquely swollen, Enoch thought he might have smiled.

"Easy now." Being a regular muscled behemoth, Justice scooped him up as if he weighed nothing. Heading back for the agency, he said, "I got ya. You just relax, my friend."

Sahara, her eyes swimming with tears, met them on the way. "Oh, Enoch, thank God." She sniffled, looked him over with something akin to horror, and the tearful expression turned to rage. "Someone will pay dearly for this, I promise you that. Do you understand, Enoch? I will make him—"

Her voice faded, his vision narrowed and he lost consciousness knowing he was safe.

SITTING ON THE side of the hospital table, Leese watched Cat as she watched the doctor stitching him. Five stitches total. Justice was either off by a little, or this doctor liked tiny sutures. Thanks to a numbing shot Leese couldn't feel the piercing of the needle, but his side hurt as if he'd taken a kick from a heavyweight.

He could see Cat holding herself tightly, watched as she repeatedly chewed her bottom lip and squeezed her hands together. He thought of how close he'd come to losing her and he, too, tensed from head to toe.

The doctor gave him an impersonal glance. "You're okay?"

"I'm fine."

Never again. Today, the second they were alone, Cat would tell him everything. No more guessing, no more fear, no more keeping secrets.

Definitely no more running.

When he heard a commotion in the hallway, he braced himself, but a second later Justice stuck his head around the curtain. "Hey, thought you should know, everyone's come to visit."

"Everyone?" Cat asked, alarm making her breath come faster.

"Friends," Justice clarified. "Nothing scary 'bout it."

Miles poked his head around the curtain too. He smiled at Cat first, then said to Leese, "Justice called, whimpering, saying you were all but slain and so everyone piled into a car and here we are, just to make sure you don't need a lollipop or anything."

Leese let out a long, aggrieved huff. "I'm fine." And he was damned tired of saying so.

Looking at her, Miles said, "I think Cat disagrees."

She whispered, "He was *shot*."

Miles strode on in and put a hand on her shoulder. "Yeah, hon, I know. But not with a cannonball or anything, right?"

While Leese appreciated the support, he needed time alone with Cat. Entertaining the masses, putting up with the good-natured ribbing sure to come, would keep him from clearing the air with her.

The doctor finished up with a bandage and stood. As if he dealt with gunshot wounds all the time, he rattled off instructions and, eyeing Miles and Justice, wished them all a good day.

The guys hung around while Leese pulled on a fresh shirt, wincing only a little in discomfort. "Where's everyone waiting?"

Justice grinned. "Some pretty little nurse hustled them off to the waiting room just around the corner."

"You can hear the muted roar," Miles said.

"And Sahara?"

"She's with Enoch." Looking pissed all over again, Justice said, "They moved him to a room."

"How is he? And how's Troy?"

"Troy is bandaged up and ready to go. He'll be in a sling and off work for a while. Sucks, I know. He already looks bored."

"Did he tell you what happened?"

"Yeah. The goons had Enoch's briefcase, claimed he'd been hit by a car. When Troy went to check on him, they tangled. He got shot, but kept going, so the second bastard hit him in the head, knocking him out. He came to tied up and stuffed in the closet."

"Damn," Leese said, frowning in sympathy. "And Enoch?"

Justice shook his head. "He hides it, but he's tough as nails, no way 'round it. He was strangled bad. His eyes are bloodred."

"Subconjunctiva hemorrhaging," Miles said.

They'd seen it before in a fight gone wrong.

"Dude's neck is bruised real bad, and it looks like he took a real ass-whoopin' before that."

Fuck. Just…fuck. "Was he able to tell you anything?"

Justice tugged at an ear. "Poor guy can barely whisper. Last I saw, he was trying to write some stuff out for Sahara, but the pricks broke a few of his fingers too, so—"

Rocking, her arms wrapped around herself, Cat said, "This is all my fault. They were hurt because of me."

Before Leese could speak, Justice did.

"Bullshit. That's just stupid talk and I'm betting Leese will tell you so."

She looked up with big tearful eyes. "They wanted me."

"Yeah, but that ain't the point." Folding his arms over his chest, Justice glared at her. "Whoever worked over Enoch is a chickenshit coward. Hell, Enoch's not much bigger than you, and you're an itty-bitty thing."

She blinked up at Justice. "I don't see—"

"You're not a coward. Just the opposite from what I can tell. So don't piss me off by comparing yourself to them."

Shaking her head in confusion, she said, "I didn't—"

Miles asked, "Should I be hearing any of this?"

"Probably not." Leese took Cat's arm and drew her from the chair. "Justice is right, but we'll work all that out later. Right now you need to meet everyone, and then I want to get you someplace safe." Where he could hash it out with her. She needed to completely trust him. Nothing less would do. Not anymore.

With a lame cough, Justice said, "Those other two? They're in comas."

Frustrated anger boiled inside Leese. "You're fucking with me. *Both* of them?" He needed one of them alert enough to answer questions.

"'Fraid so." Justice glanced at Miles, shrugged and spilled his guts. "You crushed the bones in the one guy's arm. It's pretty fucked. But I'm guessing you kicked him in the head too?"

"After he shot me."

"Well, he's out and who knows if he's going to come around?"

Fascinated, Miles looked from one to the other as he listened.

"The other one has some serious damage to his windpipe. They stuck a tube down his throat so he could breathe and they're keeping him out on purpose."

"Son of a bitch." Leese felt grim, but after all the violence, resolve coursed through his veins. "The penthouse is a crime scene so we can't go back there."

"Sahara said she's moving you both to her place. It's a huge house. Plenty of privacy."

Leese stared at him, distracted. "How do you know what her house looks like?"

Tugging at his ear, Justice admitted, "I just spent a few days there myself. Got snowed in."

No way. "You stayed with Sahara?" Huh. Hadn't seen that one coming. "For days?"

Pointing at him, Justice growled, "Get that thought outta your head right now!"

"What thought?" Leese asked, just to make him squirm.

"Stow the innocent act. You know what you're thinking, so don't bother denying it. But it's not like that. The lady scares me, and besides, there ain't a single speck of chemistry between us."

"Amen," Sahara said as she breezed in.

Justice went comically rigid, his gaze frozen forward.

That didn't stop Sahara from hugging one of his arms. "Justice was a complete gentleman, his presence made me feel safer and I appreciate him as a valued employee. Period." Her attention settled on Miles, and she went into assessment mode. "Hello."

Wearing the smallest of smiles, Miles said, "Hey, yourself."

Hoping to hurry things along, Leese did introductions. "Miles, meet Sahara Silver, owner of the agency. Sahara, Miles Dartman, a friend."

"My," she whispered, her gaze going all over him. "A fighter?"

"Yes, ma'am."

Justice tried to subtly shake her off, but she didn't let go. He glared down at her. "I don't want to be a party to your flirting."

Sahara hugged him again, then said to Leese, "We need to talk. Do you suppose these two could keep Catalina company for just a minute?"

Miles and Justice both agreed, but Leese said an emphatic, "No. She's not leaving my sight. Not here."

"Very well." Sahara turned to the guys. "If you'd both excuse us?"

"I'm waitin' right out here," Justice warned, then, while avoiding Sahara's gaze, he explained, "I'm sort of her protection for now."

"Interesting." Miles followed Justice, saying, "Guess I'll wait with him."

"So gallant," Sahara enthused, but the second they were gone, she closed the space to stand very near to Leese. "Those bastards hurt Enoch bad. He has two broken ribs, broken fingers, a concussion and he was nearly strangled to death. His throat is going to need time to heal. He wasn't able to say much, and writing is difficult, but he did manage this." She pulled a folded sheet of paper from her pocket and smoothed it out.

Keeping Cat close, Leese read the broken scrawl. *They wanted Cat. Would kill to get her.*

Cat drew in a deep breath. "I'm so sorry. I thought I was protecting you—"

"By keeping us in the dark?" Leese knew he sounded

harsh and didn't care. The rage continued to simmer. She'd come so close to being hurt, to being taken by the very men who'd brutally savaged Enoch.

She'd risked that, rather than confide in him.

"Yes," she admitted softly. "By keeping you in the dark." Eyes pleading, she carefully hugged him. "Sometimes the truth is more dangerous than not knowing."

His jaw flexed, but he put his arms around her and relished the fact that she was here, with him, unharmed and still relatively safe.

"If we can cease with self-recrimination, please, we have things to discuss." Sahara kept her voice low. "Tesh stopped Justice and me in the parking lot right before the big storm hit."

More fed up by the second, Leese waited.

"There's been no way to tell you everything, but I may have a plan."

Yeah, Leese had a plan too: go after the people causing all the problems and end it once and for all.

As if she knew his thoughts, Cat said, "Please, Leese. *Please* don't do anything crazy."

Crazy? Loving her was crazy, but no way could he stop. The close call made him realize that he wanted to spend the rest of his life with her, and he'd do whatever was necessary to ensure her protection.

Her gaze moved over his face, and she sighed. "That's why I couldn't tell you. I knew you'd want to confront them, but you *can't*." She hugged him again. "Not for me."

"It's no longer just you, is it, honey? The bastards shot at *me*. They attacked Troy, they strangled Enoch. Odds are they meant for all of us to die."

"All," Sahara said, "except for her."

Because they had something worse than death in store for Cat.

"We can't get into all that here," Sahara said in a low voice. "We need to find someplace more private. For now, I'm going to stay with Enoch. I'm arranging for two guards to watch over him throughout the night. Two others will relieve them in the morning." Her hands curled into fists. "He won't be left alone."

Cat visibly shored up her courage. "Before either of you do anything, you need to know. It's not just my stepfather behind this."

Because he already knew that, Leese demanded, "Give me a name."

With a fatalistic nod and a lot of dread, she whispered, "Senator Platt."

LEESE FELT SICK. Cat had one of the most powerful political figures in modern history after her? He wanted to believe she'd misunderstood, but given everything that had happened, he didn't think so.

Senator Platt had a reputation for being benevolent, kind and caring, one of the few good men left in politics. His constituents adored him. The elderly revered him. He championed the poor and visited the troops and did every fucking thing a politician should do to win over the masses.

All of it a ruse?

He was absolutely wealthy enough, certainly had enough influence to buy silence when needed. Had the aging senator visited Désir Island?

Had the miserable bastard raped and then murdered a young girl?

Both Sahara and Cat had stayed silent while he

led them down the hall to the room where his friends waited. Without asking any questions, Justice and Miles kept pace with them. Luckily the fighters were the only ones inside.

Leese stepped in, and before anyone else could speak, he said, "I need a minute of ensured privacy."

The guys all looked at each other, then at Sahara and Cat, and they stood.

"Three minutes, tops," Armie Jacobson said as he walked past. "My curiosity won't hold any longer than that."

As they exited the room, Cannon, Stack and Denver each had something to say, Cannon with concern, Stack ribbing him about *two* women, and Denver saying, "'Bout time, man."

Sahara, still stunned by Cat's disclosure, stared at the departing fighters with a mix of awe, appreciation and calculation.

Once they were alone with the door closed and barred by fighters, Sahara turned to Leese.

She opened her mouth twice before she managed to get out any words. "We'll talk about your friends later."

Leese didn't want to talk about them at all. "I figure the senator is a priority."

"Yes." Hand to her head, Sahara murmured, "I never imagined…but I suppose it makes sense."

Ah, so Sahara had taken the same road to logic that Leese had? "Proving it will be tough." But he refused to believe it would be impossible. He looked at Cat's pale face, stiff with a mask of control. "Tesh works for him?"

"For as long as I've known him." She glanced away while admitting, "I met the senator when I met Tesh, when I was eighteen. I've seen Tesh without Platt, but not the other way around. Far as I can tell the senator doesn't go anywhere without Tesh."

"So," Sahara surmised, "Tesh is working under the senator's orders."

"I assume so." Cat made a point of not looking at Leese. "Tesh is the one who 'took care' of Georgia for the senator. I heard him say so. When he spoke with Webb that day at the boathouse, he explained that both he and Tesh needed an alibi, because Tesh had, very necessarily, 'disposed of the girl.' Protecting Tesh, Platt said, was also protecting him, and he promised Webb he wouldn't forget his loyalty." Her chest expanded on a slow breath, and on the exhale she whispered, "That's when Webb agreed."

Leese didn't like how distant Cat felt, as if she'd already emotionally left him. "You should have told me all this immediately."

Cat paid no attention to the reprimand, keeping her gaze somewhere in the distance. "Tesh always scared me, but the senator seemed so nice. Almost like a grandpa. I never, ever would have guessed if I hadn't heard him myself. The things he said and how he said them… He was a different man than the one you see on television, definitely different from the man who offered to let me visit his stables." She swallowed hard. "I know he's awful, but still, Tesh is the scariest."

Leese caught her arm and drew her around to face him. "Platt wanted you to come to his house?" Had she been alone with the monster?

"He invited me often, and you know, I wanted to go. I wanted to see the horses, maybe ride, draw the grounds…" Her gaze, so lost, lifted to his. "Webb always refused. He was adamant that I not visit Platt, ever."

The knot of rage loosened in Leese's chest. "At least your stepfather showed some common sense."

"I wonder," Sahara mused. "Perhaps Webb always knew the caliber of Platt's character. It's possible he knew what would happen to Cat if the senator got her alone."

"Then he should have stayed away from the man," Leese insisted.

"Yes. But I wonder if he's caught up in something he can't control."

Leese didn't like the direction of her thoughts. Sahara certainly knew more about the vagaries of the wealthy than he'd ever know, but not for a second would he dismiss Webb's involvement with the senator. "You think he protected her then, but was willing to sacrifice her now?"

Sahara considered it. "I think it's worth putting more thought into this." She brightened as she took Cat's shoulders. "Please don't look so anguished. We will figure this out, I'm sure of it. In the meantime, with the police now investigating—" she made air quotes "—the 'break in,' it'll be riskier for Platt or Tesh to try anything. Hopefully that'll buy us enough time to set my plan in motion."

"What plan?" Leese asked.

Cat took in his expression with a lot of remorse. "There's only one thing for me to do."

"Hand yourself over to Platt," Sahara agreed.

Leese jerked his head around to stare at Sahara. "What the hell?"

She merely smiled.

"No." He'd die before he let that happen.

"It is the only way." Cat did her utmost to look stoic. "Once he has me—"

"Fuck that," Leese growled, his voice deepening with his outrage. "Not happening."

Through the waiting room window, the fighters turned to stare curiously.

"Of course not." Sahara shushed him. "But I have a plan that involves making him *think* he's getting Cat, while we set a trap."

Cat took a step back. "But—"

"No buts," Leese said. "You're not getting anywhere near Tesh or Platt." He glared at Sahara. "I won't have Cat in danger."

Cat blinked at him. "I've been in danger for a while now. Most of all, I just want it to end before anyone else gets hurt."

Hating the entire situation, Leese tangled a hand in his hair. He couldn't control things and it enraged him. Somehow, some way, he needed to remove Tesh and a beloved senator forever from Cat's life.

But how?

Sahara gave him a long-suffering look. "Both of you, stop being so grim. You know you can trust me, and you know I'm good at what I do. I need to go see Enoch now, but I'll talk to you both when I get home." She handed Leese a key. "Justice can tell you where I live."

Leese caught her hand before she could turn away. "You need to be careful too, Sahara."

She cocked her head. "I would tell you that careful is my middle name—" her expression hardened "—but actually it's vengeance."

ONCE THEY WERE alone together, Cat completely withdrew. She strode to the windows and looked out at the parking lot, her shoulders drooped, her posture weary and defeated. "I'm so sorry."

Knowing his friends wouldn't wait much longer, Leese needed to put his anger on the back burner for now. But first, they needed to come to an understanding. "No more secrets, Cat."

She nodded.

"Say it. Swear to me that you won't ever again keep anything this important from me."

She turned to him, her face ravaged with guilt. "Will you also promise not to put yourself at unnecessary risk?" She took two quick steps toward him. "Please, Leese. I can't bear the thought of you being hurt."

The necessity of risk was a subjective thing. Since he considered her safety very necessary, he easily agreed. "All right."

That answer stole some of the shadows from her eyes. "Thank you."

Tunneling his fingers into her hair, Leese held her head and pressed a kiss to her brow. "No more lies of omission, no secrets and don't even think about some stupid sacrifice."

That stiffened her up a little.

Good. He'd take her irritation over misery any day. "I've told you from the beginning, honey, if you run, I'll come after you. That hasn't changed. Keep it in mind for any half-baked plans you might come up with. If you face Tesh or Platt, I'll be facing them with you."

With new alarm, she gasped, "No—"

And Leese stole away the protest by kissing her.

Not a quick, easy peck. No, that wouldn't do. He took

her mouth in a devouring possession so hot, it obliterated the pain in his side.

"Get a room, already."

Leese pulled away and found Armie grinning at him.

"Hard to believe you were wounded." Armie tipped his head, looking at him critically. "Gunshot, Justice said?"

"Sloppy," Stack accused. "You sure you shouldn't return to fighting?"

"He'll have a badass scar now," Armie pointed out, then gestured at Cat. "Clearly, the ladies love that macho shit."

How had he forgotten that they were all here?

Behind those two, Denver, Cannon, Miles and Justice pushed into the room.

Cat stared at the group, her expression boggled. "Wow, that's a lot of big men."

Armie stepped forward. "Armie Jacobson, friend of Leese. It's nice to meet you."

"I told him you'd bring her to us, but he didn't want to wait," Stack explained. He held out a hand. "Stack Hannigan. Also Leese's friend."

She tried a silly smile. "Hello." And then to Leese, she said, "You fighters sure are big and buff."

Leese looped an arm around her shoulders, and with his other hand he pointed out each friend, giving Cat their names and allowing each man to make some outrageous remark to her.

Cannon said, "Good catch, Leese."

"I agree with Miles—she's too cute for you," Stack said.

Denver looked her over and announced, "No similarities. That's a good thing."

Confused, Cat blinked. "Um…similarities?"

"To my wife." Denver smiled. "Total opposite, in fact."

Cat looked to Leese for an explanation.

Put on the spot, he rubbed the back of his neck. "You remember that situation I told you about? The girl who had some trouble? Denver is her husband."

Cat's eyes widened with understanding. "Ah," she said, looking at Denver again, this time with a sly smile. "The foot-dragger."

Armie choked on a laugh. "Nailed it! In fact, he dragged those big feet so damn long, he almost lost her."

Cannon slowly pivoted to stare at Armie. "Seriously, *you* are going to accuse anyone of being slow? That's a laugh."

"Brand would have been here," Armie said, doing his utmost to change the topic. "But he's fighting soon and caught up in promo."

"Lucky for you," Stack said to Leese, "since Brand is still single." While bobbing his eyebrows, he grinned at Cat.

And on and on it went with the good-natured heckling.

The upside was that Cat couldn't dwell on problems when the guys kept teasing her, giving her extravagant compliments and doing a hell of a job distracting her.

While Denver entertained her with stories of his wife, Leese got drawn aside by Miles and Justice.

"When you leave," Miles said, "we're going to follow. Justice already gave us the address and it can't hurt to have a little backup just to ensure you get there without being hijacked."

With Cat's safety at stake, Leese didn't object. "Thanks. Appreciate it. Just be sure to be invisible, okay?"

"Definitely. I don't think a parade would help to keep you off the radar."

Justice explained how to get to Sahara's using an alternate route that was a little out of the way, which made it a better, less risky choice.

After half an hour, Leese checked the time. "I want to visit with Enoch before we go."

As far as hints went, it failed, because everyone decided to join him.

"We'll just peek in," Cannon said. "I want to thank the guy who tried to save your hide."

Leaving Cat with the group just outside Enoch's room, Leese tapped softly on the door and stepped in. Enoch was awake, and yeah, someone had bludgeoned him pretty badly. One side of his face was a mess, swollen and discolored. That eye was completely closed.

Leese had seen plenty of shiners before, cuts from a perfectly placed elbow, bruises from a hard kick, but this was something altogether different.

Through one barely opened eye, Enoch looked at him. He tried to smile, but the swelling in his face and mouth didn't make it possible.

"Damn," Leese said softly, turbulent with a mix of rage and pity.

Sahara stood from her bedside vigil. "I owe him a year's pay for this."

Enoch protested with a small shake of his head and somehow, even with the abuse making expressions nearly impossible, he looked ashamed.

Leese saw it, and it killed him. He'd been there, felt

shame for what he hadn't done, what he hadn't been able to do.

Enoch had no reason to feel that way.

"He's too proud," Sahara said, handing Leese another paper. "And he blames himself when he absolutely shouldn't."

Leese glanced at the scratchy, nearly illegible writing that partially explained Enoch's ordeal.

Wanted to know if Cat was inside. Didn't tell him but he found her picture in my case. Sorry. So sorry.

Approaching the bed, Leese looked down at Enoch. "I don't have Sahara's cash flow, but I know there's not enough money in the world for me to repay you."

Again, Enoch tried to shake his head.

Sahara whispered, "He thinks he failed."

"No," Leese insisted. "You stalled them and that gave us the edge we needed. Cat was there, by the door, and heard them coming in, so she was able to get me from the shower. If they'd come even a minute sooner, she'd have been washing dishes and wouldn't have known what was happening until it was too late. They might have killed me in the shower, or else I would have come out with no idea where they'd taken her."

Enoch slowly closed his least injured eye, then gave a small, accepting nod of gratitude.

Leese put a hand on his shoulder. "We're alive because you're a badass, Enoch. You have my respect for life." Then, grinning, Leese said, "And I hope you don't mind, but a few of my friends, MMA fighters, want to thank you too. Are you up for that? I promise they won't stay long."

Enoch's eye managed to widen, and he gave a single, uncertain nod.

One by one they filed in. Leese noticed that Denver had tucked Cat under one massive arm, while Justice flanked her on the other side.

They were all big men, but those two were behemoths. Between them, Cat looked even more petite.

She also looked a little shell-shocked.

"I like her," Armie told him. "She's funny as hell."

Yeah, Cat did have a sharp wit, usually carved from honesty. He could only imagine what she might have said.

Enoch went stock-still, very watchful, as the guys took turns assessing his injuries. Surrounding his bed, their voices low with concern, firm with appreciation, they shared fight stories and compared injuries.

"I thought I had the biggest of all goose eggs when I got kicked in the forehead," Stack said, "but damn, Enoch, you have me beat with that beauty."

"If it swells another inch," Denver added, "he could pass for a beat-up unicorn."

"Remember in *Rocky*, when his eye was like that?" Miles asked.

"Cut me, Mick," Cannon said in his best Stallone voice. "Enoch's is better than Rocky's though."

"The ladies are going to be so sympathetic," Armie added. "I almost envy you, dude. I bet you get smothered in the best kind of TLC."

They continued with the congenial joking until Enoch relaxed, and damn, he even managed a half-baked, crooked smile every so often. When he reached for the paper, Sahara quickly brought it to him.

Feel like a star, he wrote. *Thanks.*

They all laughed.

Minutes later he was given his pain meds and quietly faded to sleep.

With everyone crowded into the private hospital room, Sahara preened, flirted and did impromptu interviews in case she could sway any of them away from fighting.

To Leese's surprise, Miles had questions for her. He didn't commit to anything, but he definitely showed keen interest.

Apparently the danger surrounding Cat was a lure, drawing him in. Hell, each one of the fighters wanted to get involved.

They were protective that way.

"I'm thinking we should stick around," Cannon told him, his voice low in deference to Enoch. "Just in case."

No surprise there. Cannon and the others ran a neighborhood watch back in Warfield, Ohio. "Somehow," Leese said, "I think your wife would protest that."

"Yvette would understand."

Probably. She was every bit as caring as Cannon. Leese drew him aside to talk privately. "I appreciate it, but I'm thinking the best way to go is with a low profile."

Cannon studied him, then shook his head. "You don't want us drawn into the danger."

"There is that." The last thing Leese wanted to do was give Platt or Tesh more targets. "Sahara has some reach. I think—" *pray* "—it's under control."

Accepting that, Cannon said, "Keep me posted, then. And if you change your mind, know that we're around."

"Thanks."

Denver joined them, gave Leese a close scrutiny and smiled. "You're in love with her."

Was it really so obvious? Leese looked across the room to where Cat listened while Armie spoke to her, likely saying something outrageous since Armie didn't know any other way.

She smiled, leaned close to reply and Armie pretended to stagger with weak legs. Miles grinned beside him and Stack smirked, holding Armie upright.

Whatever she'd just said had amused his friends, meaning as usual, Cat held her own.

She'd been through hell, was living in it now and still she charmed everyone around her. She kept her chin up, optimism firmly in place.

She wanted to sacrifice herself to keep him and Sahara safe.

"Yeah. I love her." How could he do anything else?

CHAPTER SIXTEEN

BY THE TIME they reached Sahara's house, it was nearing bedtime. They hadn't eaten since breakfast. Cat felt her stomach rumbling, but didn't want to grumble.

It was Leese who'd been wounded, and he didn't complain. He just stayed grim, his thoughts contained.

His anger still palpable.

She wanted to say something to him, but what?

He had to be just as tired and hungry as her, and though she'd never been shot, she assumed a bullet wound—even a searing graze—had to be sore.

Too many hours had been spent talking to the police, waiting while Leese was stitched, visiting with his friends and coordinating with Sahara.

Keeping a good distance away, Leese watched as Justice pulled into a private drive. He had Sahara with him, so Cat assumed it was her house.

"Do you know how to get through her gate?"

Leese gave one small nod. "She shared the passcode with me."

As far as topic-starters went, that had failed miserably. "Are we trying to be less conspicuous? Is that why we're not sticking closer to her?"

Leese's brows twitched together. "Yeah."

Not very forthcoming. Cat cleared her throat and tried again. "Your friends are coming in?"

His gaze shot briefly to hers. "What do you mean?"

Looking over the backseat to see out the rearview window, Cat confirmed that the same headlights were still there. "That's them following us, right? I mean, I assume it's not Tesh since you're not worried about it."

Gaze straight ahead, Leese worked his jaw. Finally he asked, "You knew we were being followed?"

Cat gave him an arrogant glare. "You think I survived this long by being unaware?"

His mouth flattened. "No." After a glance in the rearview mirror, he said, "They're not coming in."

"So just making sure we got here safely, huh? That's so sweet."

"Downright sugary," he growled, then he turned down the long driveway. Behind them, the SUV with his friends drove past without acknowledgment. He paused at a keyless entry gate and entered the passcode. Wide, arching gates parted to let him in, then closed again once he'd driven through.

The lighted private lane wound around trees and finally opened to a sweeping circular drive in front of Sahara's home.

Another high iron fence secured the main entrance, blending into the landscaping. Sahara and Justice stood just inside the opened gateway.

When Leese parked and got out, Justice said, "Told you so."

"Yeah." Leese looked around, gauging the security and showing a little bit of awe.

Seeming pleased with her visitors, Sahara said, "Everything is wired, so if anyone intrudes, alarms are sent directly to a security company." As she led them up the front steps and to another locked door, she said,

"I want you to make yourself at home. Help yourself to the kitchen or anything else you might need."

Instead of a keyed entry, she pressed more buttons and the front door unlocked. They stepped into a grand foyer with a double staircase. It was truly beautiful and, despite its grandeur, felt somehow homier than her stepfather's estate.

Sahara turned to Cat. "I'll loan you some pajamas and tomorrow the officers said we should be able to get into the penthouse long enough for you to grab some belongings. We just can't disturb anything yet."

They'd been about to leave the hospital earlier when the officers had shown up with more questions, especially since the two men Leese had fought off were both in critical condition.

On the one hand, Cat would be relieved if the two cretins were no longer around to hurt or threaten innocent people. On the other hand, they could possibly provide a clue that would help to nail Tesh, and then the senator.

But she doubted it. Anyone working for Tesh would have been thoroughly vetted.

Such an eventful day, and more than ever before, viable solutions remained hazy.

Cat's eyes burned, her stomach churned and she wanted both food and sleep. But more than that, she wished Leese would hold her.

Forcing a smile, she thanked Sahara and went with her while Justice showed Leese around. The house was magnificent, and nearly as secure as the Body Armor agency.

Cat did her best to remain pleasant, but by the minute she wanted to collapse somewhere. She felt both physically and emotionally spent.

After yet another hour of polite chitchat, orientation and quickly consumed cheese sandwiches, she finally found herself alone with Leese in the lower level of the immense house. Justice had a room on the main floor, and Sahara's suite of rooms was on the upper level.

Everyone had privacy, not that Cat expected it to do her a lot of good.

While she showered and changed into the borrowed pajamas, Leese prowled around, getting familiar with the windows, the double doors that opened into a vast yard, and each closet and room.

At the bottom of the stairs to the right, part of the basement was used for storage; to the far left, a pool table and other games took up a big section.

But the middle had been designed for guests, providing a three-piece bathroom, a modest bedroom with a full-size bed, a sitting room with a television and computer, and a bar with a sink and microwave.

While showing them the area, Sahara had said with a completely straight face that the couch would fold out to a bed if they needed it.

For certain, Sahara was aware of their intimacy, Cat had no doubts about that. Did she think Leese was too furious with Cat to sleep with her?

Maybe she only wanted deniability in case it all fell apart. Regardless of Sahara's reasoning, Cat had no intention of sleeping alone. She needed Leese tonight, and by God, he'd hold her and make her feel safe, even if it was only a temporary ruse.

She found fluffy towels, a variety of toiletries— including new toothbrushes—and basic OTC medicines in the bathroom. Rather than shampoo it, she pinned up her hair, then lingered under the hot water longer than necessary.

Once she'd dressed in the borrowed flannel pajamas, which were so long she'd had to roll up the legs to keep from tripping on them, Cat went looking for Leese.

She found him standing at the back doors, arms at his sides, staring out at the yard. He'd removed his shirt and shoes and wore only his slacks.

Beard shadow darkened his face and his mussed hair looked shaggier than usual.

He was so gorgeous, it made her ache.

"Leese."

He turned, his gaze cutting over her, leaving her feeling small and, damn it, alone.

The stark white bandage on his side drew her attention, reminding her once again of the near-death experience.

Leese said nothing.

In an agony of suspense, Cat asked, "Are you ready for bed?"

After far too long, he nodded, but said, "I need to brush my teeth. You're shivering. Go ahead and get under the covers."

So he could sidle off to the couch? She wouldn't let him. Lifting her chin, she asked, "Which side do you want?"

As he passed her, he said, "Long as I'm close to you, it doesn't matter."

Relief almost took out Cat's knees. He still sounded angry, true, but at least he wasn't completely rejecting her.

Heart thumping, she stood there until she heard the water come on.

With renewed energy, she stalked after him. Damn it, he wasn't the only one who'd been through an ordeal. She was pretty damned upset too. If she'd been given a choice, she'd have gladly taken the bullet for him. But no, he had to play macho protector. *He* was the one who'd made her hide behind the bed.

And hadn't she offered to go to Tesh to keep him safe? What did he think, that the idea of being at Tesh's mercy didn't scare her near to death? Did he think that once Tesh turned her over to the senator, she didn't know exactly what would happen to her?

She'd been running for nearly two months because she didn't have any illusions at all.

She'd be dead. Period.

He refused to let her end this, so he could damn well start being nice again.

When she pushed open the bathroom door, Leese glanced at her. He had a toothbrush in his mouth, and he'd stripped down to his boxers. The fluorescent light gleamed over his shoulders and those boxers…well, they fit him well, hugging his tight butt, snug over his strong thighs and cradling his heavy sex.

She opened her mouth, but wow. How could she be coherent when he looked like that?

He rinsed his mouth and, drying his face with a hand towel, straightened before her. "Something wrong?"

She almost laughed. What *wasn't* wrong?

He lifted a brow, waiting. The man had the patience of a big cat stalking prey.

"You," she huffed, once she remembered why she'd

stormed after him. "I'm sorry you got shot, I really am. But I told you it was dangerous and—"

"It's a far sight from just dangerous, now isn't it?" He stepped around her and headed to the bed.

"Yes," she snapped behind him. "I'd say it's downright lethal, because the senator wants me *dead*."

His back to her, Leese halted, stiffened. His hands flexed into fists.

Cat tried to catch her breath, but it all came boiling up, all the worry and fear and anxiety.

The awful, miserable guilt.

"I wanted to spare you, Leese. From that very first day, I offered to walk away."

He spun around, temper spiked, expression livid. "You aren't going anywhere."

His tone sort of stole her breath away. "That's not what I'm saying." Taking a second to collect herself, she inched closer to him. "I'm trying to be reasonable."

Leese laughed, then ran a hand over his face.

"Stop that!" Cat tripped over the long pants when she rushed up to him. "I hate that you got hurt. I never, ever meant for that to happen. It's just…" Her composure fractured. "Being with you has been so wonderful. I wanted to just pretend the rest of the world didn't exist. Maybe Webb's right about that much. I do avoid the real world whenever I can."

Slowly Leese raised a hand to cradle the side of her face. "He's not right about anything. You're as down-to-earth and real as a person gets. But this mess…"

"I know," she whispered, leaning into him now that he'd softened. "There isn't a solution."

"Sahara has a plan."

"We both know it won't solve anything. Men like

Platt are untouchable and monsters like Tesh get immunity through association." She hated to say it because she didn't want him angry again. "The only thing I can think to do is go."

Leese lifted her, laid her on the bed, then settled over her. "You promised to trust me."

"No. I promised not to lie to you."

Exasperated, he put his forehead to hers. "All right. Then promise me right now that you'll trust me too."

"I do." With Leese covering her, sheltering her, she could almost push away the demons of reality. "I think I always have."

"Good. We're making progress." He gently kissed her lower lip, then the upper, before settling his mouth over hers, tasting her deeply, teasing with his tongue and filling her with need.

When he ended the kiss, he smiled at her. "Now swear to me you won't go anywhere without me."

Carefully, Cat slipped her hand down his side to the padded bandage. "You were hurt because of me."

"I'd die for you."

Her breath caught, her heart racing. She didn't want that, not ever. "Leese…"

"I'm your bodyguard. No one is getting past me."

So…that hadn't been a declaration of his feelings. On a roller-coaster ride of emotions, she closed her eyes and sighed.

Leese cupped her breasts, regaining her attention real fast. "Flannel," he murmured, moving his thumbs over her. "I like it."

"They're Sahara's."

"I know."

"I'm going commando."

He laughed. "That'll make things easier."

How could he laugh after everything that had happened? "I mean, I don't mind borrowing pajamas—"

"I understand." He unbuttoned the top two buttons on the pajama top and nuzzled her cleavage. "Cat?"

"Hmm?"

Through the material, he closed his teeth around her left nipple and gave a gentle tug. When she clenched around him and groaned, he said, "Promise me."

"Leese..."

He took her mouth again, the kiss rough and hot and demanding. "Tomorrow I need to head over to the agency."

"Wait—*what?*"

"Shh." He held her still beneath him. "We both need a change of clothes, I want to grab my laptop and there are a few other things to take care of."

"What other things?"

"Well, for one, I want to see if anyone is scoping out the place, maybe watching the investigation with a little too much interest." Without giving her a chance to react to that, he said, "And I want to make sure your buddy is still locked up."

Cat felt a moment of embarrassed panic before she remembered that the lockbox, with her "buddy" locked inside, was in the guest bedroom and well hidden. She scowled at Leese. "That's not funny."

For an answer, he sat up and opened a few more buttons. "I'm sure Sahara's lawyers will have the cops wrapping it up sooner rather than later, but I want to see everything for myself. Maybe there's a clue they'll miss."

Trying not to be distracted by what he did, she said,

"I guess that makes sense, as long as you're sure it's safe."

"With an active investigation? Yeah, it'll be safe, and I'll be careful." He cuddled her naked breasts. "I plan to make it back to you. Now, no more talking."

"So you don't have to make any promises?"

"How about I promise to kiss you all over."

"Um…"

He curled his fingers in the waistband of the bottoms and peeled them down her legs. To help him along, she lifted her hips and quickly kicked them off.

"And, Cat?" Expression intent, he looked her over. "I promise you're going to moan."

Cool air washed over her body, but she wasn't chilled. Not anymore. Not with Leese looking at her like that. "Okay." She shifted her legs, curled her toes and anticipated what would happen.

He parted her legs and knelt between her thighs, his gaze on her breasts, her belly and down. While stroking her inner thighs, he said, "You are so fucking sexy."

She didn't feel sexy. She just felt lost. Lost to the fear of the future. Lost to the lust of the moment.

Lost in the love she felt for him.

With her legs draped over his thighs, he leaned forward, closed his mouth around one nipple, and drew her in. He sucked gently, his hot, rough tongue rasping.

Sensation coursed through her and she closed her eyes.

He moved to the other nipple, licking, then sucking, leaving it equally wet and ripe. He caught her in his teeth and tugged, and she felt it like a direct pull to her core. Her belly tightened and tingled, and he'd just gotten started.

"I promise," he rasped, his hands now low on her hips, "to make you come."

"And you?" she managed to ask breathlessly. "You'll come too."

"No, not this time." He parted her sex with his thumbs, making her squirm as he took his time looking at her, his eyelids heavy, his cheekbones flushed. "I don't have any condoms."

"Then—"

"No. I'm fine, I promise." His gaze briefly locked with hers. "I'll just enjoy watching you."

But that sounded so…uninhibited. "I don't know about this." He wore his boxers, but she was naked, and he left her completely exposed.

"I do." His thumbs moved over her, petting, teasing. "Just relax."

If that's what he wanted, then she'd try. Breathing deeper, she nodded.

He turned one hand and briefly cupped her sex, then used three fingers to stroke her, getting her wetter. "So hot." As he said it, he began working his fingers into her, twisting, pressing.

Cat dug her heels into the bed and tightened all over. "Relax."

She gave him the moan he wanted, especially when she felt him filling her.

He looked at her breasts, licked his thumb and reached for her nipples. With the first damp glide of his thumb, she caught her breath. He wet them both, leaving her aching, then lightly pinched until each nipple was stiff, before tugging, rolling, going from one breast to the other, all while keeping three fingers pressed firmly into her.

Leese seemed tireless, determined to make her scream. She needed more.

So much more.

Like everything he had to give.

Just as she thought she couldn't take it anymore, as the rough whimper rose from her throat, he repositioned himself flat on the bed, nuzzled against her, then softly sucked on her clitoris while rasping with his tongue.

Cat held him close, her fingers in his hair, her thighs clasped around his ears as the climax exploded. Leese kept her there, on that sharp edge of pleasure, until she whimpered again.

He kissed his way up her limp body, then settled them both beneath the covers.

Cat could barely breathe, much less think. Lassitude stole her worries, and when Leese whispered, "Much better," she figured that might have been his purpose.

He drew her into his arms and held her close. Just before sleep claimed her, he vowed, "You're mine, Cat."

She smiled...and faded away.

TESH IGNORED THE code beeping on his phone. It had been going off for hours now. Over and over and fucking over until he wanted to crush it in his fist. Instead, utilizing tight control, he turned off the phone, dismantled it, then dumped the pieces, one by one, on his drive to a secure location.

It was past midnight, the sky black, the air so cold it hurt his lungs to breathe. Exhaustion tried to drag him down, but he ignored it. In his assignments for Platt, he'd spent many sleepless nights doing what needed to be done.

What he'd enjoyed doing.

From here on out, he'd be on his own—and hell, that suited him just fine.

Not that Platt realized it yet. Once he'd been picked up near the Body Armor agency, the senator had expected him to show. He wanted an accounting, maybe retribution.

Tesh snorted. Not bloody likely.

Platt could rot for all he cared. Did the delusional prick really think he still called the shots? Was he arrogant enough, *stupid* enough, to think Tesh would answer a summons at this point? Hell no.

Things had gone wrong. Horribly wrong.

The bodyguard was still alive, but Johnson and Miller were both in the hospital. By now the cops would be all over them, and no doubt Catalina had been moved.

If they recovered, Tesh wasn't worried about either of his men talking, not when they understood the consequences. But if anyone started backtracking, they could find a vague trail that led to him.

Or Platt.

Better Platt, Tesh decided. Let him take the heat.

All Tesh wanted was his kitten.

Once he got her, he'd seed the trail with information that would lead authorities straight to Platt's door. As Platt's most trusted cleanup man, Tesh had it all, every detail, dates and times and names, reservations and itineraries, everything needed to show the world what a sick, cruel, perverted bastard their favorite senator really was. He'd bury Platt so deep, there wouldn't be money enough or influence enough for him to dig himself out.

Then Tesh could live out his life in peace…with little Catalina.

Pacing in the dim interior of the bankrupt shop, a property he'd acquired on his own so Platt would know nothing about it, Tesh thought out his plan.

The easiest course now would be to shadow Platt. Eventually the senator would come after him, or he'd go after Catalina. Either way, when he moved, Tesh would have him.

Platt might suspect, and might attempt to cover himself. But Tesh had trained every man who worked for him. He knew their habits, their strengths and their weaknesses.

As an added advantage, Tesh had used the years of burying the senator's secrets and sweeping up his messes to build his own alliances, contacts that rivaled those of the senator's.

With a grim smile, Tesh anticipated the coming conflict. He knew he'd come out on top. Didn't he always?

But that was for tomorrow; tonight he had to figure out the ramifications of the massive fuck-up perpetrated at the agency. Far as he could tell there was only one loose end.

The secretary had survived.

Unlike Johnson and Miller, that diminutive man would tell everything he could. Tesh admired his guts even as he plotted ways to finish him off.

If they hadn't been in such a congested area with work crews a mere block away, Tesh would have put a bullet in Enoch's brain. But gunshot had a way of drawing attention. At the very least, he should have cut Enoch's throat and let him bleed out.

But the need for violence had gotten the better of him, and so he'd gotten sloppy, using his hands instead of a weapon.

Regret was a son of a bitch.

Maybe he should just bomb the hospital? Kill them all… No. That would bring out far too much scrutiny. He wouldn't even be able to move in the shadows without someone spotting him.

As he paced, Tesh considered his options.

The police had no doubt already talked to Webb, alerting him to his daughter's whereabouts. The fighter would be sticking to her closer than ever. And Ms. Silver would have hidden her someplace very secure.

Where are you, kitten?

He jammed his hands in his pockets and found the papers he'd taken from Enoch's briefcase. Moving to a window where the light from streetlamps penetrated, Tesh skimmed the notes, looking for something useful—

Ah, the itinerary.

Given all that happened, the schedule had probably changed, but just in case… Tesh smiled as he began to read in detail.

THE SUN CAME out with a vengeance, as if it hoped to lift the spirits of the glum group gathered around Sahara's kitchen table, imbibing massive amounts of coffee. Leese didn't always like to use the artificial adrenaline of caffeine to get his day going, but this wasn't just any day.

For half the night, he'd stayed awake in the darkness, hard and hurting because of it, wanting Cat, listening to her breathe and wondering how he was going to save her.

He never had come up with an answer.

With no other clothes to choose from, Leese had stuck with his slacks and nothing more. It might be disrespectful in front of his boss, but Sahara was now more than that. She'd seen him naked, helped him conspire to keep authorities in the dark, and had tacitly accepted his relationship with a client. They'd left the employer/employee boundary in the dust.

Justice continually yawned, his eyes barely open even though he frowned. He looked to be in a similar state of antsy unrest. His Mohawk listed to the side in an odd sort of bed-head style. He, at least, had been able to change into jogging pants and a white T-shirt.

In the too-big pajamas she'd pulled back on, Cat looked adorably small. She also looked uncertain and vulnerable.

Sahara, the only one with her eyes wide open, had her long brown hair pulled over her shoulder in a braid. Even without makeup, she was beautiful. She wore a gown and matching robe in soft gray with pink trim, and pink slippers. Very pretty.

Justice nodded at Leese's bandaged side. "How do you feel?"

"I'm fine." He gave his friend a "drop it" look. The last thing he wanted was for Cat to start fretting. He turned to Sahara. "I'm heading to the agency today. I need to grab a few things."

She glanced at the clock on the wall. "Give me another hour and I'll call the attorneys to see if they were able to hustle the cops along. The last I heard yesterday evening, it shouldn't be a problem. There's no question that those men intruded, and that you did only what you needed to do."

Justice asked, "Why do the cops think they were there?"

"They know Catalina is from a wealthy family. The

general consensus, without any truth volunteered from us, was that they hoped to rob her." Sahara shook her head. "But that's flimsy at best. Still, there's no one to tell them otherwise. Not unless we decide to share the whole truth—"

"We can't," Cat said, without looking up from her coffee.

"No, we can't," Sahara agreed. "Not yet anyway." Distracted, she glanced at Leese, down to his chest, then away. "I meant to tell you yesterday, but in the middle of the confusion, I forgot. Those two men you ran into at Catalina's house?"

"What about them?"

"They're missing."

Interest sharpened, Leese sat forward. "Missing, as in they didn't show up for work, or they're presumed dead?"

"I'd go with the latter. My PI checked into it, of course, and they haven't been seen since the day you found them at her house." She nodded at Cat. "My guess is that someone didn't like the way they'd screwed up."

Brows beetled, Cat went back to sipping her coffee.

"Also, that license plate you got back when Tesh first approached you? It doesn't match any registered car, yet it's the same plate on the car that Enoch escaped."

Well, hell. Leese sat back in his seat. "Completely fake plates?"

"On a now-abandoned car." She sipped her coffee and sighed. "Under normal circumstances, it could be days before the crime scene is cleared. But my attorneys explained that we didn't have days. After all, Body Armor is a business…" She waited a heartbeat before adding, "…and we have a party tomorrow."

Disbelief hit Leese. "You can't be serious."

"Of course I am."

Just as stunned, Justice said, "That's fucking nuts."

Cat sat frozen, silent, her eyes huge.

Sahara stood to refill her coffee. "I have important clients coming." She carried the carafe back to the table. "And it's also part of my plan."

Less controlled than Leese, Justice said, "So share the damn plan already."

"So surly." After refilling each cup, she took her seat again. "The list of attendees for the party includes some of our most important clients. Those who had high-profile cases, nothing secretive. But we executed our obligations with professionalism, so we now have their loyalty." She smiled. "And that means Senator Platt will also be in attendance."

Leese nearly lurched out of his chair. "What?"

With a casual shrug, Sahara said, "He is—or rather was—a preferred client. It's well-known that Body Armor provided security during speaking engagements and special appearances. He's endorsed the agency with other important clients." She glanced at Cat. "Of course, that was before I knew of his proclivity for rape, violence and murder. Now that I do know, I need to destroy him."

Churning with fury that hadn't really died from the day before, Leese demanded, "By using Cat as bait?"

"How else? And while nothing is without risk, I do have several ways to ensure her safety."

Done with the discussion, Leese said a flat, "No."

"It's not up to you," Sahara told him, and her gaze again shifted to Cat. Gently, she said, "Don't you want to end this? Once and for all?"

Cat drew a slow, shaky breath, and nodded. "Yes. Very much."

"I can help you with that."

"I said no," Leese repeated, the fury escalating with each second.

Pretending he wasn't out of control, Sahara said, "That dress we got for Catalina? I have one that matches. If we both wear our hair up, and her heels are high enough, we could be mistaken for each other."

"You look nothing alike," Leese argued.

"Believe me, two society women attending the same party would never be caught in the same dress. The dress alone will be enough to cause confusion. But from a distance, in dim light, we'll be able to pull it off."

Slowly, Justice sat up straighter. "So *you're* the actual bait?"

She flapped a hand. "We need the villains to see Catalina joining the party. Once she's inside though, we'll tuck her away safely and I'll wait—all isolated and alone at a chosen location in the agency—for someone to make a grab for me."

"Jesus, Joseph and Mary," Justice growled.

"It's insane," Leese agreed.

She continued without worry. "And once they do, you two can grab them. At the same time, we'll keep tabs on Platt without him knowing. He'll likely be trying to leave once he thinks Catalina is secured, and we can follow him and—"

Leese threw up his hands. "That's the most idiotic, reckless plan I've ever heard."

Sahara slowly stood to face him. "Do you forget that you work for me?"

"You want my resignation?" he challenged. "Fine. Consider it given. But Cat's not getting anywhere near—"

"I'm going."

All eyes switched to stare at Cat. She sat with her shoulders back, her chin lifted, and in her gaze Leese saw a sort of fatalistic acceptance.

"No," Leese growled, "you are not."

"It's not your decision to make."

Without denying or affirming that, he said again, "You're not going."

Cat, too, pushed back her chair and stood to face off with him.

Great, just what this situation didn't need: her stubbornness.

Justice looked around at each of them, sighed and came to his feet. "If anyone cares, I'm voting with Leese on this."

Sahara slanted him a look. "Learn when to be silent."

"Sure. But not this morning."

Knowing Cat wouldn't care what Justice thought about it, Leese said, "Be reasonable, Cat."

"I was going to say the same to you." Full of defiance, she stared up at him. "If this thing is going to work between us, you have to respect me."

This *thing*? What the hell did that mean? "Of course I do."

"Then you should know that I can make up my own mind about things. You have to understand that I can—"

Leese leaned into her space. "You have to understand that I *don't want to lose you*."

She breathed faster, then whispered, "You won't."

"You don't know that. You can't know it." He flagged

a hand in Sahara's direction. "Not with her sketchy-as-hell plan that's riddled with holes."

Using that as her opening, Sahara said, "And that brings us back to this little powwow around the table. Let's work through the details, take care of those holes and make the plan as solid as we can." She touched Leese's arm. "There's no better idea and you know it. Not if Catalina is ever going to be free to get on with her life."

A life with him hopefully in it.

Cat hugged him tight. "It'll work," she insisted.

But in her voice he heard the same desperation he felt. She only believed it'd work because it had to.

He couldn't accept any other outcome.

CHAPTER SEVENTEEN

CAT STOOD IN the spacious conference room of Body Armor and tried to relax. Not easy. More than fifty well-known guests were in attendance, filling the room and spilling out to the main hall and an entry room.

Sahara flitted about, visiting each couple, each area, playing the perfect hostess. Justice, ever vigilant, stayed within reach of her.

But Cat, following the plan, didn't budge from the conference room.

Neither did Leese—for good reason.

Across the room from her, Senator Platt held court.

Watching him speak with self-assumed importance, hearing him laugh without a care, seeing the way he casually touched others…her skin crawled. The man was a monster, and knowing he pretended otherwise only made hatred burn within her.

Those around him probably saw him as an earnest, caring, gentle soul. They didn't know the depths of his depravity or how vicious he'd be when his phony disguise was threatened.

Two staid guards flanked him. Being still, deliberately imposing, wearing severe expressions, they had nothing in common with the Body Armor team, who looked friendly and companionable. Powerful, yes. Capable, yes.

But somehow, far more *real*.

To help build up the ruse, Leese kept his distance from her, but never, not at any moment, was he unaware of her. She knew it, felt it.

Someone bumped her, and Cat, who'd been concentrating on the senator, nearly yelped.

An elderly woman patted her arm, said, "Excuse me," and moved on past.

A strained breath strangled out of Cat. Good Lord, she was jumpy...and ill at ease. The largest part of her discomfort was due to the senator. But the rest had to do with her general unease at large formal functions.

Despite the beautiful outfit Sahara had provided and the finishing touches given to her hair, nails and makeup, she still felt like a fraud.

Yes, she was as polished as any other woman there, but none of it fit her, not the real her.

Ideally she'd have done her own hair and makeup, but in order to better match Sahara, she'd given in to the professional stylist.

Currently, Sahara wore a red gown.

None of this would have worked if they'd entered the party in the same blue dress. But any minute now Sahara would excuse herself, change into the dress, shoes and jewelry that matched Cat's, and then they'd wait for a murderer to strike.

When the senator suddenly locked eyes with Cat, it was all she could do to hide her loathing and abhorrence.

Especially when he excused himself from the other guests and started toward her with the two guards following close behind. The thumping of her heart drowned out all other noise. Cat did her best not to look at Leese. He saw it all, of course, but this would work better if the senator remained unaware of the net closing in.

When Platt got close enough, he reached for her hand.

Cat snatched it away. Touching him? No, that she couldn't do.

"Catalina," he chided in his soft, grandfather's voice. He glanced at the guards and they turned their backs, watching the crowd, ensuring privacy.

"I haven't told anyone," Cat lied in a whisper.

"Of course not." His slick smile made her stomach roil. "There's nothing for you to tell, now is there?"

Pig, she thought inwardly, but outwardly, she only whispered, "No."

For only a second, the pretense of "sweet elderly man" slipped, showing the sick, deviant freak. "You need to return to your father."

With just the right quaver in her voice, Cat said, "Not until I know I won't be hurt."

"Hurt by whom?" He eased nearer, crowding her personal space. "Sweet child, tell me what you're afraid of and I'll do what I can to protect you."

Pure menace glittered in his eyes as he stared into her soul. Cat swallowed, trying to think with him staring so hard. "Tesh."

"Ah, yes. He was ruthless, wasn't he? Necessary. Very necessary."

Was? She went on high alert. Had the senator done away with Tesh?

As if confiding in her, Platt said, "There are those people who would use my public stature against me."

Anger outpaced fear and she asked recklessly, "Like Georgia Bell?"

His face pinched. Through lips that barely moved, he said, "I have no idea who that is."

Realization of what she'd just done sent a flush of panicked heat rolling through Cat, leaving her faint. "I'm sorry," she gasped. "I shouldn't have…" *Stick to the plan, Cat.* "I need to go."

"You don't need to fear Tesh any longer," he promised her. "Our association has…ended."

If he'd killed Tesh, that would be one fewer person for her to worry about.

Rather than risk asking questions, she turned away— and his cold thin fingers clamped around her wrist with crushing insistence. When he spoke, she felt his damp breath on her temple and smelled the shrimp hors d'oeuvres he'd eaten.

Her stomach lurched.

"My child, you have tried my patience enough. You either head home to your father tonight, or you're going to start losing loved ones." His grip tightened more. "Is that clear?"

No longer caring if she caused a scene, Cat jerked free and faced him again, doing her own fair share of crowding. "Who are you threatening?" she demanded to know. "Webb?" The laugh sounded close to a choke, proving she had very mixed feelings about that.

He didn't smile. Idly, as if it didn't matter to him, he said, "Or your brothers." Watching her, he gauged her reaction to that, and added carelessly, "Whoever is most important to you, my dear. That's the way leverage works."

Definitely past time for her to retreat. "Could…could

we speak privately? Please? I just… I'm afraid of being overheard and I need…" Forcing another stammer, she said, "I need…reassurances."

Triumph blazed in his dark eyes. "Of course." His attention dipped to her chest, then back to her face. "But my guards will need to accompany me."

"I understand." She looked around as if searching for the right place. "I believe there's an empty boardroom. If you give me five minutes—"

"Five minutes," he repeated, then his voice hardened. "And, Catalina? If you think to run from me, you can consider your brothers dead."

That wasn't a threat, but a guarantee, and Cat shivered with apprehension. "I won't run, Senator, not this time." *She would never run again.*

"Finally," he purred, "you're being reasonable."

Blind with determination, Cat fled his proximity, heading for the designated boardroom. She ensured no one followed. And in fact, she almost felt invisible.

Only Leese remained acutely aware of her. With every step she took, she felt his attentiveness.

She slipped out of the conference room and across the hall, then ducked inside the dim, empty boardroom. Pressing her back against the wall, her heart in her throat, Cat prayed her brothers would be okay. Bowen and Holt were good men. They didn't deserve to be pulled into her nightmare.

Remembering the plan, she quickly removed her earrings and pulled the pins from her hair, then shook it loose. At a table to her left, draped over one of the chairs, she found the long coat that would completely conceal her dress, along with black ballet flats to replace her heels. Forcing herself to go through each preplanned step, she set the heels aside and—

"Cat."

She jumped, but immediately recognized Leese's calm voice and launched herself against him, holding tight.

"It's okay now," he said, as he coasted his hands down her back. "Sahara is changing. She'll join us very shortly."

They'd used different rooms to change, to help lessen the chance of them being caught together.

Moments later, Sahara slipped through the back door that led to the restrooms. "I'm sorry, but I need one of you to zip me up."

Sahara had ducked away right before Cat had, going into the private, locked restroom where her blue dress was hidden. There, she'd switched out her shoes and earrings too.

Beneath the doors, lights from the conference room filtered in. As Leese turned to assist Sahara, he said to Cat, "Go out the back door now and into the private bathroom. Platt could be here any second and if he sees you together, we're blown."

"Please," Cat whispered. "*Please*, both of you, be careful."

Sahara said, "I'll be as careful as I need to be to nail that bastard. Before the night is over, he'll be mine."

Knowing she had to hurry, Cat said, "Thank you, Sahara."

Poised, strong in her own right, Sahara smiled with evil delight. "This, Catalina, is absolutely my pleasure."

Cat believed her. Sahara was not only a beautiful woman, she was intelligent, cunning, ambitious and a very imposing adversary. Strong enough to best Platt? Cat just didn't know, but Sahara certainly thought so.

Bracing herself, Cat whispered, "Leese?"

Leaning down, he struggled with the tiny zipper, and finally pulled it up. "What is it?"

"I love you." She needed him to know...just in case this all went sideways.

Battle-ready, prepared for the worst, Leese slowly straightened and stared toward her.

Cat didn't want or need for him to say the words back. At the moment, under the circumstances, she wouldn't believe him if he did. "I'm just saying, you better not get shot again."

His face dark with turbulent emotions, Leese nodded. "I promise not to get shot."

"Thank you." She hurried to the door.

"Cat?"

"We'll talk later." *When our lives aren't on the line.* "I'll be waiting for you." She peeked out the door, saw no one around and hurried down the short hall to the private room. Once inside, she locked the door and then...all she could do was wait.

Each minute felt like an hour. She strained her ears, trying to hear, but couldn't distinguish the sounds of the party from possible conflict.

Was the senator, at this very moment, attacking Sahara? What if he'd sent one of his guards to shoot her without warning? Sahara absolutely could *not* take a bullet for her. Cat knew she couldn't live with that.

She waffled, reaching for the doorknob then backing away again.

No, that wouldn't happen. Not at the crowded party. Not with both Leese and Justice looking after her.

Regardless of what common sense told her, Cat continued to torture herself with what-ifs.

When she heard footsteps, she went limp with relief. *Leese was okay.* And it hadn't really taken long at all. Probably only five minutes or so.

She smiled as the key sounded in the lock and the doorknob turned, a million questions at the ready.

The door opened—and there stood Tesh.

It took a split second for reality to crash into her expectations. *No!* She opened her mouth to scream and Tesh slapped her hard, propelling her into a wall. Dazed, she struggled to regain her footing, and his hand clamped over her mouth and nose.

Crushing her close, her back against his chest, he crooned, "Now, now, my kitten. None of that."

Cat kicked and struggled. Her shoes flew off her feet, her elbow hit the wall…but no one heard.

No one came.

Tesh held her so tightly she thought her jaw might break. Blackness fogged the edges of her vision, and her limbs began to go weak. Fighting him did her no good. He dragged her out the door and down to another room, farther and farther away.

He had her and he wasn't letting go. Cat knew she would die…and with her last cognizant thought, she prayed that at least Sahara, Justice and Leese would survive.

LEESE GROUND HIS teeth together.

The senator didn't indict himself. In fact, the cowardly bastard spoke from a distance, one guard next to him inside the room, the other guard standing just outside the closed door.

"You've taken us all on quite the chase, but it's time for you to quit these absurd games, stop being such a difficulty to so many and make your amends by going home."

Keeping her back to him, her shoulders rounded in a show of defeat, Sahara nodded.

"I'm glad you're finally coming to your senses." His voice dropped. "You realize there's nowhere you could have gone. That's why you're here now?"

Again Sahara nodded.

"And a show of deference? Of meekness?" The senator narrowed his eyes. "I suppose better late than never."

When the guard smirked, Leese wanted to destroy him.

These were the people terrorizing Cat, chasing her, threatening her. He could gladly kill them with his bare hands. Having to hide, hearing Platt berate her, it took a herculean amount of effort to stick to the plan and wait.

"You and I will come to an agreement," Platt promised without an ounce of sincerity. "But only if you go home tonight. Do you understand me?"

Hidden, Leese watched as Sahara ducked her head as if cowed. She didn't face the senator, didn't speak.

"Answer me, damn you!"

That tone pushed Sahara a little too far. Her shoulders slowly drew back and a new crispness entered her tone. "Will you promise not to hurt me?"

The senator was apparently too lost in his own power trip to realize it wasn't Cat. "I won't promise you anything." Breathing harder, he demanded, "Be at Webb's, tomorrow, one o'clock. That's your last chance. Now *do you understand me?*"

Sahara sighed with frustration. "Not really, no. Care to spell it out?"

After a lengthy pause filled with electric rage, Platt muttered, "You've wasted enough of my time." The door opened, and he said to the guard in the room, "Take care of her."

Leese stiffened. *Son of a bitch*. That could mean anything from actually "help her" to "kill her." He'd bet on the latter.

More than ready, Leese moved out of the shadows, inching up behind the man.

The guard was so bent on following orders, he never realized, even after getting face-to-face with her, that Sahara wasn't Catalina.

The idiot reached for her, and Leese locked an arm around his neck in a rear naked choke, squeezing to cut off the blood flow from the guard's heart to his brain.

It was an effective way for Leese to immobilize the bastard. It was a very different matter than the way Enoch had been choked, and worked as a temporary means for Leese to quietly get the upper hand.

While Leese tightened his hold, Sahara took advantage and nutted the guard, hard. A squeaky sound of pain escaped him before he passed out, going limp in Leese's hold.

"Well," Leese muttered, "that ought to teach him."

Seething, Sahara said, "We need the senator to come back. Maybe if you hold the guard—"

"Fine by me," Leese said, lowering the big man to the floor and relieving him of his weapons. "But I want Catalina out of here."

"Justice can get her." She withdrew the phone from her purse, gave Justice instructions and then knelt by

Leese. "He'll take her to one of the upstairs offices and stay with her behind a locked door."

"No sign of Tesh?" Leese asked as he fastened the guard's hands and feet with the nylon restraints he'd brought along in his suit pocket.

"He said not."

Justice opened the door, looking a little confused. "You get her already?"

Sahara asked, "Who?"

A drumming of dread brought Leese upright.

"Cat," Justice said, looking around and then drawing a breath of alarm. "Fuck. She's not in the room."

Leese strode across the floor. "She has to be. You checked the bathroom—"

"Yeah." Justice followed on Leese's heels. "The door was unlocked and open, and she's not there."

Running now, Leese surged up to the open bathroom door, and like a knife to the heart, he saw Cat's discarded shoes, not set neatly on the floor, but flung, as if she'd been kicking.

"Listen to me," Sahara said from behind him. "It's going to be okay."

But even Sahara didn't sound convinced.

"We'll find her, I promise. But first—"

"How?" Leese demanded. For him, there was no other *first*. He looked toward the boardroom where he'd cuffed the guard, and his eyes narrowed. If necessary, he'd beat the bastard to death to get the answers he needed. He started forward.

Sahara got in his way. "We have to talk to the guard. *Talk*, Leese. If it was Tesh—"

"You know it was." Leese easily lifted her and set her aside.

Justice, ever protective of his boss, said, "Umm," his loyalties divided.

Leese got two steps closer to the boardroom before Sahara was in front of him again, and this time she had that pissed-off look he recognized as gritty determination.

She grabbed him by the lapels and hissed, "You will listen to me if you want to get Catalina back."

Hell, yes, he wanted her back. "Then tell me. Now."

"I put a chip in her dress," she said quickly, "just in case something like this happened. It's why I didn't ask her to change, to just pull on the coat. We can track her using GPS."

Leese drew a breath. He could still reach her. "We have to hurry."

"I agree. But for Catalina's sake, we need to know what we're up against." She turned to Justice. "Grab the guard. Drag him somewhere. Anywhere. I don't care. Find out from him how Tesh got in, who he has with him and where he might be going. Then let me know. I'm going with Leese."

"That's nuts," Justice said. "You need to stay here, run your party, deal with—"

"I'm going." She paused for one second to say, "I already figured I'd be away dealing with Platt, so I have an assistant handling hostess duties. You just concentrate on that guard."

"What about Platt?"

"Ignore him for now." Her voice hardened. "We'll deal with him later."

Leese didn't care enough to debate it. He was already on his way, leaving Sahara rushing to catch up.

CHAPTER EIGHTEEN

TESH KEPT HIS grip bruisingly tight as he hustled Cat along, out a side door, down an alley toward the street.

She fought him the best she could but it wasn't enough. In comparison to Tesh's strength, she was downright puny.

So she did what Leese had taught her and went limp.

Cursing, Tesh quickly readjusted his hold, wrapping one arm around her throat, the other around her waist. With a huff, he warned, "Keep dragging your feet and I'll kill him. And her. Fuck, I'll kill them all."

No! Somehow, Cat would stop him.

But she knew she wouldn't manage it with fear, so she gripped his forearm and managed to loosen his hold enough to gasp, "Not if he kills you first."

Growling, Tesh turned and slammed her into the wall, knocking the wind out of her.

His hand landed at her throat, pressing against her windpipe. His nostrils flared and his gaze smoldered.

Between his choking hold and the way he'd slammed her, she couldn't draw a single breath. Her eyes watered and her lungs burned and all she could do was wheeze.

He searched her face, no doubt looking for the fear he craved. A slow smile lifted his dark expression. "I was on to Sahara and your bodyguard."

She shook her head, denying him.

"Yes." He moved up closer to her, angling his body against hers. "I have men watching them both. They'll shoot to kill if I give them the word." To convince her, he asked, "How do you think I knew to find you in that bathroom? The senator's guards are my men. Loyal to me. I was notified the second Platt went into that boardroom with you. Only other men were watching all of you too, and when Ms. Silver disappeared, and your bodyguard, I told them to check every door." Satisfaction dripped from his tone. "Only that bathroom was locked, accessible enough. It made sense that I'd find you there."

No, it wasn't possible…

His thumb stroked over her fluttering pulse. "So wild," he remarked, fascinated with the telltale sign of her terror. "You know the truth now, don't you? There is no escape from me. Not ever."

Fear pumped through her veins, destroying her attempts to conspire a strategy. Still barely breathing, she gave up and rasped, "Please."

Oh, he liked that. She saw it in his eyes, in the shift of his posture. "Please what, Kitten?"

"I don't want anyone else hurt."

The smile spread over his face. "Then quit fighting me. It does you no good anyway."

In a fog, Cat nodded. She couldn't quite ground herself, couldn't think of a way out.

Tesh stepped back just enough that his body no longer pressed hers. He reached into his pocket, whispered, "Sorry, Kitten," and then slipped something over her head.

She couldn't see a thing, but neither did she dare fight him. He lifted her roughly over his shoulder, jos-

tling her as he walked at a fast clip. She heard the creak-
ing of metal, an idling engine, and then she got dumped
on a hard floor. Before she could get her hands under
her, her head smacked awkwardly against something,
dazing her anew.

Pinpricks of light danced before her. The covering
over her head disappeared and Tesh stroked his hand
through her hair, smoothing it.

She jerked away...and her head pounded.

"You struggle against your fate," Tesh whispered.
"Shh, shh now. You're mine and you'll stay mine."

Dear God, he sounded insane. By instinct alone, Cat
flinched away from his touch.

A firm hand brought her face back around. "Always
so stubborn." The pleasure in his soft laugh sent shivers
down her spine. "Sometimes there will be pain. Sometimes not. It's natural that you'd resist. I don't mind too
much. It'll make taming you more fun."

Don't react, Cat told herself, knowing he enjoyed
shocking her. She tried to get oriented and became
aware of movement. Everything had happened so
quickly, but...they were definitely on the go.

Tesh smiled down at her, superior, smug, even giddy.

Shifting only her eyes, Cat looked around and realized that she rode in a stripped-down cargo van.

"This," Tesh said, "is the beginning of your forever...
with me."

Needing to be on her feet, *away from Tesh*, Cat
wrapped her fingers into an empty cutout of the bare-
bones vehicle and stood.

One man, a stranger, stared out the windshield as he
drove. Other than his and the passenger seat, the van
was hollow—metal floor, metal walls, metal ceiling. No

windows in the back. The streetlamps they passed lit the interior with a strobe effect that made her stomach pitch. Two empty paint buckets, a metal ladder and tarps littered the floor. A single handle secured the rear doors.

Had Tesh stolen a painter's van?

He, too, stood. "No, Kitten, no one will report the van stolen, and the driver will not help you. Resign yourself."

Never.

Cat looked around the van again, Tesh watching her closely as she gathered the facts and sorted through them. One giant question drummed against her sluggish brain and she decided, why not ask? If nothing else, it'd maybe keep him distracted.

"How did you unlock the bathroom door?"

"I took keys from your little friend, Enoch."

Fresh anger poured through her. "You almost killed him."

"You had no right to give him your artwork!" Tesh flexed his jaw muscles, squeezed his hands into trembling fists. "All your gifts belong to me."

"I didn't even know you liked my work."

That took him by surprise and he retrenched. Had he expected her to match his loss of control? Not likely. Leese had taught her that winning meant staying calm, staying in control and using what tools you had.

"I love your work."

His sincerity was as scary as his rage. "Thank you."

"Since I meant to choke him to death," he added, "don't expect me to show remorse."

"No," Cat said. "I don't." She expected him to rot in prison.

In a show of nonchalance, Tesh removed his heavy

winter coat, folded it and placed it on the floor behind him. As if there'd been no interruption, he picked up his story again. "I also got an itinerary that told me about the party tonight. Once I verified that it hadn't changed, I assumed Platt would show. He's a twisted fuck who enjoys flaunting his power."

Talk about the pot calling the kettle black. Cat just stared at him, encouraging him without words to continue talking—giving her time to think.

"I knew he'd want to rub your nose in it. And if you weren't there, then of course Platt would have enjoyed tweaking Ms. Silver with what she *couldn't* do to him." He tipped his head. "I assume you confided in her? In your fighter friend?"

"No," she immediately denied. If Tesh thought she had, it'd put them at added risk.

He glanced down at his shoes, a frown in place, then back up to meet her eyes with icy disappointment. "Just this once, I'll let you slide on lying to me. But you will quickly learn there are consequences to that type of behavior. For your own sake, don't let it happen again."

Cat rolled back her shoulders, doing her best to hide her dread. "Platt wanted me. He'll kill you when he finds out that you've—"

"Both Platt and Webb are dead."

Her knees buckled and she slumped against the wall with sudden, debilitating remorse. "You killed Webb?"

"Ah, so you do care." He seemed overjoyed by that, then said, "Not yet, no, but I plan to. Before another day passes, they'll both be gone."

Relief made her limbs even weaker. "I don't understand. Why?"

"You see, Platt was too stupid to realize it, but I'm

more powerful than he could ever be, because I know things he doesn't know."

Was that possible? She knew Tesh didn't have Platt's obscene wealth, but he might exceed him in insanity. "You said his guards work for you?"

"Some of them. Enough of them." He gloated. "It took very little persuasion on my part to get the info I needed from the guards there tonight."

Cat tried to look impressed. "You've covered all your bases." She took another look around the van, searching for any weapon she might be able to use. "But why hurt Webb?"

"The backstabbing bastard worked against Platt. Against *me*." Tesh ran a hand over his shaved head, rubbed the back of his neck and growled, "Webb was trying to find a way to bury us both."

Wait... Webb had worked *against* them? "But I thought—"

"I know what you thought." Indulgent, he shared his cruelest smile. "Poor little Cat. It's possible Webb would have tried to protect you. But you ran from him." He took a step closer. "For a while now, I've been suspicious of him, and of course, after Platt bragged about the girl he raped—"

"Georgia Bell." *She had a name, damn it.*

"Yes, whatever." Tesh softened. "She died quickly, if that makes it easier for you to accept."

No, nothing would ever make it easy to accept. "You personally killed her?"

Confirming that, Tesh inclined his head. "In her sleep. I promise you, Kitten, she never saw it coming."

Cat struggled for composure and lost. "You're a monster."

The insult made him laugh. "She came to the island willingly enough, but then fought the senator's... appetites. She demanded that he change his plans, and when things didn't go her way the spoiled twit stupidly threatened to report him. No one would have believed her, of course, but the senator always preferred the easiest route."

Cat pretended to listen while she thought about Tesh's revelations. *Webb hadn't been a part of that mess?* She'd spent so long condemning him in her head that the sudden switch threw her. "I heard Webb say—"

"That he'd help, yes. What else could he say? Open defiance would have gotten him murdered on the spot."

"By you?"

Tesh smiled his answer. "In a way, I almost hoped Webb would balk. You would have been mine for the taking, without all this fuss."

She absolutely couldn't think about that, not yet. She'd never be able to keep her head if she did.

"Unlike Platt," Tesh continued, "I cover all the bases. I'd had extra eyes on Webb for a while, and bugs in all the rooms of his house."

"You had a bug in my house as well."

He smiled. "Yes."

Going stiff to contain her shudder of revulsion, Cat waited.

Finally, Tesh continued, "I knew the bastard was searching for a way out. Your father wasn't above making unseemly connections to better his social standing, but he certainly balked at a little harmless, sexual fun."

Harmless? God, how she detested him. At the same time, she worried for Webb. For once, she didn't object to having him called her father. "I can believe you'll get to him." In some ways, Webb had never fit the role of obscene criminal, so he likely wasn't practiced in the ways of eluding the real cretins. "But Platt? That's a very different matter."

"I have my ways."

"Odds are," she continued, as if he hadn't spoken with such confidence, "Platt is already planning *your* demise. There's nowhere you can hide. Nowhere you can run. He'll still get you."

Brows flattening, Tesh said, "Now you're just showing your ignorance. Soon you will learn to never underestimate me." He removed a flash drive from his pocket, holding it between his finger and thumb to show her. "I own every detail of Platt's life. He can't do anything to me without exposing himself and he knows it."

Trying for a look of awe rather than excitement, Cat widened her eyes. "You have info on the senator? Incriminating stuff?"

"I have him by the balls, and I have decided to destroy him." He tucked the small drive back into his pocket.

Cat refused to believe it could be that easy—not that getting the drive from Tesh and then escaping alive would be anywhere near easy.

But at least now she saw an opportunity.

"You have enough information to expose the senator, and you're carrying it around as if it's nothing? I'm not stupid, Tesh. No sane man would do that." A psychotic monster, yes, but Tesh was still cagey.

His mouth flattened at the insult. "I have another copy."

"Saved on your PC?" She snorted. "Seriously, Platt would have already hacked that—"

Surging toward her, Tesh snarled, "No, damn you. I am not incompetent. I have a safe-deposit box with everything. Photos, details, dates, names, *everything.*"

His sudden nearness alarmed her. With every second that they talked, the van took her farther away—from safety, from escape.

From Leese.

But at the moment, she couldn't think of anything else to do. "If you have it in your name, trust me, the senator has already secured it."

His control snapped and he grabbed her hair, dragging her against him. "It's in my mother's name, *goddamn you!*" After that outburst, Tesh stood there heaving, his face florid, his body coiled.

They stared at each other, Cat in bone-deep fear, Tesh in shock at his own savage outburst.

His chest expanded as he visibly gathered himself. By small degrees he released her, carefully separating her hair from his fingers and still taking too many strands.

Her scalp stung from the attack, but she did what she could to keep all expression from her face.

He didn't deserve to see her fear.

Now more composed, Tesh stepped back and brushed his hands over his slacks. With impersonal command, he instructed, "Take off your clothes."

What? His mood swings changed lightning fast, making it difficult for her to anticipate.

The driver glanced in the rearview mirror, not in concern, but lewd curiosity.

"Don't worry about him," Tesh said softly. "He might look, but he won't touch what is mine."

Numb at the idea of being so exposed, Cat shook

her head and whispered, "I'm not yours." She would never be his.

Pleased to again have the upper hand, Tesh casually unbuckled his belt and slipped it from his pants loops with a quiet hiss. While ignoring her, he wrapped it around his meaty fist. When he finished, the silver buckle gleamed in the shifting light, prominent over his knuckles.

Cat tried to swallow, but fear left her throat too dry. She didn't want to be hurt—but she knew she would be.

In a singsong voice, all the more eerie for its softness, Tesh said, "Our relationship may as well start out right."

Again the driver glanced back.

"We don't have a relationship." Cat back-stepped and tripped over the bulky tarps, landing hard on her palms and her butt. As Tesh moved in, she crab-crawled away, but there was nowhere to go. She ended up backed against the rear door, scrunched in a corner against the protruding metal frame. Terror gave strength to her defiance. "We will *never* have a relationship!"

"You are so wrong." He knelt by her, grabbing her ankle when she tried to flinch away. "You belong to me now, my pet, and you will be tamed." He licked his lips in lewd excitement. "I'm looking forward to it. God, I've been looking forward to it forever."

"You're sick," she snapped, and tried to kick out with her free leg.

Prepared for that reaction, he dragged her flat and landed one heavy punch to her midsection.

The hard buckle connected with her ribs and pain exploded. She couldn't help but cry out as she curled in on herself. *Oh God, oh God, oh God.*

"I wish you wouldn't make me hurt you. But if you

do, understand that I won't hesitate." Now he gently stroked her hip, adding frightful revulsion to the pain. "Webb was always too lenient with you. For your own good, I won't be. No, I won't bruise your pretty face. But your body… Sometimes a few bruises make things more interesting."

Carefully, staying in the cowed position, Cat dragged in an uneven breath. That punch had hurt so badly, she wasn't sure she was brave enough to provoke him toward further violence.

Then again, she definitely wasn't brave enough to let him strip her naked.

"Come now, Kitten." He stood over her. "Stop hiding from me."

Terrified of more retribution, Cat uncurled enough to see him. Tears pricked her eyes and the ache from that strike continued to radiate to every nerve ending.

Tesh smiled at her. "Good. Now you will get up and you will strip away every single article of your clothing."

Each small breath hurt, but Cat didn't fight him as he took her arm and yanked her upright. Her ribs protested. Had he cracked a few?

She kept her arms wrapped around herself, her feet braced against the jostling of the van. Glancing up at him, she showed him all the fear he craved.

His gaze, devoid of sympathy, moved over her features and then down her body. "Webb tried, I'll give him that. But you were always so goddamned feral." He loosened his hold and his firm voice softened to a croon. "I will soon have you purring. That's a promise."

She tried a tremulous smile, confusing him, deluding

him. He seemed stunned but pleased, already amped up from the violence, his expression raw with lust.

He yanked her against him.

Though any movement hurt like hell, Cat reacted by bringing up her knee as hard and fast as she could, striking him in the groin with stunning accuracy.

Blank shock cleared Tesh's expression just before he moaned and doubled over.

For good measure, Cat ignored her own pain and shoved him hard. As he fell to the hard corrugated floor of the van, a guttural groan bubbled from his throat.

Please, please, please, Cat whispered to herself. She grabbed the latch on the back door. At first it didn't give, and as the driver cursed and swerved, slowing the van, she tried again, gripping it with all her might.

She cried out as pain ripped through her bruised midsection, then the door swung open, dragging her out. Her toes barely stayed inside the van and she balanced over the pavement racing beneath her.

The van kept going, but so what? Better to die from the fall to the road than be tortured to death by Tesh.

In the distance behind the van, she saw headlights. If she did survive, perhaps the passengers would call for help.

"Cat, no." Sounding truly alarmed, Tesh stretched a hand out to her.

Ignoring him, Cat considered her odds of surviving the fall.

"Stop, damn you!" Tesh barked.

Cat thought he spoke to her until he added, "She'll die!"

The driver slowed, pulling to the side of the road.

Knowing it was now or never, Cat jumped toward

the piles of snow on the berm. She hit hard and, against her will, her body rolled uncontrollably, tumbling fast.

Tires screeched.

Tesh would come after her. God help her, he'd almost sounded horrified by her probable death, which only made him more insane. *He wanted to keep her, to sexually torture her, to enslave her as his own—for the rest of her life.*

What kind of life would that be?

She had to get up. She had to run. Her hands dug into the snow, frozen mud and gravel. Her hip now hurt as bad as her ribs. Panting, she got one knee beneath her—

"Cat!"

Terror played tricks on her, because that outraged voice sounded entirely too much like Leese.

She heard the running footsteps, then the screech of police sirens and finally a gunshot. Without understanding, she cringed, covered her head and—

"Cat. Baby, it's okay now. Just be still. Where are you hurt?"

Her racing heartbeat slowed. That was definitely Leese.

Peeking up, she found him kneeling by her in the snow. He didn't wear a coat. He was dressed exactly the same as he had been at the party—meaning…what? That he'd learned of her kidnapping and run after her without a second thought?

It appeared so. "Leese?" Confusion and hope squeezed her lungs. "How are you here?"

"I'm so sorry." He touched her gently, with fear and so much more. "Paramedics are on the way. Just stay still."

To hell with that. "I'm okay." She sat up, gasped in pain and quickly looked around.

Tesh lay facedown on the ground, the headlights of a police car showing the pool of blood around him. Another officer pulled the driver from the van, already locking his hands behind him.

It appeared everything had changed in a heartbeat.

"What hurts?" Leese carefully brushed snow and ice from her hair. "You have to talk to me, honey. Let me know you're okay."

Her heart started thumping. In a whisper, she said, "You have to trust me now, Leese. Please." When he started to question her, she put her fingers to his mouth. *"Trust me."*

"I do."

She flashed him a grateful smile, then, taking him by surprise, launched away and threw herself on Tesh. "Bastard," she yelled, sounding as hysterical as she could. She pounded on him, grabbed his shirt and yanked. Cops came running, but before they got to her, she got her hand in his pocket and grabbed the flash drive. No way would she allow Platt to use his influence to buy his way out of this one. Sahara had promised to see it through, and Cat believed her. With the evidence they needed held tight in her fist, she glanced back at Leese.

"Don't touch her!" he bellowed, halting the cops in their effort to drag her away.

Now that she had it, now that she knew Georgia Bell would finally be avenged, all the pain came screaming back and her face crumpled. She shifted to her butt, moaned, and Leese carefully supported her as she stood.

"My ribs," she gasped, leaning into him. "And," she whispered, "a flash drive."

Surprise drove his brows high, but when she slipped it into his hand, he took it. Seconds later the EMTs reached her.

And Leese never left her side.

CAT LOOKED EXHAUSTED by the time they left the hospital. A fiery dawn, filled with promise, edged the sky as Leese drove. He knew Sahara had wanted to be with them, but she was still being grilled by law enforcement.

Though Cat winced with every small movement, her ribs weren't broken, just very badly bruised. The attending doctor explained that the pain actually came from the traumatized muscles and cartilage around her ribs. She'd be sore for nearly a month…but she was alive.

And by God, she was *his*.

Leese lifted her hand and kissed her knuckles. If Tesh Coleman wasn't already dead, Leese would have taken pleasure in killing him.

"I'm okay," Cat told him again, her beautiful mouth curled in a small smile. "But I don't think I'll be exercising with you for a while." She hesitated. "I mean… if I'll even be around—"

"You're not going anywhere." If he had his way, she'd never again be out of his reach. He rubbed his thumb over her soft skin, then returned both hands to the wheel.

Cat just sighed. "Good. I'm not sure I have the energy anyway."

"I'm taking you to my house." He waited, and when she didn't object, some of the tension eased from his shoulders. "The agency is under siege by investigators, and they're starting to spill over to Sahara's house too. It won't take us long to get to my place. You can nap on the way if you want."

"Mostly," she said, "I just want to look at you and know you're safe."

His molars locked and he tightened his hands on the wheel. "I was never in danger, honey. But you…"

"He threatened you. He said he had guards watching you, ready to take a shot—"

"I know what the bastard told you." As far as Leese was concerned, Tesh had gotten off easy.

Everything kept replaying in his head like a horror flick. Seeing Cat jump to the road, her body rolling like a rag doll. That was bad enough, but when Tesh had emerged too, yelling Cat's name and then aiming a gun at her… Leese shook with the memory. Leese had known he wouldn't be able to get his weapon drawn in time and in that awful moment, he'd thought he would lose her.

But the officer behind him was ready, and he'd taken Tesh's life with a single bullet.

Leese knew if he lived to be a hundred, he'd never be able to repay Sahara for her calm, commonsense thinking. She'd had the chip sewn into Cat's dress as an added precaution, and in between giving him directions on where to go, she'd notified the police. With men in the area, they'd shown up just in time.

"Webb was innocent."

"Yes. Sahara's PI knew something was up, but he didn't know what. He'd told her too many pieces weren't coming together."

"Tesh thought the same. That's why he got suspicious, I guess." She curled a little tighter in her seat, shoulders down, arms around herself. "He was in as much danger as me. Tesh planned to kill him. But I...I assumed the worst."

"For good reason, considering the evidence you had." Leese hated to see her hurt, physically, but emotionally too. "Sahara spoke with your stepfather."

Cat stared at him with big eyes. "He's okay?"

"From what she told me, he was relieved to know you're okay." *Okay* being a very relative term. "He claims he knew the rep of the Body Armor agency, so when Platt insisted that he come up with a plan to get you back, he hoped for the exact scenario that played out."

"I'd like to believe him."

Getting her life back would be good, and that would have to start with knowing her family could be trusted. "Sahara believes him, if that helps. She says when he called, he worded things in a way that made it clear you were the priority. It was ambiguous enough to get past Platt and Tesh, who were in the room with him, but direct enough that when Sahara assigned me, she told me I worked for you, not for anyone else. And Webb did pay in advance, ensuring Sahara wouldn't pull your protection for lack of funds."

Cat watched him. "Would you have—"

"Quit? No. Not after knowing you a day." It hadn't taken long at all for Cat to get under his skin. After that first night when she'd slept with him...he'd known he was a goner. "Webb claims he also has evidence that will help to corroborate everything we've told authorities. Extra details so he'd be better able to offer an alibi."

"I'll talk to him tomorrow."

"After we've all gotten some sleep," Leese agreed. "You've had a pretty momentous day."

Cat held silent for a few moments, then whispered brokenly, "I thought Tesh was going to hurt you and it almost killed me. I knew I had to do something to stop him."

She'd done something all right. She'd attacked a madman. Jumped from a moving van. Then hoisted a flash drive from a dead body with police looking on. "You're amazing. And reckless."

"I couldn't risk you," Cat whispered.

Because she loved him? She'd said so, but her timing had sucked and now Leese wanted to hear it again. "We'll talk about that after you're rested." Never again would he let her put him first. If she thought risking him was bad, she should try it from his perspective.

He'd died a thousand times while trying to get to her. And all the while he'd known how twisted Tesh was, what he might do to Cat, what he probably was doing.

The flash drive contained all the information they needed to expose both Tesh and Senator Platt as the perverted, sick fucks they were. Sahara's PI had quickly located Tesh's mother, and soon they'd have the evidence from the safe-deposit box too.

Law officials were all over it because sometime after midnight the senator was found dead in his home, poisoned by the ice in his routine nightcap. A staff member close to the senator, but apparently loyal to Tesh, had prepared the drink.

The plan to commit the murder was laid out in notes contained in the flash drive, otherwise the world might have never known that Platt hadn't died of natural causes.

When Cat dozed off, Leese let out a tense breath. He'd soon have her in his home, and if all went as planned, she'd want to stay with him.

Forever.

As SUNSHINE SPILLED into the quiet bedroom, Leese nuzzled against Cat's neck and stirred her awake. He loved the scent of her skin, the taste of her mouth, the warmth of her small body snuggled to his.

He loved going to bed with her each night and waking up with her each morning.

He loved her, period.

For far too long they'd been under nonstop interrogation. Valentine's Day had come and gone, along with much of March, and spring was fast approaching. There'd been very little downtime, and no opportunity for a romantic dinner out. But he'd given Cat the few Valentine's Day gifts he'd picked up back when Miles had stayed with her.

She'd loved the unique, handmade Andamooka Opal necklace. Once she put it on, she didn't take it off. The bright splashes of color in the gem matched her quirky, fun and beautiful personality. He'd also bought her a new knit hat, mittens and a scarf, and a new cell phone with a long-term plan.

She hadn't remarked on the implied expectation, but had accepted when he insisted.

In return she'd given him a small painting, and then, because she said she hadn't had an opportunity to shop, she gave him a lap dance.

They were the best Valentine's Day gifts ever. One memory stayed on his office wall, the other he stored away as the hottest experience of his life.

It was the first holiday that Leese had celebrated in a long while. He knew it would always be the most memorable.

Things with Platt and Tesh weren't yet settled, but they were well on their way. Because Leese and Cat told the truth, as did Sahara and Justice, there could be no cover-up of the senator's evil conduct. The world had a right to know.

And Georgia Bell deserved justice.

Leese didn't want to think about that right now though. He wanted to concentrate on the fact that he and Cat finally had a few days free. His house was a good distance from hers, but Cat was still with him, and if all his plans worked out, they'd have a lifetime together.

There was nothing he wanted more.

"Wake up, sleepyhead."

As Cat stretched, making a small, throaty sound, Leese gently touched her ribs. She'd recovered from the assault, and no longer flinched in pain. Only faint bruises remained, though he'd forever remember them.

He, too, had healed from the bullet graze. Then, to get things settled, he'd taken a hiatus from work. Soon, however, he'd return to the agency, probably next week. Before then, he wanted to cement things with Cat.

Resting on his forearms over her, Leese murmured, "Open your eyes, Cat."

Her thick lashes slowly lifted. "Mmm?" She yawned widely, stretched again, then smiled up at him with soft affection. "Someone," she teased, "kept me up too late last night."

Last night had been amazing. Every time with her was better than the last. How that was possible he didn't know, but it was still true. "Complaining?"

"Praising," she corrected as she looped her arms around his neck.

Smoothing back her beautiful hair, Leese kissed her lips, then whispered, "Stay put. I'll bring you coffee in bed."

"Oh, nice. I'll just run to the bathroom, then crawl back under the covers."

She was so incredibly cute.

And she was his.

"Sounds like a plan." He kissed her again, then said, "Be right back."

In the kitchen, he made the coffee, readied two cups and retrieved the small wrapped package he'd hidden behind the bread box, along with everything else he needed.

When he returned, he found Cat in the bed propped against the headboard with the covers pulled up to her chin to ward off the chill.

She said, "Gimme," and gratefully took the coffee he handed her. "Mmm. Delicious." After two fortifying sips, she cradled the warm cup in her hands and eyed the other things on the tray. "So...what's all that?"

Leese smiled. "A proposition." He got into bed beside her, letting her wonder while he drank a little coffee too.

Finally she set her cup aside on the nightstand and reached for the sketch of a room. She studied it a minute, then said, "This looks like your guest room, but a little different too."

Also setting his cup aside, Leese scooted over to sit closer to her. "It's the guest room, but I had a designer reconfigure things so it could be a studio."

Surprise widened her eyes. "A studio?"

"More specifically, your studio. I wanted it to be similar to the room you had set up at your house."

"Why?"

"Your art is important to you, so it's important to me." Before she could question him further, he showed her a pamphlet. "And this is from the local shelter."

She blinked, clearly confused.

Leese opened it to photos of dogs. "What do you think?"

"I don't understand."

"We both wanted a dog, right? I figured we'd get one from the shelter." He teasingly kissed her. "You're not one of those snobs who need a pet with a pedigree, are you?"

Her eyes got a little glassy and she whispered, "No."

"Good. Me either. And my yard is already fenced. So when the shelter opens up today, we'll go get us one. Or hell, maybe two? Whatever you think is best."

She bit her lip, then whispered softly, "Two."

"Perfect. Two it is. Now open your gift."

"My gift?"

Leese handed her the small box, moved the tray to the floor, then lowered the sheet below her breasts. "Open it." He liked the way the opal rested just above her cleavage.

Breathing deeper, she whispered, "You can't keep buying me gifts when I can't reciprocate."

He gave her a hot smile. "You reciprocated enough for twenty gifts, trust me."

"You're saying you liked the dance?"

"The dance, the way you kissed me and the sex afterward. But that's nothing new, Cat. You know I love having sex with you."

She swallowed, nodded. "I love it too."

Still she held the small box without opening it. Leese figured she knew what it'd be, so maybe she just needed some time. He'd give her a few minutes more.

Until then…he cupped her breast. "I also love watching you paint. And seeing you laugh. The way you argue and how you sip your coffee."

That made her laugh.

Leese bent and kissed the warm skin just beneath her left breast. "I love your heart," he whispered. "How you trust it and your instincts, how loyal and brave you are."

Cat threaded her fingers into his hair. "I love those same things about you. And your body." She tugged until he lifted his face so she could look into his eyes. "Not just how good you look, though you're seriously hot. But you're also strong and so capable."

Sweeping a hand down her side to her hip, and pushing the blanket away in the process, Leese said, "You're strong in your own way, honey, and your body is about the sexiest thing I've ever seen. I definitely love it."

"You know, Leese, that's an awful lot of love words."

She sounded worried by that, but Leese didn't relent. "Know what else I love? The honest way you say what you think and feel. Don't ever let anyone tell you that's wrong."

She took in a shaky breath and nodded. "Okay."

Lastly he kissed her forehead. "I especially love the way you think, how you deal with all the twists and turns of life."

After a fortifying breath, she whispered, "I love everything about you." Her gaze held his. "I already told you that."

"Just once," he reminded her. "And I wouldn't mind hearing it again."

With no hesitation, she said, "I love you, Leese."

God, it felt good. Because she hadn't yet unwrapped it, Leese took the small box from her. The ribbon pulled away with ease and he lifted the velvety lid. "I love you too, Catalina. Will you marry me, live here with me, adopt a pet or two, eventually have some kids and let me love you forever?"

She stared at the ring, her breath coming faster and faster—and then with an elated scream she launched herself at him, taking him to his back and kissing his face all over.

Leese hooked her legs and flipped her right back over so he could settle between her legs. "Can I take that as a yes?"

"Yes!" Tears clung to her lashes. "I know it's crazy and insane, but I love you more than I ever thought I could love anyone or anything."

He smiled, and his heart felt full. "Same here. And yeah, it's a little crazy, but in a good way." He took the ring from the box and slipped it onto her finger. "Do you like it?"

She looked at the ring as if she hadn't really seen it before. It wasn't an extravagant diamond, but a moderately sized cushion-cut diamond with opals on either side that matched her necklace.

"Oh, Leese." Tears had her blinking fast. "It's the most stunningly beautiful thing I've ever seen." Again, as if only just then catching on, she said, "You're having a room remodeled for me?"

"I want you to live with me." It'd be a big move for her, but also a way for her to start over, away from the memories of what she'd been through. "What do you think?"

"I'd like that very much." She continued to study the ring, a small smile teasing over her lips. "I'm sure my job is gone by now, and after knowing people were in my house, that they'd planted bugs to spy on me…" She shuddered. "I don't ever want to live there again."

He understood that. Her stepfather claimed he wasn't the one to plant the bug, but he was the one who'd kept up the house for Catalina, and to fend off curiosity.

"It's okay," she said, smoothing a finger over his frown. "*I'm* okay. I promise."

She would be, Leese vowed. He'd make it so. He'd fill her life with so much happiness and love, it'd help to drive away the dark memories. "What kind of puppy do you want?"

She let out a big sigh. "Would you mind if we got a more mature dog? Everyone wants a puppy, but the older dogs get overlooked. I like the idea of two."

Could she be more special? He didn't think so. Meaning it, he promised, "Whatever you want, honey."

She curved her hands over his shoulders, then lifted her fingers to again admire her ring. "I want you."

Leese groaned in physical regret. "We have to leave soon if we're going to make it to Cannon's house on time. All the guys will be there, wives and babies too. Everyone is anxious to visit with you."

She bit her lip, then nodded. "They're like your family, aren't they?"

"More so than my real family ever was. You'll like everyone, I promise. And the babies are cute as hell."

"Cannon and Armie each have kids?"

He nodded, smiling when he thought of the little

ones. "Armie has a son, and Cannon has twins, one boy and one girl."

"I can't wait to see them." Cat drew a hand down over his chest. "We're going to visit my family afterward, right?"

By the second, it got harder to think about leaving the bed. "Yes." He'd met Webb a few times now. The man was formal, quietly caring and wary. He and Cat were slowly reconciling. A private dinner at Webb Nicholson's home would give them a chance to get more comfortable, and a chance for Leese to meet her brothers.

"We're going to have a busy day," Cat said. "But tonight...tonight you're all mine."

Leese loved the sound of that. "Tonight, tomorrow and for the rest of our lives."

* * * * *

*Look for Justice's story,
HARD JUSTICE,
coming soon from
Lori Foster
and HQN Books!*

*Meanwhile, read on for
BUILT FOR LOVE,
a bonus novella
in print for the first time!*

BUILT FOR LOVE

Dear Reader

Those of you who read my stories "Love Unleashed" (in the *Love Bites* anthology) and "Love Won't Wait" (in the Turn Up the Heat anthology) have been waiting patiently for Jesse Baker, best friend of brothers Evan and Brendan "Brick" Carlisle, to get a story of his own. After all, the hot contractor is the perfect blend of honorable and charming, despite his bad-boy rep. I'm so pleased that the wait is over and that Jesse's story, "Built for Love," is available now.

You might recall that Jesse was first introduced to sexy Realtor Tonya Bloom in "Love Won't Wait"—but though their chemistry ignited from the start, Tonya had just become the guardian of her orphaned twelve-year-old nephew, Kevin...not exactly the best time to fall in love. In "Built for Love," Tonya is struggling to help Kevin feel safe and secure in his new home—and while she sees Jesse as a distraction she can't afford, Jesse's determined to prove to her that he wants forever. With a little help from some old friends and a pregnant cat aptly named Love, can Jesse convince Tonya that some loves are built to last?

I hope you enjoy Jesse and Tonya's story. Don't worry if you haven't yet read Evan's and Brick's stories, as each novella was written to stand alone.

Lori Foster

CHAPTER ONE

BACK WHEN HE'D been twelve years old, Jesse Baker had lived the cushy life. He'd played most sports, even excelled at a few. His dad helped coach and always encouraged him. His mom coddled, set boundaries and loved unconditionally.

They were both watchful with high expectations. Always positive, supportive, attentive.

Never absent, never negligent.

He'd had his own room, a comfy bed, music and games, and he'd never had to ask for the necessities, like food or clothes or school supplies.

Now, at twenty-seven, his folks were still indulgent and very involved in his life, but not in any intrusive way. Occasional phone calls, visits, big holidays together... Never, not once, had he doubted their love.

It wasn't that he'd taken them for granted, but he'd never before realized just how lucky he was to have them. Now, though, seeing the sullen boy sitting on the curb, it hit him in a big way.

Leaving his surprise on the passenger seat, Jesse got out of his truck and closed the door quietly, but still drew the boy's attention. Through a mop of messy blond hair, Kevin squinted up at him. Jesse saw a few bruises, swollen eyes and a lot of attitude resting on rawboned shoulders a little too wide for his frame. He was tall for a twelve-year-old boy, his joints prominent, especially given his slight weight.

He had yet to fill out, but when he did, he'd be a good-looking kid. If he'd smile.

Jesse planned to work on that.

"Hey." Walking closer, he wondered where Tonya might be. "Your aunt around?"

"Inside on the phone." He watched Jesse with wary uncertainty, trying to shore up the boulder-sized chip on his shoulder while hovering on the brink of crumbling.

Heart hurting, Jesse stopped beside him. For more than a month he'd been chasing Tonya, determined to have her in his bed. Maybe more. But sex first.

Only Tonya had resisted for reasons he hadn't understood—until it became painfully obvious. She liked him, of that Jesse had no doubt. She wanted him too, although she'd never admitted it.

But she had big responsibilities that made her reservations more than reasonable.

When Jesse didn't walk on, Kevin scooted back and came to his feet. Though his jeans rode low on his hips, they were still too short, his shirt too worn.

Blue eyes expressed a world weariness that no kid should ever possess.

"How are you holding up?" Jesse finally asked.

Mouth firming, eyes narrowing, the kid hunched his shoulders, turned and shuffled off without answering.

Now what? Jesse wondered. How far would the boy go? He hadn't meant to chase him off, but hell, he'd never dealt with a situation like this before.

Tonya saved him by opening the door and stepping out. "Kevin," she said pleasantly, as if he hadn't been leaving. "It's time for lunch."

Kevin stood there a minute, his lanky body stiff, his skinny shoulders rolled forward, until finally he turned back and headed across the lawn to the front door. He didn't look at either of them, and he said nothing as he went in past Tonya.

Stepping out and letting the door close behind her, she waited until Jesse had reached her. Her forced smile of welcome didn't quite reach her beautiful blue eyes.

Feeling beyond inadequate, Jesse asked quietly, "How are you doing?" He wanted to touch her, to tell her he intended to help, but damn, she didn't look any more receptive than Kevin had.

Last week she'd learned that her sister had died in a DWI. High, out of control, an absentee mother. The police had found Kevin at home alone. Apparently not an unusual occurrence.

Now Tonya had custody, and a whole lot of emotional complications to sort out.

Did she expect Jesse to bail? Probably.

He had a pretty good clue that it was issues with her sister that had kept her closed off from him, the reason she'd built so many walls around her heart.

"I'm doing okay," she said, clearly lying. "There's an incredible amount of paperwork and reorganizing and…so many things I can't even figure out yet, especially with school right around the corner. But we're getting there, little by little."

She looked overwhelmed, and no wonder. Jesse glanced back at the truck, saw all was quiet and decided to give it a few more minutes.

Leaning against the side of the house, he said, "Go over it with me. Maybe I can help."

"Jesse," she remonstrated. "You don't need to do this."

Since meeting her he'd become all too familiar with that apologetic yet dismissive tone. She liked him, enjoyed his company—unless he got too involved. Then she put on the emotional brakes and placed a whole lot of physical space between them.

Now that he knew why, he'd stop making it so easy on her. Whether she admitted it or not, she needed him, and that made a big difference.

Quirking one brow, he asked, "This?"

She avoided his gaze. "Hanging around." Keeping her voice low, she explained, "It's not you. You're... terrific."

Drily, he muttered, "Gee, thanks."

She forged on. "But I know what you want and I can't—"

"What?" He crossed his arms over his chest, more than a little curious. "What is it you think I want?"

Long blond hair cascaded down her back when she lifted her chin. Damn, she was a knockout, no two ways about it. Independent, smart, compassionate—and pretty clueless when it came to him.

It'd be his pleasure to straighten out her misconceptions.

She glanced inside to ensure Kevin wasn't within hearing range, then met his stare. "Sex."

No reason to deny it. "Sex would be great."

Her lips softened, and her blue eyes went dark. "Jesse—"

"But if that's all I wanted," he told her gently, "I could get that without you."

The sensual heat cleared away, replaced with an overdose of attitude. "Then maybe you should—"

Crowding into her personal space, Jesse kissed her. Soft, warm and so incredibly hot. Even though he kept it light, barely there, it affected him.

Because this was Tonya. Because he hadn't yet had her.

Because he liked and admired her and, hell yes, he wanted her. Bad.

From the first moment he'd laid eyes on her, he'd been physically attracted. With every minute after that he'd grown to like her more.

He'd already realized that what they had between them was special. Now he just needed her to understand. But she'd had so much dumped on her that he had to put the revving engines on idle, go slower, ease her into things.

And even thinking *that* made him tense with lust.

"Fact is, I want *you*, Tonya, and that's not the same thing as just wanting to get laid."

Nervous fingers touched her mouth. It took her a second before she whispered, "All the reasons I couldn't before—"

"Are more valid than ever, I know." He smoothed back her silky-soft hair. "You were trying to help your sister?"

"Yes." She dropped her hand, and her breath released in weariness. "And protect Kevin."

In the end, Kevin had gotten badly hurt anyway. He'd been neglected by the only parent he knew—and now that parent was gone. But Tonya wasn't, and she'd make a better life for him.

Jesse badly wanted to help her with that. "I'm glad he has you."

She took his right hand in both of hers. "Then surely you understand that I can't...can't push him aside to get involved with you right now."

A dozen replies came to mind, ways to convince her, to win her over.

He settled on being blunt. "I just got here. Don't piss me off, okay?"

Frowning, she dropped her gaze. "I didn't—"

"Number one, we're already involved. Denying it won't make it go away because I'm not budging." He smoothed her hair again. "And besides, I'm not the only one feeling it."

Lashes lifting, she stared into his eyes.

No reply was admission enough for him.

"Number two." He cupped his hand around her nape and resisted the urge to kiss her instead of talking. Given the subject wasn't an easy one, kissing would be a lot easier.

But ultimately, that wouldn't get him anywhere.

"Do you honestly think I'd expect you to do *anything* that'd bring more grief on that kid?"

She searched his face. "No."

He gave in and kissed her forehead. "Good. So stop shoving me away. Let me help."

"You are so stubborn."

"Look who's talking."

She covered her face, but still he heard the strained laugh.

"Number three," he whispered, pleased that he'd lightened her mood just a little, "you don't have to choose. Give me a chance to show you that I can help without getting in the way."

Still hiding behind her hands, she laughed again. "You distract me."

Far as he was concerned, she could use some distractions. Encircling her narrow wrists, he pulled down her hands and gave her another quick kiss, this one on her smiling mouth, then, securing her hand in his, led the way through her house.

As a Realtor, Tonya had found the perfect property. She lived in one side of the old house that had been turned into a duplex and rented the other half to Merrily—the woman now very involved with his best friend, Brick.

Brick, aptly named given his hard head, had introduced him to Tonya without realizing just how complicated things would become. He had Jesse's gratitude all the same.

He could handle complications; it was Tonya cutting him out that he couldn't handle.

With Merrily next door, so too was Brick, which gave Jesse plenty of excuses to be nearby…if Tonya didn't see reason. But hopefully his plan would work out for all involved and Tonya would invite him to stick close.

The house had a lot of character that, as a carpenter, he especially admired. But the fact that it was divided into two living spaces meant limited room to grow and add a kid. He knew she had a second bedroom, but she'd mostly used it for her office.

Now that she'd cleared everything out so Kevin would have a bedroom, where had she relocated her work space?

Thinking ahead, it was possible Merrily would be

moving out once she and Brick married, something they were currently planning. At that point, it would be easy for him to turn the house back into a single dwelling—if that's what Tonya wanted.

But maybe she needed the income from the rental, in which case he could probably convert the attic into a cozy office for her. He'd have to ask Brick about their plans. If they did move, they'd need a place with a yard for Merrily's two dogs and three cats.

It was from Merrily and her menagerie that Jesse had gotten his inspiration for how to help. Well, from her and from fate.

When they entered the kitchen they found Kevin slouched in his seat, his knees pointing outward, big feet hooked around the chair legs, his head propped on a fist. Only one bite had been taken from his sandwich.

Tonya's smile quickly faded. She became brisk and determined. "Jesse, would you like a sandwich?"

"Sure." He steered her away from the cabinet and to her seat. "But you go ahead and get started. I'm a big boy. I can make it myself."

Brows flinching with doubt, Kevin eyed him and the bread he pulled from the bag.

Jesse kept a smile on his face as he arranged a pile of meat and cheese. "I stopped by for a favor."

As if expecting something awful, Kevin turned his gaze away and drew up his shoulders again.

How many times had he had to do that? Hunker down and prepare for the worst?

Of course, Tonya noted Kevin's skewed perception of the world where any favor asked by a man was a bad thing. On top of drugs, had her sister indulged too many men? Maybe men who'd had little patience for having an adolescent underfoot?

Jesse held his anger in check. Any sign of it from him would only discomfit Kevin more.

Apparently Tonya felt the same since she forced a smile. "Sure, Jesse. What can I do for you?"

"Well, that's the thing. It'll involve Kevin too."

Kevin's head popped up and he stared at Jesse as if totally taken by surprise.

At least he'd gotten an honest reaction other than that awful emotional distance that usually shrouded the kid like a black cloud.

Tonya was liable to smack him, but damn it, he had to try. After setting his plate on the table, he turned to the boy and was struck by his expression.

Had no one ever before included him?

Jesse geared himself for arguments or outright refusal, even as he considered ways to convince him. "I know it'll be a big job, Kevin, but before you say no, let me show you, okay?"

Put on the spot, Kevin scowled, then nodded. "Okay."

"Great. I need to run out to my truck, but I'll be right back." Nodding at the sandwich on Kevin's plate, he said, "Wolf that down while you have the chance."

Tonya tipped her head, confused. He squeezed her shoulder on his way out.

Feeling a little more optimistic now that he had something to do, a way to proceed, a *plan*, Jesse strode through the house and out the front door. Sunshine blinded him. It was a beautiful day—a clear sky, a slight breeze and low humidity. His truck sat beneath a huge tree that offered plenty of shade, and he'd left the windows open, but still, he was anxious as he opened the passenger door and retrieved his package.

Inside the large carrier, the lazy cat stretched awake and gave him a rumbling purr.

Poking a finger inside, he stroked the cat's head. "How you doing in there, Love? Okay?"

She rubbed her furry little face along the sides of the carrier as if seeking more attention.

"Soon now. Let's go."

When he turned, both Tonya and Kevin stood at the door watching him. Gaze zeroed in on the carrier, Kevin popped the last bite of his sandwich into his mouth.

Huh. Well, if nothing else, he'd gotten the boy to eat.

Tonya pushed the door open and stepped out. "What in the world?"

"Good luck," Jesse whispered to the cat. "Be your charming best, okay?"

Big eyes, one yellow and one blue, stared up at him.

Hoping Tonya would accept his plan, he said, "She's pregnant, due to give birth in the next few weeks, according to the vet." He paused as both Tonya and Kevin bent to peer inside.

Kevin said nothing, but Tonya started in surprise. "She has two different-colored eyes."

"She's unique." Jesse opened the door and went in with the other two following close behind.

For once, Kevin didn't shuffle.

"I found her hiding under a woodpile at the shop." As a carpenter, he had a lot of stored supplies, both inside the building and out in the yard. It was during a rainstorm that he'd found the cat. He'd opened a tarp to cover a new delivery of wood and there she was, huddled down, soaked through and round with pregnancy.

Back in the kitchen, he set the carrier on the floor, opened it and, counting on the cat to do her part, took his seat at the table.

Kevin went to his knees in a rush, silent but more involved than Jesse had witnessed so far. Wide-eyed curiosity replaced the scowl. When the cat poked her head out, Kevin looked as if he'd never seen a pet before.

"Be extra gentle with her," Jesse instructed quietly. "She's not only pregnant, but deaf. She's been through a lot lately too. First being out in a storm, then getting used to me when I took her in, then the vet and now here." The cat had a lot to adjust to—just as Kevin did. It'd be nice if they helped each other with that.

After giving him a knowing, very pleased and finally real smile, Tonya went to the floor with Kevin, their shoulders almost touching.

Tonya was a tall woman, nearly six feet of female perfection. But Kevin, at only twelve, was probably only three or four inches shorter. Clearly height ran in their family.

"You're sure she's deaf?" Tonya asked.

"I'd suspected, but the vet confirmed it." He took two big bites of food, satisfied with the cat's reception so far. "I know Kevin starts school soon, but until then, do you think he could help me with the cat?"

"Help how?"

Both Tonya and Jesse went still at the words. So far Kevin had been mostly withdrawn, and when he did speak, it wasn't with any type of enthusiasm.

Now, though, he seemed wholly engaged.

Tonya recovered first. She tickled the cat under the chin as she spoke. "Jesse's a carpenter with his own shop. He puts in a lot of hours. With the cat pregnant

and probably a little scared, it'd be nice if she had someone looking after her. Someone she could get to know
and trust."

Sitting back on his heels, Kevin stared at the cat
with rapt fascination. After what felt like an eternity,
his attention went to Jesse. "You'd let me watch her?"

"I'd beg if needed," Jesse teased.

Kevin's attention went to Tonya. He licked his lips,
his expression painfully hopeful. "You…you wouldn't
mind?"

"Of course not." With a fleeting touch to his back,
Tonya said, "But are you sure? Cats are a lot of responsibility."

Bobbing his head, Kevin glanced back at the cat.
"I'm sure."

As if on cue, Love walked out of the carrier with her
big belly swaying. With a raspy meow, she butted her
head against Kevin's knee.

The boy breathed fast, then carefully ran his hand
down her back.

She purred loudly, and poor Kevin looked like he'd
collapse.

It damn near left Jesse choked up. "She likes you,"
he managed to say without too much smothering sentiment.

When the cat put both front paws on his thighs and
looked up into his face, Kevin went stiff.

"Aw. She does," Tonya confirmed.

In her gaze, Jesse saw the same things he felt—relief,
satisfaction…and burgeoning hope. Kevin needed a
new focus, and he badly needed a friend. So far he'd
shunned those people trying to get closer, so maybe the

cat could do what humans couldn't—or at least soften the way a little.

While Kevin and the cat cozied up to each other, Jesse ate the rest of his sandwich, content just to watch the bonding process.

After climbing into his lap, the cat curled herself comfortably and closed her eyes. Kevin continued to gently stroke her. "She's going to sleep."

Tonya blinked back tears and carefully put her hand to Kevin's back. "Yes, she is. That's how she tells you that she trusts you."

Moving slowly so he wouldn't disturb the cat, Kevin shifted to sit cross-legged, his back to the wall. He swallowed hard when the cat looked up at him, gave a high-pitched "meow" and settled again.

His gaze flashed to Tonya, and then to Jesse.

"Cat talk," Jesse said. "She likes to meow every now and then, but I don't think she realizes how loud she is." He chewed the last bite of his sandwich. "The vet told me most white cats with blue eyes are deaf. I hadn't realized that."

"How come?"

Jesse shrugged. "No idea. Just part of their DNA I guess."

"Maybe we could go to the library one day and get some cat books, do a little research to see what causes it," Tonya suggested.

Kevin froze again. "The library?"

"There's one not too far from here. I have a library card, but we could get you your own if you want."

Given his expression, Jesse would bet Kevin had never been within throwing distance of a library. Which probably meant he didn't do much reading. "I like mysteries," Jesse said. "And I own a ton of how-to books."

"I read a lot of romance and some biographies," Tonya offered.

Kevin frowned. "I don't read much."

"Then maybe you just haven't found the type of books you like. But we'll look into it," she told him.

"Cat books," he murmured uncertainly. "I guess I could check in to them."

"So." Jesse, too, joined them on the floor. "I already got her a cat box. With her pregnant, that'll need to be changed a couple of times a day."

"I'll do it." Kevin glanced at Tonya, then back at the cat. Shoulders dropping, sounding very uncertain, he offered, "She could stay in my bedroom with me."

Locking her hands together, probably to keep from hugging the boy, Tonya said, "That'd be great, honey. But I'm not sure there's room."

"Why don't I take a look?" Relieved to again have something to do, Jesse pushed back to his feet.

"A look at what?" Scrambling up to join him, Tonya laughed with her own uncertainty. "You can't make the room bigger."

"No, but I can do other things." As he started out of the room, he heard her speaking to Kevin in a rush.

"Do you mind keeping an eye on her while I...?"

Kevin must've agreed, because two seconds later Tonya was beside him. "Jesse, wait. I don't know what—"

Overwhelmed and feeling it, he caught the back of her neck and put his mouth over hers. Her soft, sweet lips took him closer to the edge, but he knew this wasn't the time and it sure as hell wasn't the place. By small degrees he forced himself to ease away.

For two seconds more, Tonya's eyes stayed closed, her lips parted.

"Damn." If there wasn't a kid only a room away, he'd definitely accept that unwitting invitation. "Soon," he promised her, knowing neither of them would last much longer. Now that he understood why she threw up barriers, he hoped to help her tear them down.

"Oh." Gaze searching his, Tonya cleared her throat and smoothed her hair. "What was that for?"

"For being so amazing." She'd not only taken in a boy with a lot of baggage, but she'd openly accepted a pregnant, deaf cat. That made her pretty damned special.

"Amazing?"

"And hot too." His gaze dipped over her. "Definitely hot."

She took the sexual compliment better than the emotional one. Pretending exasperation, she started to say something, but when he walked on down the hall, she again hurried to catch up.

Standing in the open doorway to Kevin's new room, he immediately saw the problem. Large, clunky furniture filled the space to the point he wondered how they could get to the closet.

Squeezed in close beside him in the doorway, Tonya said quietly, "These are his things." Giving an embarrassed wave at the disreputable mattress, the dresser missing a drawer, the threadbare quilt, she added, "I wasn't sure how—or if—I should replace them right away, or if he'd mind..."

"Yeah." Mouth firming, Jesse made note of the deep scratches in the dresser, the stains on the quilt.

He turned away with a purpose and called down the hall, "Hey, Kevin?"

Confrontational but cautious, Kevin peered around the corner from the kitchen only a few seconds later. "What?" The cat wound around his legs.

"Come here a sec, will you?"

Even more wariness entered his gaze until he hung his head, tightened his shoulders and, at a snail's pace, stepped around the cat.

What the hell? Did he really think Jesse called him over for something awful? If it wouldn't unman Kevin, he'd have pulled him in for a big, gentle bear hug.

He needed it even if Kevin didn't.

Going the next best route, he put his arm over Kevin's skinny shoulders and drew him into the room. "It seems your stuff doesn't fit."

Chin jutting, Kevin shrugged. "I told her there wasn't room but—"

Tonya cut him off, saying firmly, "If I lived in a one-room hut, there would still be room for you."

Damn. So Kevin mistook his meaning? Jesse allowed himself one squeeze—a move that clearly surprised Kevin—then he got down to business. "It's the furniture that's too big. But you know what I think?" Stretching out his arms and framing one wall with his fingers, he imagined it aloud. *"Loft bed."*

Tonya's eyes widened, but Kevin just looked at him with confusion.

"See, the bed will be on long legs, sort of like a top bunk bed, but instead of another bed on the bottom, we'd put a desk and dresser. And I'd even build a nook, so there'd be room for Love."

"Love?" Tonya asked, sounding a little breathless at his fast-track plans.

"The cat." Curious at her reaction, he watched her closely. "That's what I call her."

"Why?" Kevin asked.

"Because she seemed so uncertain of her welcome, but I figure there's always room for Love, right?"

As if summoned, the cat sauntered in, brushing against this leg and that leg until she reached Kevin and sat on his worn sneaker.

God love the cat, she did what Jesse couldn't—freely gave affection.

Kevin again looked like a deer caught in the headlights. He clearly didn't know how to react. "Um…so you actually love her?"

"It was love at first sight." Again he dropped his arm over Kevin's shoulders. "It's like that sometimes. The cat wasn't sure about coming into the house. I wasn't sure she'd want to. But we tried it and, hey, worked out great, right?"

Frowning in thought, maybe drawing a parallel, Kevin muttered, "I guess."

"There's stuff to work out, of course. It's always that way when things change. But we're getting there."

Kevin looked at him. "Okay."

Before things got awkward, or maybe more awkward, Tonya took control. "I love the idea of a loft bed." She tipped her head at Kevin. "What do you think?"

"It'd mean climbing a ladder each night, but tall as you are and long as your legs are, it'd probably be only one step for you." Jesse did a visual measurement. "You're what? Five-eight?"

"I dunno."

Jesse backed up to him, did a hand measurement on the difference in their height, and nodded. "I'd say at least five-eight. Maybe five-nine. Tall, for sure."

"Mom wasn't as tall as Tonya."

Jesse didn't know about the kid's dad, so he asked instead, "Your grandparents?"

Kevin deferred to Tonya.

"Dad was tall. Mom and Cissy, my sister, were both shorter. I'm guessing Kevin got my and Dad's height."

"Couple more years," Jesse said, "and you'll be taller than me."

Maybe flustered by mention of the future, Tonya launched back into the discussion on the bedroom. "Are the ceilings high enough for a loft bed?"

"Yeah. I can make it work if Kevin likes the idea." Before he could reply, Jesse said, "I'm a contractor, you know? Not to brag, but I can build anything. Especially if you lend a hand." It'd be good for Kevin to have something to do, other than ponder the rapid-fire changes in his life. "I already have the wood and supplies from leftover orders."

Kevin scowled at the old bed taking up too much room.

In a rush, just in case Kevin thought to deny him, Jesse added, "You can consider it payback for your taking care of Love."

"But I want to do that."

"Great." He gestured around the room. "And I want to make this setup better suited for you. It's great when you can enjoy your work."

Unconvinced, Kevin shifted his feet. "I don't know how to build anything."

"Well, neither did I at your age, not until someone taught me."

"Who?"

"My dad, and Brick's dad—you've met Brick, right? There was an older guy that lived next door to us too. He built furniture and he'd let me lend a hand sometimes." Shrugging, Jesse added, "Anytime someone gave me the opportunity to hold a tool, I was on it."

Tonya eased closer to Kevin. "Would you mind if we replaced these things?"

"To make room for Love?" Jesse hoped that'd cinch the deal. Damn, but he wanted to do something for the boy.

"I don't care." Kevin swept a scowl over his meager belongings. "It's all junk anyhow."

"It's not bad. I remember being your age," Jesse told him. "I'd camp out on the ground, the floor, in a tree house… I could pretty much crash anywhere."

"I guess."

Needing no more agreement than that, Jesse almost rubbed his hands together. "Tomorrow is Saturday. We can get started then. It might take a few days. It'll be best if we build the bed right in here, which means we'll have to move all this out. I have a sleeping bag you can use until we get it all done. Love will probably want to bunk down with you. You're not allergic to cats, are you?"

Tonya stared at him for that verbal outpouring, but she didn't interfere.

Kevin shook his head. "Don't think so."

"Good. I have her things in my truck. Cat box and litter—Tonya will have to decide a good place for that."

"In the alcove by the stairs to the basement?" she suggested.

"Sounds good." Again he put his arm around Kevin, ignoring it when the kid stiffened. "I have a brush for her too. She loves being brushed. And some food and her dishes."

"Those can go in the kitchen."

It almost made him grin, how Tonya struggled to keep up.

"Got her some toys and catnip too. She's *nuts* on the nip, so protect your toes. She likes to pounce."

Kevin looked at the cat and grinned—and damn, but that almost floored Jesse. That grin made him feel twelve feet tall, and at the same time it put a vise around his throat. "You have great teeth. Anyone ever told you that?"

Blinking, Kevin said, "Uh, no."

"You do." He clapped him on the shoulder. "You're a good-looking kid. Tall. Broad shoulders. Strong enough to help me with the heavy lifting."

Tonya protested. "Hey, I want to help too. I think I'm strong enough."

She had more strength than any woman he'd ever known. He smiled at her, checked her biceps and pretended to think about it. "Hmm. What do you think, Kevin?"

Ducking his face, Kevin hid a smile. "Up to her."

"Then I guess she can help. A little. But I was thinking it'd be nice to make it a surprise for her."

"I do love surprises," she said, playing along.

To Kevin, Jesse asked, "Wanna help me carry stuff in?"

"Sure."

Love jumped up to Kevin's mattress, circled a few times, then snuggled down into his pillow.

Appalled, worried, Kevin glanced at Tonya.

Reassuring him, she smiled. "Isn't that sweet? Will you mind sharing your pillow?"

"No, I don't mind." Poor dude exhaled in relief, scrunched up his brow, then blurted, "I brought this old cat in once, but Mom had a fit and made me put it back out cuz it got on the couch and stuff. She said no one wanted an old mangy cat hanging around. She said if I wanted a pet, she'd get me a cute little kitten."

Jesse and Tonya exchanged a look over how he'd suddenly shared all that.

"She never did though. We never had any pets." Still frowning, Kevin stepped over to pet Love. "Probably a good thing, I guess."

It surprised Jesse, hearing Kevin open up so much. "A lot of people like kittens more, but I think Love is perfect. For one thing, she doesn't have to be box trained, and she already knows not to shred anything with her claws."

Kevin nodded.

"And she'll have kittens," Jesse reminded him, in case that appealed to him.

"Yeah."

Going one further, Tonya said, "I know not everyone lets pets on the furniture, but it's never bothered me. You've met Merrily and her menagerie. They all go wherever they want."

"We'll have to introduce the animals to one another." Jesse watched how gently Kevin petted that cat, and how the cat loved it. "Brick might want to help with the room. He's a handyman himself. His brother, Evan, is pretty good too. Have you met him? He's a gym teacher at the elementary."

"Evan and Cinder were by a few nights ago," Tonya told him. And then to Kevin, "You remember them, right?"

"Yeah." Kevin stepped away. "Want me to just get the stuff from your truck?"

"Sure, if you don't mind. Thanks. It's on the floor of the passenger seat."

After giving the cat one last look, Kevin jogged out.

With gratitude shining in her eyes, Tonya sent Jesse a silent but heartfelt *thank you*. When she heard the front screen door drop shut, she added, not so silently, "I can pay you for the materials—"

"You heard what I told Kevin." He scooped her in close for a one-armed hug and got her moving. "I already have everything I need."

"Which you paid for."

"It's just scrap material, leftovers from other jobs. But enough to make the room work better for him."

They were in the hallway, out of sight of adolescent attention, and to Jesse's surprise, Tonya pressed him back against the wall.

Her hands to his chest, her face tipped up, she gave him a solemn smile. "You make it seem so easy."

Since she'd never before initiated things, Jesse took advantage by putting his hands on her waist and keeping her close. "What's that?"

"Dealing with him."

"I was his age once."

"It's not the same, and you know it." She took another step in and snuggled against him. "I angst over every little decision. I'm so damned afraid of making things worse for him."

"You could never do that just by caring, by trying to improve his life." By loving him.

Her hands moved over him, creeping up and around his neck. "He tries so hard to be tough when I know he has to be fragile."

"Boys that age are a lot more resilient than you think."

"He's so…moody."

"Honey, he's *twelve*." He kissed her forehead. "He's been through hell, I know. But trust me on this, moodiness is not uncommon for any kid his age."

The front door opened and dropped shut again, forcing Tonya to step back away from him. They watched Kevin cross into the kitchen, his arms loaded with cat paraphernalia.

"You gave him some direction." She looked back at Jesse. "A way to be a part of things."

"So you don't mind the cat?"

"Of course not. It's brilliant. And she's beautiful. And you're…wonderful." Her face showed many emotions. "Again, thank you."

"You'll let me help?" He wanted her agreement. He wanted *her*. Hell, he was starting to think he wanted it all—Kevin included.

"If it was just me…but you got him to smile." Her eyes glistened before she blinked fast and gave him a smile of pure happiness. "Yes, please, I would love your help."

"That's a start." Hopefully, eventually, Jesse would get her to love everything he had to offer—forever.

CHAPTER TWO

TONYA COULD HEAR male laughter coming from down the hall, and it filled her heart with hope. In such a short time Jesse had performed miracles. With the house. With Kevin.

With her heart.

There was still a long way to go, at least with Kevin. But her nephew had opened up enough to show occasional enthusiasm over the changes in his room, the addition of a cat and working with "the guys." He thought Brick, Jesse's best friend and Merrily's fiancé, was hilarious. He and Evan, Brick's brother, discussed school, making that transition easier. And in his quiet, resigned way, Kevin so obviously idolized Jesse.

And why not? The man excelled at everything he did, including getting close. To Kevin, and to her.

She'd worked so hard at resisting him, denying everything he made her feel. Then he'd shown his caring for a hurt boy, diving into a situation most men would avoid, and in the process he'd forever stolen her heart.

She already knew she loved him.

He'd been clear about wanting her sexually, and even clearer that he'd be sticking around to help with Kevin's transition.

But more than that? She didn't know. For right now

she planned to live by the motto "one day at a time." It'd have to work with Kevin.

And with Jesse.

From the glimpses they'd given her so far, the loft bed looked like it came with the house, matching the woodwork, sturdy enough for a boy Kevin's size, and all around…perfect. She had no doubt the dresser and desk would be the same once they were finished.

Jesse was good with his hands. Good with boys. Good with women…

He was especially good at making her adore him. For so many reasons—too many to count. Some were physical because, come on, he was a seriously gorgeous guy. Tall, fit, with dark blond hair and wicked green eyes that drew every woman's attention.

But the emotional reasons far outweighed the physical.

Merrily nudged her. "You're smiling like a woman with a fantasy on her mind."

"Maybe." Tonya sighed. "Jesse's been over almost every night for the last six days. How could I not fantasize?" She had a feeling he could have wrapped up the work in half that time, but dragged it out to give himself a reason to keep hanging around.

Then again, other than Saturday and Sunday, he'd been putting in full days at his carpentry shop and just coming by afterward.

"That's awesome," Merrily enthused. "You know Brick and I would love if you two became more official."

To ensure the guys wouldn't overhear, both women kept their voices low. "That's not the kind of fantasy I meant."

"I know the kind you meant, you hussy." Merrily's grin widened. "And I know Jesse is more than willing."

"That may be." Tonya put the last slice of pizza in a keeper. "But right now it'd be tough to work out."

"Hmm…"

"No," Tonya told her, her expression filled with mock severity. "Don't start plotting."

Merrily opened her mouth to reply, and just then, empty plate in hand, Kevin stepped into the kitchen. He froze when he saw they'd already put everything away. At the most unexpected times he would become wary, even about simple things like leftover pizza.

Tonya did her best to overlook his concern. "Still hungry? We've got one big slice left."

"No." He headed for the sink. "That's okay."

"Oh please," Merrily said, already reopening the plastic keeper. "Fill up! Better for you to eat it than chance it going to waste, right?"

"You might want it later." He glanced at Tonya. "Or Jesse might."

"Jesse can buy another pizza if he decides he wants more."

Unconvinced, Kevin hesitated, rocking back to his heels, until the words just bubbled out. "Mom always said I ate too much. That I'd put her in the poorhouse."

Appalled, Tonya went mute.

Thank God Merrily was there because she laughed as if it were a joke, as if Tonya's sister hadn't been a self-centered person and a miserable mother. "I think all moms of growing boys say the same thing. Shoot, my mother used to say it about me." She plopped the pizza on his plate. "She used to call me a bottomless pit."

"Really?"

Making it the most natural thing in the world, Merrily reached up to mess his hair. "Yup. She said I inhaled my food."

"My mom said that too."

"That just means you're growing and need the energy, I think. Good thing we had some left over, huh?"

"Yeah." He smiled, amazing Tonya. In the next second he said, "Thanks," and went back to the men.

Defeated, Tonya dropped into a seat and, elbows on the table, covered her face. "Everyone is so good with him—except for me. I totally suck."

"That's not true."

"I overreact to everything."

"You knew his mother better than the rest of us, so you have a very different perspective," Merrily reasoned. "But honestly, you need to stop looking for ways she failed him."

Shamed, Tonya peeked from between her spread fingers. "Do I do that?"

"I think you're worried, and you saw some terrible stuff, so you automatically put the worst possible connotation on everything." She folded up the pizza box and put it in the trash, then rinsed out the food keeper they hadn't needed, after all. "It's understandable, so cut yourself some slack, okay? You've lost a sister and gained a live-in family member, so you have a lot more to deal with."

"I want him happy, damn it." Brimming with frustration, she waited until Merrily had taken a seat. "More than anything in the whole world, I want that."

Merrily took her hand. "You both need a little time, that's all."

Jesse spoke from the doorway. "And I'll be helping." With a naturalness of long-standing, he bent to give Tonya a reassuring hug and a kiss to her temple. "Don't forget that."

Merrily beamed at him. "How's it going in there? When can we see?"

"Soon." He opened the dishwasher and put his and Brick's pizza plates away. "Kevin ate almost as much as me. I'll have to remember that next time and order more."

Meaning he planned to visit for dinner again, even though the remodel was nearly complete?

Leaning back on the counter, arms crossed, he eyed Tonya. "He said he's never had Chinese, or Thai food. Might give that a try. And do you know he's never grilled out?"

No, she didn't know that, but she wasn't surprised. Her sister would never win mother of the year, but their apartment had been small and without a balcony, so grilling anything would have been impossible.

Many times, Tonya knew, Cissy forgot to feed herself, so had she also forgotten to feed her son?

She rubbed her temples. "So many things to do…"

"But neither of you are alone." Jesse glanced at Merrily. "You, Brick and the pets want to join us for a grillout tomorrow? I thought maybe I'd set up the sprinkler, buy some squirt guns, maybe even bubbles."

"Heck yeah." Enthused, Merrily nodded. "Count me in. The dogs will love it! They have their own kiddie pool I'll fill up."

"Hot dogs and burgers, or steaks and chicken?"

Knowing she had to get involved, Tonya said, "Why don't we ask Kevin for his preference?"

"Good luck with that." Jesse eyed her a moment

more, then came forward and pulled her from her chair. "Want to hit up the drive-in tonight?"

Her jaw loosened. "The drive-in?"

"Yeah." He nuzzled her throat, uncaring that Merrily watched with fascination. "Some youth-appropriate movies are playing. And maybe I'll be able to sneak in a kiss or two."

How could any man be so incredible? Her throat thickened and her heart swelled. "That would be pretty cool."

"Yeah?" His smile went crooked. "The drive-in or the kissing?"

"Both."

"Well then…" This time when he touched his mouth to hers, he lingered for a few heartbeats before releasing her to turn to Merrily.

Her friend quickly stopped fanning her face and gave Jesse an angelic look.

"Brick said you two would join us."

"And here I was, getting all jealous."

"Is that what you were doing?"

"Sure." The teasing smile also added a twinkle to her eyes. "It's been forever since I went to the drive-in."

Curious, Tonya asked, "What did Kevin say about it?"

Jesse cupped her face, brushed his thumb over her cheek. "Haven't told him yet. But I will now that you've agreed." He kissed her one last time, more thoroughly, deeper, and ended with a soft growl. "I better get back to it before I forget myself."

As he started out of the room, Merrily mouthed, *Oh my God!*

Nodding, hand to her heart, Tonya agreed. Wow, she felt singed. "He's…"

"Potent?" Merrily dropped back in her seat. "Yes, he is."

This time it was Brick who intruded. Black hair disheveled, brown eyes narrowed, he paused behind Merrily's chair. "Talking about *me* again?"

Merrily bent her head back and looked at him upside down. "Of course."

"Fibber." Grinning, he leaned down for his own brand of kissing, and left Merrily breathless.

Tonya blushed while watching. Blushed, and smiled. She was so happy for both of them.

To break up the blatant PDA, Tonya cleared her throat. "I thought the drive-in had shut down."

"It closed for a while during renovations, but it's been back open all summer." Brushing Merrily's long brown hair aside, Brick caressed her shoulders in a pretend-massage. "Jesse is talking about it with Kevin right now."

More like Jesse was working at convincing Kevin, and Kevin was quietly listening. It was rare for him to really engage in a conversation.

Sad, Tonya thought, how they all braced for a variety of reactions beyond the expected happiness. Sometimes Kevin just took it in stride. But other times he got defensive, as if he thought he shouldn't be happy.

As if he thought no one really wanted him.

In the blink of an eye he would withdraw, become distant and uncertain all over again.

It divided her so badly—the love and, yes, the hate she felt for her deceased sister. Sometimes it knotted her stomach up so badly she didn't know how she could bear it. Cissy had been older by eight years, but for as long as Tonya could remember, she'd been the more mature one, the one with a plan, the one who accepted responsibility.

No matter how she'd tried to help her sister, it had never been enough. And because of that, because she'd failed, Kevin had been cheated.

Driven by self-loathing, she pushed back her chair and strode toward the hall—but Jesse and Kevin cut her off as they left the bedroom.

"Ah, no you don't." Jesse had a very paternal hand on Kevin's shoulder, and Kevin looked...pleased. "No peeking."

Tension drained from her spine, and as she watched them approach, her smile came naturally. "Is the room done? I'm dying to see it."

"Not yet," Jesse told her. "Brick and Merrily are going to take Kevin to the store with them to pick out some hardware for the dresser and the desk drawer."

That was news to her!

"Our treat," Merrily said from behind her, apparently having just been clued in. "Sort of a housewarming gift for Kevin, neighbor to neighbor."

The way Jesse watched her, Tonya knew he'd arranged it so that they'd have a little alone time, but for what? It wouldn't take long to pick out knobs. Unless Jesse was a wham-bam kind of guy there wouldn't be time enough for—

"Mind out of the gutter," he whispered near her ear, making her flush with guilt.

Amused and not bothering to hide it, he caught her hand and took her along with them back to the kitchen.

For once, Kevin looked excited. "We're going to the drive-in."

"I heard." Needing to touch him, she combed her fingers through his unruly hair. It was overlong, but a haircut was the least of her priorities right now. "I haven't been there in forever, but it's perfect weather for it."

He chewed his bottom lip. "Jesse said we could take his truck and sit in the back."

"Sounds like a plan." Before he got fed up with her mothering, she dropped her hand.

Love walked in, twining around each and every leg before stopping by Kevin. The cat stared up at him with her different-colored eyes.

Always attentive to the cat, Kevin immediately knelt down and scratched her head. "Think she'll be okay if we're all gone?" He stroked along the length of her back. "She might have the babies soon."

"If she does," Merrily assured him, "she'll know what to do. But what a great surprise that would be, huh?"

"I hope she waits till I'm here with her." He dropped down to sit against the kitchen wall, gently urging the cat into his lap. "I don't want her to be alone."

And even that, such a caring sentiment, left Tonya's throat tight.

"Tell you what." Merrily knelt down beside him. "How about I get my pet sitter to come stay with her, and if she goes into labor she can give us a call? What do you think?"

"You have a pet sitter?"

"I do. Sort of like a kid sitter." She patted his knee. "You had those when you were younger, right?"

Without answering, he did some quiet thinking, then

shifted his troubled gaze to Tonya. "Maybe it'd be easier if I just stayed here with her. I mean, if you want."

Maybe it was past time she actually told him what she wanted. His room was almost done, he'd been with her now for a couple of weeks and they really needed to get some things bought for school.

They needed an understanding.

Turning to the others, Tonya asked with a smile, "Could I have a second with Kevin, please?"

Brick nodded. "We'll wait in the living room." He and Merrily stepped out.

Pausing by her, Jesse cupped the back of her neck and kissed her, warm and firm, right on her mouth. That kiss felt like reassurance that she was doing the right thing. Like backup if she needed it.

Like caring, whether she'd admitted to wanting it yet or not.

Lightening the mood, he winked at Kevin and left.

Tonya's thoughts scrambled, trying to find a toehold on the *right* thing to say. She wasn't good at this, not like she'd been good at so many other things. Real estate, managing her money, planning her future—as a single woman with no children—yes, she'd been great at that.

But this...talking with a troubled boy, not so much. She felt totally out of her depth.

But then, she hadn't been good at being a sister, either. At least, not the type of sister Cissy had apparently needed.

Suddenly realizing how Kevin eyed her, she asked, "What?"

"You guys do a lot of kissing."

Her smile slipped. "Well..."

"It's not like how my mom was always kissing guys though."

Oh God. How much had he seen with his mother? "How is it different?"

"The guys, mostly." His expression hardened. "They were gross."

"Jesse's not gross."

"No." He eyed her again. "He likes you. He's nice."

"Very nice." Had the men she'd brought around not really liked Cissy? "So you don't mind him being here?"

Kevin shook his head, looked away and asked, "Does he mind me being here?"

"No!" She went to her knees beside him. "Jesse likes you, you know that."

"But—"

Shoulders back, she said with assurance, "If he didn't, then he could take a hike."

His blue eyes, so much like his mother's—so much like her own—widened.

"But he *does*," Tonya promised him. "He told me so. Heck, he's told *you* so, even if he hasn't outright said it. Why else would he want to fix up your room and take you to the drive-in and—"

"Because he likes you." Kevin concentrated on the cat rather than look at her. "And I don't want to get in the way."

"You couldn't, so please don't ever think that." Bottom lip caught in her teeth and her brows knit together, she settled herself beside Kevin there on the kitchen floor. "How come we always end up on the floor?"

"I don't know."

"Well, I do. You get down here to help make Love comfortable. That's such a nice thing to do." She brought her knees up, clasped her hands together and looked at him.

Kevin avoided her gaze.

"I figured we should talk."

He shrugged. "Okay."

"First, though, I'm not sure what kind of guys Cissy brought around, but Jesse would never use you to get to me. He's not that way. He's a really good man, because if he wasn't, I wouldn't allow him to be around you."

His brows kept twitching, but he didn't say anything, either to accept or reject her assurances.

"And he would never consider you in the way. You need to get that idea out of your head. In fact, I'm sure he enjoys your company."

Kevin looked at her like she was nuts. "He enjoys *your* company."

It hurt, but she got her mouth to smile. "Well, sure he does. I'm fun to be around, right?"

Sounding very unsure, Kevin said, "Yeah."

She didn't let his lack of conviction bother her. "You're fun too. And so is Jesse."

Kevin kept quiet.

"I like Jesse, and I hope you do too."

"Sure."

"But you know what I'd really like, Kevin?"

He shook his head.

"For you to be happy."

In his first real show of attitude, he snorted, glared at her with eyes gone glassy, then brought the cat a little closer for a hug.

Tonya waited.

"I'm happy enough."

"Oh, honey." She slipped one hand around his arm

and leaned her head on his wide but bony shoulder. At twelve he was still so young, but she remembered being his age, feeling all grown up, on the edge of the teen years.

When she was twelve, Cissy had been twenty, and already a disaster. It had been difficult—as in almost impossible—for her parents to have enough energy and attention for them both. Always, for as long as she could remember, Cissy had needed.

Everything. Time, attention, money, advice, understanding.

And that had left Tonya resentful, and so alone.

A deep inhalation helped cleanse away the memories. "Listen, neither one of us is very happy right now. We've just lost Cissy and—"

"And you didn't like her anyway." He breathed harder, the growing tension in his body obvious. Turning his face away, he muttered, "I didn't like her most of the time, either."

Ignoring his efforts to subtly lean away from her, Tonya held tight and nodded. "Okay, that's fair. Sometimes I didn't like her. Often I *really* disliked the things she did." Like refusing to pull it together for her son, rejecting all offers of help to get clean and sober.

Never, not once, making her son a priority.

"But she was my big sister, and even when I didn't like her, I still loved her. That's how it is with family."

When the cat protested, Kevin loosened his hold and let her walk away. She gave him a big-eyed look, a soft "meow," and then went a few feet away to groom herself.

Tonya could hear the ticking of the kitchen clock on the wall, and the stillness of the others in the living room, maybe listening in, but maybe just being respectful with their silence.

"Mom always said you didn't want anything to do with us."

Horrified, even though she'd often suspected Cissy had filled his head with those lies, Tonya whispered, "That's not true."

"I know." He stretched his legs out and put his head back.

He looked far too emotionally fatigued for a boy so young.

"I remember you visiting, arguing with Mom about… everything. Drugs, drinking, men." His mouth pinched, he swallowed hard. "Sometimes about me. And I know you paid the rent a few times."

She'd also twice turned Cissy in to authorities for being an unfit mother. But each time her sister made promises to get it together. She'd sign up with different programs, and Child Protective Services had let her slide. Maybe things hadn't been quite bad enough to take Kevin from her.

But they'd still been bad enough.

And God, Tonya had wanted to take him.

Now she had him, and somehow, some way, she'd make him understand.

Tonya hugged his arm a little tighter. "I've never done this before, you know? Cissy didn't want me around much, so you and I aren't as close as I would have liked. But I'm your aunt and I love you."

"You don't really know me."

"I know enough, but it doesn't matter anyway. If I'd never seen you I would love you because you're a part of me."

He gave her such a disbelieving look.

"It's true," she promised him. "From the day Cissy told me she was pregnant, I loved you. I'm sorry she's gone, I'm sorry that I could never figure out a way to make things better, and I'm very sorry for what you're going through. But I'm *glad* you're here with me. I want you to be happy. I want *me* to be happy. I think, maybe if we work together and are forgiving of each other and talk—probably a lot of talking—we can make it happen. Don't you think?"

"I don't know." He rubbed a spot on his worn jeans. "I got dumped on you."

"No." Fighting off her own tears, her throat thick and her voice cracking, she whispered, "I would have *fought* for you." He needed to understand that.

For one moment in time he looked devastated. Then he pulled up his knees, put his head down and covered it with his arms.

He was such a tall boy, his limbs gangly, but still a boy. And now he was hers. "Kevin?"

He held himself tighter.

Tonya feared the worst—that maybe he'd cry and then she knew she'd totally lose it too. But instead, still with his face hidden, he said, "You and Jesse going to live together?"

Her heart jumped into double time. "I'm not sure. We're still working on our relationship."

"Because of me."

She shoulder-bumped him. "Don't take all the credit, kiddo. A lot of it is me."

"What do you mean?"

She sighed. "Sometimes I have it together. And

sometimes I'm just a mess." She smiled. "But hey, I consider myself a work in progress."

Finally he lifted his head. "I don't belong here."

"Please believe me that you do. And, Kevin, I swear, whatever it takes, I'm going to make it okay."

Their talk had left his eyes red-rimmed and colored his nose, but he didn't cry. Maybe, even at only twelve, he considered that unmanly.

Suddenly he scrubbed the heels of his hands into his eye sockets and scrambled up to stand. "I should get going."

A little panicked, she jumped up too. "Where?"

His jaw worked, then miraculously, he smiled, a boyish smile that somehow made him look very mature. "To the store to get knobs so Jesse can finish up."

Oh. Her spine turned to gelatin. "Right."

"You guys are doing so much…"

That broke her heart too, because they hadn't really done much at all. "Don't hate me for this, okay?" Letting that be her only warning, Tonya wrapped her arms around him and hugged him tight.

Leaning away from her, clearly uncomfortable, he patted her shoulder. "Um…"

"Just a few more seconds."

"Well…okay." He patted her again.

She was still clinging to him when Jesse stuck his head back in the kitchen. "You about ready, Kevin?"

"Yeah." As Tonya released him, he sidled out with alacrity. Jesse went with him, politely giving her the time she needed to regroup.

After a few slow, even breaths, she felt together enough to join the others.

"C'mon." Brick scooped his arm around Merrily. "Let's get this show on the road."

Head down, Kevin shuffled toward the door. "I'm ready."

Jesse gave her a long look, touched her chin and said, "Be right back." Pulling a note with numbers on it from his pocket, he walked out with the others.

The urge to sneak down the hall and peek was strong. Instead, Tonya returned to her kitchen chair and dropped into it. Closing her eyes, she tried to think of all that still had to be done. She'd never gone school clothes shopping with a very reluctant, unhappy boy. How was it going to work when so far Kevin seemed suspicious of nearly everything?

Well, except for the cat. He adored Love.

And apparently the drive-in.

He also seemed to like his room…

So maybe, as Merrily had said, she was borrowing trouble, making the problems bigger than they really were—when God knew they were big enough.

She hadn't heard Jesse come back in, so when his warm hand covered her shoulder, she started.

His other hand joined the first and he carefully rubbed. "You're tense."

For many different reasons—new reasons, now that he touched her. "You and Brick are so much alike. He just did this very thing to Merrily."

"What?"

"Shoulder massage."

"He was probably just on the make."

Knowing he stood right behind her—knowing they were alone—sent Tonya's thoughts down a different path. "But you're not?"

She heard his smile when he said, "Not just yet."

Darn. She would have loved the distraction.

With a final gentle caress, he moved to stand beside her. "You're okay?"

She nodded. "Just considering things."

"Me?"

"You've made yourself such a part of everything, of course you factor in."

He drew her up and out of the chair, turning her to face him and looping his arms around her waist. "Is that a complaint?"

"Only at myself." She leaned into him, accepting his strength, his warmth and caring. *About everyone.* Was she special to him? And why in God's name was she whining about herself when Kevin had had his entire world upended? "I'm sorry. I don't mean to be mopey. It's just that you make it all seem so easy."

"Apparently I'm failing, though, given everything Kevin said."

"You heard?"

"Much of it."

Soooo... Jesse had heard her tell Kevin that she'd boot him to the curb if necessary.

He urged her head to his shoulder and rocked her side to side. "I do care for him. You were right about that."

"I know." How could anyone with a heart not care about Kevin?

"You did the right thing. *Said* the right things. He needs a lot of reassurance right now."

Of course Jesse understood. As she kept telling herself, he was wonderful. "Thank you."

"Now you can reassure me." The smile warmed his green eyes, made them darker with caring. His voice dropped, went deeper. "Tell me I'm not the only one getting in deep."

Matching his whisper, she said, "I'm in so deep it scares me."

He cupped her face, put his forehead to hers. "That's the last thing I want, honey. Don't ever be afraid of me."

"I'm not." She forced out the truth. "I'm just a little afraid of *us*."

"Relationships have been hard?"

They'd been impossible. "A little." She snuggled in closer, and dared to bare her soul. "But with you, I'd really like to try." Before he could say anything to that, she added, "At the very least I need to know what it's like to be with you."

Levering her back, his expression arrested, he searched her face. "You're talking sex?"

"Yes."

His breath caught, then his arms tightened and he put his face against her neck. After a hoarse laugh, he cupped her face and kissed her. "Damn. You make me forget myself. Unfortunately the others won't be gone long enough for everything I need to do with you."

How could he expect her to keep it together while he said things like that?

"Kevin starts school in one more week, right?"

She nodded. "Yes."

"Then for those few remaining days, I'm going to work on winning over both of you."

He didn't need to work on her. Shoot, she was already in love. But she'd yet to meet a man keen on waiting. "You really think you can be that patient?"

"I'm going to think of it as extended foreplay."

She smiled with him.

Going serious again, he drifted his fingers through her hair. "But I'm taking off work that day, and I hope you will too."

"The whole day?"

His attention went to her mouth; another, deeper kiss followed. Against her lips, he breathed, "It's going to take me at least that long."

Wow. After a much-needed breath, she nodded. "Okay." *The whole day.* She could hardly wait. "I'm on board."

"In the meantime, we continue working out the problems. Which include…?"

So now she needed to think—about something other than an all-day marathon of Jesse naked. Returning to reality, Tonya put a hand to her head and tried to order her thoughts.

Jesse watched her as if he wanted a list, so she mentally ticked off some of her priorities.

School was in the top ten. "He needs school clothes. A haircut. I need to rearrange my schedule because I don't want him home alone afterward, at least not for a while." When Jesse started to speak, she rushed on. "I know he's twelve. I was babysitting at that age. But he's—"

"A guy who needs you."

"Yes." Did Jesse need her too? More likely it was all one-sided. She needed him, in so many different ways that her independent nature wanted to rebel.

But more than that, more than anything, she valued the strong shoulder to lean on.

"Mind if I give a stab at the haircut?" He ran those strong fingers through his dark blond hair. "I'm past due, so I figure I can take him with me, introduce him to my barber and all that."

"I'm sure that'd make for an easier transition. I don't think he's ever been to a barber. My sister just cut his hair."

"Not uncommon." His grin went crooked, adding to his charm. "My mom always trimmed mine when I was younger too."

"I know. And I thought about giving it a try, but if I mess it up—"

"You are far too critical of yourself."

She drew out her chair and sat down again. "Believe me, he's got enough going on without having to possibly deal with a bad haircut from me."

"I guess you're right." He teased her, saying, "Maybe someday you can practice on me. I wouldn't mind."

She stared at him, at that sun-streaked hair, and damned if she didn't get a little warm just thinking about it. "If you're really that brave, then okay."

"Shopping decisions are all on you." He, too, sat. "But if you want, I'll go along. Assuming he's like most guys, we can break up the very painful process with lunch, maybe an hour in the arcade or something."

So many things he said and did gave her great insight and made her love expand. "You think it's very painful, but you'll do it anyway?"

"For you." He reached across the table and took her hand. "For him."

"You really are terrific." So terrific that she wanted to keep him—forever. No way could she tell him that, not right now. So instead she gave his hand a squeeze and shared a very sincere smile. "Thank you. For everything."

CHAPTER THREE

THE ROOM TURNED out perfect—in every way. The loft bed provided extra storage room that Tonya never would have had otherwise. Beneath the bed Kevin had not only a chest of drawers and a functional desk, but the coveted nook for Love.

Kevin liked it. The cat liked it.

Tonya was left speechless.

The once-crowded room now looked custom designed for a growing boy.

No one looking at it, complete with a favorite pet, would guess at Kevin's background. Tonya hoped it would help him to forget—or at least be better able to accept the future.

"This rack," Jesse said, "is for hanging anything from a jacket to a ball bat or...whatever."

Would Kevin want to get involved with sports?

With Jesse encouraging him, she believed he would.

"Look," Kevin told her. "The light for my desk is built into the bottom of the bed."

"That way, he has more surface room for his school papers and stuff."

Both Kevin and Jesse stood there smiling at her, and damn it, she felt tears gather in her eyes. "You both did an absolutely amazing job."

Kevin took one look at her and retreated—until Jesse

nudged him, muttering, "Women, huh? Always looking for a reason to get weepy."

Kevin took another look, his uncertainty palpable.

"Happy tears," Tonya promised. Arms open, she closed in on Kevin, giving him a big hug despite his unease, then she moved to Jesse and did the same.

Keeping her close, Jesse said in an aside to Kevin, "When she sees the plans we have for her office, she's going to melt down. Just wait and see."

She playfully punched him, caught Kevin's grin and hugged them both once more. "Show me."

They climbed the attic stairs for the unveiling, just so, as Jesse claimed, she could "get the real visual."

And oh, did she get it. They were so incredibly awesome, she truly did want to melt down.

She didn't know how it was possible, but Jesse assured her it would be an easier task than the bedroom since the space was wide open and "begging for a remodel."

They would move the stored items down to the basement and do some hard-core cleaning, he'd replace the old window with an easier-to-open model that still matched the character of the house, and then they'd get busy building.

Jesse's offer to create the office space appealed in a big way, for a variety of reasons.

Yes, she wanted her own work area. Right now she had her desk crammed in her bedroom, and there was barely room to move. When using the phone for client calls, she had zilch for privacy. And as an organized person, it made her a little nuts having files stacked around instead of neatly arranged in a file cabinet.

She also liked the additional time for Jesse and Kevin

to bond over power tools. On a very basic level, she knew it was good for Kevin. She wanted to coddle him, and Jesse treated him like a young man—surely that was a good balance?

Selfishly, the biggest reason she loved it was because it'd mean more time with Jesse. And honestly, she wanted every second she could have, for whatever reason there might be.

Putting a hand over her head so she wouldn't bump it on a beam, Jesse indicated the wall. "Where the ceiling slopes down, we'll add lower cupboards and shelves. Your desk and main flow area will be here in the center so that we tall people can move around without cracking our noggins."

Since he was taller than her, and Kevin was certainly growing, that made perfect sense.

Kevin nodded. "You'll have a lot of places to put... stuff." He seemed unsure what stuff she'd have.

"It's an office dream," she assured him.

Expression eager, he told her, "Jesse says this'll be even better than your office being in the room I took."

"Much, *much* better. And the fact that you're in the room now...well, I couldn't be happier about all of it."

Both guys looked pretty satisfied with her enthusiastic reaction, so they all exited the attic with grins.

That seemed to set the tone, and the drive-in was a wonderful adventure that went by with nary a bit of uncertainty.

The good times even carried over to the next day for the grill-out.

For the first time since she'd gotten the awful phone call about her sister, Tonya felt optimistic that the future would not only work out, it'd be easier than she'd imagined.

And she owed it all to Jesse.

A WEEK LATER, they again congregated in Tonya's back-yard for games and grilled food. Jesse was feeling pretty damned good. Earlier that day he, Kevin and Tonya had finished clearing out the attic. Yeah, he was dragging his feet, taking more time than necessary. But so what? Kevin enjoyed helping out, he didn't want Tonya over-worked and, on a more personal level, he loved spend-ing time at her place.

Mostly because he loved her.

Kevin too.

When with them, life felt more perfect. He didn't want to let that go, but neither did he want to rush ei-ther of them. Both Tonya and Kevin were still reeling from having their lives turned upside down; he had to respect the frailty of the situation.

But damn, it was getting more and more difficult to leave each night when what he really wanted was to move on in.

"You playing or daydreaming?" Brick asked.

Daydreaming, but he got it together and grinned. "Playing." Holding the badminton racket loosely in both hands, he indicated Brick should serve.

After already defeating Evan and Cinder, he and Kevin faced off against Brick and Merrily. It pleased him, made him feel like a proud dad, how Kevin showed his competitive edge, but in a nice way.

For what the kid had gone through, no one would have been surprised if he'd refused to play, or if he'd had a temper tantrum when they lost.

Instead, when they'd started playing last weekend, he'd gotten very serious and knuckled down. He had a natural athleticism that seemed to surprise him. Both Brick and Evan had commented on his speed. Jesse saw his dexterity.

All over simple badminton.

Jesse would like to get him to a bowling lane, or on a baseball field. Kevin took instruction with the same gusto most kids used when opening presents on Christmas morning. He possessed natural talent just begging to show. Jesse wanted to give that talent free rein. It'd be interesting to see which sports he liked.

It had been a busy but successful week. In his mind, Jesse repeatedly ticked off accomplishments.

Kevin had enjoyed the drive-in, including the popcorn and colas and corn dogs.

He'd worked hard helping Jesse on the attic project.

He'd tolerated the haircut, and had gotten to know the barber.

And best of all, he'd endured the shopping that had taken more than a few hours. *Endured* being an apt word given how it apparently pained Kevin to see Tonya buy him things.

Doing his part, Jesse had taken him aside and clued him in on how to accept his aunt's shopping spree with graciousness, explaining that it was important to her, so even if he felt he didn't want or need the clothes, he should just accept it and thank her.

Jesse knew it was more about Kevin thinking he didn't deserve them, but the boy had taken the advice to heart and mumbled his thanks over every shirt, several pairs of jeans and two new pairs of shoes. He'd even swallowed back his complaints and embarrassment over new underwear and socks.

This was now their last weekend before Kevin started school on Monday. And that meant Jesse had to fight to keep his gaze off Tonya.

"No offense," Merrily said, "but we're going to win."

Jesse laughed. "Keep dreaming."

Kevin got into position and said, "We'll see."

After losing the first game today, they'd won the second. Tiebreakers were tough on anyone who liked to win, but even as they all taunted each other, they laughed.

Off to the side, Tonya watched them along with Evan and Cinder. All around them animals ran loose, enjoying the chaos. Love rested a safe distance away in the warm grass. The poor thing looked ready to pop, so Jesse hoped it wouldn't be too much longer for her.

The sun shone down on them, he was surrounded by friends and Kevin was enjoying himself.

Jesse didn't have to fake his pleasure. Yes, he was dying to get Tonya alone. He wanted her. Needed her.

Had to have her.

But he wasn't a kid. He knew how to prioritize. Tonya and Kevin were definitely priorities.

In so many ways, Tonya had been more contained than Kevin. Little by little, though, she was coming out of her shell.

Same as Kevin.

Damn, but it filled him with satisfaction to be a part of that.

He was still thinking about tomorrow, about having her all to himself, when Brick sent the birdie sailing toward them. Kevin ran hard, diving forward and managing to catch it with just the tip of the racket. But that sent him into a roll, and he sprawled on the ground like a fallen warrior. Jesse jumped to keep him from plowing into his legs, then gave the birdie another awkward smack. He, too, landed on the ground.

The birdie shot over the net—directly into Brick's racket. Taken by surprise, Brick tried to recover but fumbled it, and it landed between him and Merrily.

On a mock wail, Merrily collapsed in defeat—then got trampled by the dogs as they rushed her to play.

Grinning, Brick ducked under the net and came to stand over them.

"Either of you get hurt?"

Jesse groaned theatrically. "My pride more than anything."

"You won, so your pride will recover."

Shoving up to sit, Kevin checked a scraped elbow, shrugged it off and grinned. "I'm okay."

"You sure?" Brick hauled him up, looked at his arm and winced over the raw spot. "Can't have you going to school tomorrow with badminton injuries."

"Yeah," Kevin said. "This school doesn't know me so it might surprise them."

Both men froze.

Heart in his throat, Jesse sat up too.

Realizing what he'd said, Kevin scowled—and focused on Love. "I'm going to check on the cat." And off he went.

Brick and Jesse shared a look. Damn, but every time things started to even out, he felt the awfulness of Kevin's past all over again.

After squeezing his jaw tight a moment, Brick visibly tried to relax. But Jesse heard his low, muttered, "Fuck," loud and clear.

"Yeah." Thoughts roiling, he stared toward Kevin. Had his mother left marks on him? One of her boyfriends? He wanted to talk to Kevin about it, but uncertainty held him back.

Held them *all* back.

As if she'd felt the tension, Tonya immediately went to Kevin. Jesse knew that, like him, she would chat about the cat, about school—about everything other than the mistreatment he'd suffered before his mother's death. Unless or until Kevin wanted to talk, they'd all keep it cheerful. Or at least as cheerful as they could.

Merrily came up to lean against Brick. "He's such a great kid."

"Yeah." Brick put his arm around her.

Evan and Cinder walked out to the yard. "Everything okay?"

Jesse knew Brick had already filled his brother and sister-in-law in on Kevin's background, so he said only, "It will be," and went to join Tonya.

Like the Pied Piper, Jesse drew the attention of the dogs and cats alike. They all followed along and, eventually, so did the people.

Love didn't mind the attention. In fact, she seemed to crave it…right up until she lumbered to her feet, meowed at Kevin and stood on his sneaker.

"I'll take her in," Kevin announced, gently lifting the cat into his arms.

"Wait." Merrily fetched a camera that Tonya had left sitting on the deck and took a few photos of Kevin and the cat.

Grinning crookedly, Kevin mugged for the camera until she'd finished, then he carried Love inside.

Tonya had started taking photos last weekend at the drive-in, and she hadn't stopped yet. Already she had filled her house with photos of Kevin, as if trying to make up for the fact that none had been found at his mother's apartment.

She'd included Jesse in many of them, and some of their friends, as well as the various animals.

Kevin kept a photo of Tonya, himself and Jesse in his room, tacked to a corkboard over his desk. He hadn't made a big deal of it, but when he'd looked at the photo overlong, Tonya had handed it over to him, and it had been on his wall ever since.

Like so many other things, it was a start.

Twenty minutes later, Cinder announced that she wanted ice cream. Brick and Merrily decided they should all go to the local creamy whip, and they invited Kevin along.

Like every kid everywhere, he didn't turn down ice cream.

When she started to speak, Jesse caught Tonya's hand and held her back. "We'll pick up the yard, but the rest of you go, have fun."

Though she didn't disagree, Tonya started blushing, which amused Jesse. Did she think he planned to jump the gun by one measly day?

Tomorrow morning Kevin would catch the bus to school.

The rest of the day belonged to him.

He could wait…barely.

Kevin got Love settled in her nook beneath his bed where he'd put a few of his old shirts for her to nestle into. She enjoyed the familiarity of his scent, something Kevin found very odd but clearly liked.

With his hand on Kevin's shoulder and a knowing glint in his eyes, Brick faced Jesse and Tonya. "Want us to bring you back anything?"

Tonya had gone very quiet, so Jesse smiled and said, "We're good, but thanks."

Evan said, "Banana splits are on me. It can be our last hurrah before school starts tomorrow morning."

Kevin asked, "Banana split? They have those?"

"Ooh," Cinder said. "Are you in for a treat!"

As they left, Jesse could hear Evan regaling Kevin on the wonders of bananas, ice cream, chocolate sauce and whipped cream.

Going to the window, Jesse watched until both cars had left the driveway.

Then he turned to Tonya.

Cheeks still warm, gaze soft and dark, she watched him. "Um… I'm not sure we have time—"

"We don't. At least, not for what you're thinking."

She relaxed a little, her expression now teasing. "What am I thinking?"

"Sex. With me."

She slowly inhaled and nodded. "Nailed it."

"I know, because I'm thinking it too. Pretty much around the clock."

"So then—"

Moving away from the window, he got close but didn't yet touch her. "We need to talk."

Groaning, Tonya dropped back against the wall. "You're a terrible tease." A sexy, hard-to-resist tease. "At the very least, I figured we'd do *some* kissing."

"All right, we will. *After.*"

"After?"

He looked at her mouth and said, "If I start kissing you now, we'll get off course in a big way. But this is too important—to me, and to you and Kevin."

That sounded pretty heavy.

Especially when he added, "To our future."

Her knees almost turned to noodles. She wanted to cheer because he'd just stated, out loud and plain as day, that they did have a future. But given the serious look in his green eyes, this was something important.

And maybe not cheer-worthy.

So maybe it had to do with Kevin. Had she missed something serious? Jesse had spent almost as much time with her nephew as she had.

Worried, she braced herself. "Okay. I'm listening. What is it?"

Cupping her neck, he drew her closer and whispered against her lips, "I want in."

"In...?"

Trailing his hand down her shoulder, along the side of her breast, her ribs and her hip, he boldly cupped her between the thighs. "Here, for sure."

One simple touch should never have so much impact, but when it was Jesse touching her, she felt it everywhere. Slowly, heating with sensation and need, she closed her eyes and swallowed back a groan. "Here?" she tried to say as casually as he'd spoken. Instead she sounded all raspy and turned-on.

Because she was.

His fingers curled, his voice dropped. "I definitely want in here."

She nodded. "I already told you I'm on board with that."

He released her and touched below her breast, his hand big and warm and firm. "And here."

He wanted…into her heart? She could have told him he already took up far too much space there.

Lastly, he trailed his fingertips up until he brushed them over her forehead. "But for right now, I want in *here*."

Denying that, she tried a laugh that fell flat. "I don't know what you mean."

Jesse's expression went sympathetic, but also determined. "Will you tell me about your sister?"

She really, *really* hated talking about Cissy. Heaven knew she'd spent far too many years with the focus on Cissy's problems. What Cissy wanted, what Cissy needed…

An awful bubble of unhappiness rose up to her throat, choking her. Oh God, her sister was gone. *Forever.*

Tonya looked away. She felt awful. Selfish. Even mean. How could she still resent a sister who had lived such an unhappy life?

Jesse's fingertips on her chin brought her face back around. "Tonya?"

She could still hear her mother telling her that she was stronger, more independent than Cissy. She dredged up that strength now and straightened her posture. "What do you want to know?"

At close range, his gaze searched hers, stealing her thoughts right out of her head. "Everything." He brushed his thumb over her jaw. "But mostly I want to know how it was for you."

"Me?" No one ever asked her that. She didn't have Cissy's problems. No, her problems were small and insignificant in comparison.

"There were only the two of you?"

"Yes." Although often she'd felt invisible in Cissy's gloomy shadow. "She was eight years older." Trying for a careless smile, she added, "Pretty sure I was a mistake, you know?"

Rather than reply to that, he asked, "Was she always troubled?"

Laughing without humor, her expression pained, Tonya shrugged. "For as long as I can remember." Somehow, without her really realizing it, Jesse steered her to the kitchen. Why did all big discussions take place there?

He pulled out a chair. "She must've gotten a lot of the attention."

"The squeaky wheel gets oiled." Tonya winced over that blatant complaint, but then went ahead and expounded on the truth. "Cissy didn't just squeak, she screamed. Trouble. All the time. Over *everything*." As if a dam had burst, her words came rushing out, her hurt and resentment mixing together. "My parents had to work, and they had to always help Cissy. Financially, emotionally, in every way you can imagine."

"I guess that didn't leave much time for you?"

"It left *no* time. I was expected to be the easier child, and so I was."

"That's pretty impressive, you know. You could have gone the opposite way and followed Cissy's example."

"Ha! Not likely." She covered her face with her hands, embarrassed over her pettiness, hating her own resentment of the past, but it felt so good to say it aloud, to get it out of her head. "I got in trouble at school once. You'd have thought the world ended. Dad lectured me, telling me how unfair it was to my mother to burden her that way because, after all, I already knew she had her

hands full with Cissy. He was so disappointed in me.
And Mom cried. I think the idea that two kids would
cause problems just overwhelmed her. She was in bed
sick for two days—until Cissy had another meltdown
and needed her."

Appalled, Jesse took her hands and stared into her
eyes. "What did you do to get in trouble?"

"I skipped a class, went out with a friend and tried
smoking." Remembering her own ridiculous attempt at
rebelling, she wrinkled her nose. "It was so dumb. The
cigarette was awful, the repercussions worse. Believe
me, I never tried anything like that again."

"So you never got to sow your wild oats?"

She shrugged. "Did you?"

"Sure."

She would love to hear all about Jesse and his mis-
spent youth. "Admittedly, I'm starting late. But here I
am, sitting at the table with a bona fide gorgeous hunk
who, starting tomorrow, will let me wallow in lust. Better late than never, huh?"

Her joke fell flat, leaving Jesse frowning instead of
smiling.

"When did you lose your parents?"

She rolled a shoulder, wishing they could move
on from her tale of woe. "I was twenty. Cissy wasn't
around. I knew how badly my folks would have wanted
her there, but she didn't answer my calls or even show
up for the funeral." Anger swelled. Anger and hurt. "She
accepted her half of their estate though. For a while
there, I hoped it would make a difference for Kevin.
He was only five then. I'm not sure he even remembers
Mom and Dad since their last year, Cissy got really bad.

She lived with this one creep that my parents hated. So many nights they'd miss sleep worrying."

"And what about you? Did you worry?"

She averted her gaze. "About Kevin. But I got so angry at Cissy, especially after she blew the nice sum of money she got after I settled their affairs. Sometimes I wished…" Swallowing down that awful thought, she shook her head. "Mom had always said that Cissy couldn't help it, that she needed our help, but she made *everyone* miserable. Even her son."

Slowly, Jesse reclaimed her hand. His thumb moved over her knuckles. "Kevin still loved her."

"Because he's supposed to! I know because it's the same way I feel." She pressed a fist to her heart. "If she'd been a stranger, a neighbor or a friend, I'd have cut her out of my life and moved on. But we were related, and right or wrong, I couldn't help but love her. Not because of any closeness, or fond memories—there was none of that. I just…"

"Loved her because she was your sister."

Breathing harder, she nodded. It made no sense, not then and not now. "It's a burden that Kevin shouldn't have to bear."

"I agree it's unfair. But that's life, honey. We play the hand we're dealt."

She wanted to throw away that hand and get new cards. Except…that would mean throwing away Kevin too. And Jesse. And she didn't want that. Ever.

"I hate what you went through, what you didn't have, and what you had to put up with. But however your life used to be, you're exactly what Kevin needs now." His fingers laced in hers. "And you're who I want."

Sexually. But he'd also mentioned her head and heart…

Lifting her hand, Jesse kissed her knuckles. "I'm glad you're you," he whispered. "And, Tonya?"

Very uncertain, she said, "Yes?"

"I promise to help you sow plenty of wild oats."

CHAPTER FOUR

TONYA WANTED EVERYTHING to be perfect, and so far, so good.

Kevin looked relaxed enough wearing jeans and a pullover shirt, with lime green sneakers he'd chosen himself. She'd surprised him with a new backpack, and he still looked boggled by it.

"Do you want to pack your lunch or buy?"

His brows came together and he busied himself putting pencils, notebooks and such in the backpack.

"Kevin?"

"I think the school gives me lunch, right?"

Well, of course he'd gotten that supplemented. Why hadn't she realized? Smiling, she came to sit beside him on the couch. "Not this year. We can either pack you something, or I can give you the money—"

"Packing is fine."

Keeping her smile in place, Tonya silently vowed to look into a meal plan at the school, perhaps a prepay of some sort so he'd always have the option. "Okay. What's it to be? I can do a sandwich with that lunch meat you like, or there's PB&J, or—"

He pushed to his feet. "I can do it."

She started to follow along when a knock sounded on the door, and a second later, Jesse stuck his head in. "Hey."

Good Lord, he was early! Heat rushed into her face, making him grin widely.

"I wanted to catch Kevin before he took off."

"Oh." So he hadn't been impatient?

Kevin stuck his head out of the kitchen. "Hey, Jesse."

"Hey." As he went past Tonya, he chastised her, whispering, "Mind in the gutter again? Naughty, Tonya." He stole a quick kiss. "I like it." Then he went into the kitchen.

She stood there in the middle of the room, listening to their low conversation until she felt steady enough to walk.

"I would have packed that for you," she told Kevin.

"Why?" Jesse leaned back on the counter. "He's a big boy. He can do it."

Kevin grinned.

Ridiculously proud, Tonya got out a paper bag for him, along with an apple and a drink and a bag of chips.

Jesse eyed it all and, now as familiar with her kitchen as she was, went to a different cabinet to get out some cookies to add to the pile.

Kevin laughed. "Okay, that ought to do it." He began stuffing it all in the bag. "I've never gotten this much for lunch before." He caught himself and clarified, "School lunch, I mean."

"We should go shopping," Tonya said, making both guys groan in unison.

"For *food*," she stressed, amused by their identical forlorn expressions. "So you always have your preferences here for packing."

Kevin stuffed the lunch bag into his backpack, hefted it over his shoulder, surveyed her a moment while shifting restlessly—and in one big step he reached her, hugging her right off her feet.

"Thanks, Aunt Tonya."

Her heart almost exploded from her chest. Clasped hands at her mouth, tears welling up, she nodded and gulped, "You're welcome."

He shared a man-to-man look with Jesse. "I better go so I don't miss my bus."

She nodded hard again.

Jesse laughed. "I'll walk you out."

They were no sooner out the door than Tonya rushed behind them to peek out the window. Together, they stood on the porch chatting, occasionally laughing. A few times Jesse put his hand on Kevin's shoulder, and at one point Kevin gave him a laughing push. When the bus started down the street, Jesse faded back, then came in.

He found her there at the window, but he didn't say anything. He just nudged her over a little so he could join her, and together they watched Kevin get on the bus.

"He'll be okay," Jesse told her, his arm now around her waist.

Words still stuck in her throat, so she only smiled and nodded, staying there until the bus was out of sight.

Jesse smoothed his hand down her long braid, let his gaze trail over her body from her loose T-shirt and casual shorts, all the way down to her bare feet.

She waited for him to kiss her, but instead he stepped back.

Pulsing with expectation, she stood there as he went to the door and turned the lock. That near silent "click" ramped up her heat and made her knees tremble.

Until he headed down the hall.

What in the world? She rushed to catch up. "Jesse?"

Into her bedroom he went and she stalled, stopping just outside the door. She wanted this. She wanted him. So much.

But she didn't know how she felt about being rushed.

He sat on the side of the mattress and smiled at her. "Come here, Tonya."

Hesitation warred with excitement.

Excitement won. Steps tentative, she approached, and when she got close enough, he reached out and caught her hand, drawing her in…and onto his lap.

"You okay?"

Oh no, no, no. If he got sympathetic over her emotional overload, she'd turn weepy in a heartbeat, and seriously, that'd add nothing to the awesomely sexual moment. "Of course."

His big, warm hand moved up and down her back. "You're really good for him. You know that, right?"

"I'm trying." Was she good for Jesse too? That thought led to more uncertainty. To change the subject, she leaned into him and kissed his jaw. "You didn't shave?"

"I was in a hurry to get here."

"I like it." His whiskers rasped her fingertips, and she had to cup his face, hold him still for a deeper kiss that turned hot and wet and left her breathless.

Turning her, he lowered her to the mattress, then lifted away. His attention on her mouth, he slipped a hand up under her shirt to touch bare skin. "You want to talk a little?"

"That's your thing." She moved one leg up and over his, hooking her heel over his muscled thigh. "This is my thing."

"Yeah?" He pressed more firmly against her. "What exactly?"

"Wanting you. Needing you." She nipped his chin. "I swear it feels like forever."

"Because it has been." He bent to nuzzle her throat, making her toes curls. "A lifetime." His open mouth ate gently over her neck, down to the special spot where her neck blended into her shoulder muscle.

More than her toes curled. Her stomach did a flip-flop, her heartbeat breaking into a race. "Jesse."

Under her shirt, his hand slid up to her breast, cuddled carefully before his thumb finally played over her nipple.

She started to whisper his name again, but his mouth took hers, his tongue stroking deep, and she forgot everything except holding on to him.

For the longest time, that's all he did, touch her, kiss her. But they were both still dressed, and she moved restlessly against him, trying to get him to hurry it up.

Finally, finally, he levered to the side of her, reached back with one fist and peeled away his shirt.

"More," she whispered.

He treated her to a crooked smile. "You first." And with that, he peeled away her shirt. Breathing harder, he stared at her, her breasts and her belly, her legs. "What do you say we lose these shorts too?"

"Sure." She wanted to be naked with him. "Soon as you take off your jeans."

He bent to kiss her belly, took a soft bite and sat up. Still looking at her body, he kicked off his shoes and opened his jeans.

When he stood, Tonya fisted her hands in the bedding to brace herself. Jesse still didn't look at her face.

No, his attention remained on her body, totally absorbed as he pushed down his jeans and boxers, taking off his socks at the same time.

Casual as you please, he stood there naked at the side of the bed, one hand blindly digging into the pocket of his jeans until he found a few condoms that he put on the nightstand. Tossing the jeans aside, he parted her legs and stepped between them, trailing his hands up and down her thighs.

Neither of them said anything as he opened the snap on her shorts, eased down the zipper and curled his fingers into the waistband.

At last his gaze lifted to hers. "You're okay?"

She nodded and helped him by lifting her hips while he slowly tugged down the shorts. He'd left her in her panties, which didn't mean he'd left her much. The lacy, barely there underwear didn't conceal as much as they... decorated.

"Damn."

Tonya licked her lips. "You like them?"

"Yeah." But he eased them down too, all the while looking at her. Releasing a big breath, he murmured, "Like you naked even more."

Yes, she knew she wasn't a troll. But Cissy hadn't been a troll either and yet men had always—

"Shh." Jesse came down beside her, turned her into him and whispered, "You, me and a bed. That's all that's here, Tonya."

How had he known the direction of her thoughts? "Finally."

"Finally." He put his mouth to her forehead, the bridge of her nose, her cheekbone. "It's been a long time coming, but I won't rush you."

"You haven't." She nestled closer. "And I don't want to wait."

"Okay then, kiss me."

She tried to make it a scorcher, hot enough to get him rushing just a little.

Instead, with one arm under her head, he kept her close, and with the other he explored, his hand cuddling her breast, fingers tugging on her nipple, before petting over her waist, down her spine and to her bottom. He lifted her leg over his hip, leaving her open for him.

Making a small, rough, hot sound of appreciation, Jesse teased between her legs, over her sex, briefly pressed his two fingers into her, and then used her own wetness to stroke higher—over her clitoris.

Shocked by the intensity, she tried to free her mouth to gasp, but he didn't let her. He took her groan, returning it with a satisfied, "Mmm," rumble of pleasure.

When he was damn good and ready, he freed her lips to kiss his way down to her breast. "I owe Brick big-time."

That made no sense to her. Arching against him, she breathed, "Why's that?"

He licked her nipple, suckled for a heart-stopping second, then blew against her. "He gave you to me as a gift."

As he sucked her in again, she sank under sensation... until his words registered.

Wait, *what*?

Grabbing his shoulders, Tonya pressed him back. She could still feel his breath on her now-wet nipple, and he again had two fingers buried into her, stretching her, filling her, making clear thought more than difficult.

When she said nothing, he licked her again. "You're wondering about the whole Brick/gift thing, right?"

Eyes closed, breath suspended, she nodded, and given that his fingers were now slowly stroking in and out, she considered that a major accomplishment.

As if making love to her didn't affect him at all, Jesse spoke calmly. "Brick was after Merrily, making moves, and then he met you. Most guys would do an about-face for you. You know that right?"

No, she refused to answer that.

"They would," he assured her. "But Brick was already in it for Merrily. Hook, line and sinker. So he asked me out here with a trumped-up excuse of needing help with a door and promised me a really awesome 'gift' if I played along."

"Me?"

"Yeah, you." He kissed her hotly. "I wanted you the second I saw you."

Threading her fingers into his sun-streaked hair, Tonya admitted, "I wanted you too."

"Took me a while to figure that out though. You were friendly enough in a group, or as long as we were talking weather or improvements on your house. Anything personal, you turned cool as a cucumber."

He meant cold. And withdrawn and distant…a total drag.

Apologetic, she hugged his head to her breasts. "I'm sorry. You scared me, Jesse. *This* scared me."

"You didn't think you should risk getting involved."

It was love she hadn't wanted to risk. "It didn't seem fair when my life remained up in the air, the future so uncertain."

"I know." Another kiss, and then he half sat up and reached for a condom.

Tonya watched as he opened the packet, rolled on the condom and came down over her.

Kneeing her thighs apart, he whispered, "It's not uncertain anymore."

"How can you say—"

With one thrust, he entered her, burying himself deep. She sank her fingertips into his solid shoulders; he closed his eyes and groaned.

They stayed like that, holding the moment, until Tonya couldn't take it anymore and shifted under him.

He locked an arm around her hips. "The future," he murmured, and three deep breaths later, he continued with, "It is set, you know. There'll be ups and downs, good times and bad. But Kevin isn't going anywhere."

"Never."

He smiled, kissed her softly. "I see you," he told her gently. "You and your responsibilities. The challenges you'll face. The *fun.*"

Fun? Yes, with Jesse, everything was fun. But with or without him, she planned to make it so for Kevin. He deserved it. "Okay."

"You need to understand, honey. None of it scares me."

Nothing scared Jesse. From the moment she'd met him, he'd been rock-steady. "Maybe I'm afraid enough for both of us."

"You don't have to be. I'm here with you." He started a slow rhythm that sent heat spiraling through her. "And no matter what, I'm staying put."

For how long? Tonya wanted to ask. But with his slow, heavy thrusts, her every nerve ending sparked.

It had been so long since she'd been held, even longer since she'd been loved.

"Jesse…"

He kept her hips tilted up so that each slide of his body on hers gave the perfect contact. "God, you feel good."

"You feel better." She put her legs around him, lifted into him and whispered, "Harder."

Growling, he lifted up to his elbows, watching her as he gave her what she asked for. The bed rocked.

Jaw tight, color high on his cheekbones, Jesse stared at her with glittering green eyes until she cried out at the start of her climax.

Done fighting off his own release, he gathered her closer, his face in her neck.

She felt the coiled tension in his shoulders, the heat pouring off him, and she let go.

Seconds, maybe minutes later, Jesse lazily kissed her shoulder, her neck, her temple.

"Don't move yet," she begged, wanting to hang on to this moment…forever.

"Not yet," he agreed. Then he surprised her by saying, "Soon though."

"Soon?"

"So I can look at you some more." He lifted up to see her. "And kiss you some more."

And love her more?

He touched his mouth to hers. "And love you more."

He was *so good* at that—at reading her mind, and making love to her.

"What?" he teased, smoothing his thumb over her brows. "You're frowning—but I know you came."

"I did," she confirmed, not that there was really any question. "You're amazing."

"And it's been a long time?"

A lifetime. "Yes."

"We have—" he rose up to see the bedside clock "—several more hours. Plenty of time."

"For what?" She liked him like this, all mellow and sated. But she liked him ramped up and turned-on even more.

"I ended up rushing things, after all. But I'm blaming you for that."

Pretending outrage, she said, "Me?"

"Mmm. The way you smell, how you taste." He bent to her and whispered, "Those sexy sounds you make."

"I don't—"

"Totally set me off." He sat up beside her, his attention on her breasts. "I wanted to spend a lot more time on these." So saying, he cupped each breast, using his thumbs to tease her nipples into stiffening again.

Tonya breathed harder. "Okay."

"And your belly." He bent to press one soft kiss there—while wedging a hand back between her legs. "And here…" He kissed his way downward; the fingers already there opened her, and he licked her clitoris. "I especially wanted to spend some time here."

Fresh excitement curled in her belly, then spread heat out everywhere. "Yes." She had no doubts she'd like that. A lot.

"Don't move," Jesse told her as he stood. "I'll be right back."

She watched him walk out to the bathroom, heard the water run, and in less than half a minute later he was back.

Expression intent.

Wicked smile in place.

Good thing she hadn't moved.

SPRAWLED ON THE bed on her stomach, Tonya tried to catch her breath while Jesse trailed his fingertips down her sleek spine, down to her sexy tush. God, she was amazing.

And he wanted her still.

He wanted her *always*.

Squirming, she murmured, "Mmm. That took the edge off."

Jesse cupped one cheek in his palm. "You think so?" Her open thighs drew his attention, and he went to one elbow to look at her anew. "Because I think it only stoked the fire for me."

Groaning, she opened one eye to peek at him. Gathering herself, she pushed up to her elbows too, in a pose guaranteed to make his blood burn.

"Really?" Her gaze went over him. "Well, then maybe—"

With a loud meow, Love came to the door.

Most of her "cat sounds" were loud, maybe because she was deaf. But this time was different.

Jesse sat up and found the cat staring toward him anxiously. He and Tonya shared a look.

Almost as one they scrambled out of the bed and began pulling on clothes.

Jesse checked the clock. "Kevin will be home in an hour. Damn, I hope she holds off until he's here."

Tripping herself while pulling on panties, Tonya asked, *"What do we do?"*

He shucked up his jeans and grinned at her. God,

she was sweet. And serious. And so incredibly loyal and bighearted.

Not to mention amazing in bed.

Long ago she'd lost her braid, and now her long blond hair tumbled everywhere. He took his time smoothing it down, then tucking it back behind her ears.

Just...touching her.

After the afternoon they'd had, he should have been sated, and in some ways he was.

In other ways, he knew he'd never get his fill of her.

Twice he'd brought her to climax, once with his mouth, then again with his fingers, before using the second condom and joining her in a release so strong it had pretty much rocked his world. A world he wanted to share with her.

"Jesse?"

He kissed the tip of her nose. "We don't do anything except make sure she's comfortable."

"Okay, I can do that." Tonya looked around. "Oh my God. Where did she go?"

"I can guess." And sure enough, Jesse found her in her nook—on Kevin's old shirts. "Hang on, Love. Kevin will be home soon."

It was a guess who was more distraught—Tonya or Love. The cat knew what to do, and she went about it naturally. But Tonya was a woman who needed to help, only she was totally out of her element now.

"You've never seen kittens born?"

She shook her head, her worried gaze remaining on the cat as Love occasionally cried, shifted, squirmed. "My parents didn't allow us to have pets, not when they already had their hands full with Cissy. And after

I moved out, well, it never seemed fair to have an animal when I put in so many hours."

"Then you're in for a treat." Jesse prayed there wouldn't be any problems. He wasn't sure Tonya, or Kevin, could handle it.

Not much later, when he heard the bus, Jesse went to the front porch to wait for Kevin. Soon as he stepped off the bus, Jesse said, "Love is giving birth. Hustle!"

At first Kevin froze, then he busted into a run up the driveway and through the front door. He dropped his backpack in the living room on his way down the hall and didn't put on his brakes until he reached the bedroom door.

Eyes enormous, the boy stood there staring. Jesse could almost see his heart thundering. When Love meowed, he bolted into the room the rest of the way and dropped hard to his knees.

Tonya smiled at him, rubbed his back. "I'm so glad you got home in time."

"Yeah."

Poor kid could barely breathe. Jesse knelt down beside him. "You can pet her a little if you want."

He did, his touch gentle, his eyes still round as saucers.

Love had just finished cleaning the first kitten when she started squirming, cried a few times and another slid out.

Kevin withdrew his hand. With awe, he said softly, "That is so gross."

Jesse couldn't help but laugh. "Yeah, especially watching her clean them up."

"Yeah." Kevin's lip curled, but he went back to carefully petting the cat. "How many will she have?"

"No idea," Tonya said, her expression almost identical to Kevin's. "But she's going to have at least three, because I see the third one coming now."

"Wow."

"I'm guessing this isn't her first litter," Jesse said, hoping to reassure them both. "They're coming pretty fast and easy." *Thank God.*

True enough, within fifteen minutes, Love had given birth to three kittens. Kevin hadn't moved, had barely blinked the entire time. And when Love looked at him, almost as if she wanted his approval, he scooted in closer and started talking to her, telling how great she'd done, that she wasn't alone, how he'd take care of her and how much she meant to him.

He said all the right things, maybe things that had never been said to him, things most twelve-year-olds wouldn't think to say but definitely needed to hear.

Damn, but he was a good kid. Despite his upbringing, or maybe because of it, he was gentler and more understanding than most adults.

Jesse couldn't recall ever getting that attached that quickly to another human being. He wanted to be in Kevin's life, now and always. That the boy was also a part of Tonya only sweetened the deal because, yes, he loved Tonya. Like, crazy-loved her.

Somehow he'd work it out, and in the end, he'd have Tonya, he'd have Kevin.

He'd have it all.

Rather than stay and watch Love finish cleaning up, Jesse made an offer. "How about I order pizza for dinner?"

Kevin scrunched up his nose and swallowed hard. "I was starving when I first got here, but now..." He rubbed his stomach. "I might need a little while before I can look at gooey pizza."

Jesse grinned. "Bucket of chicken then? It'll take me half an hour to go get it."

"I could eat that," Tonya said. "Kevin?"

"Sure. Thanks." He went to his dresser and took out another old shirt. It was two sizes too small, stained, but clean. "Do you think she'd mind if I changed that bedding for her once she's all done—" his face scrunched up again "—licking that up?"

Now it was Jesse who put a hand to his stomach. "I'm sure she'd appreciate it. Give her time to finish though. She might not want you touching them yet."

Tonya nodded. "When she's ready, I'll help."

Pausing in the doorway, Jesse surveyed them both. "You guys realize you have four cats now, right?"

Kevin looked at Tonya, but she didn't miss a beat. "We'll keep any that we can't find good homes for. But first we'll get them all fixed. No reason to keep them multiplying."

Relieved, Kevin went back to reassuring Love.

"I think Merrily uses the same local vet as Cinder and Evan. Given their menageries, they probably get a discount." And if they didn't, Jesse thought, well then, he'd figure out a way to foot the bill.

He was an integral part of this family unit, whether Kevin and Tonya realized it yet or not.

CHAPTER FIVE

To Tonya's relief, the following Monday went much the same, minus the drama of new kittens being born. She and Jesse spent the day in bed, burning up the sheets until it was time for Kevin to return.

Then Jesse took them all to dinner.

And so started their routine. Tonya knew that Kevin had quickly become as attached to Jesse and his visits as she had.

At least one day a week, usually Monday, Jesse switched his hours so he could spend the day alone with her. When Kevin got home from school, Jesse took them out to dinner.

Like a family.

Other days, he often came by after work.

He and Kevin worked on the attic around school, grill-outs, movies and a host of other fun activities that always seemed so new to Kevin and, because of that, felt new—or at least better—to her too.

Amazingly, one remodel led to another.

They no sooner wrapped up her office in the attic—which was truly a thing of beauty—than Jesse suggested a game room in the basement. By the time they were done with the plans, the space would be turned into a casual family room.

Brick donated a gaming system, saying he and Merrily had the same one and definitely didn't need two.

Evan brought by a laptop he said he no longer used. She planned to splurge on another television.

Jesse even said he could add in a second bathroom. At times it boggled her mind the amount of work he put into someone else's house.

Her house. And Kevin's.

Oh how she wanted it to be Jesse's home too. But so far, as invested as he seemed in their relationship, he didn't push for more.

Damn it, she sort of wanted him to push a little.

Six weeks went by, and it felt like things were falling into place. Kevin waited until they were all seated at the table, halfway through dinner, before he pulled a folded paper from his pocket.

Purring loudly, Love curled in the one empty seat with a kitten, and around Kevin's feet, the other two kittens played, fighting over his shoestrings, occasionally climbing his leg.

Like Love, they each adored him. He'd named all three, kept them fed, their bedding and box cleaned, and never seemed to tire of playing with them.

Tonya had already decided to keep them all, and not just because Kevin was attached to them, although that played a part.

In truth, she, too, was attached. And she loved watching Kevin with them. With Merrily and Cinder as examples, she knew multiple animals meant more work and expense, but also more love. And that's what she wanted to fill her house with—love for the pets, for Kevin.

And for Jesse.

"Hey." Brushing his hand up her forearm, Jesse smiled at her. "Best meal I've had in a long time."

The compliment warmed her. "It's just roast and potatoes."

Mouth full, Kevin nodded. "Really good roast and potatoes."

If there was one thing she didn't like about Kevin, it was that he was too perfect for a twelve-year-old boy. Too polite. Too grateful. Too quiet and accommodating.

She wanted him to be comfortable enough to be himself. To maybe complain now and then, make a few demands.

Be a kid.

But she had no idea how to reach him, how to reassure him enough that he'd let loose and just accept his changed circumstances, so she returned Jesse's smile instead. "Thank you both." Hoping for some confirmation on their relationship, she said, "I could get used to this, getting compliments from my two favorite guys."

Jesse gave her a quick glance, then winked at Kevin and said, "Anytime you want to cook for me, believe me, I'll pour on the compliments. All of them sincere. Right, Kevin?"

"Heck, yeah."

But Jesse went one further. "Long as you know Kevin and I don't take your hard work for granted. Whenever you don't feel like cooking, we're fine with takeout." And he said again, "Right, Kevin?"

Tonya loved how Jesse always included him.

Scooping up his last bite of mashed potatoes, Kevin nodded. "Sure."

Watching him, Tonya could tell he had something else on his mind. She put her fork aside. "Everything okay?"

Startled, he looked up at her, blanched, glanced at the paper he'd put beside his plate, then nodded. "Yeah."

"What do you have there?"

He smoothed out the paper, taking an inordinate amount of time to get a fold out of the corner.

Done eating, Jesse pushed his plate back and crossed his arms on the table. "What's up?"

Loudly clearing his throat, twice, Kevin handed Tonya the paper. "I was thinking about, maybe, well…"

"Sports?" Tonya prompted, after glancing at the activity details. "Football or soccer?"

Jesse leaned around to see the athletic sign-up form. "You'd be terrific at either one."

Appearing anxious and somewhat embarrassed, Kevin said, "I've never played."

"No one could tell," Jesse assured him. "You're naturally athletic."

"Really?"

"Absolutely. You can learn the rules, piece of cake. But you're already fast and strong, and you have good moves. No one can teach you that."

His ears turned red, but he fought a grin over the praise. "Thanks."

"If you want, I can go over some of the basics with you."

"For football or soccer?" Tonya asked him.

Jesse shrugged. "Whichever he wants. I played just about every sport through high school."

That didn't surprise Tonya. Jesse was definitely a guy's guy, very physical and macho. But he was also incredibly intuitive and, at all the right times, exceedingly gentle.

Toying with his fork, Kevin avoided eye contact. "It's kind of expensive."

Tonya went back to the paper. Indeed. The sign-up fee, the cost of the uniform, did add up.

"Uh-oh," Jesse said. "I think this qualifies as another one of those times for talking."

Tonya elbowed him but said, "He's right." She tipped her head, giving Kevin a direct look. "We're in this together, right?"

Kevin halfheartedly lifted one shoulder.

"We're a family, and families have expenses. Like the school clothes, there will be dentist and doctor bills, school photos, sports, birthdays—"

Scowling, Kevin hunched his shoulders—his self-defense mechanism.

Jesse recognized it too, because he gave her a quick look. Tonya kept her attention on Kevin.

"There will be times when I need to budget things out. *All* families do that, Kevin."

"My mom didn't."

"Your mom wasn't well."

His shoulders went tighter.

"I'm not her. I have a good job, and while we're far from wealthy, I don't ever want you to hesitate to bring things like this to me. Okay?"

He picked up a kitten and cuddled it close. "I was thinking I could try to get a job cutting grass or something."

"Kevin," Tonya said, wanting—*needing*—him to accept her in all the important ways.

Jesse grinned, drawing not only Tonya's attention but Kevin's too.

"What?" Kevin asked, shifting in his seat.

"I'm just proud of you, that's all."

Suspicion brought his brows together. "Proud? Why?"

"And you," he said to Tonya. "Damn, but you're both pretty special."

Tonya and Kevin shared a look, prompting Jesse to laugh.

He wrapped a hand around Tonya's neck and pulled her in for a loud smooch. "I know you want to do everything you can for him."

"Of course I do. We're—"

"Family. I get it." Next he clasped Kevin's shoulder. "You get it too, right?"

Still frowning, Kevin nodded.

"Great." Jesse squeezed his shoulder and then sat back in his seat. "I was sixteen before I got my first job, so I'd say you have a little time for anything too consuming, but cutting grass is a great idea. I remember how terrific I felt earning a little money of my own."

Tonya started to protest, but he cut her off.

"He knows you love him, honey. That doesn't mean he can't lift a finger. Look at him. He's healthy as a horse. Cutting grass won't hurt him."

Kevin straightened his shoulders. "I was going to make some fliers and hand them out on our street."

Pride swelled inside her. "I think that'd be pretty awesome." She braced herself and said, "I'll need to walk with you when you do."

Kevin went still, his gaze darting helplessly to Jesse. "When I do what?"

"Hand them out."

Brows going high, he asked, "Why?"

"Because you're only twelve, and while I know the

people right next door to me, I don't really know anyone else and—"

"I'll be careful."

"And so will I."

Flummoxed, he again looked at Jesse.

Jesse shrugged. "When I was sixteen—*sixteen*, Kevin—
I started working at the grocery story. I remember my
mom came up every day to buy something, just to make
sure I was okay."

That only left Kevin more horrified.

"One night," Jesse said, "I had to bring in carts from
the parking lot. It was raining."

Tonya grinned, just knowing where this story might
be headed.

"Yeah," Jesse said with a shake of his head. "She and
my dad came with raincoats and insisted on helping."
He laughed. "Back then, it embarrassed me. Now, I just
appreciate how much they cared."

Like a bottle of cola that someone shook up, Kevin
looked ready to explode. But he still had the lid screwed
on tight.

Too tight, Tonya decided.

Keeping her tone soft, she told him, "You can get
mad, you know."

Showing just a *hint* of mad, he glared at her. "You
want me to be mad?"

"No, of course not."

Jesse took his shoulder again. "She's just saying it's
okay if you are. I got mad at my mom and dad, but it
didn't change anything. They still loved me, and still
insisted on doing what they thought was right."

The pressure built. Kevin worked his jaw. "She's
not my mom."

Tonya was about to address that—she had no idea how—when a knock sounded on the kitchen door. She twisted to look behind her and found Brick and Merrily standing there, both smiling hugely. Knowing it was dinnertime, they'd crossed the backyard rather than walk around to the front door.

"Are we interrupting?" Merrily asked through the screen.

"Nope." Jesse stood to let them in. "We just finished dinner."

"We did too," Brick told him. "A celebratory dinner."

"Yeah?" Jesse lifted Love to give the chair to Merrily. "What are we celebrating?"

Too excited to sit, Merrily clapped her hands together. "We bought a house."

Tonya had been about to stand, but that had her dropping right back into her seat.

"I know, I know," Merrily rushed to say. "You're a Realtor. But it was for sale by owner and you've had your hands full, so we didn't want to bother you."

"We paid for a house inspection," Brick explained. "All good. It can use some updating, but I've enjoyed helping you here, and we've already got some ideas, so—"

"Count me in," Jesse told him.

"You're moving?" Tonya felt Jesse rest his hands on her shoulders. "You're really moving?"

Bubbling over, Merrily clapped again. "Yes, and I'm sorry because you know I love you, and I love it here, and you've been the best landlord ever. But I also love, love, *love* the house we found. It has more space and a fenced yard and it's only five minutes from here so we can still visit often and—"

To shush her, Brick kissed her, making Jesse laugh.

Now that she'd subsided, Brick picked up the explanations. "We're getting married one week after we close on the house. The honeymoon is on hold until Merrily has a break in her classes. It's going to be crazy enough just getting everything moved over."

Merrily smiled at Tonya. "Be happy for me."

"I am!" She jumped up to draw Merrily in for a big hug. "So very, very happy for you."

"You don't mind that we're moving out?"

"I'll miss you, and no other tenant will ever be as wonderful as you, but all that aside, I'm thrilled to see you so happy!"

Jesse nudged Brick. "To hear them talk with all that landlord and tenant stuff, you wouldn't know they were friends."

"The best of friends," Tonya corrected, and she hugged Merrily again.

Jesse put his arm around Kevin and drew him into the group. "Just let us know how we can help."

"Thanks," Brick said. "Because I'm counting on you to help haul boxes and furniture."

"We'll be there."

Merrily smiled at Kevin. "Weeeelll… I was hoping Kevin might help out with the animals while we move and get set up. Not overnight or anything, but of course the front door will be open a lot and—"

"I'll do it."

Merrily mussed his hair. "Thank you, kiddo."

"I'd offer to take you to dinner to celebrate, but we just finished," Jesse said.

"No need," Brick assured him. "We're heading over to see Evan and Cinder next."

There was another round of hugs that this time included Jesse and Kevin, and then they were alone again. Tonya wanted to get back to Kevin's earlier comment, that she wasn't his mother, but Jesse derailed her.

"So." He didn't sit at the table with her, choosing instead to stand there, arms crossed and feet braced apart. "You're going to have the other half of the house open."

"I'm sure I'll be able to find another tenant."

Far too serious, Jesse watched her. "Maybe you could hold off on that."

Shrugging, she said, "The rent is a big part of my monthly budget."

Slowly nodding, he turned to Kevin. "Would you mind having me around more?"

"What?" Heart pounding, Tonya pushed back her chair. "What are you talking about?"

"I'm asking Kevin if he likes me enough to have me around more."

Put on the spot, Kevin hoisted his shoulders. "I like you a lot more than I liked my mom's boyfriends." He laughed without humor. "A lot more."

"No comparisons, okay?" Jesse braced his hands on the tabletop. "Forget all that, and just think about us. About this."

His ears went red again, but Kevin nodded. "I like it when you're here."

Beaming, Jesse turned to Tonya. "I love you."

"You...?"

"Love you." He winked at Kevin. "Love him too. And I love the idea of us as a family."

A million responses went through Tonya's mind. She wanted to squeal in excitement. She wanted to grab

Jesse and kiss him senseless. But she became aware of Kevin's stillness.

Cautiously, he came out of his seat.

"You want to marry her."

"Yes, I do."

Hearing it confirmed sent that jumbled elation spiraling through her again. "Jesse."

"You'll get married and have more kids."

Pretending nothing was wrong, Jesse told them both, "I wouldn't mind that. We could open up the other side of the house and use all the space. There'd be more than enough room."

Kevin backed up a step. A kitten clung to his jeans, and he bent to quickly pry the tiny claws loose, then set it aside.

It came right back.

Smiling, Jesse told him, "You'd make a terrific big brother."

"Cousin." Face pale, he lifted the kitten again and this time just held it. "I'd be a cousin."

"Technically," Jesse agreed. Then he narrowed his eyes, his expression intent. "But mostly you'd be a big brother."

Kevin shook his head, and his voice went thin. "You're not my dad."

"No." Jesse took a step toward him. "But I wish I was."

Face crumbling, Kevin took off down the hall and into his bedroom.

Tonya and Jesse both heard the door slam.

When she started to go after him, Jesse caught her to him. "First things first."

She fretted.

"It'll be okay, honey. Will you believe that?"

He looked so confident, so strong, that she nodded. "We can make it so."

Pleased, he lightly kissed her. "Yes, together we'll make it so."

Oh God. Hugging him tight, Tonya said, "I love you, Jesse. So much."

"Finally." He pretended weak knees, making her laugh while grabbing for him. Just as quickly he straightened, lifted her high in his arms and turned a circle while kissing her. "You ready to go tackle our first priority?"

Tears stung her eyes. *Happy tears.* She nodded.

Jesse set her back on her feet, took her hand, and together they went down the hall. She knocked on Kevin's door.

"Go away."

Hearing the break in his voice, she and Jesse shared a look. But despite her breaking heart, she smiled. "We did tell him it was okay to be mad."

"That's something, I guess."

The cat wrapped around her leg. Tonya looked down to see the other two kittens had also followed them.

"Kevin," she said through the door, "Love wants in."

The seconds ticked by and then, reluctantly, he opened the door. Immediately Love pushed her way in, and naturally the kittens followed.

It devastated her to see the tears in Kevin's eyes.

She started to reach for him, but he turned away, going to his desk and dropping into his chair.

Jesse propped a shoulder in the open doorway. "I know you won't believe this, Kevin, but it's okay to cry."

"I'm not!" He scrubbed both fists over his eyes. "I'm not a baby."

"No."

"I'm not a wuss, either."

"I would never say you are."

Kevin stared up at him with red eyes and a watery nose. "Mom said only babies cried."

Tonya loved Jesse even more when he said with conviction, "You'll never hear me say it."

"Or me."

"I should miss her," Kevin insisted.

"And you will," Jesse told him. "There will be memories good and bad. Unresolved feelings. But, Kevin? You have to know, you're one of the strongest people I've ever met."

Fretfully, Tonya held back as Jesse strode in and stood over him. "I mean that. I have a lot of respect for you. Respect that I hope is mutual. Crying won't change that. In fact, I'd say you're past due."

Suddenly the dam broke and Kevin curled in on himself, his head to his knees, elbows over his ears, rocking back and forth.

Rushing in, Tonya embraced him, holding him as tight as she could, so tight she heard his protesting grunt—and still she didn't loosen up. "I love you, Kevin. I love you so much."

He tried to draw a breath, choked and said, "I feel so bad."

She rocked him, her hands locked around him. "About what? Tell me and we'll work it out."

"I'm happy here."

The whispered words stole her strength, and she slumped, letting him put a few inches between them.

Sniffling loudly, angry and defiant, Kevin pulled away. "I like all *this*." He waved a hand—at everything. "All of it." He stabbed a finger toward Tonya. "You." And then at Jesse. "Him."

"You like me?"

His bottom lip quivered before he clenched his jaw and nodded.

Such an amazing gift. She tried on a gentle smile. "It's okay for you to be happy."

He shook his head hard, shoving out of his chair and turning his back on them. "It's so much better here. I like it so much more." He scrubbed at his face with his forearm. Choking out the words, he said, "I love you guys."

Looking pretty solemn himself, Jesse said, "We love you too."

"Mom never did any of this." He faced them again, his shoulders bunched in insistence. "She cared, though!"

"Of course she did," Jesse said. "It's just that people are different."

"How could she not?" Rubbing his shoulder, Tonya said, "It's okay for you to cry. To get sad and mad." Needing him to believe it, she kept her voice firm. "And it's more than okay for you to be happy."

Unconvinced, he swallowed. "It's not that I'm glad she's gone."

She nodded her understanding. "I honestly tried my best to save Cissy. I really did. But it was never enough. Now you're mine, and I need you to know that however the situation worked out, I'm so glad you're here with me. I will never, ever let you go."

He surprised her again by giving her a big hug, his skinny shoulders shaking only a little. "Thanks."

"Thank you."

Awkwardly, he pushed away and dragged in a strained breath. Using his shoulder, he wiped his eyes. When he realized Love was staring up at him, he bent to give her a pat, whispering, "Sorry, Love. I'm okay now."

Tonya hoped it was true, that he was okay. "We're a family."

"Yeah." He straightened again, slanting an embarrassed glance at Jesse.

Jesse put his arm around Tonya. "So what do you say? Okay if I marry her so I can be an official part of the family?"

This time it was his nose Kevin scrubbed with his forearm. When he finished, he caught a broken breath, quirked a smile and said, "Guess that's up to her, but I hope she says yes."

Tonya took her time fixing Kevin's hair, then she kissed his cheek, turned to Jesse and said, "Yes."

Jesse surprised her by pulling both her and Kevin into a group hug. The awkward laughing, reciprocal hugs and overall sense of well-being left her heart full.

Love nudged her way in, and Kevin scooped her up along with a kitten. Tonya picked up the other two.

Jesse watched them both, his satisfaction plain.

"Guess you were right," Tonya told him.

"Glad to hear it," Jesse said. "But about what?"

"I know." Even though Kevin ducked his face against the cat, Tonya could see his smile. He shoulder-bumped her, then went to put the cat and kitten down in their nook. "There's always room for love."

An explosive new series by
New York Times bestselling author

LORI FOSTER

*These sexy bodyguards will do anything
to protect the ones they love...*

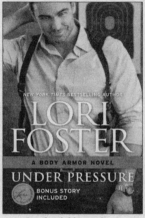

Available now!

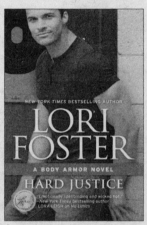

Available March 21!

"Storytelling at its best! Lori Foster should be on
everyone's auto-buy list." —#1 *New York Times* bestselling
author Sherrilyn Kenyon

www.LoriFoster.com

www.HQNBooks.com

The first full-length novel from
USA TODAY **BESTSELLING AUTHOR**

ALEXA RILEY

A strong, possessive man finds the woman of his dreams, and takes fate into his hands. He'll do everything to make her his.

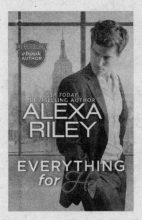

"Alexa Riley crafts a deliciously sexy…story, complete with dark and manipulative undertones." *–Fresh Fiction*

Available now, wherever books and ebooks are sold!

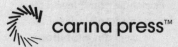

HARLEQUIN
Desire

Powerful heroes…scandalous secrets…burning desires.

Save **$1.00**

on the purchase of ANY

Harlequin® Desire book.

Available wherever books are sold, including most bookstores, supermarkets, drugstores and discount stores.

Save $1.00

on the purchase of any Harlequin® Desire book.

Coupon valid until April 30, 2017.
Redeemable at participating outlets in the U.S. and Canada only.
Not redeemable at Barnes & Noble stores. Limit one coupon per customer.

52614604

5 65373 00076 2   (8100)0 12262

HDCOUP0117

Turn your love of reading into rewards you'll love with
Harlequin My Rewards

Join for FREE today at
www.HarlequinMyRewards.com

Earn **FREE BOOKS** of your choice.

Experience **EXCLUSIVE OFFERS** and contests.

Enjoy **BOOK RECOMMENDATIONS**
selected just for you.

PLUS! Sign up now
and get **500** points
right away!

Earn **FREE REWARDS** Join Today! HarlequinMyRewards.com

MYR16R